A Tree Lighting in Deathlehem

A Tree Lighting in Deathlehem

Edited by
Michael J. Evans
and
Harrison Graves

A
Grinning Skull Press
Publication

A Tree Lighting in Deathlehem

The Skull logo with stylized lettering was created for Grinning Skull Press by Dan Moran, http://dan-moran-art.com/.
Cover designed by Jeffrey Kosh, http://jeffreykosh.wix.com/jeffreykoshgraphics.
Interior graphic created by daver2002ua.

ISBN-13: 978-1-947227-44-6 (paperback)
ISBN: 978-1-947227-45-3 (e-book)

DEDICATION

As always, to all those who enjoy embrace
all things Christmas, light and dark.

ACKNOWLEDGMENTS

As always, we would like to thank Jeffrey Kosh for another stunning cover, and an extra special thank you to Scott Deegan for providing the chilling verse that graces the back cover.

TABLE OF CONTENTS

Scary Christmas and a Bloody New Year

One of the earliest memories I have of Christmas is setting up the tree on Christmas Eve. For many, if you don't have an artificial tree that you recycle year after year, this involves the time-consuming—and sometimes horrifying—task of going to the local tree farm (or stand) to pick out a tree. Too tall, too short, too fat, too thin, not full enough, until you finally find the "perfect" one. For those familiar with Deathlehem, you know how dangerous real trees can be. For those who are new to town, you doubt me? Just check out Dan Foley's "Aianna" and R. A. Goli's "Bloody Christmas Tree."

But let's see... Where was I? Oh yeah, naked trees! That's what we had. There were no lights, no ornaments, no tinsel. Nothing. Just a naked tree in the living room, blocking the windows and any light that might filter into the room through the gauzy curtains, giving the room a somewhat gloomy air. Then we were ushered off to Midnight Mass, and upon returning home, we were rushed off to bed with the threat of, "Right to sleep, otherwise Santa won't come and there'll be no presents under the tree." I'm sure you're familiar with that situation.

Like most kids waiting for the jolly old elf, I couldn't

sleep, so I stared up at the ceiling and listened to my older brothers whispering in the next room, wondering what presents they'd be getting. Every so often, I would hear the jingle of sleigh bells and what I thought to be somebody tromping around on the roof. I often wondered about that when I got older and sort of convinced myself it was my Grandfather adding to the wonder and magic that is Santa. Although what Santa would be doing on our roof was a mystery because, like most houses in New York, we didn't have a chimney. So how was Santa getting in? It was a question I frequently asked my mother, and her response, as though it explained everything, was, "Magic."

And explain everything it did, because when the sun came up and we were allowed to go downstairs to have breakfast and open presents, the tree was decorated to the nines, as was the living room, and you couldn't see the floor for the number of presents stuffed under the tree. There were the usual gift tags that read "From: Mom and Dad," "From: Grandma and Grandpa," and a gift from each of my siblings, but a majority of the gifts were "From: Santa."

At that young age, it was indeed magical, although I should have guessed at the time that Santa didn't exist because I never got anything that I had asked Santa for (I don't recall any of us kids ever getting what we asked for). Mom never had an explanation for that, but she did have a way to make sure we continued to believe in Santa. It was blackmail, if you want to know the truth of it, and so many people think what she did was horrible, but she told us once—and reminded us every year—that if she ever heard us say Santa didn't exist or we no longer believed in the Big Man in the Red Suit, that would be the last time we would find any presents under the tree. Thus, if you asked my twenty-one-year-old brother if he still believed in Santa Clause, he would tell you that he did.

Looking back on it, I can understand why she did it. She wanted to keep the magic of the holiday alive for as long as she could. Did that make her a terrible person? Some would say yes, but I don't think so. But I often wonder what would happen with kids whose parents were a little more upfront and told them at some point that Santa wasn't real, or if the child found out the truth through friends that Santa wasn't real and their parents did nothing to deny it. I'm sure some kids would be disappointed, but they'd shrug it off and move on. But what if the child wasn't right in the head? The so-called Bad Seed. The one who harbored dark thoughts no one knew about, not even the parents. How would they respond? This year, some of the authors dared to venture into the minds of these children to see how they handled the bad news. And trust me, it ain't pretty. Want proof? Just check out Tristan Ryan's "The Santa Revelation" and "That's the Spirit" by Kurt Newton. Rose Blackthorn and Karen Thrower tackle things from the opposite end of the spectrum: poor children who must deal with the fact that Santa and his helpers are very real. Which do you think would be more terrifying? Finding out there was no Santa or that Santa is real but he's not the jolly old elf you've been led to believe he is.

The Santa argument aside, I'm sure the one thing we can all agree on is that Christmas is about family, which is why we were happy to see so many family stories this year. But just because the stories are about family, that doesn't mean that they're happy crappy or that they're so sweet they'll send you into a diabetic coma. This is Deathlehem, after all, but I would suggest having tissues ready for some of the stories you'll be reading. Scott Deegan's "Chris Miss, Mama" is a bittersweet tale of two little boys separated from their mother at the holiday and want nothing more than to spend

Christmas with their mommy. In "Song of the Hunt" by Pierce Skinner, a father overcomes the greatest obstacle ever to make certain his daughter gets what she wants for Christmas. Sheri White ("Christmas Eve on the Rudolph Express") also weaves a tale of a family torn apart at the holidays and a father desperate to get his family back together and keep it together. And Jeffrey Kosh takes us overseas on a family holiday in "Bloody Bones," where the holiday celebration turns from happy to hellish in the blink of an eye. And no, it's not Krampus that terrorizes the family here, nor an evil Santa and his blood-thirsty minions.

In fact, Krampus doesn't even make an appearance this year. What? No Krampus for Christmas?!? But don't worry; there are plenty of other scary creatures to keep you chilled through the long winter nights. W. Brice McVicar opens this year's collection with a visit from Perchta, the Christmas witch, in "Silver and Straw." She makes Krampus look like a kitten. And while she has a preference for children, she's not opposed to terrorizing the adults during the twelve days of Christmas. The fairy folk also pay us a visit this year, and it's only fitting that James Carlson closes out this year's collection with "The Vices and Virtues of Gideon Thomas." It's a story you won't soon forget.

So get a fire going in the fireplace, grab a cup of hot cocoa, snuggle up under the blankies, and brace yourselves for yet another chilling visit to Deathlehem.

Michael J. Evans
and the staff at
Grinning Skull Press,
Best Wishes for a Happy Helliday
and a frightful New Year!

Silver and Straw

W. Brice McVicar

D*ecember 25, 1914*

It all started with that stupid silver coin.

In the middle of the Great War, freezing our asses off and celebrating Christmas in the most bizarre way, thousands of miles from our wives, our children, our lovers, and our mothers, the strangest battle I ever saw came in the midst of an unofficial ceasefire called, just for a short time, so we could all feel like men again instead of monsters. We had laid our weapons down but still within reach, and so had the small battalion of German troops who had joined us to trade a few fags, sip from communal bottles, share some laughter, and even dine together with whatever rations we could pull together.

Even in war, there is civility.

Thomson had noticed the white flag the Krauts were waving, hunkered down behind a ridge less than a mile from the trenches we had called home for the past few weeks. We, in turn, raised our own flag with hesitation, fearing we were being pulled into a trap, but Thomson said he'd heard of similar actions on the battlefields, enemies agreeing to a brief break from the blood and the bullets so they could either collect the bodies of their fallen brethren in that area referred to as No Man's Land, where neither force had claimed the territory yet, or, in some cases, simply allow for the human spirit to rebuild itself, a necessary relief from the atrocities being carried out. Regardless of the reason, the troops respected the flag and watched the Germans suspiciously, but also with a sense of gratitude. It was Christmas Day, after all, and it seemed an insult to Baby Jesus to be killing on his birthday.

So, the muzzles on our rifles cooled, and we watched with trepidation as an unarmed German soldier crested the ridge and, with his hands high, advanced on our location.

"Christ… Do we shoot?" Harris called, sighting the man with his rifle.

I reached out and gently pushed the barrel of Harris's gun toward the frozen earth. I could sense the young man's fear and understood its cause, but shooting an unarmed man on any day, let alone the holiest of days, wasn't a part of my war.

"Let him come," I said, spotting a German soldier providing cover from the ridge. "I don't think they want to fight."

The men watched patiently as the man approached, occasionally hollering something in his language, and when he was close enough that we could see the fear in his face, I told him to stop. I crawled out of the trench, the wind coming down from the Alps biting into the exposed skin of my face, and turned around slowly to show the man I too was unarmed.

We sized up one another for a few heartbeats before beginning to approach one another.

The man began speaking to me as he neared, and I called for Harris to tell me what the hell the German was saying. I hadn't learned enough of the language to understand, but the tone told me it wasn't threatening.

"He said, 'Merry Christmas'," Harris hollered. "He said we should celebrate."

It wasn't intentional; it was natural, the smile that crawled over my face. It was reflected in the German soldier's face, and I could see the fear evaporate, mostly, from his eyes as he extended his hand toward me. I shook it heartily and looked over my shoulder to see a dozen faces watching intently, some also smiling at the moment of camaraderie shared between two men who, by the virtues of war, were sworn enemies.

They invaded our camp. Yes, their rifles were slung over their shoulders, but only so their free hands could carry boxes of food, biscuits, dried goods, and other perishables we could, as brothers, share. We sat there, in the midday sun, sharing laughter and edibles with the very men who, just a few hours before, we had shot at, cursed, and vowed to send home in boxes or in pieces, both in some cases.

Recognizing the season, we asked the German men about their Christmas traditions, the gifts their children would find from Father Christmas, and what they missed the most about being home during the holidays. It seemed surreal to literally break bread with these soldiers, but we left our animosity outside the trenches that gave some shelter from the cold winter winds and, for those brief hours, enjoyed the company of our protagonists.

As the sun lowered and the shadows stretched, the rations lessened, and the vodka and whiskey became our source of warmth; the small fire we'd lit in the trench kept the cold mostly at bay provided we remained well within the circle of light thrown by the flames. Taylor, a young gunner from London, grabbed a tin of biscuits his mother had sent and, pulling a few of the pastries from the box, expressed bewilderment as he peered into the tin.

From within, Taylor pulled out a small silver coin, not smooth like something from a mint, but roughly hewn, with obvious hammer markings on both sides, the silver glinting in the fire's light. Taylor rolled the coin in his fingers and held it up for closer examination.

"I've no clue why me mum would send me this," he said, his voice slightly slurred from the evening's drink.

One of the older German soldiers, a grizzled old man with a gaunt face and months of beard growth on his chin, backed away from Taylor, his eyes on the silver and his lips stammering. Once his back was pressed to the trench wall and half his face enveloped in shadow, he began muttering and slowly shaking his head.

"What in the 'ell is he sayin'? What's got 'im all worked up?" Wilson asked, smiling drunkenly.

Harris leaned in, his square jaw jutting out like a bayonet, and listened to what I heard only as gibberish.

"*Perchta. Perchta. Das ist ein schlechtes omen,*" the man said.

Harris shook his head and said the soldier was discussing bad omens. He said he couldn't understand all the words because the man was talking too quickly, but he sounded scared.

"Well, I can tell that much," I said, taking a pull on the bottle in my hand. "What's got 'im so riled up?"

Harris shrugged his shoulders and followed the German man's eyes to the silver coin in Taylor's hands. He snatched the coin from the young man's hand and held it out to the German soldier, offering it to him.

"Here... Take it. Merry Christmas," Harris said.

The man moved quickly, swatting Harris's extended hand and sending the silver coin tinkling off into the deeper shadows of the trench.

"*Perchta,*" the man repeated. "*Perchta ist hier gewesen.*"

Harris flinched, his hands balled into fists, and he lunged toward the older soldier, a look of determination spreading across his face as the seasonal cheer dissipated from his features. A younger German soldier, Klein, reached out quickly and placed a gentle but authoritative hand on Harris's chest.

"He is scared," Klein said in broken English. "He said there is a bad omen and Perchta has been here. He's scared there's something bad here."

Klein lowered his hand from Harris's chest and took a few steps toward his friend, holding his hands out in a signal for the older man to calm down. He spoke softly, in German, and shook his head lightly as he spoke.

"He says we should leave. He said Perchta has been here and will come back for us because of what we do here," Klein said, translating for those of us who couldn't understand what he was saying.

"What in the 'ell is a purse ta?" Harris asked.

Klein turned and smiled coyly. He shrugged his shoulders and bunched up his face, trying to choose the English words carefully. "Perchta is...Christmas demon. She comes down from the mountains before Christmas and gives gifts—like silver—to the good boys and girls. The bad... They get taken away sometimes, but mostly hurt," he said, his face carrying a coy smile, suggesting he didn't believe the fairy tale. "It is old stories parents would tell to frighten children. A joke."

He turned back to the old man and spoke calmly, waving out toward the darkness beyond the fire's reach. He shook his head and smiled, obviously telling the old man not to believe in such tales and that nothing was waiting in the shadows.

"*Nein. Nein,*" the older man said, having nothing of Klein's reassurances. "Perchta. Perchta."

I leaned back against the frozen wall of mud and watched the man closely, mesmerized by his fear. Here was a grown man who, much like myself I assumed, had witnessed the many atrocities of war, had likely taken others' lives, and was rattled by the mere sight of a silver coin supposedly delivered by a fairy or ogre or some other creation of the imagination. I watched him, his eyes flitting back and forth as he desperately tried to see something in that darkness that was not there, and contemplated how, on Christmas Day, I could find myself in this hell.

The older man's rant over, we returned to our bottles and laughter. The mood returned to one of cheerfulness, some of the German soldiers obviously rattled by their comrade's outburst. Like all regions, folk tales aren't uncommon in Germany, and many of these men had obviously been warned about the Perchta as children. Mind you, I highly doubt any of them had ever imagined, as children, they'd one day be celebrating Christmas hunkered down in deep ruts in the earth, sharing drinks with men who, in only a few short hours, they'd once again aim to slaughter in the name of the war machine.

The evening turned to night, and the temperature continued to drop. My breath crystallized in the air before me, and I took a slow pull on the bottle of vodka one of the Germans had offered. My lips were becoming numb, and I debated on the cause: the cold or my slow advancement toward inebriation. My thoughts returned home, where I could picture my Katherine eating our traditional yule feast, her family surrounding her, and the large dining table set with her mother's finest dishes. I could smell the pies baking, the goose, the mincemeat... Home. I allowed myself to linger there in my mind and later kicked myself for allowing my guard to fall. I was naïve to think a simple ceasefire would protect me and the others, but perhaps the spirit of the season had played into my foolishness.

Spirit.

That's what it appeared as at first. Let me quantify that. That's what I *thought* I first saw. I'd spent, perhaps, too long in my own imagination, pictures of Katherine and the seasonal celebrations occupying my mind. I was staring into the night's depth, watching the clouds moving across the sky, blotting out the stars only to reveal them again as they passed overhead. From the far corner of my eye, I watched a large cloud, with wisps of white trailing its progression, dip down out of the obsidian sky, and it appeared to filter into one of the trenches to our west. I shook off the notion as alcohol-induced and briefly listened in as the men around the fire chuckled and, from what I could decipher, shared tales of their womanly conquests.

Laughter bounced off the hard earth walls, and the dancing light from the flames washed the area in an orange glow. I sat forward, the better to hear the men's conversation and, pushing my thoughts of home down, to participate in some of the merriment. I was about to share a tale, albeit a made-up one of the night I spent in a Paris brothel, when a small, round object embedded itself in the earth just inches from one German soldier's head.

Every man in the trench visibly jumped, myself included, and, like second nature, scrambled for his gun. The ceasefire, it seemed, was now null and void as men found themselves with barrels sighted on them. There wasn't a man in that trench who wasn't both pointing a rifle at a man and wasn't, in turn, having a rifle pointed at himself. The Germans were hollering unintelligible demands at us, and we were returning the favor, voices running over voices.

"*Nein. Nein*. Perchta. Perchta."

Out of the symphony of chaos the voices created, I heard the old man's frantic screams, and ensuring my own gun didn't waver from the man who I had targeted, I turned my head to look at him. His face was scrunched up in terror, and instead of aiming a gun at anyone, he used one hand to point at the earth where the item had embedded itself. I followed the imaginary line his finger tracked through the air and stared at the object.

It was Taylor's silver coin, its edge glinting in the fire, and the frost on the soil sparkled beside it like millions of diamonds catching the sunlight. Someone had decided to play a dangerous trick and throw the coin back into the light, frightening the old man and, in turn, throwing all of the men into a frenzy.

"Enough! Lower your guns! Put down your goddamn guns!" I shouted at the men. The command was directed toward my own troops, of course, and I repeated the demand before a few of them followed the order. I lowered my own and raised my hands in a sign of surrender.

"Perchta. Perchta. *Sie ist hier*," the old man hollered, pointing at the coin in the trench wall.

A few of the German soldiers heard the old man's comment and took notice of the coin in the wall. They looked at the coin and then peered into the dark where it had come from. Slowly, with guns seeming to be forgotten and the perceived threat changing in their minds, men on both sides turned to look into the shadows. Smiles crept on the faces of some men, catching on to the joke, but I noticed the majority of the German soldiers, at least the older ones, didn't appreciate the joke and remained stone-faced as they looked into the shadows.

If the coin created concern, what happened next created a hell within those trenches even war itself had never produced, nor would it replicate.

I leaned forward like the others, waiting to see what smart-ass soldier had wandered off to retrieve the coin and pull the prank. I was hoping it wasn't one of ours because I thought the Germans might lynch him and because I hated to think anyone in our battalion could be so stupid and careless.

"Perchta."

I turned to hush the old man, but the words died on my tongue when I realized this time it was a different soldier who had muttered the word. This soldier—his name was Neumann, if my memory was correct—had shifted the focus of his gun and aimed it into the trench's oily blackness. I noticed, with fear for my men's safety, the gun trembled in his hand.

"Enough," I said as I stood. "Whoever the hell is out there better come forward before they need a field medic."

With no response coming, I grabbed a lantern and held my hand out, the lantern's flame illuminating six feet down the trench where nothing revealed itself other than a few sandbags and a munitions box.

I took a step forward but was stopped by a German soldier who gingerly placed his hand on my leg. I looked down at him, ready to scold him for stopping me, but held my tongue when I saw the terror on his face.

"*Geh nicht da runter. Sie wird deinen Bauch stopfen,*" he said in a quiet voice.

"Harris? What the hell did he just say to me?"

I turned my head to Harris. He looked at the German soldier, who still has his hand on my leg, and shook his head. He looked at me and, with a wry smile, explained the soldier had said there was a woman in the trench who would stuff my stomach.

"Stuff my stomach with what?" I asked, looking at the soldier but directing the question to Harris.

Harris informed me the soldier said my stomach would be filled with hay if I had been bad.

"What is he on about?" I asked. I shook my leg gently, indicating for the German to let me pass and took two steps further into the trench's darkness. The lantern's glow illuminated deeper into the pitch, and I involuntarily took three quick steps back as I saw something scuttle back into the shadows, avoiding my light. My eyes barely had time to adjust to the receding shadows, but the gray, waxen flesh and long, white hair I glimpsed gave me reason to pause and for my free hand to fall onto the pistol in my waist holster.

"What the hell was that?" I whispered. I looked down at the German who had been trying to prevent me from going farther and watched as he crab-walked backward toward the fire. He, too, had seen something in that trench and wanted no part of it.

"Perchta. Perchta," he said, his eyes remaining on the shadows.

I did my best to step over his legs as he scurried backward but stumbled as he quickly changed direction, his hands trailing in the dirt behind him as he was pulled violently into the shadows of the trench, the same shadows I had just chased off with my lantern.

The trench erupted in gunfire, the noise nearly loud enough to drown out the German soldier's screams as he was pulled deeper down the trench, out of the light's illumination. German soldiers, still holding their rifles after the scare with the coin, unloaded freely into the dark, the sound and the bullets ricocheting off the mud walls. I crouched, pressing myself against the trench wall in the hope of avoiding a bullet, stray or otherwise, but never letting my eyes leave the darkness. I can't say, though, whether I was watching with the hope of seeing something or the fear that the shadows would reveal what they were hiding.

The gunfire faded, the smoke from gunpowder making the trench hazy, and we sat, as a collective group, listening for anything. The air seemed to still around us; no sounds emerged from the trench's depths nor from the night above us, and our breaths we held in with quivering lips and clenched jaws.

"Somebody want to tell me just what the fuck that was?" I whispered, turning my head slightly to the soldiers behind me but leaving my eyes trained on the trench's narrow path before me.

"Perchta," muttered Klein. He pointed down the trench's path with a shaking hand, and with the other, he made a cross over his chest. He said the word a few more times before he fell silent once again.

"Okay. Someone better tell me, now, what the fuck that is and what the fuck it's doing here," I said. I ensured the lantern in my hand remained steady so its light would shine into the trench, but not too far into the darkness. If my eyes had been true, and I saw what I thought the light had shown me, I needed to see no more.

Harris turned to Klein and, in the man's native language, drilled him with questions. I couldn't understand what was being said but understood enough to know Harris was trying to find out what was in the trenches with us.

"It's the Perchta," Klein said, drawing the word out slowly to emphasize each syllable. "It's the old woman who comes down at Christmas to visit the children. She hands out silver..."

"And...? She just dragged one of your friends off; I suspect he's not getting silver coins." I said.

"She steals the bad and cuts them open and stuffs their

stomachs with hay." Klein said it matter-of-factly and without hesitation. It wasn't a time to question local superstition or to mock the men for their beliefs, beliefs that I, myself, had just adopted.

"How do we…?"

I was interrupted when one of my own men, Gordon, screamed from his perch in the back of the group. I twisted my head quickly, the lantern extended just short of where my pistol rested in my other hand, and watched his feet disappear into the air above the trench. His boots kicked in the open air like a marionette having its strings pulled violently, and his scream trailed off as he was carried higher into the black sky. Men fired crazily into the air with no regard for whether their bullets would hit the old hag or find a home in Gordon.

The bullets stopped. Gordon's screaming stopped. But we didn't stop watching the sky. We sat in the trench, staring up into the nothingness above our heads. I could hear only my own heartbeat thumping in my ears until a small, metallic clang came from a few feet to my left, followed by another and another and another throughout the trench. I looked to the ground and saw a silver coin, much like the one Taylor had found, lying on the dirt. About a half dozen of the rough coins had fallen from the sky like rain into the trench.

One of the younger German soldiers leaned forward, picked up one of the coins, and held it up to the sky, hollering, "*Vielen dank*! *Vielen dank*!"

Harris hissed at the man, telling him to shut up and asking what the hell he'd be thanking the creature for after it had taken and, I assumed, killed two men in a matter of minutes. If the myth were true, it would seem some of us in the trench had been good and were being rewarded with the silver coins. Others… I swung my light to destroy the shadows before me.

I took a few hesitant steps into the trench, the lamp's light making long shadows of the munitions boxes and sandbags piled there. The lantern cast a yellowish light into the dark as I chose my steps carefully and proceeded deeper into receding darkness. I wanted to find the German soldier to see if he was still alive. The silence before me told me everything I needed to know, but what my hearing relayed I needed my eyes to confirm.

With the light of the small fire fading at my back and the anxiety-riddled chatter of the men getting quieter, I stepped further into the trench. The earthen smell was fainter here, with no fire to thaw the frozen soil and evoke the dank stench of earth, and the ground crunched beneath my boots. My nose, though, began to decipher a familiar scent. The tangy smell of blood, like orange juice left to ferment on a warm summer's day.

I slowed my pace and scanned the edges of the lantern's glow, not wanting to scare the creature if it were lingering in the dark, and sighed heavily as I recognized the form of a body lying in the dark. I thrust the lantern out as far as my hand would go from my body and flinched when the shadows created by its own light danced on the mud walls and wooden beams erected to fortify the trench.

There was no doubt the soldier was dead. His head was turned away from me, dead eyes staring into the trench's darkness. His arms remained extended above his shoulders, just as they had been as I had watched him be dragged away, and I noticed with casual observance that one of his boots had come off and was lost somewhere in the shadows. The heavy, gray parka he'd been wearing remained but was tattered along its bottom. Sections of the coat were stained with a fluid that looked black in the night, but I knew it was blood. Portions of the tattered cloth were obscured by the fleshy ropes of intestines that were erupting from the long wound on his abdomen like fresh sprouts in a garden's furrow. It was easy to make the comparison considering the pieces of straw that had been pushed down into the wound. Handfuls of the material had been pressed into those stretches of intestines, forcing them out of the man's body to make room for the creature's violation. Small tendrils of steam rose from the man's opened stomach.

I stepped backward slowly. I fought the urge to get closer to the body to check for a pulse, but the image of his ruptured gut was ingrained upon my retinas, and I had no desire for further details to dwell there. I quickened my pace and, feeling somewhat sure the creature wasn't lurking in wait for me, turned my back on the man's body and ran back toward the group of men and the fire's safety, whether it be authentic or perceived.

I caught my breath as I approached the fire, the huddled men watching me apprehensively with the question each one wanted to ask written in their eyes. I slowed my pace and shook my head at them. I need not say what I'd found in the trench, the details weren't necessary, and I supposed the fact I'd returned alone provided enough answer for their collective query.

I had questions of my own, and I scanned the faces until I saw Klein. He was sitting near the fire, his rifle across his lap. He stared back at me without expression and watched as I stepped closer to him.

"What the hell is that thing, and how do we fight it?" I asked.

Klein looked up at me, his breath creating a halo around his head. His eyes moved from my face to the shadows deep in the trench at my back. Despite his calm demeanor, the nervousness rolled off his body in waves, and I felt myself getting caught in their ripples.

"I told you. It is Perchta. She is here for Christmas. Silver for good, something else for the bad," he said. "She is like your Santa Claus, but much different. Naughty and nice? Santa gives...coal? Perchta takes the bad children."

I looked over my shoulder, into the trench. The other men had gathered behind me, listening to Klein's explanation of what was with us. The German troops were looking down at the ground, kicking the dirt with the toes of their boots like little boys caught doing something bad by their parents while my men had a mixture of disbelief and terror on their faces. Regardless of beliefs, they knew something had come to us of this Christmas Day.

"Okay," said Harris, his voice heavy with irritation, "so how do we kill the bitch?"

Klein smiled and looked at Harris with bafflement. He shook his head and shrugged his shoulders. "You don't. She does not die. Perchta can't die. I don't know how old she is, but she will not die. We just wait. She will bring her gifts and take what she wants. We just wait until she is done."

Harris snorted in disgust, or maybe defeat, I couldn't tell which of the two.

"Okay, smartass, when do we know she's done?" he asked.

The sigh Klein released turned to a plume of white mist in the cold night, and he looked toward the sky, which was already showing tinges of purple as dawn crept along the far horizon. "Perchta comes for the days of Christmas," he said.

It was my turn to sigh. With Christmas Day already fading into the past, I felt relief.

"That's good, right?" Harris said, stealing my thought and vocalizing it. "Christmas is over. The old bitch is gone. Right?"

Klein smiled. He looked at Harris with sympathy and shook his head before lowering it.

"No. Perchta visits for the twelve days of Christmas," he said in a low voice. "The twelve days of Christmas. They start on Christmas. She has eleven days left."

Christmas Sinner

Dave Jeffery

Daniel Clift groaned as his fingers kneaded the nape of his neck, palms clammy, the skin cooled by the frigid air about him. He felt a lump; it moved like an egg under his shivering fingers.

He really wanted to open his eyes, but at that moment, courage was a waning commodity, and he had to dig deep. His body may have been sluggish, but his mind was gearing up, his capacity for recall now greased and rolling.

A sigh in the gloom. "Merry Christmas, Danny."

The voice made him gasp in surprise. His eyes sprang open, and he was thankful that the only light came from a splay of twinkling Christmas lights to his left.

In the creamy glow, he could make out the skeletal shape

of a cheap tinsel Christmas tree. To one side of the spindly plastic trunk was a stack of boxes, each wrapped in metallic paper and finished with bows of reds and silver. Tiny starbursts exploded under the touch of the fairy lights. It looked both sinister and beautiful.

A figure sat opposite him, thin, and dressed in an oversized Santa suit. The man's head was small, his body slim. There was so much surplus material he looked as though he'd deflated in his chair. One hand scratched at his stubbled chin. The other hand, perched on the armrest, held a gun.

Dan looked into the guy's gaunt, pale face, and thought for a split-second that he only had empty sockets for eyes. Then he realized what he'd thought to be gaping holes were merely sunglasses, the whole thing adding to the surreal, unnerving moment.

Dan's voice was thick with fear and confusion. "Who are you? Where am I?"

"Questions, questions, Mister Nosey Parker." There was a lilt to his captor's tone. Mocking.

Dan tested his bonds, shaking the handcuffs and the length of chain dropping from his wrists down to his feet. After a few seconds of wanton struggle, the only thing he'd achieved was to almost upend the dining chair to which he was fettered. In a panic, he stopped, breathing ragged, not with exertion but terror.

"Let me out of this chair." Dan hated how pathetic he sounded, whining like a child in the chocolate aisle of a supermarket.

"All in good time, Danny. All in good time."

"How'd you know my name?"

The man in the Santa suit nodded as if this was expected. "I know a lot more about you than your name, Danny. I know all your *dirty little secrets*. It's part of what I do, all part of the service. You can call me Nick. Not my real name, but it'll do for tonight's proceedings."

Nick pushed a hand into one of the big red pockets, working his fingers beneath the white, furry trim. After a short time, he pulled free a phone and hit a few keys. An image came up on the screen.

It was his wife.

Dan felt sick. "Jenny."

"She's a fine-looking woman," Nick said as he turned the screen back so he could stare at it. "No doubt about that. You're a lucky guy."

"What the hell have you done to my wife, you bastard?" Dan went to stand, but his chains wouldn't allow for it.

"Easy, now. You don't want to take a tumble. You might hurt yourself before the fun starts. Don't worry about Jenny's well-being, I'll get to that in a little while." He nodded toward the tree.

"Be of good cheer, Danny. Even though you've been a very naughty boy this year, I've still brought you presents."

Dan tapped into a rage that he never knew he possessed. At that moment, he was imagining stamping the life out of Nick with his bare feet.

Unaware, his tormentor continued, his tone cordial. "Now, if you sit still and be a good boy, things won't need to get messy."

Dan shuffled uneasily in his seat. Despite his cordial disposition, Nick gave off a menacing air. Dan's feet squeaked on the smooth floor. He looked down and saw he was center stage of a large rectangle of sturdy plastic sheeting.

"What's this?"

"Gift wrap. No bows, I'm afraid. Just a shallow grave out in Lickey Woods if you don't play nice."

"You're fucking insane."

"*So* not true. Sociopathic, maybe, but not insane. I do what I do for money. Although I'm damn good at it, I take no joy out of my work. I am a wage slave. There, I've said it, and it can't be taken back."

"And what is it you do, for money?"

"I make people *pay,* Danny. I make them pay for being *naughty.*"

"Look, I have money put aside, fifteen grand. You let me go and it's yours. I won't go to the police, I give you my word, okay? My goddamned word."

"Can't do that, Danny."

"Fifteen grand, for Christ's sake."

"In my line of work, reputation is everything. If I go reneging on a contract, then I'd be out of work PDQ, *comprende*? I have some instructions for you to follow. My client was very specific. If you don't do as I ask, I'm going to have to give you a little incentive. And by that, I mean putting a bullet into each kneecap."

Head bowing, Dan felt despair take hold of him, tears fell into his lap.

"Aw, now don't cry. All you need do is co-operate. It's Christmas, and you get to open all those wonderful presents."

"Great."

"Well, that does sound a tad ungrateful, Danny. Just putting it out there. A lot of work went into giving you the most memorable Christmas ever."

Nick stood and walked over to the stash of presents. He stooped, the Santa suit making him appear like a flaccid, mutant tomato. When he came back to Dan, he carried a gift the size and shape of a shoebox. He held one hand under it, the gun held steadfast in the other.

"Here. Let's start small."

"What's in there?"

Nick laughed. "Are you for real? It's a surprise, silly!"

Dan lifted his shackled hands and reluctantly took the glittering red carton from Nick.

"I've added a little tissue in there, just to stretch the suspense. You don't think it's overkill, do you? Sometimes I just get carried away with my work."

Apprehensive, Dan began to tear away the layers. Sure enough, the paper revealed a shoebox, and he reluctantly lifted the lid, tossing it to the floor. He didn't hear it land.

There was tissue paper, dark like sackcloth, but it had shifted in transit. In the box, Dan could see clawed fingers and an upturned palm streaked with blood.

"Argh! Jesus, Jesus! You sick fuck!" He threw the parcel away from him, and it skittered across the floor. The hand, severed at the mid-forearm, slapped against the plastic sheet. Dan couldn't tear his eyes away from the carnage.

"Is that my wife? Is that my Jenny?"

"Not your Jenny. Not anymore." Nick was matter-of-fact, almost rueful.

"Why?" Dan snarled with rage, finally turning his head towards Nick. "What the fuck did we do to you?"

"I'm not usually one to point fingers, but you're going to have to pin that one on Jenny."

"What?" Rage gave way to confusion. "What are you talking about?"

"Well, Jenny did kinda employ me."

Confusion became bewilderment. "I... I don't understand."

Nick went back to his own chair and sat down. "Your wife, Danny," he sighed. "She signed on the line, sir. She splashed the cash. She wrote out the contract."

"I don't believe it. She couldn't do this; she just wouldn't," Dan muttered.

Nick gave out a mirthless laugh. "I'm not going to argue

about the finer points of healthy relationships, but I'm guessing Jenny took you boning another woman pretty hard."

"Another woman?" Dan said weakly.

Once again, Nick retrieved his phone and scanned it as he clicked buttons. "One Caroline Edwards, I believe." He double-checked the display. "Yep. That's the gal."

"Shit."

Caroline Edwards, his mistress of three years, his bolthole from the drudgery of a stable, married life, a spark of light in the gray days.

It had started out as sex, wild and rampant. Mutual lust servicing mutual need. Then emotions seeped in, a connection, long talks after sex, deep discussions as they learned more about each other, and lust became love, and love became guilt. She had a partner, Dan had Jenny. Neither had intended it to be any more than an aside, a little fun to buff up the dull days.

Now it was something else. Now it was the collision of worlds, and the fallout was catastrophic.

"I guess the brevity of the situation is probably dawning on you about now," Nick interjected. "Jenny found out about your gal Caroline, got pretty down about it all. But, fuck, how she loved you, mate. Seemed she was about ready to forgive you and then finds the note."

"The note?"

"The one she found when she was getting the suit ready for dry cleaning. The one you had squirreled away in your pocket, the one telling her you were going to leave her for Sweet Caroline after Christmas."

"I..."

"Yes, I know. It's a lot to take in. The betrayal, the level of hatred it takes to get a guy like me involved in redressing the balance. She's a talker, your Jenny, no doubt about it. She told me everything as she was signing the paperwork."

Dan looked back at the severed hand. "Oh, my God. Caroline..."

"I can give you my word your mistress didn't suffer," Nick said hastily, as if this made any difference at all. "The *cutting up* happened after she had expired. And I packaged her up with care and respect. The way all gifts of love should be."

"Jenny didn't have to...do this..."

"I'm thinking Jenny is not big on being spurned. *Hell hath no fury* and all that. She was keen that you follow the instructions."

"Fuck her. Fuck you!" Dan spat the words, each coated in contempt.

The gunshot was loud, and the muzzle flash exploded in the air, leaving a smear of light imprinted in Dan's corneas. The searing pain in his knee helped him focus on the reality of the situation; his manacles allowed him to grasp his mashed patella, blood and denim mixed with shards of bone, grating against his palms.

His breath came as short, sharp gasps, and the pain rose and fell like an ocean in a really bad swell.

"Just for clarity, you did that to yourself. The terms were made pretty clear from the outset, behave or pay the piper." Nick spoke as though reading a child a bedtime story, slow and clear. "Time to focus, Danny. Jenny's instructions. Look at me. You looking? You listening?"

Dan was able to let go a growl of pain and fury.

"Good. You still got a backbone, always a doozie to see."

Nick folded in the middle and reached under his chair. When he sat upright, he brought with him a black bowling bag, which he placed on his lap and put his hand inside. When it came free, Dan gave out a tiny whimper, his hands clutching his knee made the bones pop and grind, his teeth squeaked as he mashed them together in pain and grief.

"Now, you get to give dear Caroline a nice, big farewell kiss."

"No, no, no..." It was a mantra of despair, but even with the horror of it, Dan couldn't look away as Nick brought out the head of his lover. Only one of her eyes was open, and this was rolled back to reveal white.

"I never fail to be amazed by just how heavy these things are," Nick said as he walked over to Dan.

He held Caroline by her dark hair, lank with dried blood. Her mouth was slack, the tongue lolling over her dark lips. Dan was mesmerized by just how white her skin appeared, like an alabaster bust he'd seen in museums up and down the country.

Caroline's face, her ragged stump of a neck, seemed to fill his vision. Nick held it out and made it dance in the air as he shook it.

"Pucker up, lover boy. Your girl wants her Christmas kiss. *Mwah, mwah*!"

Dan began to cry, the tears a visceral manifestation of despair, fear, and boiling anger. Like acid, they scorched his cheeks, and he tipped back his head to scream his frustrations at the ceiling.

"Back in the room, Danny boy!" Nick said. "You're offending our guest."

Snapping his head back down, Dan sneered in physical and emotional agony. He allowed his anger to drive him, but there was something else, the absolute desire to live, to exact vengeance on the piece of shit across the room, and his fucking bitch of a wife.

He pouted, placed his mouth on the dead lips of his lover, ignored the faint smell of feces and bleach, fought against the contents of his stomach that wanted to launch itself into the room.

"Now, now," Nick chuckled, pulling the head away. "You two should get a room."

He dropped Caroline's head back into the bowling bag, where it landed with an unceremonious *thud*. There was a moment when Nick looked down into the bag, his face calm and serene, then he zipped the bag shut.

"Final instruction," he said to Dan with a smile. "After that, you get to call an ambulance, and the police if you're inclined, but I'll be long gone by then. And given the funds Jenny was planning to swipe from the family coffers, she will be, too."

Dan was on autopilot. "Let's just get this shit over with."

"Good man!" Like a child on Christmas morning, Nick went to a door to his left. He opened it and went briefly inside, the gun aimed in Dan's general direction through the open doorway. When he came back into the room, Nick had a plate in his hands. The cling film covering the contents was misted with red.

"Now then, Dan, I couldn't figure if you were a leg or a breast man, so I cut you a little of both."

This time Dan had no say over what his body needed to do. He vomited fast and hard.

And it wasn't to be the only time that evening.

Christmas Wish

Rose Blackthorn

The shrill, eardrum-piercing screams brought Tess out of a sound sleep. She stumbled out of bed, nearly tripped over a pile of laundry left scattered in the hall, and flipped the switch to light her daughter's bedroom as the shrieking cut off.

"Linz, you okay?" she asked, squinting in the sudden glare.

Lindsey stared at Tess, eyes wide and shocked. She had a bad case of bed-head and was hunched up against her headboard with her covers clutched under her chin.

"Honey, what's wrong?" Tess crossed the room and sat beside the girl.

"Monsters," Lindsey whispered, her voice ragged and rough.

"Oh, sweetie—"

❄ ❄ ❄

"You look like shit."

Tess gave Ryan a dirty look. "It's that time of year."

He raised one eyebrow, a wordless question.

She downed the rest of her coffee and poured another cup. "Most kids get scared and have nightmares around Halloween. Not mine. Only kid I know who starts freaking out the week before Christmas."

Ryan grinned, obviously unsympathetic. "On the first day of Christmas, my true love gave to me—a kid who's afraid of the Christmas tree."

"Funny. We'll see how much enjoyment you get out of it tonight."

"What's that supposed to mean?"

"She's not a one-night show."

❄ ❄ ❄

"So, what did you ask Santa Claus for?" Miriam placed a teddy bear at the small table set in the corner of Lindsey's room. A doll with a plastic face and cloth arms and legs sat in another chair across the table. Miniature plastic cups and saucers were placed before each chair.

Lindsey shook her head.

"You have to ask for what you want. Or who knows what you'll end up with!"

Lindsey pressed her lips together. She hated this time of year, not just because of the thought of some fat old man sneaking in during the night while they slept.

"Momma says if I'm real good, Santa might bring me some ice skates. And then, Momma and Daddy might let me take lessons," Miriam went on, pouring make-believe tea from an old copper teapot.

"Not asking for nothing," Lindsey whispered. Her throat still hurt from the night before.

"You'll feel left out, then," Miriam advised, then picked up one of the empty teacups. Her pinky-finger stuck out just like it was supposed to when you were drinking make-believe tea.

Lindsey didn't argue; she just slumped tiredly in her chair. All she wanted was to lie down and take a nap, but Miriam wanted to play. So, rather than sulk, she listened to her friend prattle on about Christmas, and Santa Claus and his elves, who she'd visited at the mall, and the pretty pink ice skates she had asked for and just knew she would get. Then again, after a while, maybe Lindsey did sulk just a little bit.

❄ ❄ ❄

When the high-pitched scream started, Ryan managed to fall out of bed before he could get his feet under him. Tess had warned him, but he'd thought she'd been exaggerating. He staggered down the hallway toward Lindsey's room, trailing a hand along the wall as he searched for the light switch. The overhead hall light came on just as he swung into the little girl's room and, for a moment, he was completely blinded by the darkness before him.

"No!" Lindsey shrieked, and something rushed past Ryan's ankle. He jumped, slamming his shoulder into the doorframe before he found the light switch for the bedroom.

"Hey, hey," he tried to soothe, still catching his breath and attempting to ignore his goosebumps. It was chilly in the room, and he was only wearing the shorts he'd gone to bed in. "It's okay, Lindsey. I'm here."

"Where's Mommy?" she asked, a note of fear evident in her soft voice. Her eyes were wide and filled with barely controlled terror. She kept looking around her room as though searching for someone else.

"She's at work. Remember? She's scheduled for the night shift this week." He pushed his hair out of his face, the adrenaline rush that had ripped him out of bed already beginning to ebb. "That's why I'm here." He and Tess had been dating for six months, but he still had his own place. He stayed over now and then, and occasionally babysat when she had the night shift and couldn't get her regular sitter. And this, the week of Christmas, her regular sitter was out of town. "Were you having a nightmare?"

Lyndsey shook her head quickly, eyes still seeming shocked. "No. I was awake."

"So, what happened?" Ryan crossed to her bed and sat down facing her, wishing he could make her feel better. He wasn't a dad, and Tess was the only woman he'd ever been serious with who had a kid, but Lyndsey was cute and smart, and he was becoming quite fond of her.

"Monsters," she whispered, clutching a purple teddy bear tightly to her chest. Her eyes still darted around the room, seeking something that she couldn't find.

"Hey, you know there aren't any monsters. You're old enough to know that, right?" He reached out to pat her arm, feeling completely inadequate.

She shook her head again and looked directly at him for the first time. "You're wrong. It ran past you when you opened the door."

Something had brushed against his ankle when he came in, but he figured it was probably just one of the stuffed animals tumbling onto the floor. "Linz, there's nobody here except you and me. Your mom will be back before you wake up in the morning, but you're safe here with me."

She didn't answer, but the set expression on her face said she clearly didn't believe it.

"Why don't you tell me about it, then? Maybe if I know what you're scared of, I can help you get rid of it." He didn't know if it was a good idea to play along with it, but he couldn't do anything if he didn't know what was frightening her. Tess had said it happened every year before Christmas, but she hadn't gone into any details.

"It won't do any good," she whispered, her grip on the teddy only getting tighter. Tears welled in her big blue eyes, and her bottom lip began to quiver.

Don't cry, don't cry! he thought, and tugged lightly on one of the bear's fluffy feet to distract her. "But it won't hurt, either, right? Give me a chance."

❄ ❄ ❄

He woke when Tess came in, walking on the balls of her feet and attempting to make no noise. The clock on the bed-side table said 5:45 a.m.

"Morning, babe," he said, and she jumped.

"Shit!" The shoes she carried in one hand dropped to the floor with a muffled thud, and she covered her mouth with the other hand. "What are you doing up so early?"

Ryan leaned up on one elbow and yawned before answering. "Didn't really get much sleep."

"Oh, no." Tess sat on her side of the bed, turning toward him. "Bad night?"

"That kid has a hell of an imagination." He leaned forward and pressed his forehead to her leg. "I think she finally went to sleep about an hour ago. She'll be on your schedule before long."

"I'm sorry, Ryan. It seems to be worse this year." She ran her fingers through his hair, working gently through a few snarls. "What happened?"

Sitting up, he met her eyes. The only light in the room came from the clock, and it was hard to make out her expression. "Santa doesn't have elves, Tess. He has little boogeymen who break into people's houses to check for naughty kids. Apparently, they're really interested in this house. That's why they keep coming back."

Tess shook her head, rubbing her eyes tiredly. "I don't even know where she gets this from. And I don't know how to stop it. It's not like she's a bad kid, so why would she be worried about being naughty?"

After a moment, Ryan slid over and put his arms around her. "Christmas is almost here, and once it's past, this will pass, too."

She nodded against his shoulder but didn't say anything.

❄ ❄ ❄

The next three nights were repeats of that night. Ryan had agreed to stay over and watch Lindsey while Tess worked. If anything, the girl's night terrors only got worse, but he did everything he could to comfort her. In return, she gave him more details about the monsters she claimed were skittering through her bedroom every night.

"They're little, even littler than me," she described while Ryan made her funny face pancakes for breakfast and hot chocolate with mini marshmallows. "I've seen people dressed like elves at the mall. At least, that's what Miriam said they were." Miriam was the next-door neighbor, a year older than Lindsey, and she was as excited about Christmas as Lindsey was dreading it. "And these aren't elves. They're skinny and boney, and they have sharp teeth."

"So, how do you think they're getting in?" Ryan asked. He put chocolate chips on the pancake on her plate, making a smiley face with another mini marshmallow for a nose.

She shook her head, wiping at her shadow-circled eyes. "I don't know. We don't have a chimney."

Hiding a smile, Ryan sprayed whipped cream across the top of the pancake, making fluffy white hair. "Okay, that makes sense. Do you want syrup?"

She considered for a moment, then nodded. "Strawberry."

Ryan let her pour the syrup herself and asked casually, "So do they talk to you? Or just sneak around and try to be scary?"

Lips pursed thoughtfully, she made circles with the syrup on both cheeks of the smiley face and then outlined the chocolate chip mouth like lipstick. "They talk to me, but I just cover my ears."

"Hmm." He flipped out another pancake onto a plate for himself and scattered a handful of chocolate chips on it. "Well, maybe you could talk to them. Tell them you want them to go away 'cause you're trying to sleep."

She shook her head, peeking up at him from beneath her bangs. "Mommy said to never talk to them."

Tess had said she told Lindsey to just ignore these *monsters,* to pretend that they weren't there in hopes that eventually she'd outgrow them. Obviously, that wasn't working. Ryan glanced toward the hallway leading from the kitchen back to the bedroom, where Tess was still sleeping after her last night at work. He leaned closer, keeping his voice low. It wasn't his place to undermine Tess, but the last few nights, he'd gotten a lot closer to Lindsey. He was tired of hearing her screams, seeing her terrified face in the sudden light when he raced in to check on her. What Tess had suggested was not working, so he thought it was time to try something new. "So here's an idea. If they come back tonight, just go ahead and talk to them. Maybe they keep coming back because you're ignoring them. If you tell them what you want, maybe they'll listen to you and leave you alone."

Lindsey didn't say anything, just started to eat her pancake before it got cold. But she gave him a level glance, so much more mature than her age, and nodded once.

Ryan grinned at her. "More marshmallows?"

❄ ❄ ❄

It was Christmas Eve, and Tess was off work until after the holiday. Ryan made sloppy joes for dinner, and they watched cartoon Christmas specials in the blinking lights of the tree. Per tradition, Tess and Lindsey each picked one present to open before going to bed. Lindsey made sure Ryan participated by bringing him one of the gifts from where it had been hidden beneath the tree. When he opened it, he was surprised to find a hand-tied friendship bracelet with a tiny silver charm. *RYAN* was impressed in it, and he looked at Tess, who seemed surprised to see it, too.

"Did you make this?" he asked, and Lindsey nodded with a shy smile. "It's beautiful. I love it." He didn't think any child had ever made something for him before, and it was amazing how much it affected him.

"That's so cute!" Tess took it, studying the bracelet while Ryan leaned over to hug the girl. "You did a great job, sweetie."

Then it was time to clean up the dinner dishes and tuck Lindsey in. Neither of the adults said anything about Santa coming tonight, but Ryan was pleased to see a determined look on Lindsey's face. After brushing her teeth and changing into pajamas, she climbed into her bed as though she hadn't awakened screaming every night for the last week.

"Sweet dreams, sweetie," Tess said and dropped a kiss on the girl's brow.

"Sleep well," Ryan added and held out his fist to bump Lindsey's. The little silver charm on his bracelet swung, catching the light before Tess turned it off.

Back in Tess's bedroom, Ryan kicked off his shoes and fell back on the bed. "I'm looking forward to a full night's sleep."

"You may have to wait one more day for that," Tess warned, pulling her shirt off over her head. "But at least we're close."

"Come here, you," Ryan commanded and grinned at the raised eyebrow she gave him. "Time for your Christmas Eve present."

After a moment, she laughed lightly and joined him on the bed.

❄ ❄ ❄

It was after three in the morning when the screams started. Out of the habit born of the last week, Ryan lurched up out of bed, but Tess pushed him back. "I'll get it," she said, making sure he lay back down before she hurried out of the room.

Down the hall, not bothering to turn on the light, she went into Lindsey's room, where the screaming had already stopped. There was a rustling sound on the far side of the bed, but in the dark, Tess couldn't see anything. "Linz?" she called quietly, searching for the light switch by the open door. "Honey, are you okay?" The switch clicked, but the overhead light didn't come on. "Damn bulb," she muttered and cautiously moved toward the twin bed with its pink and purple quilt. "Sweetie?"

The door to the hallway closed. It didn't slam, just clicked as it was pushed shut, and Tess jumped. "Lindsey?"

More rustling noises and something scurried past her bare legs.

She started again, tripping on something—the stuffed bear?—and smacked the edge of the footboard before hitting the floor. A groan escaped her at the sudden pain, and she grimaced. "Linz, turn on your lamp, okay? Mommy fell down."

"Miriam said I'm supposed to ask for what I want." Lindsey's voice was soft coming from the far side of the room between the bed and her window. "Santa's elves won't know what I want unless I ask."

"Honey, turn on the light." Tess pushed herself up, hissing at the scrape on her elbow and feeling something warm and wet sliding down her face from where she'd struck the footboard.

"You told me to ignore them, but that just made them angry. They just wanted to know what I want for Christmas."

"Lindsey, turn on the light." Tess made her voice firmer, yipping as something scratched at her in the dark.

"So, I told them I want Ryan to stay."

"Linz—" She cut off as sharp claws or talons grasped her ankle and yanked her around on the floor. There were whispers and mutters, the sounds of little hard feet running across the hardwood, and then the window was opened, letting in a blast of frigid air. "Lindsey!"

She clutched at the bed, trying to stop herself as she was dragged to the window. A streetlight from outside let in a little light, enough to see her daughter crouched against the wall beside the head of her bed, a teddy bear in one arm, and a dark angular figure with glowing green eyes held in the other. The thing smiled, dark lips pulling back to bare sharp white teeth, and then Tess was lifted up and pulled out the open window. She tried to brace herself for an impact with the ground, but it never came. Instead, carried in the wickedly sharp talons of Lindsey's monsters, she was spirited away. Her screams faded even more quickly than Lindsey's had.

❄ ❄ ❄

Daddy had disappeared when Lindsey was four. Grandma Joan went missing when Lindsey was five. There had been a couple of Mommy's friends, whom Lindsey didn't really remember, who had just stopped coming over when she was six and seven. The elves, for surprisingly, that's what they told her they were, had been so happy when she spoke to them instead of hiding her head and screaming. All she had to do was tell them what she wanted. They would make her Christmas wish come true. Mommy never made the elves go away or stopped them from tormenting her every Christmas season. But Ryan made it okay by explaining that she could just tell them what she wanted. Just like Miriam had said.

"You have to ask for what you want, or who knows what you'll end up with?"

Cold Edge

Damascus Mincemeyer

The day was created for the good of mankind; the night was made for murder.

It had been snowing for half an hour when Sal pulled the van off the narrow roadway, and already the asphalt was covered in a quickly accumulating white blanket. In the headlights, the flakes were dizzying as they spun around the endless acreage of tangled woodland, and in the passenger's seat, Frankie ground out his dying cigarette in the stuffed ashtray with a shivering fat hand.

"Too fuckin' cold out here," he grumbled, turning the collar up on his tailored overcoat; there was a dark stain on the lapel, and Sal was unsure if it was blood from the evening's events or pasta sauce from the enormous plate of ziti Frankie ate before they headed out. For Sal, getting the call to work a hit killed his appetite along with the mark, but Frankie Two-Chins' considerable gut had no such reservations. His mouth didn't either, and the complaints continued.

"Too fuckin' cold," he repeated. "Too fuckin' long a drive. Too fuckin' many trees out here. Too fuckin' quiet. Jesus, what a way to spend Christmas Eve," Frankie paused, looking into the rear of the van. "I tell you, Tony, you caused more trouble tonight than you were worth."

Sal glanced over his shoulder to the large, ornately woven oriental rug rolled up on the floor behind him; with the way it seeped crimson splotches onto the vehicle's upholstery, the tapestry looked like a giant, misshapen serpent devouring a rat whole. He knew what the bulky form burrito-wrapped within the rug was, and if he didn't, the throbbing from his freshly broken nose was more than enough to remind him. Part of Sal wondered what Tony "Sticks" Salerno had done to earn the order to end his life but knew enough not to ask. That was the way of the wiseguy: no questions, no mercy. *Omerta.* You get the call, you do the job. The why didn't matter. The who didn't matter. Not even if it was someone you'd known for a dozen years, played cards with, shot the shit with, ran schemes with. Not even if it was Christmas Eve. None of that counted. When the capo said it had to be done, it was done. Maybe Tony made a pass at another guy's broad or didn't let the capo in on earnings from a side-hustle. Maybe he'd been a snitch. Maybe it didn't matter.

Sal touched his face, wincing at the burning cauldron his nose had become. Usually, when a wiseguy came to be whacked, for whatever reason, the execution followed a routine path: go out, wine and dine him, bullshit with him, then as you leave, sneak up behind him and put two large in the base of his skull, quick, clean, and cruel. The first part of the night had gone that way, too, with Sal and Frankie inviting Tony to Patistio's restaurant, and together the three of them talked, laughed, ate, drank, just like always. But when they stepped outside into the alley, things went awry. Maybe Tony had gotten wise to the hit or heard the cocking of Frankie's .44; either way, in the split-second life and death hung in the balance, Tony knocked the piece from Frankie's hand and fought back like a demon, caving in Sal's nostrils with an elbow before trying to make a break for it. But Frankie had caught him, mauled him, the pair wrestling until Frankie finally bashed Tony's skull with a length of pipe he'd found, so savagely the face was unrecognizable pulp. Afterward, they folded the body into the rug they'd brought and headed downstate to where Tony's pre-dug grave awaited. The trip itself only aggravated the evening's chaos: true to Frankie's gripe, the drive was long and cold, made harder by the snow, and when the van's heater decided to quit, the frigid temperature worsened, increasing the misery.

"Let's put this motherfucker six feet under and get goin'," Frankie said, pulling a flashlight from the glove compartment. "I'm sicka this shit already."

"How're we gonna bury 'im, Frankie? The ground's probably frozen by now."

"It wasn't when we dug the hole," Frankie snapped. Sal shook his head; two days prior, their initial expedition from Newark to the Pine Barrens area had been made in one of New Jersey's warmest December's on record, but a holiday-week Arctic cold-front had changed things, even if Frankie couldn't comprehend it. Opening his door, he only sneered. "Just get the goddamn shovels, Sal."

The snow outside was already ankle-deep and coming down faster with each passing second, making the five-acre march to the gravesite a challenge of endurance; the snow, the dark, the difficulty in hauling both body and digging tools sapped Sal's strength, and even Frankie, usually sturdy as a bear, showed fatigue, and what would've been a fifteen-minute hike instead became an hour-long polar endeavor. By the time the beam from Frankie's flashlight illuminated the crude burial pit, Sal's hands and feet were numb, and he stumbled, dropping the head-end of the bloody rug to the snow.

"Watch what the hell you're doin'," Frankie snarled. Sal staggered upright, his Armani coat caked with sloppy, wet, white powder. Below him, the rug had opened up, Tony's disfigured head suddenly exposed in the flashlight's beam, and Sal recoiled at the gruesome sight.

"Jesus, Frankie, you think you worked him over enough?" he asked.

Frankie set his end of the rug down on the snow and smirked. "My old man always said I hadda talent to be a ballplayer. Maybe he was right." He looked from the pit to the rug then, frowning. "He ain't gonna fit, Sal. Too fuckin' tall."

"They didn't call him 'Sticks' for nothin'," Sal said, sizing Tony up; the body's legs were indeed too long for the hole they'd created, but while he stood there, Sal noticed something else and asked, "Do you hear that?"

"We're in the middle of goddamn nowhere. Ain't nothin' *to* hear."

Sal furrowed his brow. The empty wilderness had, as Frankie groused, a cemetery stillness to it, but after a second, he shook his head again. "No, it sounds like...*breathing."*

"Whatta you talkin' about?" Frankie scoffed. "We're both huffin' and puffin' from carryin' his dead ass."

Sal squatted next to Tony's torso. "Shine the light over here, Frankie," he commanded; when Frankie complied, Sal saw the slow, steady rise and fall of Tony's chest, a soft, icy fog of shallow breath coming clearly from his toothless, split-lip mouth.

"Fuck," Sal said unsteadily. "Frankie, I don't think he's dea--"

The sentence never finished. Below Sal, Tony's eyes, startlingly white against the raw blood red of his face, flipped open, and he screamed a wordless animal howl, grabbing at Sal's coat and lurching up, his hands clawing towards Sal's throat.

"Jesus!" Sal reeled back, breaking Tony's hold on him, but the snow was slick, and Sal's footing slipped, sending him tumbling down into the grave. He landed hard at an odd angle, heard a crack from his left arm; above him, the silent snowfall was punctured by unfolding violence—thrashing limbs, Frankie's screams, and Tony's agonized, angered grunts, the beam from the flashlight swinging wildly back and forth. Then there was a final shout, a deafening gunshot, and the light died altogether.

Sal struggled to his feet, and now it wasn't just his nose that hurt; his left elbow shrieked with pain, and it took more effort than he expected to climb from the pit. Once above ground, the quiet darkness was as disorienting as it was unnerving.

"Frankie?" he whispered. At first, there was no response, but then the flashlight flipped on, blinding in the black, forcing Sal to shield his eyes. Frankie stood there, shaking and short of breath, flashlight in one hand, his .44 in the other, clothes rumpled and snow-covered, nose leaking a stream of blood all the way down his double chin. After adjusting to the light, Sal saw the rug, crumpled, fully open, and empty, the snow around it torn up from the fight, and then spotted the trail of bloodied footprints in the snow snaking out into the woods.

"What the fuck happened?" Sal asked. "Did you get him?"

"I think I plugged him one," Frankie said, dabbing his

nose.

"You *think?* Jesus, you're a shit of a shot," Sal scorned. "Yeah, *hell* of a ballplayer you woulda made. Next time you go to kill a guy, make sure the sonuvabitch is *dead,* will you?"

"I don't see you doin' no better," Frankie spat back, shining the light along the path Tony had fled. "We gotta find him. We don't, we're fucked."

Sal cradled his arm; with his growing list of injuries, he didn't feel like trooping further through the cold, but he knew Frankie was right: the penalties for failing to complete a hit were savage—Sal envisioned being strung up by a meat hook in his ass, severed scrotum shoved in his mouth, and didn't treasure the image.

"How far do you think he can really get?" Frankie asked.

"Dunno," Sal said, withdrawing his own revolver from his coat. "But I guess we'll find out."

Tony's wounded route zigzagged around trees and rocks, up slopes and across a frozen creek bed, where the path was almost lost, and in the isolated forest, all sense of time was obliterated; to Sal, how long they toiled was not measured in minutes or hours but in stabbing throbs from nose and arm, and when the snow kept coming in thickening waves, it made him feel like an Eskimo. Ahead of him, Frankie looked the part, his coat and gel-slicked hair frosted white, and the farther afield they ventured, the more Sal heard the laughter from other wiseguys cackling in his mind at the debacle the night had become. If he escaped without a meat-hook enema, he'd laugh, too.

Just when Sal didn't think he could take another step, a clearing opened up in the forest, on the far side of which a narrow lane led uphill to a small country cottage, its quaint wood-paneled exterior aglow in the swirling snowfall by the candy-colored shine of Christmas bulbs, and from the edge of the road, Tony's footprints disappeared from the halo of Frankie's flashlight in the direction of the house.

"Look at that. Winter fuckin' wonderland," Frankie grunted. "Got the bastard cornered now."

"Wait, you wanna go *in* there?" Sal asked. When Frankie nodded, Sal examined the house; there was a pick-up and sedan, both snow-covered, parked in the driveway. "You fuckin' crazy? What about the people inside?"

Frankie shrugged, hefting his revolver. "We ice 'em right along with Tony. No witnesses." He gave Sal a callous glare. "Problem with that?"

Uneasily, Sal shook his head; he'd seen that malicious look before, whenever murder became the answer to whatever obstacle was in Frankie's path, and as they went up the lane, a dozen scenarios unfurled in his head, none of them good and all of them bloody.

Near the house, Frankie flipped the flashlight off; in the brightness from the holiday decorations, Tony's tracks were plainly visible, ending at a broken basement window, and Sal's thoughts were then less about Frankie's increasingly itchy trigger finger than what Tony was apt to do now that he'd gained entry. Yet when Sal took a step towards the opening, Frankie pulled him back.

"Don't be a fuckin' mook," he growled. "Tony ain't stupid. He wants us to follow him right in there. Ambush us." Frankie eyed the house like a lion stalking a wounded gazelle. "I say we split up. I'll take the front, you do the back."

He continued on towards the porch, and after some hesitation, Sal went around to the rear of the house, stood on the back stoop, and stared at the door, envious of Frankie's assuredness. He may have been an oversized slob of a man, but Frankie's appearance belied nimble criminal skill; his sausage fingers were delicate when it came to picking locks and opening safes, something that still marveled Sal after all the years they'd hustled and thieved together, and he had stern faith in Frankie's ability to slip into the place undetected. Sal's own method of breaking and entering was far less dexterous: he smashed the door's window with a sharp hit from his good elbow, reaching a hand through the hole to unlock the deadbolt. Inside was pitch dark, but a dim glow creeping down a nearby hall gave enough light for Sal to see he'd entered into the kitchen. Like the house's exterior, the room was cozy, the sudden warmth at once comforting and distracting, the sting of recirculating blood to his frostbitten extremities almost causing him to forget his actual intent.

The floor was slick with quickly melting snow from Sal's ice-crusted shoes, every step noisy with the crunch of shattered glass, and carefully he listened for other sounds in the house—of people, of dogs, anything—but when he heard nothing, he half-wondered if Tony had already accomplished what Frankie had intended to do to whomever lived there. Slowly, Sal moved into the next room; it, too, was dark, but he could make out country furnishings and a long dining table set with finery for a Christmas breakfast he doubted anyone living there would get a chance to eat.

There was the soft creak of floorboards behind Sal, and he turned, grunting in pain, leveling the .38 at the shadows of the dining room's entrance. From the hall, there was another shuffled footstep, and Sal tightened his grip on the revolver.

"Frankie?" he whispered unsteadily. There was no reply, only the sound of breathing, and then Sal asked, more cautiously, "Tony?"

Again there was no answer, but when a shape emerged from the gloom, Sal was startled to see a girl, eight, maybe nine years old, dressed in pajamas, cherub-faced with sandy hair pulled into a pony-tail, her eyes huge saucers, and for a few long moments, the two quietly stared at each other, mirrors of surprise.

"Are... Are you Santa?" the girl stammered quietly. When he didn't respond, the child repeated her question, and Sal's mind raced. *No witnesses,* Frankie had said, but as Sal looked at the girl, the knowledge of what should be done and the reality disconnected.

"Are you Santa?" she asked again.

Sal shook his head. "No, kid, I ain't Santa," he said, scrutinizing the child. There was something on her clothes, her face, her hair; he thought, at first, it was a shadow, but when he moved closer, he saw more clearly:

Blood was spattered all over the girl's nightwear. A streak of fear quaked through him, the worry alive that Tony had accomplished what he, like Frankie, was capable of committing, and somehow had overlooked one member of the household.

That's why it's so quiet here—the sonuvabitch already took everyone out and now is just lying in wait for us. Sal glanced at the girl; broads, wiseguys, thieves, and killers were his life's bedfellow, not children, and for the first time in a long time, uncertainty gripped him. Reluctantly, he tucked the revolver at his waist and reached for the girl. "C'mon kid, it ain't safe here. You gotta find a place to hide for a while. Seriously."

She pulled away from his intended touch, stepping back into the shadows of the doorway. *"No,"* she refused stubbornly. "You're *not* Santa. You said so."

"Jesus, enough with the Santa shit," Sal said, rougher than he intended, and immediately felt bad; the girl obviously was in shock, traumatized, something. *And why the hell not? Going through what she probably has would fuck with anyone's head.*

He was about to reach for her again when a crash, then a scream, shattered the black stillness, and a surge of adrenaline coursed through Sal when he realized he recognized Frankie's voice as it wailed in agony from somewhere nearby within the house.

"What the *fuck*?" he said, instinctively grabbing the revolver and pushing past the girl. Unfamiliarity with the house blinded him, and Sal haphazardly knocked into furniture following Frankie's screams to the end of the hall, where the front door was ajar and the twinkle of lights—gold, red, green—lit the adjacent room enough for him to see what was happening.

Seeing was one thing; comprehending was another. Sal stood at the threshold to the living room, its furnishings comfortable and homey; in the far corner was a Christmas tree, resplendently decorated, a mountain of unopened, carefully wrapped presents piled underneath, its bulbs illuminating the bizarre tableau opposite him: Frankie lay writhing before an unlit fireplace, howling a vicious stream of obscenities, flashlight and .44 dropped just out of his reach, his face curdled with a mixture of fury and pain, and after a moment Sal saw why—like a wild beast, Frankie's left leg was caught halfway up the shin in the mouth of a bear trap placed on the hardwood floor, his pants shredded and stained crimson, the snapped fibula protruding from the fabric, a growing pool of blood spreading beneath his huge frame.

"Sal! Sal, for fuck's sake, get me outta this fuckin' thing!" Frankie shouted, frothing, clawing desperately at the trap, but Sal remained motionless despite the profane pleas for help, his eyes glued instead to the further atrocities on display in the room: a family of corpses—father, mother, two teenage girls—sat rope-bound, grimly upright on couch and loveseat in pantomime of existence, though Sal knew instantly from the grisly injuries sustained they were far beyond living. All were peppered with stab wounds, yet each bore distinct desecration: the father's throat was slashed wide, gaping where a hand had rummaged in the wound, the tongue pulled out and left dangling down the neck through the gash; next to him, the mother's cheeks had been crudely hacked away to the meat, leaving a shapeless crimson hole from which her teeth protruded in a lipless smile. Across from them, the teenagers were tied together on the loveseat; their hair torn out in bloody clumps to the scalp, each neck slit from severed ear to severed ear. In one girl's mouth, a round Christmas ornament had been violently stuffed, while the other's lower jaw hung from one mandible, chopped loose from the joint. Despite the overpowering bloodshed, Sal noticed the mutilation was oddly incomplete: every victim's eyes remained intact, the lids held open with strips of duct tape, giving them a grotesque look of anticipation amid the amputation.

The brutality of the sight choked Sal's urge to speak, to scream, though his bewildered thoughts remained clear—*How the fuck did Tony do this so fast?* To Sal, the overkill was senseless, the posing of the bodies pointless when a simple slit throat would've accomplished the task just the same.

Speech at last returned, and Sal stammered, "Frankie...? Frankie, what the fuck? What the fuck's going on?"

Frankie grimaced and swore, but when he looked again at Sal, the sadistic glare so common in his gaze was gone, replaced with a wide-eyed terror that Sal had never seen on him before. A breath later, Frankie's screams began anew, so frantic the warning in his words was almost lost: "Behind you! Fuckin' *behind* you!"

It took precious seconds for Sal to understand, but before he could turn, it was already too late, and the first jolt of pain from the opening wound behind his right knee thundered up his leg, so quick and unexpected he hardly felt the blade twist, then remove; suddenly his leg buckled and he collapsed awkwardly to the floor, landing on his crippled arm, screaming, the .38 bouncing from his grasp. There was another stab, then another and another, to his lower back, and each time Sal felt the cold length of steel parting muscle and piercing tissue. Then, with one last thrust, something struck bone, and though his assailant tried removing the weapon, it remained wedged deep in Sal's flesh, and he lay helplessly squirming and bleeding on the floor.

Despite the pain, Sal still managed to prop himself up enough with his good arm to look over his shoulder, but the form towering over him in the entranceway wasn't the one he expected to see: the young girl he'd abandoned when Frankie's screams began stood there, an indifferent, dead-blank stare on her face. Not hate or rage or cruelty, just an emptiness that Sal had only rarely seen on the hardest of killers, the ones to whom murder meant nothing more than pouring a cup of coffee or picking up the morning paper.

The girl knelt down and, with strained effort, finally wrenched the blood-smeared butcher knife from Sal's vertebrae; he screamed again, trying to push away from the child, and panic set in when his legs refused to respond to the urge. Above him, the girl prepared to plunge the blade down once more when a burst of Frankie's profanity drew her attention, the blankness dissolving when she saw him caught in the trap.

"Santa?" she asked, lighting up. Then, ecstatically: *"Santa!"*

The girl rushed to Frankie, knife still in hand, smothering him with as huge a hug as she could, her minuscule body dwarfed by Frankie's grizzly size. She pulled back, looked him square in the face, smiling eagerly. "I *knew* you'd come. That's what they say—believe and be good all year and Santa will come on Christmas Eve and leave presents and toys for you." She cast a sneering glance at the corpses in the room. "My sisters tried to tell me you weren't real, but I knew if you came down the chimney, I could catch you and they'd have to believe, but then Mommy and Daddy started lying to me, too, so I made sure they'd all be able to see you tonight."

The girl stood, her free hand gently picking a chocolate chip cookie from a platter set on a small nightstand near the Christmas tree that Sal hadn't initially noticed, then sat cross-legged next to Frankie, offering the sweet to him. "I made these for you. All by myself. I know you like cookies, Santa."

Frankie's enraged growl was the only warning before he backhanded the girl, the force of the blow tipping her over, and he roared, "I'm not Santa, you fuckin' little psycho bitch! Get me out of this fuckin' thing!"

The girl didn't move at first, but slowly she sat up, one small hand clasped over her jaw, a shocked, hurt look on her face, and to Sal, she looked primed to burst into tears. Instead, that emotionless veneer returned, and she said, *"You're* not Santa, either. Santa's jolly and wouldn't *hit* little girls."

Sal saw Frankie eye his fallen .44, and without warning, he lunged for it with a sudden heave, jerking the trap with him, falling just shy of the weapon. Frankie groaned, jerked forward again, fingers straining for the revolver, but the girl, faster, leaped at him, launching a streak of stabs to his chest, his arms, his face; Frankie's howls filled the room, but the child's frenzy kept on until there was only silence.

The girl stood, panting, glaring at Frankie's punctured, bleeding body. From where Sal was, he spied his own revolver mockingly within arm's length; despite the numbness spreading throughout his body, he fumbled for the gun. Shaking, he cocked the revolver, tried to aim, but there was a banging in the hall, and Sal glanced over his shoulder; a door opposite the living room had opened, and from the darkness beyond, Tony staggered up the stairs from the house's basement, leaning on the wall for support, his face a mangled graveyard nightmare, eyes rage-fueled, drying blood caked on his expensive suit, one shoe missing. He walked stiffly, like a dead man, but only when Tony moved into the living room's entrance did Sal see the claw hammer clenched in his battered fist.

The girl, startled, stared at Tony. "Who... Who are you?"

"Santa Claus," he snarled, words from his toothless mouth more garbled gravel than language. "And these pricks have been very naughty this year."

Sal attempted to roll, to raise the revolver, but his body wouldn't obey the commands, and Tony struck him along the skull with the hammer as smoothly as ringing a bell; Sal's cheek-bone surrendered beneath the blow, his right lower jaw shattered, a dozen teeth freed from their sockets, and the world blurred blood-red before sliding to black.

Sometime later, the snow lifted, the living room filled with the soft gloom of daybreak, and Sal surfaced from the void like a swimmer rising through deep water, a bone-splitting cacophony of white noise between his temples. Vision only came to one eye, and the more his surroundings focused, the more Sal wished he'd remained sightless.

He sat sandwiched on the couch between the carcasses of the girl's parents, arms roped tautly to his torso, the coffee table in front of him carefully arranged with a medieval inquisitor's assortment of work tools and kitchen cutlery. Tony stood next to it, a faceless monster in the ambient holiday lights; beside him, the blood-spattered girl was wrapping something bulky in garish holiday paper.

"You sure brought us a lot of presents this year, Santa," she said, creasing and taping a fold. "You'd think Mommy and Daddy would've appreciated having someone like you to help them out at Christmas time and all, but I guess not. Oh, well. Their loss."

Tony glanced at her, then to the corpses around him. "Did you really do this all by yourself?"

The girl nodded. "I put some of Mommy's sleeping pills in the orange juice at breakfast, and when everyone fell asleep, I tied them up. When they were awake again, I did the rest. It made everything messy, but it was worth it. I mean, now they *know* you're real, Santa." She smiled proudly then, holding up the crudely wrapped package. "I'm finished. Can I open one of my presents now? I tied up the bad man and wrapped up your gift like you asked."

Tony's rasps deepened as he struggled for breath. "What's your name, kid?"

"Rachel."

"Well, Rachel, Santa's got one more gift to wrap, and if you do as good a job on it as you did on this one, I promise you can open your presents after. You still wanna be my little helper?"

"Absolutely!" The girl—Rachel—enthusiastically bounced to her feet, setting the wrapped parcel aside. "But who are these gifts for, Santa?"

"Some people I wanna let know I don't take kindly to bein' treated like a rat," Tony said gravely.

Rachel giggled. "Who would think you're a *rat,* Santa?"

"It don't matter none. Just get the gift and wrap it up real pretty. And remember, you don't have to push too hard on the neck. The blade's designed to go through the bone by itself."

Sal's lone eye shuddered when Rachel excitedly plucked a scarlet-spattered electric carving knife from the tabletop, terror rising as she brought it to motorized life. His instinct was to struggle, to try and break his bonds, but strength, like hope, had gone. He looked to his left; near the fireplace,

Frankie's body still lay trapped like a dead bear, only now the hunter's trophy had been taken: where there should've been a head, only a jagged stump remained, and Sal knew then what Rachel had busied herself wrapping.

Across from him, the girl smiled, gently hugging Tony. "This is the best Christmas ever, Santa. Thank you."

Sal believed his body numb, but the first thrust of the knife into his throat proved otherwise; his demolished jaw prevented a scream, and he choked instead on a final anguished cry that was lost below the sound of the whirring blade. Outside, birds sang, the clouds broke, and the first rays of sunrise sliced through the morning just as easily.

Chris Miss, Mama

Scott Deegan

"Mom."

The word bounced around the cell several times before landing in Susan's sleeping ear.

"Mom."

It came again, this time pulling her from the inky depths of sleep.

"Mom."

The word faded to blend with the other sounds of the cellblock: the snoring, the whispering, the farting.

Susan sat up on the bottom bunk and looked out into the dimly lit corridor that made up cellblock W4. Hurried footsteps echoed past the bars that held her. They sounded small and quick. Not those of a guard, but of a child running in play.

A child lifting their short legs high at the knee. But she saw nothing.

Joey ran like that.

She chided herself at the thought of her child.

Everyone knew who Susan was, what she did. Everyone knew she was the woman who drowned her two little boys, still strapped in their seats in the back of her car. She had blamed it on a mysterious black man she said carjacked her and took her boys. The truth was she couldn't stand the little shitheads. She only had them to keep David happy, and he fucking left her for someone else. She'd dated Steve for a while, but he only came around for a piece of ass. Maybe if she didn't have two kids, they could be serious, he had told her, but he wasn't ready to be a Dad to someone else's kids. That, too, was a lie; she'd gotten rid of the fucking brats, and he hadn't done shit. Men were scum, but that was no longer a concern. Her concern now was getting some sleep.

She had kitchen duty tomorrow, and it was Christmas. Christmas in prison wasn't a big deal, just another day. Most inmates didn't give two shits what day it was; they weren't going anywhere, so it didn't matter if it was Christmas. Most inmates who weren't mothers didn't care. Mothers who had young children on the outside cared that it was Christmas. They also cared that they were inside on Christmas with a woman who had killed her own kids. That was the reason they'd put her on Kitchen duty.

Out of sight, out of mind. That was Warden Richter's thinking, not that he personally cared what they did to her. He just didn't want anything reflecting badly on his tenure as Warden. He always thought of Warden as a capitalized word; he was important, after all.

Again, the footsteps moved past her cell, probably someone on the walkway above doing rounds. Susan lay down on her bunk and closed her eyes. A hand caressed her face. A small, cold hand. She opened her eyes, ready to scream at the guard to keep his filthy mitts to himself, but the cell held only her, and the other side of the cell bars was even lonelier. She touched her cheek, and her finger came away wet. Had she been crying? She didn't think so. She thought that maybe a toilet had run over in the cell above, but that made no sense. There wasn't any way for the water to make it into her cell.

Movement on the other side of the bars drew her attention. Someone stood just past her circle of light, waiting in the shadows. Someone with small feet. Someone with small feet wearing the same sneakers that her four-year-old had on when she watched the car roll down the embankment and into the lake. A puddle was forming beneath them.

"Josh?" she whispered into the darkness. "Joshua, is that you?" She felt a tightness in her throat, and her eyes began to water. Fear crept into her mind, and she glanced around the cell for something to use as a weapon. That's when she saw Joey, her five-year-old, squatting on the end of her bed, staring at her. His flesh was gray and his body swollen with water; he resembled Gollum from the 1977 Rankin Bass animated movie *The Hobbit* she watched with her father when she was a kid. He was crouching there with his dark hair plastered to the top of his head, looking intently at her.

"Mom." As he gurgled the word, water ran from his little blue lips. He cocked his head like a bird and continued to stare at her.

She felt cold hands wrap around her shoulders from behind.

"Mama, I cold. I cold, Mama."

She tried to scream, but no sound came out.

"No wanna swim no more, Mama." Josh tried climbing into her lap, and she pushed him away.

Joey duck-walked closer to her. "We want to be with you and sing the reindeer song when Santa comes, Mommy."

"You can't be here; you're dead," Susan said, barely audible in the silent room.

"We know 'cause you killed us, huh, Mama?" Josh said, taking her hand.

"Get away from me, you little fuck!" She pushed him away.

The little boy looked at her with a sad face. "It's Chris miss, Mama. You will get on the naughty list."

"Don't be on the naughty list, Mommy!" Joey said, pushing her into the corner. "Santa won't like that, and you'll get something bad."

Susan tried backing away from the older boy and his spongy touch, but her feet caught on each other, and she fell hard. Her ass hit the toilet, and she slid off the side onto the floor.

"Mama, you fall down?" Josh giggled. "You go boom?" He walked over to her and sat on her lap.

"Leave me the fuck alone. You're dead. I don't want you here!" Susan fought to get away from Josh and tried scrambling over the toilet. Joey waited on the other side.

"Don't you love us, Mommy?" he asked.

"No, I hate you," Susan screamed in his face. "I always fucking hated you. I never wanted either of you. Now leave me alone!"

"But we want to spend Christmas with you, Mommy," Joey said. "Don't we, Joshy?"

"Uh-huh. Chris miss," the younger boy answered. "Don't you want to spend Chris miss wish us, Mama?" His watery voice intensified his lisp.

"No! I don't want to spend Christmas with you little bastards! I'd rather be dead," Susan screamed at the little boy.

"But Mama, that's how we spend Chris miss together!" Josh started clapping his puffy, wet hands together. "Mama, spend Chris miss, Joey. Yay, Chris miss!"

Susan slowly turned to look at Joey, who was smiling at her. "Merry Christmas, Mommy!" Joey said and shoved her head into the toilet. Susan tried to fight, but he was incredibly strong for his size and age; he held her fast. Her struggling slowed and then ceased.

❄ ❄ ❄

Edward Kline was pissed he had to work on Christmas. He hated being away from his family on the holiday that excited his two boys. It was his four- and five-year-old sons who occupied his thoughts as he walked from the mess hall to cell-block W4 to find out why the child-killing bitch hadn't reported for kitchen duty. He hated that woman. Every time he looked at her, he saw his two boys and wondered how anyone could do that to a child. He smiled to himself when he saw her face down in the toilet. He considered pulling her out but figured she deserved to be there, so he left her in that undignified position. When he turned, he noticed the small, wet footprints all over the cell floor and all around Susan's body. He looked for just a second longer before grabbing the hand towel and wiping them away. Whoever or whatever visited her in the wee hours of Christmas morning gave her the present she deserved.

"Merry Christmas, boys," he whispered as he left the cell to go alert the medics. As he walked, he found himself with the sudden urge to sing "Rudolph, The Red-nosed Reindeer." He gave into that urge with a smile.

The Christmas Angel

Dan Allen

I don't need an introduction, and you're better off never knowing me...but you do. Trust me, you do. And it's too late to change that now, but if you're good, I mean deserving of my attention, I might just send you a pretty, little gift.

Ebenezer says Christmas is harvest season for the money lenders. Christmas is my favorite season as well—harvest season for the soul takers. Picture an angel with golden hair wearing a long, flowing dress and hands clasped together holding a candle. She is a Christmas decoration, nothing more than a toy. She is also my ride, my way in. Don't blame her if you think she is a sharp knife. I'm the one who thrusts the blade into your soft underbelly and eviscerates your soul. I'm the one who pulls the trigger and puts a bullet in your heart.

I don't judge; they don't have to be good or bad to enter my kingdom. I take 'em all, and I don't discriminate. To amuse myself, I cast Angel into the world and wait for someone to take the bait. Five months ago, she showed up at a school rummage sale and called out to a boy.

At craft sale prices, Tim could easily afford her. She was the perfect Christmas gift for his sick grandfather.

❄ ❄ ❄

"Do you think that looks like him?"

"I'm not sure. He changed a lot recently."

"I know, but his face looks too thin."

"It's his skin that looks wrong to me. It doesn't look real."

"You're right. It looks fake, like something out of a wax museum."

"You going to take a picture?"

"No, that's not right. Who'd want to look at it? Nice job with the suit. Where'd you get it?"

"It's all I could find in his closet."

"Gray pinstripe? I don't remember him ever wearing it."

"I know. Dad wasn't much for suits. You sure you don't want one last picture?"

"Nah. What would we do with it? Display it in the front hall? Dad hated getting his picture taken."

"He looks stupid with his glasses on. Are they going to bury him with those?"

"No, they'll take them off, and his ring, too. Do you want any of the flowers?"

"Hell, no, let the church have them, except for that one. Throw that fucker in the bin. Who the hell sends a Christmas wreath to a funeral?"

"What about the doll and the picture of Tim?"

"Leave the picture in the box but get rid of the Angel. Dad thought she brought him good luck. Filthy thing gives me the creeps. You would've thought he'd have changed his mind after Tim died."

"Nah, he treasured the damn thing even more because it was a gift from Tim. Superstitious old fart really believed it saved his life. He lives five years longer than the doctors gave him, and he thinks the doll was responsible."

"Whatever. I still don't want it in the box. Donate it to the Salvation Army with the rest of his stuff."

"You want to go downstairs and get a coffee?"

"No, they're playing Christmas music. How fucking inappropriate."

❄ ❄ ❄

Two brothers, upset with how their Christmas worked out, don't know the part I played. They didn't even like the Christmas wreath I sent. Well, I got my gift. Another daily double. One pledged to me for the promise of a reprieve, and one I took as a bonus payment. Let me show you something more current, a little work in progress.

I've had my eyes on Nonna Rosa for a few years now. I'm always recruiting, you know; it's a relentless job. Now, Rosa is an interesting case. Old Italian ladies have their ways, complaining about the food, complaining about the neighbors, even telling you about relatives who you have never met and never will. Rosa does all this and more, but even still, there is something not right with her. She shows signs of dementia, and I'm damn sure I'll be hanging around to see this through. The key is to be there for them in their time of need and offer them what they can't refuse. I visit her in her sleep and whisper some suggestions.

"Rosa, can you hear me?"

"Who is it?"

"There's something wrong with you. Something in your head, gnawing on your brain, eating your memories. I can make it go away for a while, buy you some more time. You can trust me. Let's make ourselves a deal."

"Whaddya talkin' about? There's nothing wrong with me. Get outta here and let me sleep."

I go to her on several nights, and each time she refuses to bargain. I'm not discouraged easily, and time is on my side. They can agree to my contract and make a trade for mercy, or they can hold out and go down hard, but either way, the water is leaking out of the bucket. Rosa is stubborn, and she's going to ride it out.

❄ ❄ ❄

It's the festive time of the year, and she's at her daughter's house for Thanksgiving. The turkey smells wonderful, and Maria already has the Victorian village displayed on the credenza and the fancy candles lined up on the mantel.

"Hey, Joey, you're never going to believe it. I saw this movie last night," says Rosa.

Joe looks at his wife and raises an eyebrow. He and Maria have heard about this same movie every day. I'll help relieve them of this annoyance, but not yet. I have other things to do first.

"You know, Joey, that good one about the man."

"The old black and white one, Mom?" asked Joe.

Rosa doesn't seem to hear him anymore.

"Joey, Joey, you know. It has that guy in it. You know. That George guy who jumps in the river. Well, you're never going to believe it, I gotta tell you."

Joe tries to keep her on track, but there's futility in his efforts, and it makes me chuckle. Rosa soon forgets about George Bailey and all that sentimental hogwash. She stands by Joe, trying to see the giblet gravy simmering on the stove and oblivious to being in his way.

"He's good looking!" she confides to Maria.

"Oh my god, Joe, she would hit on you if she were a few years younger." Maria is amused and a little disturbed. I'm indifferent because Rosa isn't my priority anymore. I believe I have a date with Joe. I can smell him and hear his body rhythms. He doesn't know it yet, but if he was a car, he would need more than a tune-up.

A few minutes later, Maria's older sister arrives, and Rosa sees her coming into the kitchen. "You're getting fat." Rosa has lost her filter. Delightful.

Later, in private, Maria will laugh at this. Sibling rivalry, you know.

At dinner, Rosa insists on reciting her children's names in their birth order. Joe is embarrassed for her, but I listen with interest. She struggles with the names *and* the order, but she corrects herself and works through it.

"Holy hell, we're all here, we know who we are," whispers Maria. One day I plan to show her there's nothing holy in hell, but for now, I let it slide.

When Rosa gets to Maria, she pauses and makes eye contact with Joe. I can see the fear in her eyes. She knows she can't remember her own daughter's name.

"It's Maria, Mom," Joe tells her.

That Joe, what a party-pooper; Rosa's struggle was fascinating.

"I've been having some dreams lately. I want to tell you about them, but I can't remember." The old lady randomly changes the topic.

Joe's twin boys, Tony and Vince, think Nonna is funny. They don't fully realize the eventual implications of her memory loss. I'm on their side. This stuff keeps me young.

"Watch any movies lately?" Vince goads her on.

Rosa takes the bait and struggles to recall the story. It's the ridiculous black and white movie again, the one about Clarence getting his wings. Let me tell you... If it was that easy to get wings, I'd get me a pair, too. The boys laugh at Rosa's attempt to recite the lines. Mischievous little devils, boys after my own heart. I watch Rosa's reaction. She appears ignorant of being the brunt of their jokes; however, I believe she is aware they're making fun of her, and I relish her pain.

❄ ❄ ❄

Over the next few days, I watch Joe's energy level drop. He has trouble climbing stairs and is often out of breath. I plant thoughts in his head, telling him he's alright. I have my own motives, and the last thing I need is him seeing a doctor. No sense prolonging things. One crisp morning, with the grass dusted with white frost and a blue jay watching from the fence, my man, Joe, has a wee little heart attack while hanging Christmas lights from the eaves.

The emergency department runs its tests and confirms his heart is shot. My prize awaits. The doctor explains surgery is needed, but Joe is reluctant.

"What if I don't have the surgery?"

The doctor smiles. "Then, you'll probably have another attack and die."

I think the doctor has a very strange sense of humor. Strange and wonderful. I make a note to keep tabs on the doc. He may be useful.

A few days later, Maria tries to explain to Rosa. "Mom, Joe had a heart attack."

"I need to get my haircut. You have to take me". Rosa looks at Maria, showing no acknowledgment of the bad news.

Maria is devastated. Nona's reaction only proves how fast she's slipping, but the worst is yet to come. It's time to send in Angel. She isn't my only way to broker a deal; far from it, but I do find her useful, especially around the holidays.

❄ ❄ ❄

Christmas arrives, and with it, all the globs of gaudy decorations. It looks like someone puked up a pile of green and red trash. I detest the sparkling lights driving out the gray gloom of winter, and nothing grinds my teeth more than the tasteless music. The same songs, over and over again, hypnotizing the masses and uniting them in this insane gift-giving cult.

Joe has deteriorated some, Rosa, even more. It looks like a race to the finish, and I have bets on both. Rosa finds Joe in the kitchen.

"Joey, I got something to tell you. You're never going to believe it. It's so funny, you're gonna laugh."

Joe has heard her stories before. They are never funny, and he doesn't laugh, but he foolishly tries to help her remember when she gets stuck. It's like a constant game of charades for Joe and a comedy show for me. Rosa talks with her hands and with sound effects. Joe fills in the missing words.

Dinner is the usual festive feast, and it's the only part of the season I appreciate. The smells of the succulent bird float in the room and blend with the baking apple pie, so yummy you can taste the air.

I whisper in Rosa's ear, and her eyes light up; she remembers something important.

"Hey, Joey, come here. I got something for you." She pulls out a brown paper bag. "I got you a Christmas present. I saw it at the store. She told me she was for you."

"Who told you, Mom?" Joe and Maria catch each other's eyes. Rosa hasn't brought anyone else a gift, not even the twins. Joe pulls Angel out of the bag. She is dirty, and her hair is tangled and matted. One wing is broken and hangs down a little. My girl isn't aging well. Joe sees a price of twenty-five cents scribbled on a piece of masking tape stuck to the base.

"Thanks, Momma, she's beautiful."

Later that night, Maria has a moment alone with Joe.

"Why would she give you that gross thing? It looks like she took it from a bag lady."

"Come on, Pumpkin, it's an angel!"

"More like a fallen angel, don't you think, Joe?"

"I think it is wonderful your mom even remembered Christmas presents."

"Sure, wonderful. She only remembered a present for you, a present she bought at the second-hand thrift store. Who knows where it came from? I'm going to throw it out."

"Please don't, Maria, I kinda like it, and I need all the angels I can get right now."

The next day, Maria puts Angel on the top shelf of the bedroom closet. She thinks Angel is repulsive and feels dirty after touching her. Later, when the angel appears in the front room window, Maria assumes Joe put her there. Wrong. Maria takes a closer look, and I see the corner of the doll's mouth curl up ever so slightly. My angel looks like she might belong on a treetop, but she is a little too big and has a solid wood base. She wears a full-length gown. The dress is dirty and stained now, but once it was beautiful. Her two hands were intended to come together to hold a candle, but one has become detached and hangs down. Maria grabs the tiny hand and attempts to put it back in place. She is rewarded with a sharp prick, painful enough for such a little scratch. A small drop of blood appears on her finger, and she drops the tiny arm.

"So, you got some claws on you, eh, you filthy piece of shit." Maria knocks the angel over and leaves her lying face down on the floor.

❄ ❄ ❄

January drives an icicle through the Christmas spirit, and all signs of the dreaded ritual are cleansed from sight. Joe is getting weaker and gulps at each elusive breath. In the wee hours of the morning, he wakes up with chest pains and prays to his God. And just so we're clear, I can be whoever they want me to be. They don't need to guess my name.

"Please give me ten years. That would be enough, just ten more years," he begs.

I plant the seed, water and nurture it, give it a little hope, show what is possible, and then when it's ripe, I harvest. Perfection.

Joe gets stronger every day, and Maria begins to think differently about Angel. I whisper the idea that maybe Angel is a good luck charm, that maybe she is helping Joe get better. Joe certainly thinks so.

❄ ❄ ❄

Spring escapes through the iron bars of winter, and it's time to turn up the heat. Maria's cell phone goes off while Joe is getting ready for the day, and he overhears the call.

"Oh my god, is she alright? Is she breathing?"

Joe is alarmed. "What the hell, Maria? What's going on?"

"Shhh Joe, it's the superintendent from mom's apartment."

Rosa was found unconscious on the floor. They figure she had a fall and was lying there all night. Okay, I'll tell you the truth; I was a little rougher than that. It's simple. If you won't make a deal, I have no time for you. I need you out of the way, finished and scratched off the prospects list.

Two days later, Rosa is transferred to a special care nursing home. Maria visits her daily, and Joe goes when he can. Rosa has regressed and only speaks in Italian. She looks at Joe and talks very fast, very animated.

"Mom, you know I don't understand you, right?"

She laughs and says something else. Joe knows enough to know that she said something dirty. I could show her some mercy, but her fate is already sealed.

❄ ❄ ❄

Maria gets a call. Her mother is having an episode. Joe gets to the nursing home in time to see the staff holding a sheet up in front of the TV.

"*Puttana cattiva*! *Puttana cattiva*!" Rosa is hysterical.

"Evil whore? Mom, who's the evil whore?" asks Maria.

"L'angelo, the angel." Rosa struggles to get the words out, and she points past the bed sheet to the television. A commercial is playing, and a scruffy faced man is pushing a travel booking website. Rosa sees something very different.

The nurses lower the sheet, and Rosa's English comes flooding back.

"Keep the sheet up; you mustn't let her see me." Her face is contorted, and her trembling hands are white.

"Who, Mom? Who can't see you?" asks Maria.

"L'angelo della morte!" Rosa is terrified. Her eyes bulge,

and tears run down her cheeks. I got the old lady right where I want her.

Joe looks at Maria for a translation.

"Angel of Death," explains Maria.

"Mom, I can shut the TV off." Maria looks for a way to help calm her mother.

"You mustn't, Maria. She'll come for me. You mustn't."

They take turns holding a bedsheet in front of the TV until Rosa falls asleep. *The Sound of Music* is playing, and Joe turns it off.

❄ ❄ ❄

In the wee hours, the room is quiet, and the night nurse is tucked away in her hole playing games on her cell phone. She is too far away and too distracted to notice any sounds of the harvest.

"Rosa. Rosa, wake up," I whisper deep in her ear so only she can hear. This is going to be fun, and there's no way I'm letting her sleep through it.

The next morning Maria gets a call. Rosa died in the night. Give her some credit. Rosa held her ground, never made a deal. I don't always get their soul, but either way, I get my kicks.

❄ ❄ ❄

The river of time flows downstream, and the days grow bitter with the approach of another holiday season. Joe has recovered enough to take his family north for a ski trip before the big day. He believes the Christmas gift from Rosa was responsible for his health. He remembers asking for ten more years, and he is content with that. He has a vague memory of making a deal, but the details escape him. He was pretty messed up at the time, but I feel no shame. Hey folks, all's fair in heaven and hell.

"Who knows. Maybe it was a dream."

"What was a dream, honey?" asks Maria.

"Oh, nothing, babe. I just had an odd thought."

Everybody loves the mountains. The skiing is good, the air fresh, and they even find the perfect Christmas tree. They soak up every minute of fun, and it's long after dark when they load the truck and head for home. The kids see the large deer moving out of the ditch. Joe doesn't. He's too focused on the road ahead and watches a large Indian chief walk down the centerline just beyond the reach of his headlights. A glorious headdress hangs down the chief's back, and feathers adorn the headband, creating a suitable crown for such a magnificent king. Joe struggles to see. The image is blurry, transparent. I bring it into focus for him. Slowly, not too fast now, making sure to take away his time and space.

"No shit..." he mumbles. "That's not an Indian. Those are wings. That's an angel. A goddamn angel in the middle of the highway."

It all happened so fast. You know, I hear it every day. Crying they didn't have time to slow down. Well, Joe has time to brake. I give him a chance, just a second or two, but he hesitates, and it's because of her.

Joe sees her clearly. It is his angel, my angel. She glows purple and stands over eight feet tall. Her luxurious golden hair floats on a phantom breeze, and her gown, no longer ripped and soiled, flows down to her feet. Her arms spread wide in a welcoming gesture, and she smiles at him. Her face elongates as she reaches for the truck. A grotesque vein bulges from her collarbone and stretches over her impossibly long neck. Patches of hair and scalp fly from the back of her head as if pulled off by an invisible turbulence.

Angel is close now. Her face fills his entire windshield, and her lips roll up, showing jagged, rotting teeth. The rest of her skin peels away from her face to reveal a blood-stained skull. Joe can hear her screech. The noise explodes inside his head; his chest tightens, and he can't breathe.

The truck hits the deer without braking and caves in from the impact. The vehicle spins over an embankment, slamming into a line of old-growth pines and bursts into flames. The Christmas tree in the back resists at first but soon succumbs to the blaze.

"I didn't get my ten years. It's not right, I was promised," Joe complains. He feels betrayed, then he feels nothing. He doesn't hear the sizzling crackle as the fire finishes off their treasured tree and moves on to consume the rest of the truck.

He didn't get his ten years. I know, I lied. What did you expect? You know who I am. And yes, it was ruthless to take them all, but what can I say. It's a job. I do love a bonfire in the snow.

❄ ❄ ❄

Maria's sister cleans out the house for the realtors. A pile of unopened gifts waits for a tree that isn't coming, and among them she finds an angel with a soiled dress and a broken wing. She tosses the angel in the trash and drags the bin to the curb.

❄ ❄ ❄

A young girl is out catching snowflakes and pulling her sled. She sees a doll on top of the garbage and stops. It's an angel, a Christmas angel with a red and green gown and a wreath for a halo.

"Why, aren't you the most beautiful thing?"

The girl has a brother, and he is very sick. She knows this

angel is for him; it'll be the perfect Christmas gift. The angel told her.

❄ ❄ ❄

Well, my treasured friend, it's been a pleasure chatting with you, and I look forward to seeing you again. And I will, you know, rest assured—and very soon. There is no doubt about that. In the meantime, if you see an angel grasping a candle and perhaps nursing a broken wing, don't be afraid to say hello… I'll be close by, and there's no point in wasting time.

Bloody Christmas Tree

R.A. Goli

Lydia pressed her foot against the accelerator as she sped through town. The streets were quiet, everyone already enjoying festive meals and cold beers.

"I said I was sorry," Pete said. "You need to get over it."

"It's nearly fucking Christmas, and you've been putting this off for weeks. Then you can't even get home from work early."

"I told you, we had a couple of drinks, and I lost track of the time. Can you please slow the fuck down?"

"I'm trying to get there before it closes."

"Whatever," Pete muttered as he cranked up the air conditioning. Though it was nearly 8:00 p.m., it was still muggy, and he was sweating through his shorts and t-shirt.

As they neared the Christmas tree farm, he could see it was closed and risked a glance at Lydia. She was shaking her head, fuming. She pulled up in the carpark and turned to him. "Are you happy? Christmas is ruined." Her bottom lip quivered, and she turned away.

"It's not ruined. We'll jump the fence, it's not that high."

"Are you serious? What if we get caught? What if they have guard dogs or something?"

"Well, let's go see."

She turned off the engine, and they both got out. Lydia winced as Pete slammed his door. "Shhhhhh."

"Chill out, we're twenty kilometers from the nearest town. Besides, it's a good test to see if there are any dogs around."

They stood quietly, listening. All they could hear were the cicadas, and then the crunch of pine needles and gum leaves underfoot as they started walking. They climbed the fence and weaved between the sparse selection of remaining trees.

"Oh crap, I just realized... We don't have an ax. I'll just have to rip it out of the ground with my bare hands and brute strength."

Lydia laughed.

"Okay, so pick one. A weak one," he said.

A rustle and loud thump froze them in place.

"What was that?"

Between a row of trees, a dark shadow stood just as still, watching them. It burst into movement, escaping between the trees, followed by three smaller shadows.

Thump. Thump. Thump.

Pete breathed a sigh of relief, and Lydia giggled, placing her hand over her racing heart as the family of kangaroos sped off.

"Well, that scared the shit out of me," said Pete.

"Me, too. Did you see the size of him! Almost as tall as

the trees."

"Oi, what are you two doing?" a booming voice shouted.

Pete and Lydia shielded their faces from the torchlight the stranger shone directly at them.

"We just wanted a tree, and we got here too late. We haven't done anything. We only just got here," said Pete.

"Sorry, we'll leave," said Lydia.

The stranger began laughing and lowered his torch. Pete could see the man was thickly built and wearing overalls, boots, and an Akubra hat, but no shirt underneath. His bare arms were large and hairy. Pete guessed him to be a farmer. "Mate, that's what I'm here to bloody do as well."

"Nice one. We forgot to bring an ax, though. Can we borrow yours?" said Pete.

"No worries, it's in the ute. Come on." The farmer headed back to his car. Pete helped Lydia over the fence, then they followed. A kelpie sat chained in the back. It growled softly as they got near.

The man was leaning into the utility's tray when they reached him. He swung around, pointing a rifle at them. "Get in the back."

Lydia gasped, an icy fear twisting her gut. Pete bolted, quickly leaping the fence and disappearing between the pines. She watched in disbelief as he ran, leaving her with the madman. "Fucking prick."

"Hey, mate, you better get ya arse back 'ere unless you want me to shoot your girlfriend."

Pete crouched low, peering through the branches at the silhouettes, barely visible. He watched as the farmer bashed Lydia across the head with the butt of the rifle, and she collapsed to the ground, screaming and holding her face. The man dragged her onto her feet and shoved her into the back next to the now-snarling dog. He unclasped its collar and wrapped it around Lydia's neck, then tied her hands behind her back. Pete could still make out the sound of her panicked crying over the sound of the dog, now standing guard. It barked every time she moved.

Then the man turned and looked straight at him, or so Pete thought. Chest heaving, he sucked in a breath as the beam of light passed over him. "I see ya, boy." To his dog, he said, "Get 'im," and the dog leaped from the truck and raced towards Pete, barking as it scaled the fence with ease.

Pete ran. Cold fear surged through his limbs as he pushed through branches. He couldn't outrun a dog. He scrambled up one of the pines just as the kelpie clamped his foot in its jaws. He screamed, and he and the dog played tug-o'-war with his leg. He yanked it free and climbed, branches poking his stomach and scratching his arms and legs. The dog circled the tree, barking and jumping on hind legs in a vain attempt to reach him. Pete heard an engine start and saw the utility pull away.

"Fuck."

He sobbed then, for his own life and because of his cowardice. He shouldn't have left her, but his instinct was to save himself. He patted his pocket for his mobile phone, but it was gone, likely fallen out during his desperate run or climb. He scanned the ground but could barely see a thing. Except for the dog. His only hope was to wait it out and pray it left.

❄ ❄ ❄

Time crawled by. An hour, Pete guessed, judging by how the moon had shifted in the sky. His arms and legs were losing strength. He had already slipped twice but managed to right himself; each time, the dog went crazy. Now, the kelpie sat quietly, as though asleep, but even the slightest sound sent it into a frenzy, its murderous intent threatening to cause Pete to release his bladder. His foot slipped, and the dog responded with a series of barks. He had to do something or he was going to fall. He fished his wallet from his pocket—thankfully, that was still there—and flung it as far as he could into the trees. It worked; the dog sprinted towards the sound. Pete prayed as he gingerly climbed down the tree, trying to hurry, yet not make a sound. When he reached the ground, he resisted the urge to run, hoping the dog wouldn't hear him and assume Pete was still clutching the trunk of the pine overhead. He heard the barking in the distance, and he ran, the weight in his chest growing heavier with each step. He heard the thump of paws behind him and wished it was only kangaroos again. Gelid fingers crawled down his spine as he ran. He felt like he was drowning in his own fear as he gasped for air, legs pumping, arms flailing to push branches from his face as he maneuvered through the pines.

The sharp bark behind him caused him to turn, and the dog leaped. Pete crashed to the ground on his back, the snarling dog on top of him. He held the dog's front legs and turned his face away from the snapping jaws. The dog tore off his left ear and part of his cheek. Pete screamed as a searing heat engulfed the side of his head. His heart seized, the rush of blood in his ear so loud he could barely think. The dog bit at his face again. His own blood splashed into his eyes. Pete tightened his grip and jerked the legs apart. The dog yelped and rolled off. Pete crawled away, heaving in breath after breath. The animal lay a few feet away, panting and whining on its back, its front legs sticking out at unnatural angles. Pete had almost ripped its ribcage apart. Normally a dog lover, Pete felt no sympathy for this one. He got to his feet and shuffled away.

Completely disoriented, he walked, unsure if he was heading back to the road or further into the bush. When he cleared the Christmas trees, he realized he had been heading away from the road. A light in the distance gave him hope. It was a house light, he was sure. Much too bright to be a torch, though he did consider it could be the farmer's house. He would tread cautiously, only approaching it if he was sure it was safe.

The light was like a beacon, his own Star of Bethlehem to lead him to safety. It felt like he had walked for hours. As he got closer, he saw it wasn't a house but some other structure. Not as large, but he couldn't make out the detail between the gum trees.

Then he could hear music. A Christmas song about a winter wonderland. He grinned at the irony and wiped sweat from his brow with the back of his hand. It came away pink. He stumbled into the clearing, willing his panic to stop as his eyes took in the monstrosity.

Then he felt a rifle muzzle press into his spine.

"Where's me dog."

Blackness fringed the edge of Pete's vision, and he thought he would pass out, but the man pushed him forward, close enough to hear the agonized moaning. He stared in horrified awe at the sickening structure before him. Arms were broken and strapped together. Legs were intertwined, many had been crudely separated from their torsos. Blood coated the leaves that poked out from under mutilated body parts. It dripped down bare skin and splattered onto the leaf litter below.

Then he saw her. Lydia was near the top of the tree, tied down to the rest of the bodies. Well, half of her was, at least. Her arms were outstretched, like Christ on the cross, head lolled to one side. Her legs had been hacked off and presumably added to the make-shift tree somewhere else.

She lazily lifted her head to look at him, and he dropped

to his knees and screamed.

"You'd be surprised how many cheapskates try to steal Christmas trees at night. My cousin Jasper owns the farm. He'll get rid of your car, don't ya worry 'bout that."

Pete finally released his bladder. "Please, no."

"No point, mate. I need me some more ornaments."

Pete felt the rifle move away from his back and knew what was coming. He felt the whack, and his vision blurred, then darkened.

"And you're going to be my star."

The Other Side of Giving

Christopher Stanley

The children of the village are sledding when the stranger appears. They race down the slopes, carving great arcs through three days' worth of snow, their whoops and cheers as clear as church bells on Sunday. Their faces are hidden under layers of hats and scarves, but their eyes sparkle like the flecks of ice in their eyelashes.

A few of the children have sleds, but most improvise with dinner trays and anything else they've managed to sneak past their parents. Sofie Lehne has a length of bark she found in the forest. She's small for her age but has the fierce look of someone who has grown fast, who knows that life is not something to be taken for granted. Her family lives in a little shack on the edge of the village, where her father repairs furniture to keep food on the table and her mum makes their clothes with material she's scrounged from the market.

Something hits Sofie in the back, and she falls face-first into a deep drift of snow. As she climbs back to her feet, hands bruised with the cold, she hears laughter behind her. Aksel Barstad. Her cheeks flush with anger. Most of the children are decent enough to leave her alone, but Aksel has been mocking her and throwing snowballs all afternoon. *Enough,* she thinks. She isn't scared of Aksel or his friends. They might be bigger than her, but three meals a day and a comfortable mattress have made them soft. She balls her hands into fists, ready to retaliate. And then the pine trees at the edge of the forest start moving, their branches flailing and sending up a thick fog of powdered snow.

Sofie watches until the snow-fog has cleared. And gasps.

In the village below, the parents stop what they're doing and look up towards the slopes, wondering why their children have fallen silent.

❄ ❄ ❄

The children shuffle warily, like a herd of sheep in the presence of a wolf. And maybe that's what the stranger is. He has the eyes of a predator—unblinking, determined, merciless. His lips part in a snarl the children feel more than see.

Sofie's never seen anything like him. Not alive, anyway. His few remaining teeth chatter somewhere deep in the nest of his gray beard. His ragged clothes are black with grime, and his hair falls in long, wild strands. She wonders if a man can be haunted by his own ghost because that's how he seems to her. His body looks like it wants to die but his spirit won't let it. She steps closer. She doesn't attend the village school, and the other children aren't her friends, but today they've let her join them on the slopes, and she feels a debt of gratitude. Maybe not to Aksel, but certainly to the rest of them. If the man turns out to be trouble, Sofie will stand in his way. She might even slow him down while the other children escape.

"The parish council," says the stranger, his vowels drawn out, his accent suggesting some distant, unfamiliar landscape. "You will take me to them."

The children remain silent, none of them wanting to be the first to speak. The stranger regards them, his gaze flitting from face to face until it eventually lands on Sofie. Then he barks a single word.

"Now."

❄ ❄ ❄

The parish council isn't due to sit until after Christmas, but a special meeting is called for all who can attend. The stranger says it is a matter of "great importance," although later Sofie can't remember whether he said "great" or "grave." Unseen by the adults, the children sneak up the polished wooden steps to the gallery and peer over the balcony. Sofie hangs back in the shadows.

"It is Christmas Eve," says the stranger. "Your children will be expecting gifts." His voice is haggard, and the act of speaking seems to cause him discomfort. "The world is growing. Costs are rising. Sacrifices must be made."

The children exchange anxious whispers. Is the man saying there'll be fewer presents to go around? Or that some children will have to go without?

"Tonight, you will take one of your children to the center of the forest," says the man, "and tie them to the fallen pine tree. They will join the ranks of the elves to work for the remainder of their natural life. That is Santa's price."

The parish councilors talk fiercely among themselves, faces aghast. Where is the Spirit of Christmas in this man who claims to be an agent of its father? What right does he have to suggest such an arrangement?

On the balcony, the children have a different conversation. Who wouldn't want to join Santa in his factory of colors and candy? Surrounded by toys. Feeding the reindeer. Dressed as one of Santa's elves.

"We need more time," says Leah Espensen, long-serving chair of the council. She's an elegant woman, if a little severe.

"You have one hour," says the stranger.

"And why should we trust you?" she asks.

"Because I was a child in this village," he says. "I was chosen."

❄ ❄ ❄

"What you are asking is unconscionable," says Leah when the council reconvenes. "How could any of us celebrate Christmas knowing an innocent child has been taken from their parents and forced to adopt the unnatural ways of the elves?"

"It's a hard existence," says the stranger. His skin is grayer than it was before, and he sits because he no longer has the strength to stand. During the recess, he was offered broth for his hunger and ointments for his sores, both of which he declined. "But there is satisfaction in knowing you make other children happy."

"And we commend you for that," says Leah. "We'd gladly reward you for your service."

"All I require," says the stranger, "is the name of a child to take my place."

Aksel's father, who also sits on the council, says, "There

is one child who might be offered so that others may be spared."

Leah looks at him, shakes her head.

"She lives in a shack on the edge of the village," says Aksel's father. "She's poor and of little consequence. Taking her would be a kindness."

"What is the girl's name?" asks the stranger.

"Sofie Lehne."

On the balcony, Aksel cries out. "You can't do this, Dad," he says. "It's not fair."

Confused, Sofie stares at Aksel, wondering why he, of all the children, would stand up for her. And then she runs. Down the stairs and out into the night, past windows lit with candles and gently glowing trees. Heart pounding. Head spinning. Her feet slipping on the ice. When she reaches her home, she thumps her fists against the door until her mum answers, and then she curls up into her mum's warm embrace, tears in her eyes, thinking she'll be safe.

❄ ❄ ❄

Sofie's parents won't let her stay up. She can hear them arguing in the lounge, her mum guarding the front door. Their fight isn't the result of a disagreement. They're afraid, and so is Sofie.

Outside the wind picks up, hammering the walls with icy snow. The air in Sofie's room grows cold despite the candles by her bed. She tells herself to sleep. No one would take a child out in this weather. It would be murder.

Eventually her parents fall silent, and Sofie surrenders to her tiredness.

And then:

Her mum screaming.

Her father's voice, high and angry.

Her bedroom door bursting open and four men from the village marching in.

And before Sofie is awake, before she knows what's happening, the icy wind is biting at her flesh and running its fingers through her hair. In her panic, she can't catch her breath. She's lifted and dropped against something hard. Wood—cold wood. A pony trap. The men climb in around her, and she hears the strike of a whip against flesh.

"Mum!" she calls. "Dad!" She blinks to clear her eyes, and there they are, outside the shack, their arms held behind their backs by folks from the village, their haggard faces saying everything. They are powerless. There'll be no rescue. No final embraces or tearful goodbyes. Sofie's head bounces against the floor of the trap as she watches her parents shrink into the distance. "Where are you taking me?" she asks.

The men's faces say everything. They don't want to be here. They don't want to be doing this. They have no choice.

Sofie remembers Aksel's plea in the town hall. She entertains the idea that he might execute some daring rescue. But why? He never liked her. And he's just a boy. He's probably asleep and dreaming of Christmas.

By the time they reach the fallen tree, Sofie is shivering uncontrollably. Her feet are numb. After they've tied her to the trunk, the men do what they can to wrap blankets around her, urging her not to struggle. She's going to die out here. They know it, and so does she. The only question is: how soon?

She listens to them leaving and sobs quietly in the frozen darkness.

And then she hears voices. Excited, whispering. Hundreds of them. All around her and moving closer.

❄ ❄ ❄

Church bells.

Sofie peels open an eye, but it refuses to adjust to the light. Her head is sore. Her shoulders and wrists, too.

But she can hear church bells, and that means it's Christmas morning.

She's hit by a wall of memories. Sledding. A stranger. The meeting of the parish council. Aksel. Her parents. Stolen in the night. Cold and left for dead.

Is she dead?

Or is this the realm of the elves?

She tries her eyes again, squinting until they focus.

A ceiling.

A wall.

The stubs of burned-out candles.

She's in her bedroom. She sits up on her elbows and looks around. In the corner of the room, she sees a pile of blankets. Lots of them. Too many.

Moving stiffly, her body wracked with pain, she crosses the room. They aren't her blankets; they're the ones the men brought.

It wasn't a dream.

Feeling dizzy, she pulls the top blanket to one side. Underneath, she sees the edge of a box. She has no idea what it is. She pulls away the rest of the blankets and sees the corner of her room is piled high with boxes, dozens of them, all wrapped in different-colored papers and finished with tags and bows.

Christmas presents. For her. More than she's ever seen. She feels tears gathering in her eyes.

She has been spared.

Her parents' faces light up at the sight of their daughter.

For the rest of the morning, they open presents and sing carols together until it is time to eat. Christmas never tasted so good.

❄ ❄ ❄

Leah Espensen visits the boarding house where the stranger spent the night. Wracked with guilt for the part she played in the council meeting, she hasn't slept at all. She needs to confront the stranger. She wants to know if Sofie was taken and, if so, how do they get her back.

Ms. Tandberg, the owner of the boarding house, shows Leah to the stranger's room. The door is unlocked. The stranger is on his bed, eyes open, staring at the ceiling. He is cold and unresponsive, but finally, he looks at rest.

❄ ❄ ❄

In the center of the village, where the finest properties look down on the streets below, Aksel's father sits on the edge of his son's bed. He has the same blond hair and broad shoulders as his son, but today he looks much older than his age. A single tear creeps from the corner of his eye, and he brushes it away before it can make a mark on his cheek.

He rereads the letter, trying with every ounce of resolve to stop his hands from shaking. Aksel's words, revealing Aksel's heart. "I love her, Dad. I must rescue her. Punish me in the morning, but please don't stop me tonight."

It is morning. The house is here, and so is Aksel's bed. The sheets are neatly creased, and the pillow is still plump. But there's no sign of Aksel. No sign at all.

Lovely Weather for an Unseelie Ride Together

Matt Cowan

"It's no wonder Harper killed himself," said Roger as he emptied the remainder of the coffee pot into his Styrofoam cup.

"What a horrible thing to say," said Caroline from the cluttered break-room table.

"I'm just saying Dolan drove him to it. Who fires someone a week before Christmas?"

Seated across from Caroline, Frank swallowed a bite of his sandwich before joining the conversation. "Why do you think he fired him anyway? I mean, does anybody believe that stuff about too many complaints? We're telemarketers.

All we get are complaints."

Dolan listened, hidden from view, from the hallway just outside the door. "Ungrateful bastards," he mumbled to himself. Harper's contract called for significant raises every five years and an extra week of vacation at ten. Finding an excuse to get rid of him before the month-end would save him thousands.

Caroline's voice carried to him from the break room. "Whatever the case, Harper should have taken it to court. Killing oneself is never the answer."

"Of course, it isn't, but he let Dolan off the hook. He should have…" Roger let the comment drift as the door opened.

Adjusting his belt, Dolan eyed them. He relished the tinge of fear in their eyes. "Since your breaks are about over, I thought I'd address the…tragic news of Harper's passing. I was sorry to hear of his death, and I realize some may blame me for having to dismiss him. Unfortunately, far too many customers complained he was harassing and combative with them. I was left with no other choice but to let him go. I was hoping to wait until after Christmas, but his conduct was causing too much damage. Let this be a lesson; you are all valued, but if outside problems arise—and I understand Harper was hitting the bottle—I'll do whatever's necessary to maintain this company's image," said Dolan as he forced a smile he hoped was reassuring while being stern enough to remind them of his authority over them. "Any questions? Good. You should probably get back to those phones then."

❄ ❄ ❄

Dolan expected further discussion, but hearing nothing by 5:45, he decided he might engender a little good will, so he went out to address his employees. "Everyone finish the calls you're on and give me your attention." A few minutes later, they were listening from their garland-adorned cubicles.

"It being Christmas Eve, I'm going to let you all go home a few hours early, so wrap everything up and get ready to go enjoy your holiday."

Caroline started to raise her hand, dropped it for a second, and then thrust it up again.

"Did you have a question?" Dolan asked.

"I was wondering…um… Will we still be paid for the full day if we leave now?"

Dolan's smile slipped. He'd hoped he would be able to slide that past them by claiming he thought they knew they wouldn't, but that was no longer an option. They'd stay if he didn't agree to pay them, but he still needed to buy a gift for Nora's party. "Of course, you'll be paid for it," he assured, smoothing his mustache as he spoke. Later, after it was too late for them to do anything about it, he'd tell them that those paid, unworked hours were their Christmas bonus. That way he could at least get out of purchasing the discounted gift cards to his brother's restaurant that he usually gave them.

They mumbled "thank you" as they shut down their computers and donned their coats. He held the door as they made their way into the frigid outdoor air. Once they were gone, he locked up the office, bundled himself in his winter coat, and made his way down the sidewalk of businesses decked out for the season. A few people wished him "Merry Christmas" as he hurried past them. Each time he nodded but kept moving.

An unhealthy-looking Santa stood at the east entrance to Masterton Mall. Dolan briefly considered moving on to the next set of doors, but time was working against him. He held his breath and pretended the foul-smelling irritant wasn't there.

He hadn't anticipated the disheveled Santa reaching out to grab his arm. "Do you have anything worth contributing this Christmas?" he growled.

"Excuse me!" Dolan said, trying to yank his arm free, but the man wouldn't let go. He must be some vagrant who'd found the Santa suit in the trash. His oddly shaped body reeked of turned earth and overripe fruit. His build was thin and wiry everywhere except for his grossly distended belly.

Pulling him closer, the Santa glared at Dolan. "You're on my list," he grunted, breath reeking of spoiled milk.

Dolan looked around. Surely people could see that he was being accosted. A few glanced his way as they passed through the front doors, but none stopped.

"Let me go!" Dolan yelled, trying to yank his body free. The Santa suddenly released as he did so, sending Dolan sprawling into a pile of dirty snow.

The Santa loomed over Dolan. "I know when you've been naughty, and I'd have known if you'd ever been nice," he chuckled with a wink before turning to stalk away.

Dolan stood up, thought about yelling after the figure, but a glance at his watch sent him swiftly inside the mall instead. The storefronts inside Masterton's looked like presents competing to be the first one opened on Christmas morning. Someone dressed as a smiling Christmas tree attempted to get him to try some shoes, a scantily clad woman dressed as an elf called to him from a lingerie store, but he ignored them.

He had less than an hour left when he arrived at *The Book Haven*. An attendant showed him to the Young Adult section, where the book Nora's son wanted could be found. A loud thumping pulsed against the wall from the music store next door as he perused the titles for *Fae-Clopedia: An Encyclopedia of Elves, Fairies, and other Mystical Beings* and grabbed a copy as soon as he saw it. He flipped through its pages and saw displayed images of tiny beings with sprouted gossamer wings, stumpy men with heavy beards, and a variety of hideously deformed creatures. When the picture of a goblin that bore a strong resemblance to the fat-bellied Santa who had assailed him earlier caught his eye, he slammed the book shut. He couldn't imagine why Nora's child would want such a lurid book, but he needed the boy's approval to have any hope for a chance with her. A glance at the forty-dollar price tag made him swear loud enough to elicit angry looks from his fellow shoppers. Ignoring them, he made his way to the front register.

"Would you like to contribute a dollar to those less fortunate?" asked the heavyset woman wearing a snowman sweater.

"Certainly not," he grumbled. He then added, "Being forced to pay your ridiculous book prices will have me joining them soon enough."

Her smile faded. "I assume you don't want the two-dollar gift wrapping service then."

He gritted his teeth as he told her that he did want the service. He had to go straight to Nora's and hadn't thought about needing to wrap the present.

After signing the credit card receipt, Dolan snatched up the glistening red paper package and raced toward the mall's exit.

Heavy snow was falling when he exited Masterton's. Cars whizzed by on the streets, throwing slush onto the sidewalk at him. When the light on the corner turned red, Dolan crossed between them the cars, then dodged the oncoming traffic in the next lane before following a loud family laden with bags to the parking garage, where his hatchback sat alone on Level 6. He cringed at the loud cracking sounds his footsteps made on the cement. Images of the grizzled Santa and the wild-eyed creatures depicted in the book teamed up and invaded his thoughts, causing him to quicken his pace.

A sigh of relief upon entering the car caught in his throat when he spied a candy cane hanging from the rearview mirror. The vehicle had been locked. He always double-checked it, so there was no way anybody could have got in. A tag held by a strand of green ribbon dangled from the cane. He flipped it over and read the crude handwriting:

"Say your prayers because Santa Clause comes tonight."

Again he thought of his earlier assailant before dismissing it and throwing the cane into the back seat and starting the car. He couldn't help but check to ensure he was alone before finally driving down the garage's spiral ramp to merge with the throng of traffic.

***

The drive took longer than he'd hoped due to the worsening weather conditions that caused bumper-to-bumper traffic, which didn't dissipate until he turned onto Hartley Drive. Its long stretch of lonely, barely visible road was clogged with snow, slowing him down even more. As he moved as quickly as road conditions would allow, Dolan noticed himself paying more attention to his surroundings than usual. The absence of visible life among the cold, white hills flanking his route stirred unpleasant thoughts. He didn't relax until Nora's upscale house emerged from the darkness. No other cars were parked in the driveway. It appeared he was the first to arrive despite being thirty minutes late. Stepping out into ankle-deep snow, he trudged toward the glowing warmth of the house.

The front door opened as he mounted the colonnaded front steps to see Nora, wearing an elegant red dress, standing there. "Dolan, I'm glad the weather didn't keep you from coming," she said while looking past him down the road.

Dolan smiled as he stomped off clinging snow. "Nothing could prevent it," he said, leaning forward to kiss her on the cheek.

Nora turned away, looking into the house and calling out, "Carl, Mister Dolan's here!"

Dolan frowned. Perhaps he'd moved too quickly, but no matter, it could wait until later, he thought as he followed her into the house. The smell of a glazed turkey mingled pleasantly with a scent of pine that wafted in from the living room.

"Why don't you put your presents under the tree?" Nora suggested, pointing toward a huge pine glimmering with lights. "Help yourself to some eggnog and cookies by the fireplace while I see to some last-minute preparations in the kitchen. The others should be arriving soon. They've obviously been delayed by this weather, but I'm sure they're coming," she said before disappearing through an archway.

Setting his presents under the tree, Dolan hoped the others decided not to come at all. He filled an ornate crystal glass with eggnog and took a seat before the crackling fire. The rippling flames entranced and relaxed him. The rushed, nerve-wracking journey from work, to the mall, then to here had exhausted him more than he'd realized. He was starting to nod off when a red blur shot past the window to his left. Sitting up, Dolan looked around at the rest of the room's many windows but saw nothing until he glanced back over his shoulder. Something had just shifted away as he was turning, leaving behind a slowly dissipating handprint on the glass.

Dolan sprang from the couch with a yelp before recovering enough to see through a window something mounting the front porch steps just as a set of headlight beams swept across the driveway, illuminating with a flash of a goatish face before blinding Dolan. When his sight adjusted, the window was empty.

"Hey, Mister Dolan," came a child's voice from behind, causing him to jump.

"Whaa..." Dolan gasped, feeling a surge of anger before catching himself. "Oh... Hey, Carl. You startled me."

"Why?"

"You just did," he snapped, then noticed Nora approaching the front door.

She opened it to admit a tall, dark-haired man who was a good ten years younger and forty pounds lighter than Dolan. The hug they shared was more affectionate than seemed appropriate for friends or coworkers.

"Jason," Nora exclaimed with a broad smile. "I'm so glad you made it. Now I can stop worrying."

"You don't know the half of it," the man answered, brushing snow from his overcoat. He glanced at Dolan and nodded with a smile. "There's a bad accident near the Hartley exit. I just missed it. I'd be surprised if any of your other guests can get through."

Nora placed a hand over her mouth. "I hope it didn't involve anyone coming here. Why don't you join Carl and Dolan? You remember Mister Dolan, don't you? I mentioned him earlier."

Dolan didn't appreciate the smirk the two shared.

"I'm going to call our missing guests to make sure they're okay," Nora said as she retreated to the kitchen to retrieve her phone.

Dolan noticed Jason didn't carry any presents. Glancing at his own gift under the tree and remembering how much he'd spent on the necklace he bought for Nora returned his confidence.

"Jason!" Carl squealed as he ran into the man's arms.

"Hey, Sport," Jason said, lifting him into the air.

Dolan turned to hide his scowl from view. Taking a minute to compose himself, he regarded the man. "Jason, is it? Did you happen to notice anyone lurking around outside when you drove up?"

Jason's frowned. "No, should I have?"

Dolan didn't like his tone. "I suppose not."

Nora re-entered the room, still holding the phone to her ear. "I understand," she said. "No, I wouldn't want anyone risking their life for my party. We'll plan on getting together sometime after Christmas," she added before hanging up with a sigh. "Looks like we're going to be the only ones tonight."

"Is everyone alright?" Jason asked.

"Yes, but the weather's getting too bad for them to make it. We'll have to reschedule, I suppose. I'll understand if you guys want to head home."

"Nonsense," Jason said before Dolan could speak. "We couldn't leave even if we wanted to. Between the snow and the accident, the road's going to be blocked for a while. We may be stuck here for the night."

"Here, here," Dolan chimed in, wishing it sounded less like an afterthought.

Nora's face brightened. "Thank you! I'm sorry you're trapped here, but I'm glad for the company." She'd been addressing them both, but her eyes were focused only on Jason. "What should we do first?"

"How about we open presents," Dolan quickly suggested, smiling to himself.

"Yeah!" Carl agreed.

"I'm afraid my gift hasn't arrived yet," Jason said. "I found something perfect for you, but it's being shipped from France and hasn't arrived yet."

"France!" Nora gasped. "I'll be on pins and needles wondering what it is."

"You know what would be fun," Jason said, leaning forward. "We should play a game."

Nora clapped her hands. "That does sound like fun. What sort of game?"

"Hide-and-seek!" Carl yelled.

"I bet Carl already has the best hiding spots picked out, don't you, buddy?" Jason said, leaning in to tickle the boy.

"You can't be serious," Dolan muttered.

The look Nora shot him made Dolan regret the outburst. "You don't have to join us, of course," she said.

"No, I'll play, but I thought Carl wanted to open presents first."

"That's okay," Carl said. "We can do that after. I want to play hide-and-seek, and... Not it!" he yelled as he shot out of the room.

Two more "not its" came from Nora and Jason.

"I guess that leaves you as the seeker," Jason told Dolan. "Unless you don't want to."

Dolan felt trapped. "I said I'd play, didn't I? How high do I count?"

"One hundred," Nora said with a giggle as she and Jason left the room together.

Dolan counted silently. He needed to get control of the situation. There must be some way to discredit this Jason fellow. Perhaps he could take something from the house and hide in the man's coat that was hanging by the door. If she thought his interest in her was a ruse, she'd cast him into the night whether the roads had cleared or not.

He'd only reached the count of fifty when he opened his eyes and began to survey the room for something that might work. He settled on a silver praying angel statue on the sill of the front window. It was the right size for Jason's coat pocket and was obviously valuable. He was moving toward it when a face appeared in the frosted pane behind it. An elongated, bulbous-nosed face wearing a Santa hat stared in at him, with a clawed hand pressed against the glass.

Dolan stumbled backward, barely avoiding the Christmas tree. "Nora!" he yelled, but there was no answer. The dim, festive lighting of the house projected too many shadows. Wherever the others had gone to hide, they'd done so silently. "There's somebody at the door," he added, hoping to draw her out.

The face moved away. Something large and red swept past the windows toward the back of the house. Dolan ran to the front door to make sure it was locked. Through the sidelight, he noticed the fresh snow where he'd seen the thing was unblemished. He risked opening the door enough to look at the spot where it had stood. There was no sign anyone had been there. In fact, other than Jason's and his own diminishing footprints, there were none to be found. Dolan pulled himself back into the house before slamming and locking the door.

Something moved down the dark hallway behind him. Dolan had planned on beginning his frantic search for the others, but whatever was down the hall had cut him off from the rest of the house. "Alright, I've seen you there in the hall," he said, a tremble in his voice as he backed into the living room. "You can come on out now." He refused to take his eyes off the shadow taking shape. It was too large for Nora or Jason, and it was moving closer.

"Who are you?" Dolan yelled, stepping back.

A swelled belly preceded the misshapen creature into the room, wearing a dingy Santa suit and smelling of decay. Its long, gnarled arms drooped to the floor. The gray flesh of its elongated face was pocked by sprouting fungi. Dead, pupilless eyes floated within its ocular cavities, burning with unholy intellect.

"Those who cherish Christmas in their hearts are blessed

with miracles," the repugnant thing growled in a cavernous voice as it lurched toward him. "Those who pervert it for their own detestable desires eventually bring forth...something else."

"I don't understand," Dolan chattered, his retreat halted by the heat of the fireplace behind him.

The Santa-thing stood close enough for Dolan to smell its fetid breath as it spoke. "You're about to be consumed by a Christmas spirit... of a sort?"

It charged, wrapping its bony arms around him before leaping into the searing flames of the large fireplace. Dolan's flesh bubbled like boiling wax. His hair erupted like dry straw, and his skin dropped from him in chunks. Somehow they both stretched, elongating enough to squeeze up through the chimney to Nora's snow-covered roof. Through a haze of intense pain, he saw an opened ebony casket with sleigh runners attached to its undercarriage, a pack of horse-sized beetles hitched to it.

Slipping in and out of consciousness, he felt himself thrust into the coffin-sleigh, then they were flying through the night sky. The wrought iron gates of Cedar Crest Cemetery appeared before them, and they dove downward. The flying beetles met the ground and began to furiously churn into the earth, tunneling a path beneath the surface and the tombstones. The rotting Santa-creature dropped the reins and leaped free of the sleigh to stand above the hole Dolan's blistered body was being pulled into.

As he continued to descend, the view of snow falling from a Christmas Eve night sky was replaced by frozen earth pouring down on top of him.

The Santa Revelation

Tristan Ryan

I was ten years old, and I still believed in Santa Claus. No one could change my mind, not even my friends. No one could sway me from my belief in the magical man in red, who had given me more than God ever could. Santa Claus showed results.

"Don't you believe in Santa Claus?" I asked my two friends as we walked through the snow on our way to the library.

"Not really," Ethan admitted.

I could tell by their voices that they were afraid to say no to me.

"My mom told me he's not real," my other friend, Vincent, said.

"Your mom told you that?!" I said in disbelief. "And you

believe her? Don't you get presents from Santa?"

"No," he replied. "I've never gotten presents from him. My mom told me the truth about it right away. She said she didn't think it was right to lie to me."

"That's not right," I argued. "Your mom is making it so Santa can't even leave you presents. If you just believe in him, you'll get presents from him. You'll see. Then your mom will know she was wrong to keep that from you."

"Why do you believe in Santa so much?" Ethan asked me.

"Because he gives me presents that my parents couldn't afford," I said. "So I know for a fact that he's real. I'm always going to believe in Santa. I don't see why it should change just because you get older."

I had so much more I wanted to say to my friends, but I decided to let it be for the moment. Getting them to believe in Santa Claus was not going to be as easy as I thought it would be.

The next day, I talked to Vincent again about Santa.

"Just believe in him until Christmas," I begged. "He'll bring you presents as long as you believe in him."

"Okay," Vincent finally said. I thought he really seemed to want to believe. I felt relieved that I may have saved Christmas for him.

It was Christmas Eve, and I was anxious to see what I would get from Santa this year. Probably just what I asked for. This year I had decided not to show my parents the list of presents I was going to ask Santa for. That would be more proof I could show my friends after Christmas.

I went to sleep early and woke up at four in the morning. I lay on my bed, excited to go downstairs to the living room to see all the packages Santa had left for me. I decided I would go down and take a peek, but I wasn't going to open them yet. I would be considerate and wait for my parents to wake up.

As I crept down the stairs, I heard someone snoring. My mom was sleeping on the sofa! How could she do this to me!

There were no presents under the tree. I looked at my mom as she slept on the sofa and narrowed my eyes at her. I could have punched her, I was so angry. It was all her fault that Santa hadn't left any presents. How could he while she was in the room? She might see him. And nobody is supposed to see him. Everyone knows that. So why was she sleeping on the sofa?! She was such an idiot!

I went back to my room and sullenly sat on the floor. I just sat there for an hour until I heard someone moving around downstairs. Was it Santa? Had he come after all?

I heard a closet door open, and the crinkling noises that came after told me it was just my mom taking out presents that had already been wrapped.

I had a bad feeling in the pit of my stomach. The thought occurred to me that my friends may have been right. What if Santa wasn't real?

I waited half an hour to go downstairs. Just as I had feared, the tree was surrounded by presents that hadn't been there an hour and a half ago. And they were all signed as "From: Santa."

I knelt down by the presents. My expression wasn't quite blank, but it was close to it.

"You want to open your presents?" my mom asked.

I nodded my head dully. "Okay," I said.

I unwrapped the largest one from "Santa" first. It was a football. Why would Santa get me a football? I never liked sports.

The next present wasn't much better. It was a collector's set of baseball cards.

If Santa were real, he would know better than to give me such plain, generic gifts. One thing I was certain of was that my parents *didn't* know any better. There was a lot they didn't know about me. That never mattered in the past because I could always count on Santa.

But now I knew the truth. Even Santa didn't know me. There *was* no Santa. It had all been a lie.

Before I had even finished unwrapping my presents, I stood up and slowly began walking out of the room.

"Everything okay?" my mom asked. "Don't you like your presents?"

I slowly turned around so I was facing her.

"These presents aren't from Santa Claus. He isn't real, is he?" I said and gave her a good stare down. My nostrils were flaring. I never felt as upset as I did at that moment.

"You don't believe in Santa anymore?" my mom asked. Before I could respond, she laughed and added, "I guess you're kind of old to believe in Santa."

"You lied to me!" I screamed. "Everyone lied to me!"

"Keep your voice down. Your dad's still asleep," she said.

Was that all she had to say? Not that she was sorry for lying to me my entire life?

I ran up the stairs and into my room, slamming the door shut behind me. I curled up on the floor and cried for what seemed like forever. I cried so much I was out of tears.

I lay there and thought about what had just happened, what I had learned about myself and the people around me. My entire life had been a lie. Of that, I was certain. If Santa Claus wasn't real, what else had I been lied to about? Was God even real? As hard as it was to think of losing God, it was nothing compared to losing Santa Claus. I suppose the Easter Bunny wasn't real either.

How could parents lie to their children, especially knowing that one day they would learn the truth? Didn't they realize how disappointing it was to learn that you'd been basing your beliefs around a lie?

I heard my dad walk downstairs. He was awake. They were both awake. I could hear them talking. Were they talking about me? About how gullible I am?

I crept back down the stairs so I could hear what they were saying.

They weren't even talking about me! They were talking about what time we would be going to Grandma's for the Christmas get-together.

I clenched my teeth as I imagined going to my grandma's. She would probably have more presents for me, and at least one of them would say it was from Santa. I'd always known the presents at Grandma's weren't from Santa. For one thing, they were always signed in her chicken-scratch handwriting. Thinking about all the times that my mom told me to just go along with it and pretend that I believed the gifts at Grandma's were from Santa made me even angrier.

They had *all* been lying to me all those years. My entire life had been built on lies.

I walked past the living room unnoticed by my parents and went into the kitchen. I searched the back of the silverware drawer for the large cutting knife my parents thought they had kept hidden from me. I pricked my finger with the tip of the blade and watched the blood slowly drip down my finger and onto the floor.

I went back into the living room with the knife in my hand.

"Morning," my dad said. "Why don't you open the rest of your presents?"

"I don't care about presents," I said with a dead tone.

"Then you must not have opened the one from me yet," he said, somehow able to keep up with a cheery disposition.

But I could sense his unease. They'd always been wary

of me. Afraid of me.

Had they known just how afraid they should have been, they would never have lied to me in the first place.

I stabbed the small square pillow on the sofa next to my dad with the knife. My dad didn't seem as worried as he should have been.

"Woah," he said. "Easy. Calm down."

"Calm down!" I screamed. "You lied to me. You lied to me! You liiiiieeeeed!"

As I repeated the four words over and over, the knife in my hand became covered in red. I stabbed my dad in the neck so many times, I couldn't say for sure how many. My mom screamed. Her arms flailed about, but she didn't move off of the sofa.

Why didn't she move? I've often wondered. She could have given herself a chance. All she would have had to do was kick the knife out of my hand. Instead, she just sat there and screamed, as if she could not be harmed.

The knife saw more blood as I brought it down to my mom's stomach. Again, I don't know how many times I stabbed her. I just remember doing it over and over.

She deserved it. They both did. And once I was done with them, I felt a new love for Christmas. Christmas wasn't dead. It had just become something different to celebrate. The death of my parents. The death of all liars.

I decided right then and there that I wasn't going to let any other parent lie to their kids the way mine had lied to me. They could try, but they wouldn't live for very long. Not if I could help it.

A Christmas Eve Visitor

Kev Harrison

Sally tied the last glimmering bow with aplomb and placed the gift under the branches of the towering pine tree. She sat back and admired her handiwork. It was going to be a wonderful Christmas for her and little Oscar, even if Steven wouldn't be back until the 27th.

She reached back to the coffee table and took a sip of prosecco, relishing the warmth and glow of the roaring fire. She picked herself up from the rug and trudged over to the sofa. Christmas Eve and everything was ready, but not without its price. She was exhausted. She slumped back in the chair and clicked the remote on to the Christmas channel. She glanced at her watch. A quarter to eleven and *Miracle on 34th Street* was just beginning. It was the sort of saccharine nonsense that would've turned her stomach just a few years ago, but she'd mellowed since Oscar had been born. Embraced the holiday season and all the schmaltz that came with it.

As snow floated down on the screen and the gentle jingling of sleigh bells rang, Sally's head lolled forward, her breathing drawing out long and calm as she dozed off. There she stayed for an hour or so, quietly snatching at a rare chance of uninterrupted sleep. She didn't hear the tinkling of glass as the gloved hand punched through the kitchen window. Nor the footsteps as the heavy, snow-laden boots traversed the tiles to the muffling carpet of the lounge. Only when the gloved hand, chilly from the harsh weather outside closed over her mouth did her eyes spring open.

"Mmmmrrmmrmrrmmr," she tried to speak, her heart rate rocketing up, chest heaving under her heavy jumper.

"Be quiet or I'll break your fucking neck," a voice said from behind her, his grip tightening around her face as if to assure her he was serious. "Stand up, now."

Sally felt a body shuffle around the edge of the sofa and press into her back. She swallowed hard and squeezed her eyes closed.

"I'm going to take my hand off your mouth, but if you scream, I will stab you. Nod if you understand."

Sally nodded, a tear tracing its way down her cheek. The man removed his hand one finger at a time. Sally bent double, wheezing, her heart still racing, then stood up and turned to face her attacker. The man was tall, athletic build, wearing a balaclava, piercing green eyes staring her down from behind the eye holes. In his left hand, he clutched a serrated combat knife. Sally backed away, toward the tree.

"What do you want?" Her voice was hoarse after hyperventilating.

"Think of me like Santa Claus, only I'll be filling my sack

with presents instead of leaving them." From the side pocket of his black cargo trousers, he pulled a bundle of material, which he unrolled to reveal a large hessian bag. He held it out to Sally. "Put the presents in there."

Sally stood still, hands held close to her torso.

"Fill the bag!" Though his voice was quiet, there was a firmness, his jabbing knife-hand adding menace to his words. Sally reached out one trembling hand and grasped the bag. She opened it and crouched down beside the tree, keeping the robber in her line of sight. She reached out to the pile of presents on the right first. On top of the small stack was a tiny model sleigh with a hand-written card on the back, which read, "Mummy."

She shook the parcels as she lifted them, one final guess at what might have been, before placing them in the cloth sack. As she stuffed the fifth and final gift in the bag, she reached out to pass the bag back to the man. "Here," she said. "Take it. There's probably some jewelry in there. Maybe some perfume. Valuable stuff."

The man crouched down in front of her, the knife glinting in the firelight as he gestured to the tree. "All of it," he said. "Don't make me hurt you."

Sally bit her lip, fighting off another wave of tears. "Not little Oscar's things. He's three years old. This is his *first* proper Christmas."

The man grabbed her chin in his free hand. "Do I seem like a bleeding heart to you, eh? Do you think I give a shit about your little *Oscar*?" He shoved her backward. Sally lost her balance, tumbling into the wall and hitting her head, causing the dammed-up tears to overflow their banks and stream down her face. "Now fill this bag!" the man spat.

Sally righted herself, rubbing her sore head. She moved the shepherd scene, Oscar's name etched on a card in the felt grass, and began to bundle his gifts into the bag one at a time. The *My First Music Maker*. The light-up fire engine. The fluffy penguin with the cute sounds when you squeezed it.

Impatient, the man stepped closer, waving the knife. "Hurry up!"

Sally looked up into his eyes. "I'm sorry. This is just... This is difficult." She leaned forward and wrapped an arm around the man's leg, sobbing into his thigh. The man stood motionless. The sound of the fire seemed to increase in volume as the quiet sound of Sally's heart breaking escaped, staccato, from her quivering lips. "Oh, Oscar," she said.

She lowered her left hand, then forced it up with all her strength, connecting with the man's groin and sending him sprawling backward. He tripped on the sofa and fell back. Sally was quickly on her feet, lunging at him. Her right arm shot out to block the knife swipe, catching him in the center of the forearm with a painful crunch. His hand flexed open against his will, the knife clattering to the floor. Sally leaped up, her knees pinning his shoulders to the sofa. She wound up and brought her closed fist down on the man's neck, then his temple at the other side. His head lolled back, dazed.

Sally sprang to the floor, reaching for the knife. She closed her fingers around the handle as the snow boot connected with her midriff, sending her careening across the ground. The knife skittered across the floor. Still she crawled after it. She was about to grasp it when the man grabbed at her loose hair and tugged her back. He let fly with a punch into the middle of her back and left her rolling on the floor, back arched, pain distorting her vision.

The attacker stepped over her and scooped up the knife. "You almost had me," he said, and spat on the carpet next to her. He rubbed the side of his face where her punch had connected, scrunching his eyes shut against the pain. He sat back down on the sofa, waited for Sally to sit up.

"There's one more present under that tree," he said, pointing with the curved tip of the blade. "If you put it in the bag quickly, I'll wish you a merry Christmas and be on my way. Any more bullshit and...well...I think you can guess what might happen." He turned the blade in the air, Sally's reflection glinting across the surface.

Sally felt the back of her head, bringing her hand back to her face to check for blood. She found none and returned her eyes to the man. "That one's for my husband. He's missing Christmas. It's not valuable. Please...just leave that one here. Please."

The man stood. "Seems you didn't understand my warning about *bullshit,* did you?" He circled the sofa and stood at the bottom of the stairs. Tell me, which room is little Oscar in?"

Sally leaned forward, defeated, her hands up in surrender. "Okay... Okay, you win, you win!" She picked up the small, rectangular box and looked at the card, the neat handwriting. "My beloved husband," it read, with a love heart drawn beside it. She carefully slipped it into the bag and hauled herself to her feet. She carried the bag to the man. "Now, you get the *fuck* out of my house."

"And a Merry Christmas to you, too," the man said, somehow transmitting his self-satisfied smile from behind his woolen mask. He strode quickly to the door and let himself out, slamming it behind him, leaving only a chilly blast of winter wind.

Sally staggered to the window and crouched, watching the shadow of the man move along the street. He approached an alleyway between two houses on the other side of the road and disappeared into the darkness. Something held her there, staring out into the night.

❄ ❄ ❄

Meanwhile, the man was emerging at the other end of the alley. He crossed the road and scrambled over a verge into an old waste ground. There, he unlocked a battered, silver car, looked around, then climbed inside. He switched on the light and took off his balaclava, revealing pale skin and a ginger beard. First, he opened the toys, tossing them on to the back seat of the car. Next was the jewelry, a necklace of pearls, which he bit like an old movie gangster checking his swag before stowing it and the matching earrings in the glovebox.

He rummaged through the remaining three presents, casting the contents aside, then came to the final box. Steven's box. He tugged at the bow, the most intricate of all of them, then lifted the perfectly-fitted lid. Inside, on top of some crinkled crepe paper, was a scroll tied with string. He tugged at the string and unfurled it. He held the paper up to the light and read the beautiful calligraphy.

Dearest Steven,

What a pity you couldn't be with your wife and child this Christmas. It must've been such an important business trip. I know all about Madeleine from the office.

See you in hell.

Sally

The man rubbed his beard. Confused. He looked over his shoulder and, finding he was completely alone, he peeled back the crepe paper. There was a faint beeping before the inside of the car was consumed in a maelstrom of heat and noise and flame, the windows exploding outwards onto the street, followed by tiny scraps of flesh and bone.

Sally's house shook with the force of the blast, the flash of the explosion glowing in her eyes from above the houses in front. "Merry Christmas, you thieving bastard," she said, as the porch lights along the road switched on one by one.

The Widowmaker

P.A. Sheppard

Virgil closed his eyes and rolled his head from side to side; the stiff motion produced several loud popping sounds from deep within his neck. New York to Hagerstown wasn't a long flight by any stretch of the imagination, but cheap seats and long delays were a poor combination on the best of days. And Christmas Eve was not the best of days. For most passengers, getting off a budget airline was a pleasure, something to look forward to before grabbing a coffee and starting the next leg of their journey. Not for Virgil, not this time.

The landing had been smooth despite the blizzard, and the plane was currently being taxied away from the main runway, where it would wait for a shuttle to collect the passengers and their belongings. Yeah, right, his kid brother would be waiting for him, and he knew it. He closed the shutter on his window and wondered whether airport security would wait for him to disembark or board the plane to arrest him. He hoped for the latter; they were far less likely to shoot on sight if he was still buckled into his seat, surrounded by innocent civilians. He looked between the seats in front of him. The little terror who'd somehow managed to cry throughout the entire journey was now staring back at him, her squashed, ketchup-stained face pressed tightly between her parents' headrests. He imagined a stray bullet passing through the back of her seat. Annoying as she was, he couldn't risk it.

He stretched his arms above his head and yawned. "Here we go."

Freeing himself from the cramped seat, he cracked his neck once more and walked as casually as possible along the narrow aisle.

"Excuse me, sir. Please, could you remain seated until the seatbelt lights have been switched off." The air hostess bit her lip, and her forehead glistened as she waited for his response. The poor girl was terrified. A magnetic name tag hung heavily on her polyester waistcoat and revealed her name was Donna.

"It's alright, Donna, I know you've had a call from the sheriff's office, but there's no need to panic. Everything is gonna be alright. But I'm gonna need a little help. Okay?"

Donna nodded but didn't speak.

"Good. Now, I'm gonna walk toward the toilets at the back of the plane where no one will see me. Then I'm gonna lay down on my stomach an' wait for the police to take me into custody. No commotion, no trouble, Alright?" He smiled at her and nodded as he spoke.

Donna nodded in return.

"Good, very good. You're doin' brilliantly. Now follow me, an' close the curtains behind us; if anyone asks what's going on, just tell them not to worry, everything's under control. A passenger's having some difficulty breathing an' needs a little privacy."

Donna's brow furrowed, but she nodded once more.

Virgil turned and strolled towards the back of the plane with Donna close behind. As far as the rest of the passengers were concerned, he was just another traveler who'd been sitting too long and couldn't hold it in any longer. They reached the end of the aisle, and Donna calmly closed the synthetic velvet curtain behind them.

"Good, it's almost over. Now, the last thing I need you to do is to radio out an' explain the situation. Tell them that Virgil Parsons has given himself up. Tell them I'm laying on my stomach at the rear of the plane, waiting to be taken into custody. Can you do that for me, Donna?" He waited for her to nod. "Good. Keep calm, an' this could be the best day of your life. Tomorrow you'll be eating mince pies an' telling your family all about it. They'll call you a hero for this; get this right an' you'll be able to get a job with any airline in the world."

The air hostess's hands trembled as she lifted the radio to her head. Virgil knelt for a moment, listening to the radio conversation, before laying down and closing his eyes.

❄ ❄ ❄

"Well, you took your damn time. Stop for doughnuts, did ya?" Virgil asked as his little brother stepped into the interrogation room. They were the first words he'd uttered since handing himself in, knowing that his high-and-mighty kid brother would eventually show up.

Ignoring the jibe, U.S. Marshal Otis Parsons strolled to the center of the room and pulled out the empty chair opposite

Virgil away from the table. Leaning over it, he folded his arms on its back. "You're lucky they called the Regional Fugitive Force, boy; FBI woulda shot you dead."

Virgil stared up at his little brother, noticing how the years, the stress of the job, and an apparent lack of exercise had taken a toll. "Luck had nothing to do with it, an' don't call me boy. I might not look it, but I'm still your elder, always have been, always will be. Now, are you sure it's her? I took a big risk coming here."

"Sure as water's wet, and trust me, I'm the one taking the risks," he said, sliding a set of handcuffs across the steel table between them. "Put these on while I sign you out. The storm don't look like it's planning on stopping anytime soon, and it's a long drive to the cabin."

"The cabin? Is that where you found him?"

Otis shook his head. "Come on, I'll fill you in on the way."

The two brothers walked through the airport police station, the U.S. Marshal and his compliant prisoner; they were a contrast in appearances. Otis had gained some extra pounds since they were last together, but he still had his easy smile and gentle expression as he joked with the local officers on their way out. Virgil, on the other hand, looked like he'd been cutting wood and lifting logs for the past fifteen years. Weathered and strong, he was like an extra from a black and white film—shapeless jeans, worn cotton shirt, and the same shabby leather waistcoat he always wore.

"I'll drive," Virgil announced as they stepped from the station into the cold parking lot.

"Like hell, you will."

"Shotgun then."

"You'll sit in the back like every other felon in transport, at least till we get out of here. Besides, there's some warm clothes and a few other bits waiting for you in the footwell."

He opened the rear door and ushered Virgil inside, carefully bobbing his prisoner's head out of habit.

A mile or so later, with his cuffs off and a fleece-lined jacket draped over his shoulders, Virgil rummaged through the rest of his brother's supplies. Headtorch, hand torch, Glock-19. "Chemical hand warmers?"

"They ain't for you; they're for old Sal. An ounce of prevention is worth a pound of cure, especially at her age," answered Otis, slowing down to navigate a twist in the steep road. "Sal's waiting for us at the cabin."

"Alone?" asked Virgil, raising his head from the rucksack.

"Well, she is now that Pop's gone. She ain't left the building since he was killed. Says she saw the whole thing through the window. And judging by the position of his body when I found him, I dare say she did."

"Sal saw it happen? She sat there an' watched while that bitch killed Pop?"

"Now steady on, Virg; she's seventy-eight years old. What was she gonna do against something like that? Best thing she coulda done was call me, and that's what she did."

"Did she get a good look at her?" he asked.

"Yup, described her just the way you did all those years ago."

Virgil's heart sank as a large lump grew in his throat. "How'd ya find him?"

"Frozen solid," said Otis, shaking his head. "Still standing with his shotgun raised and braced. The bitch covered him in ice before he could squeeze the trigger."

"He went after her with a shotgun?" Virgil's eyes and mouth were open in an expression of stunned surprise.

"Yup. He knew as well as we do that it wouldn't do squat, but something made him step outside to give it a go. Perhaps he saw a weakness? Could be he just got fed up with her teasing."

"Teasing?"

"That's the word old Sal used. She reckoned they'd been trapped in the cabin for a week before it happened, listening to her banging on the door, or staring at them through the windows before Pop boarded them all up."

Both brothers fell silent as the car plowed onward through the growing storm, climbing into the highlands of Appalachia and bringing them closer to the homestead that had seen the deaths of so many family members. An image flashed in Virgil's mind, a childhood memory burned into his brain like a photograph. The scene was vivid as the killer turned to stare at him, still hovering over his mother's body. He heard her laughter in his mind and imagined her twisted face teasing his father forty-five years later. Shuddering at the thought, he turned to watch his little brother as he concentrated on the icy roads. A stream of familiar thoughts rose to defend is actions. *He had to leave; he would have gone to jail if he'd stayed. Otis and Pop could take care of themselves.* He knew he'd made the wrong choice when he had to work so hard to justify it. It wasn't right to leave his little brother with such a burden, but really, what choice did he have?

He leaned forward and patted his brother's shoulder. "Hey, there was nothing you could have done. He knew she'd get him one day, just like she'll get us. Best we can hope for is to take the bitch down with us."

Otis grunted. "I reckon that was Pop's thinking. Trying to take her out before she found us." It looked as if he was going to say something else but decided against it. His eyes never left the road. "I'm gonna pull in to a motel so you can get some rest. It will be better if we arrive in the morning, and I doubt Sal would open the door this late anyway." He fiddled with the radio for a second or two and set the volume to just high enough to end any further conversation.

Twenty minutes later, Virgil stepped into the stuffy front office of the Copperhead Motel while Otis parked the car.

"I'm telling you, it wasn't the cold that killed him. That family's cursed, an' he got what was coming to him!" an elderly woman in an even older fleece jacket said to the boy behind the counter as Virgil walked in. "Only people who freeze to death up here are the outsiders, ill-prepared city folk who breakdown an' freeze to death in their cars waiting for help to arrive. Us mountain folk can deal with the cold. It was his little girl that got him. The Widowmaker."

The agitated elder turned to face Virgil, her clouded gray eyes peering through him. "Boy, was you born in a barn? It's airish enough in here, close that door."

"Widowmaker?" asked Virgil, closing the door and stepping up to the counter.

"Trees 'n' branches," said the young man behind the desk, answering before the old-timer could scare away his potential customer. "It gets so cold up here that water freezes on the trees, builds up so, you think that the wood can't support the weight. After a while, it gets heavy enough that the branch, or sometimes the whole tree comes down. Y'all hear them falling when the wind dies down. If ya staying, that is? It's a bad night to be out, but I got plenty of rooms t' spare, and we're serving turkey in the morning."

"I know what widow-makers are," he said to the attendant. "I was asking the lady what she meant by it. And who froze to death?"

Virgil could see the wrinkles in the woman's forehead knitting together as she studied his voice. The lines around her eyes made crosses as she struggled to recognize the newcomer with a local accent.

"Jethro Parsons, if you must know. One of his boys found

him frozen stiff not twenty yards from his own front door. Authorities are calling it a tragic accident, but folks my age know better. We remember what he did to that poor little girl. We know she finally got him."

"Jethro Parsons had a daughter?"

Biting her lip, the old woman nodded.

"And she's the Widowmaker?"

"Aye. She ain't been seen for nearly fifteen years, but we ain't had a winter like this for nearly that long either. But I knew she'd show up again sooner or later, an' so did Jethro." She raised her chin, and her eyebrows furrowed once more. "Say, don't I know you?"

"What happened to the daughter?" he asked, ignoring her question.

"Murdered, that's what happened to her. Jethro Parsons might have convinced the sheriff that it was an accident, but those who knew him know better. We all saw how he treated that poor girl."

"Gran," the kid behind the counter tried to interrupt, but she was having none of it.

"That swine threw his own little girl in the lake an' left her to die. He killed her on Christmas Eve an' let his poor wife find the body in the morning."

"So she drowned in the lake?" asked Virgil.

The old woman shook her head and swallowed, "Oh no, she didn't drown. Backward as she was, that girl was a Parsons, and that family's as tough as they are dumb. Jethro may have left her for dead, but that girl had the grit to drag herself out of that lake and crawl right up to his front door. An' that's where her mother found her, frozen stiff on Christmas morning. Her fists still clenched from beating on the door."

Virgil blanched, knowing full well that the old woman's story was probably true. "You're sure it's her?"

"Can't say that I've seen her myself." She tapped her white cane on the floorboards. "Wouldn't want to either. I've heard her, though, and I'd recognize that voice anywhere; sometimes, she drifts on the breeze, laughing down at us. Other times she howls through the storm, fit to be tied."

"You recognize her voice?"

"Well, I ought to. I'm the one that brought her into this world. I dropped in every week to help her mother when things were bad. Lord knows Jethro didn't do a damn thing to raise that child. *'Stupid girl,'* that's what he called her!"

"How'd you know she was coming this year?" asked Virgil.

"The first frost was late in coming, but when it did, it hit the mountains with a bitterness usually saved for the big, midwinter freezes, just like the one that killed her. An' it's been getting worse since. She always comes when the season's bad. These are the winters we've been saving our firewood for. These are the winters we fear."

A violent blast of freezing wind nearly ripped the door from its hinges as Otis burst inside. Feminine laughter echoed in the wind behind him, and the temperature in the room suddenly dropped beyond the opening of a door.

"She's here!" Otis shouted, turning to shut the door against the gale. Virgil spun to help him, and the two brothers pushed together, managing to close the door just as something solid crashed into the other side. With their shoulders pressed hard against the thick oak door, the brothers could hear her rasping breath and twisted laughter coming from the other side like shards of broken glass grating against their memories. It didn't last long; within moments of them closing the door, the maniacal laughter switched to panicked sobs as the beating became more frantic. Almost like a child pleading to be let in.

"Quick, slide the bolt," Virgil yelled at the attendant. It was taking all of their combined strength just to keep the door shut against the presence on the other side; neither of them could risk shifting their weight to lock the door. "Come on, damn you!"

The man ran from behind his counter, but it was the old woman who got there first. She dropped to her knees and twisted the cold iron bolt and let it drop securely into place. With the door locked, the brothers slumped and backed away from the door. The wind and the sobbing stopped the moment the deadbolt had dropped, and all was silent. Then the screaming started. Like an animal caught in a snare, the old woman thrashed on the floor, struggling to free her hand from the cold metal bolt. Before anyone could react, a thick layer of frost formed on the inside of the door. Swirling patterns of ice crackled and grew, encasing the woman's hand and arm. Her screams continued even as her body ceased its doomed struggle to break free.

Otis moved forward, the cop in him desperate to help, but Virgil held him back, keeping his brother from taking the bait. They watched helplessly as the woman's cries of terror intensified and the ice crept further up her arm. It reached her shoulder and seemed to stop as she lifted her head and locked eyes with them, pleading for help or mercy. Her expression tugged at Virgil's heart, every muscle in the woman's face strained and held rigid with agony. It was the same expression their mother had died with all those years ago. The old woman screamed again, but it was cut short as her entire body froze solid. Encased in ice in just a few seconds. Her agonized features preserved in death to haunt the living. Outside, the sound of laughter returned, malicious and taunting. The winds howled once more, and the Widowmaker's shadow shrieked past the window, frosting and cracking the glass as she left.

Virgil sighed and cracked his neck loudly as the young man moved passed him with faltering steps before slipping to his knees, his hairless face deathly pale, his entire form shuddering.

"Gran?" His words formed a cloud in the chill air.

The two brothers exchanged a look behind the kid's back, silently agreeing that this conversation was better left to Otis. Comforting talk had never been Virgil's strongest suit.

The rest of the night was spent with the three men sitting side by side with their backs to the radiator and motel duvets pulled tight around themselves. The two brothers took it in turns to sleep while the kid sat and stared at the blanket they'd draped over his gran's frozen form. The Widowmaker stayed away for the rest of the night, and the brothers knew better than to go looking for her without a plan.

The following morning Otis called in the old woman's death from his car radio and warned the kid to get as far away as possible. His calming police officer voice was the epitome of authority as he handed over the cash from the motel register and made the boy promise to buy a flight with it, to somewhere warm.

Within an hour of the sun rising, they were back on the road and heading for their father's cabin. Another hour passed and a rusted tin sign proclaimed that they'd arrived at Deadpike Lake. The weather-worn sign was faded and looked as if someone had used it for target practice at some point in the past. Fifteen more minutes of careful driving and they were outside their old family home on the west side of the lake.

Virgil stepped out of the sedan and stretched, taking in the familiar, if somewhat dilapidated, scene. The woodland surrounding the cabin seemed ominously quiet as he stared at the full salt feeders from across the driveway, the valuable winter calories left untouched.

"Listen to that," he said after stopping to pop the vertebrae in his neck.

"What? I can't hear anything," answered Otis.

"Exactly, not a single bird in sight; they know what's coming. Tonight's gonna be a cold one."

All around them, gnarled trees previously unyielding to the worst that winter had to offer now lay bent and broken in the wake of her fury. Metal stakes that had once held police tape where their father had been killed were the only markers remaining. Virgil walked over to the spot and looked out across the lake.

"I guess this is where you found him?"

"Yup. Frozen solid like the old girl we saw last night. Only his face didn't look frightened like hers. Pop went down fighting; by the way he was squinting, I'd say he was still taking aim when she got him."

Virgil turned to face his brother. "What was he aiming at?"

Otis shrugged. "The Widowmaker, I guess. What else?"

"You found him frozen, right? With his gun still raised an' braced to take a shot?"

"Yup."

"An' he was squinting like he was aiming at something?"

"I don't like to chew my cabbage twice, Virg. What are you getting at?"

"Well, you saw what happened to the old gal last night. The Widowmaker froze her solid 'cause she was touching the metal bolt. Y'all might not remember the details, but she froze Ma to death by touching her."

"So?"

"So, she can whip up a storm whenever she likes. But I reckon she's gotta be touching a person to freeze 'em solid, or at least touch something they're touching."

"Okay, but I still don't see what you're getting at?"

Virgil huffed. "An' you're supposed to be the smart one? Why would Pop be squinting down the barrel of his gun if she was hovering right in front of him? If she was close enough to make contact and freeze him up, why was he fixin' to shooting something in the distance?"

Otis's face fell as he followed his brother's logic. He stepped forward, moving Virgil aside with the back of his hand and stood in the exact position where he'd found his father's body. He drew his pistol.

"Is that where he was aiming?" Virgil asked as his brother lined up the sights with the memory. His pistol was pointing at the end of the jetty where their Ma had sacrificed herself to save them forty-five years before.

"Head up to the cabin an make sure Sal's alright. I'm gonna take a closer look at that decking, see if I can figure out what he was thinking," said Virgil, setting off before his brother could argue.

Ignoring Otis's complaints, he walked until he reached the edge of the dirt path, his memories preventing him from stepping onto the aged planks of the pier. He'd avoided this place for most of his childhood; he hadn't even stepped foot on it as an adult. Standing in the exact spot where he'd stood as a twelve-year-old boy, his mind flashed back to that awful day with his infant brother in his arms, watching his mother beg for their lives. He remembered the look on her face and the way she kept apologizing as if she'd done something wrong. He remembered how she turned to him when begging failed, screaming with her final breath for them to run. That was the last thing she ever told him, and that's exactly what he did. Gripping little Otis in his arms, he'd sprinted back to the cabin, locked the doors, and prayed for Pop to return and make it all right. Only praying didn't work. Pop came home from work the following morning, but nothing was ever right again. It was the first time he'd run from anything in his whole life, and in a way, he'd been running ever since. He ran then, and he ran fifteen years ago, but not anymore. Running and hiding had saved them when they were little, but it wouldn't work now. His brother might not get to see his own kid as often as he liked, but at least Otis had a family and something to live for. He didn't. Tonight was going to be his last chance; tonight, it was finally going to end, one way or another. The wooden boards creaked beneath his feet as he walked down the ancient decking, weathered by decades of freeze–thaw cycles. He already had a good idea of what was in the barrels at the end of the jetty, but he needed to be sure. His father might have been a lot of things, but he was no idiot, and he certainly wouldn't have started a fight he didn't think he could win.

As he drew nearer to the rusty barrels, the noxious odor of gasoline filled his nostrils.

"Shit." He'd been hoping for gunpowder. Would a drum of gasoline even ignite if he'd managed to take the shot? Hell, would it even burn in these temperatures? He hoped his brother had a better plan.

The sound of footsteps crunching on the frozen dirt path announced his brother's return.

"How's Sal?" he asked, tapping the side of the metal drum to see how full it was. When Otis didn't answer, Virgil turned to see his brother shaking his head, his slumped shoulders telling him everything he needed to know.

"Well, we got about eighty gallons of gasoline here. I don't think Pop's plan woulda worked, but if you've got some flares in that fancy squad car, I bet we could come up with something before night falls."

"You think fire will kill her?" asked Otis, wiping his cheeks dry as he spoke.

"I reckon it's the best chance we got; even if it don't work, I'm starting to think I'd rather go out hot than cold."

"This ain't no suicide mission, Virg. I'm pissed enough that Pop tried taking her on by himself. Don't you go—"

Virgil failed to hear the rest of what he was saying, or hear much of anything for that matter. Behind him, the thick ice that covered the lake exploded upward, cracking louder than gunfire and sending jets of water shooting up on either side of the jetty. The broken-glass sound of fractured ice carried with it the familiar sound of laughter as Virgil made for the safety of the bank. All around him, the jets of water froze in the air, snapping and shimmering like blades, raining down on him like a thousand tiny darts. The smaller fragments shattered as they landed, the larger ones impaling the deck all around him. The ones that made contact tore through clothes and sliced his flesh as he ran. Throwing his arms up in an attempt to shield his face, he charged toward his brother. He'd almost reached the end of the jetty when a thick spike of ice rose in front of him, splintering the frozen wood from below. Launching himself over the gap, Virgil caught a glimpse of Otis as he flew through the air.

The moment played out like a movie scene, one brother smashing through a wall of ice before colliding with the cold hard ground and rolling awkwardly, the other, a trained cop, with his gun drawn and his feet firmly planted. The sound of two shots fired in rapid succession filled the valley. But unlike the movies, there was no explosion to follow them up. The bullets passed cleanly through the drums, leaving four streams of gasoline pouring harmlessly into the lake. Virgil scrambled to his feet as Otis fired off another couple of shots before turning and running back to the house.

"She didn't follow us. I thought she only came at night," panted Otis once they were both safely over the threshold.

Virgil rose unsteadily to his feet. "Me, too," he replied, pressing his hand against his forehead and swearing as blood oozed freely between his fingers.

"Did you see her?"

Virgil shook his head.

"I did." Otis's fingers twitched erratically as he spoke. "Just the way you an' Sal described her. It looked like she was trapped, though, like she was banging against the underside of the ice." Despite the cold, a bead of sweat trickled down the side of his face.

"Perhaps she can't leave. Maybe she's stuck down there 'til nightfall."

"But why?" Otis's brow creased.

Virgil thought back to what the old woman in the motel had said but decided against sharing his thoughts right now. "Hell, I don't know. All I know for sure is that shooting the gas didn't work. And somehow, in all that commotion, I've lost my gun." He looked around the little room, "What did you do with Pop's shotgun?"

Otis's words seem to catch in his throat as he pointed into the next room. "Sal's still holding it." The pain in his voice was raw. Old Sal must have been more of a mother to his younger brother than Virgil realized.

He nodded sympathetically. "I'll get it. You just wait here, keep an eye on the jetty, and holler if anything moves."

Still bleeding and limping badly from his dive, Virgil entered the cabin's second room, where his stepmom sat by the window, her rigid body gripping his father's gun. He'd always hated the woman for trying to replace his mother and moving in so quickly after her death. But now, as he pried and cracked the gun loose from her frozen fingers, he couldn't help but regret the things he'd said to her over the years. She didn't have to put up with the crap he'd given her, and no one should have to die like this, especially in their own home. He paused for a second, the realization chilling him to the core; she was inside her own home. Inside. Why, after Pop's death, could the Widowmaker suddenly enter the house?

He walked back into the front room, cocking the repeater and resting it against his shoulder.

"Something's not right," he said. "Let's get the rest of the gear from the car and see what else we can salvage from the house before she shows—"

"Vuh... Virg..."

He stopped talking when he heard the whisper of his brother's voice and saw the terror in his eyes as he stared behind him. Suddenly cold, like ice water had been poured down his back, Virgil's breath caught in the frigid atmosphere as swirling tendrils of fog and ice whipped around him, announcing her presence.

Without turning, Virgil raised the stock and squeezed the trigger, sending an unexpected ball of fire and sparks over his shoulder and directly into the Widowmaker's face. Smoke filled the room, followed by the pained screams of the tormented spirit. The screaming went on, desperate and terrified. As if she was somehow wailing with her entire being.

Taking advantage of the distraction, Virgil spun and backed away from the injured phantom. And there she was, the object of all his nightmares, floating a foot off the floor and writhing in midair as the hazy blue tendrils that had surrounded her a moment ago now burned red with fire. Her skin bubbled and blistered in front of him, reacting violently to the heat of the shot. It was like her very substance was flammable.

Suddenly it made sense. Incendiary shells. That was Pop's plan all along. Pumping the shotgun one more time, Virgil released a second fiery blast right into her chest as they scurried backward out of the room. It was like spitting whiskey into a house fire. The Widowmaker wailed louder, this time exploding towards them in a giant ball of fire, blasting through the timber wall and sending both men flying. A trail of fiery smoke followed her back to the water's edge, where a plume of steam marked her retreat.

The impact knocked the wind from his body and set his shoulder at an angle it simply shouldn't be in. Ignoring the pain in his shoulder and the searing burns across his exposed skin, Virgil climbed to his feet clutching a badly broken arm. Half stumbling, he picked up the shotgun a few feet away from where he'd landed.

"Otis." His voice was raw from the explosion. "Otis!"

He scanned the burning debris for his brother. The residual smoke from the fireball hung in the air, obscuring the lake like fog.

"Otis," he shouted, spinning around and searching the dirt yard, hoping to find his little brother standing. Instead, he spotted him, laying on his back barely five feet from the jetty. He staggered toward him.

"Otis..." His knees gave way as bent over his brother. "Otis?"

His brother's eyes opened at the sound of his voice, looking directly at him instead of the burning wreckage all around them. The fear and confusion in his eyes as he tried to speak but couldn't was almost too much to bear. Virgil's gaze wandered then, moving down to where the spike of wood protruded from his brother's chest. He tried to fight back the tears, but there was no stopping them this time. He knew that this meant.

Otis's eyes looked pleadingly up at him. "Virg..."

"Stay with me, boy. Don't you dare give up now. Don't you dare." His voice trembled as he spoke.

Otis's eyes glazed over for a second before blinking open again. His body was shaking; he was slipping away.

"Finish her..." His voice was barely audible, but his face held stern. He looked up and tried to say more, but the words just wouldn't come. He tried again, but his throat gurgled as he struggled to breathe. A second later, his head rolled to the side, and Virgil knew his brother was gone.

With both fists and jaw clenched, he set about doing what needed to be done. Using his gun as a crutch, Virgil fought his way back to his feet, never taking his eyes off his little brother's face. He no longer felt the pain of his broken arm or the burning sensation that tightened his skin. He simply didn't care anymore. His brother had given him a final instruction just as his mother had all those years ago. *"Finish her."* His hatred boiled like acid in his veins, fueling his actions and giving him strength as he staggered towards the ruined jetty. He pumped the shotgun singlehandedly as he reached the first broken beam. Struggling past the hole he'd vaulted earlier, he spat and cursed as he hobbled along the remaining deck, the ice shards from her previous attack crunching beneath his boots.

"Come on out," he shouted, striking one of the half-empty drums with the barrel of his gun. "Come on, Haint. Come an' finish what you started."

Nothing. His breath rose in miniature clouds as he waited.

"Hey, *stupid girl!*" He smacked the gas drum a second time and got the reaction he was looking for. All around him, icy blue tendrils started to shimmer upward between the planks of the jetty. The silvery wisps swirled in front of him, colder than arctic air. Foxfire and faint blue mists spun together and rotated in the air, coalescing until she appeared, almost translucent, in front of him. She looked different now, weakened somehow. He knew instantly that the fire had hurt her, but now he could see she'd been damaged, too. The thought brought a smile to his cracked and bloody lips.

Gradually, she came into sharper focus, her image becoming more and more solid as she drew closer. But there was no laughter this time; her gaunt soulless eyes seemed almost timid amid her newly disfigured features. *Was she wary of the gun?* The thought made Virgil laugh. *Well, she ought to be sacred because it's gonna be damn hot where we're going. And god knows, we both deserve it.*

To test his theory, he lowered the weapon, slowly pointing it downward until the gun's barrel rested on top of the half-empty gasoline drum. It worked; the moment the gun was gone, chill mists flared around her, and the air was filled once more with her piercing scream. She rushed toward him.

"Merry Christmas, bitch!" he pulled the trigger.

The incendiary sparks ignited the fumes and sent a column of orange-red flame high into the winter sky. A split second later, the remaining full barrel blew, and a fiery ball of yellow engulfed both of them. The blast threw burning fuel in all directions, obliterating everything and everyone in its path. The sea of flames that now covered her watery retreat left the Widowmaker with nowhere to hide. Her tortured screams tore through the valley as her malevolent soul perished in its own flammable substance.

A pillar of fiery smoke and ash marked the location from miles around. The blaring alarm of the abandoned squad car served as the only eulogy for the last of the Parsons. Police reports were filed, and the local newspaper covered the explosion. Some of the old-timers on the mountain might have remembered what happened back in 1953, but none of them were willing to talk to the reporters when they came calling. The Widowmaker was gone, folk felt safer, and that was all that mattered.

A Tale of St. Nicholas

Joseph P. Pietris

'Twas the night before Christmas and all on the street
People were shopping, that great holiday feat.
I stood on the corner, just ringing my bell,
Wore my best suit, but no one could tell.

When from the crowd, a small child now stood
I gave her a smile, but it did her no good.
With sadness in eyes and a shake in her knee
She made a quick movement, handing a letter to me.

I watched as she ran, grabbing the hand of her mother
And I stood for a moment with a feeling of bother.
Opened my hand and unfolded the note,

I read the small paper with a lump in my throat.

I was up like a flash, to my house at the pole.
I had to work quickly and play an old role.
I read all my books, triple checked all my lists,
"Justice was coming," I said, beating my fists.

I considered my options, as this night was for all,
But all nights were miserable for one who's so small.
As protector of children, I can't let this stand.
For that girl had been hurt by her mother's new man.

I was quick with my things and picked up an old friend,
For my primary duty, I still must attend.
I flew to her house in the nice part of town,
And it illed me to think that here he was found.

For these acts have no race, nor color nor creed.
These foul hearts are found in every breed.
I looked in her room and quiet she slept,
And I wondered how many nights she had wept.

I stepped from my sleigh and onto the roof,
I wondered what man thinks, with this visit as proof,
Of Santa's existence, of the jolly ol' elf.
Never thinking he comes to judge anyone's self.

I slipped in the house, down the chimney I leapt,
Finding the sick beast on the couch where he slept.
The sack was then placed at the edge of his feet,
My deeds may be dirty, but my suit must remain neat.

I knelt down beside him, pushing bottles aside,

Moving so he'd see me, my vice being pride.
I woke the man up and saw fear in his eyes,
And covered his mouth as pain flashed in his thighs.

I muffled his cry as Krampus's claws had set in,
"Santa protects all the kids, Krampus collects on your sin.
For too long your actions have been out of rein,
Now it is your turn to be fearful of pain."

Now, teeth! Now, claws! Now, hunger and elation!
Then, cuts! Then, blood! Then feast and satiation!
"To the back of the bag!
To the back of your hole!
Hide away! Hide away! Hide away, Troll!"

He begged for his life, but it fell on deaf ears,
Krampus pulled the man in with giggles and cheers.
He was pulled toward the bag and out of my sight,
And I knew of one child who'd have a good night.

I lifted my sack and knew she was one
Of the millions of others, a hurt daughter or son.
All year I will struggle and do what I can,
But a Saint is still mortal, a singular man.

BLOODY BONES

Jeffrey Kosh

"From ghoulies and ghosties. And long-leggedy beasties.
And things that go bump in the night,
Good Lord, deliver us!"
–traditional Scottish prayer

1

Sylvan Pines Psychiatric Hospital, Hingham, Massachusetts, December 20, 2019

"What's wrong with her?" asked Josh while wheeling the woman into the padded room. "I mean, it's quite rare we use these nowadays. Not here, at least."

Barney, his colleague, scoffed. "She has been like this for more than thirty years. She doesn't talk, she doesn't walk. But at Christmastime, she becomes nervous; and worse, she makes the other patients nervous."

"But a padded room?" protested Josh. "Ain't it too much?"

Barney chuckled. "You haven't seen her at this time of the year, dude. She changes. You see her like this, and you think, hey, she ain't dangerous, right? But I tell you what, man. I saw what she did to a greenhorn orderly like you five Christmases ago. And it wasn't nice."

"What happened to her?"

"I don't know. She has been like this since they brought her back from England."

2

Exmoor, Somerset, England. December 23, 1988

Ashcombe Manor perched atop Crest Hill in the same fashion as an ancient Norman castle. It didn't look down to the valley and the boggy countryside; it dominated it. The manor itself was a typical Georgian mansion: squarish, with its dark brown bricks, its row of five windows across the second story, and the tall gabled roofs topping the main structure.

Yet, on that cold afternoon in December, two elements told Gary the house had been rebuilt and probably expanded at a later time. And Gary Henry Ashford, one of the most talented architects in Boston, was an expert on the matter. The first was the tall, four-storied, octagonal tower flanking the left wing. It had been built with the same kind of material as the rest of the structure, but it was clearly not Georgian in style, but rather Queen Anne. The second was a small but bold Second Empire porch that descended to the grounds using a flight of eight marble steps and barely covered a tiny landing.

"Is this it?" Courtney asked abruptly, breaking the silence inside the cab. "Is this the place?"

Gary felt apprehensive. He scrutinized the large house, perfectly conscious that his wife was going to disapprove of his choice of a Christmas family retreat. Too big. Too isolated. Too dangerous for their six-year-old daughter. But hey, it was just for a couple of nights.

"Yes," Gary said, "this is Ashcombe." Another wave of uneasiness washed over him before he asked, "What do you think?"

Courtney tilted her head to look up at the tower. "I think it's a beauty." She turned to Elizabeth, who wasn't at all interested in her surroundings as she was too busy playing with her brand new Dolly Surprise. She kept twisting the doll's right arm up and down, growing and shortening the ponytail. "Isn't it cool, Beth? We are going to wait for Santa in a real mansion."

Gary relaxed. It was as if a huge rock had been removed from his chest. Courtney, usually anxious and extremely protective of her daughter and always afraid of new places where she could put herself in danger, seemed to be totally in love with that old, but well-maintained Somerset manor. He could see it in the way she was looking at it as the driver turned the car onto the pebbled driveway and stopped just in front of a large, circular marble pond. She was running her eyes over the large rectangular windows on the second floor.

"Daddy?" Elizabeth said. The doll was now on the cab's floor. "Is this our incestral home?"

Gary and Courtney burst into laughter together.

"Ancestral, honey," he corrected her. "It means that this place once belonged to our family. At least a branch of it. I think."

He turned to the taxi driver, a burly man with a thick West Country accent that made it hard for Gary—a New Yorker transplanted to Boston—to understand whatever he said on the first go-around. "Do you happen to know if this place still belongs to any living Ashford?"

The driver killed the engine and stared at Gary through the rearview mirror. "Arr, reckon so. Though technically that bain't roit. Plaice's in the hands of some international fund, me thinks."

This time Gary managed to get most of what the driver said. In the short period he had spent with Martha Mullens (the local realtor that had met them at Dunster station to give them the place's keys, instructions, and brochures) and this guy, he had learned that 'bain't roit' meant 'is not right' and 'arr' meant 'yes'.

"Same people that manage the cassle, me thinks," he added while getting out of the car. He then proceeded to unload the family's bags.

The ticking of the cooling engine was the only sound breaking the silence surrounding the house. A silence that was immediately broken by the voice of a woman.

"Welcome to Ashcombe."

An old lady stood on the porch.

That has to be Missus Lessey, the housekeeper, thought Gary.

The small woman stepped from the shadows and showed her bright smile. She was wearing a long black dress with a white collar, paired with flat-soled shoes. Her silvery hair was tidied in a formal bun, and circular, gold-rimmed eyeglasses perched upon her pixie-like nose. Gary could not guess the lady's age, for she was clearly past her prime but looked energetic and lean, with a strong, straight back.

"You must be Missus Lessey," said Gary, walking toward

the house. "Missus Mullens told me you would be meeting us."

Still smiling, the housekeeper stepped down the porch, extending her hand. "Yes, Mister Ashford." Her icy hand closed firmly around Gary's. Closer, she looked older than at first glance.

"Do come in," she said after releasing her grip and turning toward the mansion. "I'll have tea and scones ready in a jiffy. In the meantime, would you like some cucumber sandwiches?"

Gary was about to reply that there was no need—they had had a light meal in Dunster before taking the taxi, after all—but was interrupted by the loud slamming of the cab's trunk. He turned and saw the driver standing just behind him.

"I wooden mind some tea meself," he said, winking at Beth. "But I didn't do a proper job today and must hurry back to the village." He removed his right glove and extended his hand to Gary. "I wish you a lovely Christmas."

"You, too," Gary replied warmly.

After paying the fare—to which Gary added a generous tip even if the man insisted that none was due—Gary turned to the mansion and noticed that the housekeeper was gone. She hadn't waited for his answer regarding the tea.

Courtney had followed the old woman inside the mansion while Elizabeth had stayed behind and had resolutely grabbed Gary's left hand tightly, as if looking for comfort. She was evidently tired from the long railway trip and a bit nervous about the manor's overwhelming size.

The driver seemed to notice. He lowered himself down to her level and smiled.

"Oi, little lady, you make sure to stay with your family at all times. The moor bain't a plaice for chilren. Sure, Father Christmas is on his way down here. Reckon you wrote a letter to the old man, bain't so?"

Elizabeth looked at her dad, confused. Gary smiled at her while squeezing her hand.

"Thanks, mister. We'll be okay," he said to the driver.

The driver went back to his cab, opened the door, and then stopped just before climbing in. "Little lady," he said. "You don't go looking into wells, roit? And stay away from dark spots. Especially tonight. Don't give a chance to old Tommy Bloody Bones."

"What do you mean?" Gary asked, now irritated by the guy's admonishment to his daughter. He and Courtney were absolutely opposed to the use of scary fictional monsters to keep children on their toes. Yes, Santa was an exception to the rule, but the jolly fat man wasn't going to put you inside a sack and carry you away.

The taxi driver saw Gary's hardened eyes and immediately changed his tone. "Oh, nuthin'. Just a local legend, sir. Just some local chinny, a hunkypunk, that's it. Anywhen, have a safe and jolly Christmas, and I wish you a sweet 1989."

Then he quickly climbed into his cab, started the engine, and drove down what he had called a drangway—the country lane.

Gary looked at Elizabeth. "Funny guy, uh?"

"Arr," she said, imitating the driver. "Reckon so."

Gary laughed. "Come on, girl, let's go inside."

3

Before Gary and Elizabeth joined Courtney in the parlor, she'd had one of the weirdest conversations she could recall.

It started nicely, with Mrs. Lessey leading her through the house and politely asking about their trip. They had crossed a foyer with a big, wide staircase of polished wood leading to the second floor; to its right, a long hallway decorated with holly led to the back. Two identical open archways flanked the foyer. Mrs. Lessey led her to the one on the right. Here, a typical Victorian sitting room awaited. Lavishly furnished with an elegant white couch and two leather armchairs, a colorful braided rug of Persian design covered the marble floor. In one corner stood a large, lacquered cupboard, its glass doors revealing a beautiful set of porcelain birds. In the opposite corner was a small fireplace—cold at the moment—that the housekeeper had adorned with Christmas decorations. There was a lovely oval-shaped coffee table covered with lace in the middle of the floor. Delicate cups and saucers were set on it, along with a plate of scones and some cookies. To the side, a white porcelain teapot, enameled and with red depictions of a hunting scene, puffed mild steam from the spout, spreading the fragrance of Earl Gray. The only things missing were the cucumber sandwiches.

"Sit down, please," said Mrs. Lessey. "I will be back in a jiffy."

She then opened a pair of double doors (leading to the kitchen or the dining room, Courtney assumed) and disappeared into the darkness beyond, leaving Courtney to look around. However, she just managed to notice a darkened room beyond the archway to her right before she heard the doors open again. Mrs. Lessey returned with a full platter of white sandwiches.

The housekeeper gently placed the tray alongside the cookie plate, then poured a cup with a dexterity that surprised Courtney, given the woman's advanced years.

"Wow!" said Courtney. "That's impressive."

Mrs. Lessey appeared confused. "What do you mean?"

"That thing you did with the teapot. It was—"

"I just served you a cup. Nothing so special about it." The weird expression on the elderly woman's face made Courtney feel uneasy.

"Anyhow... Your honeymoon," Mrs. Lessey changed the subject. "Was it good?"

It was Courtney's time to look confused now. "Honeymoon? What honeymoon?"

"Your honeymoon, Missus Ashford. Didn't you just got married?"

Courtney laughed softly. "Oh, no. We've been married for almost six years. I was pregnant with Beth when—"

The housekeeper's eyes became as hard as stone as she fixed her gaze on the younger woman. Yet, her mouth kept smiling. "A child? You have a child?"

Again Courtney felt uncomfortable. There was something in the old lady's smile that seemed suddenly forced.

"Beth? She's here, with us. Didn't you see her outside? She's with my husband now." Courtney stood up and went to the bay window. She moved the heavy curtains aside but found that the glass was dirty and greasy. She couldn't see outside clearly, yet the shapes of three people—one small and two larger ones—were outlined by the dying light.

"Is Beth a good girl?" Mrs. Lessey pressed. "She's not a naughty girl, is she?"

Courtney turned to face the woman. She no longer looked kind and cute to her eyes. She looked malicious and wicked. "Excuse me?"

The elderly woman seemed to regain her composure. She straightened and folded her arms behind her back. "Oh, I'm sorry. I guess my questions sounded funny. I should mind my own business. I just wanted..."

Mrs. Lessey appeared really contrite now, and Courtney felt almost guilty about it.

"No. It's okay." She went back to the armchair. "I mean... yes, Beth is a good girl. But then it depends on what you mean by—"

The old woman interrupted her again. "Does she bite her nails? Is she obedient?"

It is like a rollercoaster with this woman, Courtney thought. One moment she's sweet, the next she's more nosy than a cop.

"She's a good kid," she said firmly, staring at the housekeeper to underscore that that conversation was over. "She is a good kid."

"Of course, she is." The old lady went for the teapot and poured the deep amber brew into two more cups. "But—"

"I said she is a good girl, Missus Lessey. Can we talk about something else, please? I hate to tell you, but these questions sound too personal to me." Courtney was tired. First, the long train trip, then the crowded streets of Dunster. Now, this... this interrogation? What was all of that about?

Her husband and Beth stepped in at that moment.

"Why, what a nice welcome! Thank you, Missus Lessey." Gary walked toward the table and took a cup. He put his hands around it. "Mmm... Nothing better to warm you up in this cold." Then he must have noticed her face. "Is everything okay, hon?"

"Yes, I'm just tired." She turned to the housekeeper. "We shouldn't keep you here so long. Tomorrow is Christmas Eve, and I guess you have family waiting for you. Please, show me the essentials."

"Oh, don't worry about me. I don't live far from here. In fact, my house is just down the drang—the driveway. You probably spotted my cottage coming up here." The woman's eyes ran to Beth. She seemed worried by her presence.

This made Courtney even more nervous. "Anyway, I insist. We're going to fly to bed soon."

"As you wish," said Mrs. Lessey, bowing her head.

The housekeeper showed her the rest of the house. Though

it looked creepy from the outside, the old mansion was in excellent condition with modern amenities and a state-of-the-art shower cabin in the master bedroom's private bath, which Courtney craved to use as soon as the old woman was gone.

The second floor (The first in England, Courtney reminded herself) had three bedrooms, including the master one, numerous closets, two bathrooms, an old nursery (Mrs. Lessey had remarked that no babies had used that room for at least a century), and a library filled with musty volumes. The third floor was mostly storage, and the housekeeper recommended leaving it alone, for it contained nothing useful and was probably full of spiders. Yet, Courtney could not fail to notice that not once had they passed an access to the side tower, and she asked Mrs. Lessey about it.

"There is no access to the tower. And it's better that way. Not a safe place," she said bluntly.

Back to the first floor, a beautiful dining room and a large kitchen charmed Courtney. Though full of modern amenities—including a brand new Korean microwave oven (she took note to talk Gary into buying one like that once they were back home)—the kitchen still had a medieval feel with its brick and wood cabinets, work tables, and iron stoves. But the real centerpiece of the mansion was the living room.

The first thing she noticed was the giant fireplace dominating the east wall. It was so big that a man could walk inside it without crouching. Its mantel was made out of the same rectangular bricks of the exterior walls, and the frames were of some kind of dark gray stone that Courtney couldn't identify.

Just to the right of it, there was a seven-foot-tall Christmas tree, beautifully decorated with twinkling lights, colored glass baubles, and strings of shimmering tinsel. It looked old but in good health.

Halfway up from the rug-covered floor, the dark wood paneling lining the walls gave way to a floral wallpaper. Oval Victorian paintings of all sizes studded the walls, except for a large, rectangular landscape, done in oils, that hung above the fireplace. This one attracted Courtney's attention because it seemed to be a reproduction of Ashcombe Manor. Seemed, because only the side tower was there. There was no manor.

"Missus Lessey? What is this? It looks like Crest Hill, but not quite."

The housekeeper came closer. "Oh, that was made by Oliver Larcombe, a not-so-talented painter who stayed on here during the last century. A dodgy individual, if you ask me. He gifted the late Lord Ashford this painting but went off after having nicked a fair amount of antiques. Especially the silverware."

Courtney stepped closer to get a better look at the painting. "That looks like the tower, but made of a different material."

"Ashcombe Manor was built in the seventeenth century, but the tower is much older. Before that time, it was a solitary thing made of stones. More circular in shape—more similar to a classic donjon than an observation tower. Some historians say it was built by Romans. But there is much debate about that. Guess the painter wanted to show it as it was."

It was now past six o'clock, and a strong wind was growing outside; it rattled the windows as though to hurry the housekeeper along.

"I think it's better you leave now, Missus Lessey," said Courtney. "Seems like a storm is coming."

The old lady looked out of the large bay window and nodded. "You are right, dear. To be honest, I'm a bit cheesed off with the weather. They said it was going to be cold, but no rain was expected." She moved toward a rack and retrieved her long, black coat. "Anyway, no need to faff about more, I'm surely filching too much of your time."

Courtney didn't understand much of what the woman just said but got the feeling she meant to leave at once.

"Do you want my husband to walk you to your house?" Courtney said, more out of politeness than with any heartfelt intentions. She didn't like the woman.

"Oh, no need. I'll be home in a jiffy, and then I'll be at a knees-up at the Stag's Head. Unless Mister Baily doesn't have it going pear-shaped like last year," replied the old lady.

She had no idea what Mrs. Lessey was talking about. "What's a 'knees-up'? Wait! The Stag's Head? The pub in Dunster? Are you going to walk down there? Alone?" Even if she didn't like her, Courtney couldn't avoid being a bit worried about that old lady.

"Oh, don't be daft, dear. I have a car. Do you think I come here three times per week on my old legs?" Mrs. Lessey scoffed. "Ah, and to answer your question: a knees-up is a party."

She finished buttoning her coat, then headed for the foyer, where Gary and Beth were waiting to wish her happy holidays.

"Mister Ashford," said the housekeeper, opening the front door. "I'll be back on Boxing Day to check on you and bring you some treats. In any emergency, there's a list of numbers you can call just beside the phones in the living room, in the kitchen, and on the first landing. My number is on that list. You can give me a bell at any time." Then she turned to Beth. "Miss Ashford, please promise me you will not go up to the attic. It's a bad place, full of dangerous stuff. I keep asking Mister Hall to fix that hateful door, but the man is so gormless that he forgets every time. Be a darling and listen to your parents."

"Goodbye, Missus Lessey," said Courtney, leaning on the archway. She couldn't wait for the woman to be gone.

"Goodbye, Missus Ashford. Merry Christmas."

Then she was out.

4

Elizabeth Ashford didn't like the house. It was dark, cold, and scary. The tall window panes in her room kept shaking under the strong winds assaulting the hill. There was a funny smell coming from the fireplace, and the closet door wouldn't lock properly. Trying to sleep was almost impossible.

She fluffed up her pillow, then forced herself to settle back down and closed her eyes. When she couldn't sleep, Beth used to think about the events of the day to let her mind drift away, so she recalled memories of the train trip and of the deer she had spotted out the window. It was tan in color, with white spotting on its flanks. Dad had said it was a Fallow deer. She had been so excited at the sight of it—her, actually, because Dad said it was a doe. Then the Dunster Christmas fair, with its medieval jugglers, hawker, and the smell of candy…

She yawned loudly.

The big clock down the hall had chimed eleven times, and though she was tired, she just couldn't find a way to fall asleep. She turned on her side…on her back…nothing. She was uncomfortable. Something was decidedly wrong. Yes, it wasn't her own bed, but it wasn't the first time she found herself sleeping somewhere else. No, it wasn't the bed.

Was the room too big? Yes, it was so large and empty. Shadows seemed much darker here, but not enough to justify her discomfort; grandma's bedroom was even darker, and she always slept peacefully at her home.

So all she had to do was wait for sleep to come.

But sleep wasn't coming.

I'm going to be awake forever, she thought. I'm never going to be able to sleep.

But by midnight, she finally drifted off without realizing it. However, it was a light, restless sleep.

Then something woke her up.

She sat up straight, startled and feeling cold. Weird, the heating was on. She could hear the purring of the old thermal unit.

Looking to the foot of the bed, she noticed that she had kicked off the sheet and the comforter. She reached down for them but stopped when she realized someone was in the room.

"W-who's there?" she hazarded in a tiny and frightened voice before snatching the covers and pulling them up to her chin.

No one answered.

Her eyes slowly adjusted to the darkness. She scoured the room.

Nothing.

Still, she could feel a presence right there; someone—or something—was hiding in the dark, waiting for her to lower her defenses, and then...

Stop scaring yourself, Beth!

There was nothing there. Nothing hiding in the dark. Just her wild imagination.

Santa, maybe?

Nah, Santa wouldn't come to her room, not today. Anyway, he would just go downstairs and put gifts under the tree. And drink the milk and cookies. But there were none tonight.

Then she heard the whispers.

Shocked, she reached for the switch of the bedside lamp.

Do you really want to see whatever is whispering around

in your room? Do you really want to see the thing?

Thing? What thing? Why did it have to be a "thing"?

Another voice inside her head now, a cautionary voice, something like a dark twin warning her about the horrors of the night.

You know it, Beth. You know what it is. It's gonna be ugly, scary, with blood running all over his old bones. Crouching like a predator, ready to coil and spring. A monster that was so hungry. Hungry for girlmeat.

"Shut up!" she cried.

Then she switched on the light.

And she saw the source of the whispers.

The curtains. The stupid curtains were fluttering at the window.

Releasing a sigh of relief, Beth climbed out of bed and walked across the cold floor to close the window.

That explains the whispers and the cold. Take that, stupid dark twin.

Yawning, she pulled the curtains aside and reached out to close the—

The window was closed.

Crap! she thought. How's that possible?

The curtains were fluttering just an instant ago; she hadn't imagined that.

The whispers started again, and this time she could clearly distinguish the words.

"Elizabeth... Elizabeth..."

She turned to her right and noticed for the first time a strange brass tube coming out of the wall. The voice was coming from there. Along with a draft of cold air that carried a peculiar smell, a sickly smell, the smell of...

The smell of dead things. Her dark twin was back.

She ignored that thought and moved closer to the strange

object. It was funnel-shaped and disappeared right into the stone wall.

"Elizabeth... Elizabeth..." the voice repeated.

It was definitely a child's voice. A boy. Not scary, just a bit creepy.

"Who's there?" she asked reluctantly.

"A f-f-frrriend. A f-f-frrrriend in neeeeeed of help. Help me, please. Elizabeth..."

Am I really having this conversation? she thought. Could I be dreaming?

"Who are you? How can I help you?" Even if it was a dream, there was no need to be rude to whoever was asking for help. "What happened to you?"

"M-mmm-me n-n-name is T-ommy. I got me-me-meself t-trapped. I ne-ne-need y-your help."

"How do you know my name?" she asked suspiciously. "And I'm not supposed to talk to strangers. My mom said so."

"I-I-I'm not a st-stranger. I'm Tommy. I'm a boy yah... yahr...your age. Got trapped in the t-t-tower. Please, help," insisted the voice.

Beth decided she was dreaming. A weird dream. A boy trapped in the tower? How come?

"How can I help?"

"Come to the attic," said the boy. "C-come. Juh... juh-just in front of the landing, you'll see a bi-bi-big door. It can be o-o-opened only on your s-s-side. M-m-make sure you don't get tr-tr-trapped, too. Block it with the st-st-stopper. Inside, you'll see another, smaller door to y-y-y-your r-right. Unlock it. I'm t-t-there."

"I'll ask my dad to—"

"No!" the boy cried. "Don't tell anyone! Please. Come now. Come at once!"

Beth didn't like that. "I can't come alone. I'll come with

my dad. If you want me to help you."

"I said to not tell anyone. I c-c-can't explain it now, but if you d-d-do that, I'm d-d-dead."

"Why?"

"I can't tell you."

"Then I'm not gonna help you. Goodnight," said Beth. There was no way that she was going to act recklessly. Not even in a dream.

"But I have s-s-something he-he-he-here..."

Beth couldn't fail to notice that the voice sounded older now, as if it were no longer a boy speaking, but a man.

"What? What do you have?"

"I've got a mogwai," Tommy replied, without stuttering. "Yes, right here, right with me. That's why I got trapped here; I was trying to get meself this new friend."

Beth couldn't believe it. A mogwai? One of those critters from the Gremlins movie? She'd always wanted one, but her mom dad told her they didn't exist; they were just furry puppets like the Muppets. There was no such thing as Gizmo.

"You're lying. Mogwais aren't real. And why would—"

The cooing gibber of the movie creature came through the tube. Beth's stood there agape. How was that possible?

This has to be a dream.

"See? I'm no liar. I've got one right here. And if you come help me, you can get one, too," said Tommy.

Suddenly, she could smell buttered popcorn, like the one she had when she watched the movie with Mom and Dad on a VHS tape last Christmas. And Mom's perfume. The draft from the brass tube was carrying the aromas now.

"Come up here, Beth. Come up here, and I'll give you what you have always dreamed of," said Tommy.

Beth wasn't listening to him anymore; now, she was just thinking about the movie and how that had been a perfect day for her. She remembered how horrible the months before had been, of how everything she loved had seemed to break apart. But mostly she remembered the fights. Those terrible fights between Mom and Dad. She had hated those. She had hated that Mom had called Dad names for something he had done. They had been fighting all the time. Dad had kept coming home late, and mom had been sick of it. By the end of the summer, she had told him he had to choose between his family and something called booze. Dad said that she couldn't make him choose, that he was the one wearing pants (that wasn't true, for Beth had seen her mom wearing pants all the time), and he'd do as he wanted. After that, Dad was gone for a while.

There had been talks of a thing called 'deevorce,' something that scared her more than Grandma's dark cellar. Ayesha, her best friend, told her what happened with deevorce. Her parents had it, and now she was living with her mom in another town and was seeing her dad only on the weekends. Ayesha liked it because she said she was getting more toys, more attention, and double the fun. But Elizabeth didn't want that; she just wanted her family back. Then the winter holidays came, and things had changed for the better. Dad had changed. And they had been a family again. And there had been that perfect Christmas.

Some said that the night before Christmas was too long and the night after too short. But Beth wanted that Christmas Eve to last forever.

"I know what you wish for, Beth," said Tommy. "I know why you stare out of the window every night, your eyes set on the twinkling stars. I know..."

Instinctively, Beth looked out of the window. The storm was gone, and she could see the sky over the English moor. It was full of stars. And one was blinking more than the others.

It looked red at first, but then changed to yellow, then blue, then green.

It was a magical star.

"What if…you could have Christmas all the time, Beth?" Tommy pressed, his voice huskier now, like that of the Big Bad Wolf. But Beth didn't care; she just wanted to look at the magical star. To drift into it.

"Nothing but f-f-f-fun and games forever. And Mom and Dad together. Always happy together. Like that night, Beth. Like that Christmas night when you watched Gremlins. When Dad was finally home…"

Now Tommy's voice sounded like the English barker down in Dunster, the one operating the Fun House. The one who made her laugh with his droning. "It's f-f-f-fun, f-f-f-for all ages!"

Beth snapped out of her trance. "You're not a kid. You're not trapped. You know everything about me. You know all my secrets. Who are you?"

Tommy chuckled. "You're a clever girl, aren't you? Well, let's see how clever… Who might I be? You tell me."

"Santa?" she hazarded.

"Got me. Ho-ho-ho…"

Can't be, pondered Beth. Santa doesn't talk to children. He sneaks in during the night. He doesn't want to be seen.

"No, you're not. You don't sound like him." Beth was feeling tired and uncomfortable, and now she really wanted to wake up, for she was sure she was dreaming. "Stop lying to me!"

"I'm not lying. I'm Father Christmas, I swear on it! I'm Père Fouettard and Zwarte Piet. I'm Belsnickel. I'm all of them and none. But most of all, I'm the wish-granting Leipreachán."

"The leprechaun isn't Santa. And it doesn't exist!" replied Beth. "Why are you doing this to me? Leave me alone!"

"Oh," said Tommy. "I see. Santa exists, but the leprechaun doesn't... Still, you're talking to me. You think you know better. Well, I tell you who knows better, you insolent little brat; I know better because I have been here longer than you. I have been here when your breed was no different than mice, huddling in the dark, afraid of everything." He sounded angry now. "I was here when the Devil went for a walk on Winsford Hill and decided to dig a hole to find water. The hole became the Punchbowl, and the spoil he discarded over his shoulder became Dunkery Beacon. And I was here when the pixies built Cow Castle."

"I... I didn't mean to—" Beth tried to apologize, but the Tommy-thing wouldn't stop.

"I am Jack of the Lantern. I am the Hunkypunk. I am the Unseen Cat, and the Hob of Brent Knoll."

"I want to wake up!" screamed Beth. "I don't want to be here anymore!"

It was at that point that someone grabbed her.

5

Gary found himself in a horrible nightmare. A nightmare he knew all too well because he had actually lived it as a child.

He was ten when his mom got sick and had to stay home.

Only his dad was working, and they could barely make ends meet. Barely. And things got worse. They fell behind on bills, the mortgage. Gary remembered the yellow envelopes, the way they stood out among the mail stacks.

"We're going to go fucking bust," his dad would say. "We're going to lose the house." He did that when he thought Gary wasn't around, whispering to mom and looking extremely worried.

But Gary knew.

And then there were the calls. So many of them that Dad had to unplug the phone. Eventually, he got rid of it altogether, and then they got rid of the TV.

Dad lost his job, and things took a dramatic turn.

Gary was sent to live with his uncle while Mom and Dad tried to fix their lives.

"It is only a temporary thing," Dad had said. "We'll come get you as soon as we can."

But that had never happened.

Mom had left, turning her back on Dad and her own son. She had bailed out of her family without once looking back. Gone. Vanished.

Two days before Gary's birthday.

And Dad... Dad had simply faded away, swallowed by a cruel, indifferent world.

They found his body floating in the Hudson.

Gary hated living at his uncle's; he tried to sneak out every time.

Once, he made it down to his old house. It was empty now, the lawn where he used to play basketball with Dad overgrown and full of dead leaves. The walls, once full of pictures, were now scrawled with graffiti done by squatters. And there was a big sign outside declaring the house "For Sale."

He had cried thinking about the big Christmas tree his mom used to put up every year, right by the fireplace.

Then Uncle Ben and Aunt Shelly had shown up.

He knew they were going to be mad at him, but when they got closer, all he could see was fear. And sadness. Aunt Shelly had reached out and had tenderly pulled him close. At other times, Gary would have pushed her away. But not that day. That day he let himself fall into her arms. And his life had changed.

But in this nightmare, this new nightmare, he was again at the house, looking at the overgrown lawn and the empty rooms.

It started like the real thing, but then the car that arrived in the driveway was not Uncle Ben's rusty red clunker. It was a black limo with darkened windows. The passenger door opened, and Gary squinted to look into the vehicle's darkness. He got closer and smelled something unexpected. The car smelled like Central Park. The smell of elms, beeches, and sycamores. The scent of freshly pruned roses. And wet grass. And yes, even the stench of horse manure. Gary loved Central Park.

He heard someone talking. In the darkness.

"Oi." The voice was kind and sounded familiar, with a thick British accent, but Gary couldn't put a face to it. "Are you the Ashfordses boy?"

Gary leaned closer, trying to get a better look, but the shape inside the car just retreated further into the darkness.

"Yeah," he nodded, curious.

"Me name's Tommy. I'm a chum of your mother, Gary. She ever talk about me?"

Gary found himself at a loss. He couldn't remember his mother ever mentioning a male friend. He shook his head.

"Fiddlesticks and porkies! That cheeses me off. She talks about you all the time." The shadowy man chuckled. "Gary this, Gary that..."

A strong wind started to blow; the dead leaves on the overgrown lawn began to play boisterously like children in a playground. Gary turned toward the house and discovered it had changed. It was no longer his family home. No, it was Ashcombe Manor.

"I came to bring you to your mum, Gary," said the voice in the car. "And there's your dad, too. We are all waiting for you up here. And it's always Christmas here."

Now the smell of Central Park had been replaced by that of rotten vegetables and spoiled meat. The smell of Uncle Ben's cellar. The cellar he hated.

Gary shifted on his feet. He wanted to turn back around and look at the man—no, the thing, because he knew it was a thing—inside the car, but he couldn't because he knew that if did, he would go mad. He knew that whatever was inside the vehicle was not human. So he forced himself to be still, but the voice from the car continued.

"You know why they left you, boy, don't ya? You know that they hated you."

Gary turned. "That's not true! They loved me. They loved me!"

Then he saw the thing inside the car and screamed.

6

Courtney woke up with a start to her husband screaming.

"Gary! Gary! What's wrong, Gary?"

He was standing upright, his arms crossed in front of his face as if protecting himself from some invisible assailant. His eyes were closed, but the rest of his face was tightened into a mask of terror.

"Gary?" she called again, then grabbed him by the shoulders. "Gary, you're having a nightmare."

He opened his eyes. At first, he looked confused, as if he didn't know where he was. Then his eyes met hers and he relaxed.

"My God, Court... It was terrible."

"You scared the crap out of me." She was still shaking. "I've never seen you like that."

His breathing was labored but was slowly returning to

normal. He left and went to the bathroom. She heard the sound of running water.

"What was it, Gary? Tell me."

The water stopped running. "Just a nightmare, Court. Go back to sleep," he said from the other room.

"A nightmare that made you shriek like a frightened child. Don't you want to talk about it? You know, when I was little, I used to have terrible dreams about my family dying, and it really helped to talk to someone."

It was true; when she was about twelve, she had started having these horrible dreams where she was the only survivor of a massacre. Once it had been robbers busting in and killing everybody except her. Another time it had been a plane crash. Or a shipwreck. She never understood why she had been having those nightmares, but the shrink she had been sent to said that she had been internalizing her feelings of inadequacy because her parents had expected too much from her and were always ready to belittle whatever small successes she had achieved. And then there was Audrey. Audrey had been her little sister and the apple of her dad's eyes. Audrey was perfect. Audrey never disappointed him. Courtney had felt like she was in a competition from the time her sister was born. And it had gotten worse as time went on. So much so that she started to think her parents didn't love her anymore. Her mom kept saying it wasn't true, but she knew it was. She felt it in her bones. At every failure, her dad would say that she was letting them down, that the Crosbys were a breed of winners, not losers. They yelled at her all the time.

Gary returned to bed.

"You okay?" Courtney asked, concerned.

"Yeah, sorry, Babe. But it was so..."

"Real?" she finished for him.

He cracked a sad smile. "Yeah. So real."

"Wanna talk about it?"

He passed a hand through his hair. "I was back at the house. In White Plains. The day when I discovered that my parents had left me."

"Oh, I'm sorry..."

"No, it's okay. It's been a long time since I dreamed about that, you know?"

She hugged him close. "I know, I know."

"Except," he continued. "Except this time it was different. Instead of my aunt, there was someth...someone else there."

He was about to say something, not someone, thought Courtney.

"Anyhow, nothing special, Courtney, just a stupid nightmare." He lay back down and pulled up the blankets.

Courtney stared at him, her mind going back to her memories.

"You know, my dad was always working, Gary. And when he wasn't working, he was in the basement playing with his 'big-project-that-would-make-us-rich.' That's what he called it. All in one word." What the hell am I doing? Why am I telling him that? Now.

Gary looked at her with a quizzical look on his face.

"He didn't want to spend time with me. Really. I was the black sheep, the failure, the prototype on which Audrey had been designed and perfected."

"Your dad was an asshole, you know that," said Gary. "But what does that to do with my nightmare?"

She ignored him and went on. "I started going out. Alone. Without telling them. They didn't seem to notice. I went to a place where there were all grownups, a place I had been warned against so many times. I started smoking, then drinking. And I did other things there. I would go out every evening, at any opportunity. And then I would come back, expecting my father to be mad at me, my mother in tears. But it never happened, you know? It was like I was invisible."

Gary touched her gently. "That's why you left, hon. I know."

"What was I supposed to do? I would just come home from school, or after my evenings out, and stay in my room contemplating the shitty wallpaper. Or listen to my mom droning about Perfect Audrey. Or watch my ghost of a dad building something that was not only pathetic but utterly useless. He was building this revolutionary thing while he was losing a daughter. I was having nightmares, for fuck's sake. I was having these really terrible nightmares every night, and all they did was to send me to a shrink."

"Honey..."

But she couldn't stop. "So, what choice did I have? I packed my things and left. I left. They probably did not even notice. And it was fucking Christmas Eve."

Courtney swallowed hard. With terrible effort, she brought it out. "They never went after me, Gary. The never reported my disappearance to the police. Can you believe that?" Her voice became teary and childish while she re-lived the experience. "I ended up in a stranger's car. I was lucky, really lucky because the guy was an honest-to-God eighteen-year-old musician going to the Big Apple for the chance of his life. I was fourteen. And pretty. He could have taken advantage of me. He didn't." Courtney took a deep breath.

Her husband took her hand and squeezed it tightly. "Okay, that's enough, honey. Don't go too deep into it. Not now."

For a long moment, there was silence in the room.

Then Gary turned his head to the door as if he had heard something. "I think Beth is awake. I'd better go check on her."

"Why, thank you," said Courtney, exasperated. "I'm here

telling you that everyone let me down, and here you go." She shook her head. "You'll never change, Gary."

"Hon, I'll be right back. I just told you that Beth is awake. This isn't our home, and I don't want her stumbling about this old mansion in the middle of the night. This has nothing to do with—"

"Oh, shut up."

He looked at her dourly. "We'll talk about this later. Now, if you don't mind, I'm gonna check on our daughter."

She turned on her side, showing him her back. He left without saying a word.

The bastard, she thought. After all we have been through.

She still did not understand why she had allowed him back into her life. Did she still love him? She honestly couldn't tell. She had loved him intensely at one time. But then, after the crisis, she had been more cautious. Deep inside, she knew she had given him a second chance because of Beth. Beth needed her father.

But did she need her husband?

Again, she couldn't tell.

A strange smell reached her. It was disgusting, like something left to rot under the sun. No, like something decomposing in the dark. In a cellar, maybe.

She felt chills running up and down her back for no apparent reason. And then she understood why.

There was someone behind her.

Someone struggling to breathe. She decided not to turn because whoever was behind her was not her husband. And they stank—stank like an open grave.

Courtney stayed still on her side, unwilling to move, steadying her nerves, trying to not scream. She felt the heavy breathing on her neck, and a waft of that nauseous odor engulfed her. Her stomach rebelled. But she would not move.

She was too terrified.

She couldn't say how long she resisted the urge to move, but then she inched toward the edge of the bed. Slowly, she slipped one foot from beneath the covers and lowered it to the floor.

The wheezing increased.

She eased the other foot out and down, then stood up. Her heart felt like it was trying to burst through her chest.

Don't panic, she told herself. It's not real. You fell asleep. You are alone.

But she was not alone, was she?

She heard a step behind her.

She panicked and ran from the room.

7

They say falling to sleep is far easier than waking up. It is as if sleep is an ocean and the sleeper a diver wearing weights. The sleeper falls into the dark abyss of deep sleep within minutes. However, when the sleeper wakes, they have to come up slowly, like they're decompressing. From the abyss, to twilight, to sunlight. The last stage—the sunlight zone in the ocean—is called waking sleep and is a stage in which the sleeper can hear sounds and will incorporate them into their dreams or even react in reality without being aware of it later.

So Beth heard Tommy's voice gradually turn into that of her father. She heard him call, "Beth! Beth!"

That was followed by the feeling of a pair of strong hands grabbing her shoulders, which Beth reacted to by opening her eyes. The first thing they saw was her own reflection in the window. Then she saw her dad. He looked worried.

"Beth, answer me."

"I'm alright, Dad," she said feebly. "I was just having a

nightmare..."

But her dad's expression didn't change into one of relief. "You're not in your bed, Beth. You've been sleepwalking."

It was true. Beth could see that she wasn't in her bed; instead, she was standing by the tall window overlooking the manor's driveway. It was still dark outside.

She drew in a deep breath and let it out; then she turned to face her daddy. "I... I'm scared..."

Her father hugged her tight. "Oh, don't worry, you're not the only one having nightmares. I had one, too."

"Really?"

"Yes."

"What was it about?" asked Beth while her dad carried her back to bed. "The nightmare, I mean."

"Oh, just a stupid dream, nothing really scary. You know how it works, right? When you are deep inside it, you feel scared and everything—even the most unrealistic thing—seems real. Then you wake up, and you realize that there is nothing to be scared of."

She let her dad tuck her in, her mind still running through her own bad dream. Only a dream. For as much as it looked real, it had all been a dream.

Yet she had woken up close to the window, which was exactly where she'd been in the dream.

"Dad?" she asked. "Why do we sleepwalk?"

"Well... that's a million-dollar question," he said. "I'm not a doctor, but I know that, at the moment, science hasn't found a cause yet. Some say it is due to hormonal fluctuations—and that would make sense because you are growing, and at this stage, your body is a true chemical lab."

"Homo what?"

Her dad laughed. "Not homo... Hormonal. Hormones are molecules. You know molecules, right? We talked about them last year, remember?"

She nodded.

"Well, hormon— "

Her mom ran into the room, startling her and Dad. She looked pale, and her eyes were wide, as if she were afraid of something. She was wearing her white nightgown, the one Dad had bought her for her birthday, the one Beth found very pretty. She sat down opposite dad, on the other side of the bed.

"Hey, Sweetie, are you okay?"

"Yes, I just had a hormo-thing. Or so Dad said." Beth felt embarrassed now; she had woken up the whole house. "I'm sorry, Mom."

Mom glanced at Dad with a perplexed face, then returned her eyes to Beth. "A what?"

"I found her sleepwalking," said Dad.

Something was going on between them, Beth could feel it. Her mom looked wretchedly white, and her eyes were red, as if she had just been crying. Dad's face was equally pale—minus the red eyes.

"What's wrong, Mom?" Beth asked. "You look scared."

"Of course, I look scared, you silly girl." She smiled, but it was a forced smile. "You scared me. What's this story about sleepwalking?"

Dad explained to her what had happened, of how he had found Beth standing by the window, at which point her mom had freaked out, afraid that Beth could have hurt herself by climbing out of it. Dad reassured her that the window had been closed, and Beth confirmed it. She told them that she had dreamed about Santa (for some reason, she didn't feel like telling them the whole truth) and that he'd been speaking through a tube coming out of the wall. This reminded her of the darn thing. She climbed out of bed, ignoring her parents' protests, went to the window, and pulled aside the heavy curtains.

"This." She pointed at the brass funnel. "It was in my dream. What is it, Dad?"

"That's a speaking tube—or a voicepipe. They were used in the nineteenth century to summon the servants." Dad came closer and looked around. "Actually, there should be a handbell around here to complement it..." He found it. "There!" He pointed to a piece of discolored, frayed cord dangling from the ceiling above the tube. "It has been cut, but you can see it going inside."

"What was that for?" asked Mom.

"Back then, there was no intercom, or any kind of electronics, of course. Now, if you were living in one of these big mansions, you had to think of a way to summon your servants. Imagine you are old and sick, and you need to call your butler or the maid." He mimicked pulling an invisible rope. "You pulled that thing and, because it was connected to a handbell in the servant's quarters, it would signal for someone to get on the horn. At that point, you could have a conversation."

"So this must be connected to the servant's quarters, right?" said Beth.

"In theory." Dad seemed unsure about it. "But I don't know the layout of this house, honestly. Looks to me that a lot of changes—what we architects call modernizations—have been done to this old building."

Mom kept asking questions about the voicepipe and the old times, and it soon became clear to Beth that whatever had scared her was now forgotten and was fading away. The same was happening to her dad. He was smiling, had been laughing at Beth's jokes about Victorian butlers farting in the speaking tube, and seemed to have forgotten the bad dream that had visited him. Also, Beth could not fail to notice—by the clock on the fireplace mantle—that it was almost two in the morning, and her parents were not upset about her being up.

It's really the magic of Christmas, she thought.

She decided to not tell them about the boy in the tower.

8

The next morning, instead of eating in the too formal—but still messy—dining room, the Ashford family sat in the living room by the bay window to have a magnificent breakfast. It was a typical English winter morning, hazy, with cold, drizzling rain.

After breakfast, the three of them planned to spend a happy and old-fashioned country Christmas. They walked around the property, exploring the old gardens of Ashcombe. There were a couple of gigantic oak trees that really impressed Gary, and in the back, a gray stone mausoleum—with a sturdy iron gate—hosted the final resting place of generations of Ashfields.

"My ancestors sleep here," he said.

"What?" Courtney looked at him.

"Well, that's the reason why we are here. Last September, I had one of those genealogical searches done." He pointed at the tomb. "And I found out that I am descended from these people. The American branch of the Ashfords was started by Jonathan Henry—the youngest boy of Edward George Ashford, the Earl of Ashcombe."

"What's an earl, Dad?" Beth asked.

He took her in his arms. "An earl is a nobleman. It's a rank, like Count Dracula, you know? Actually, it's the English equivalent of a count. From what I learned at school, it's an Anglo-Saxon word similar to that used by the Vikings: jarl."

"So we are noble," said his daughter matter-of-factly.

"I wanna be a princess," Courtney joked. "Can I choose my title?"

Gary chuckled. "It doesn't work like that. In theory, you'd be a countess. But we aren't noble. British peerage is quite a complex thing, and whatever right we might have had to this land was lost when Jonathan left England to make his own fortune in the colonies."

Courtney kicked a rock. "Do you know why he left?"

"Honestly, I don't know all the details, but it seems that he had...let's say... grown weary of his family's reputation. So he decided to leave. This happened in the seventeenth century. It seems that the Ashfords were suspected of being in league with an infamous local clan that was terrorizing the moors."

His wife's face darkened. "What do you mean by terrorizing?" She huddled closer and whispered in his ear, "No spooky stories, please. Not today."

"Oh, they were bandits, that's all." He put his daughter back down. "You can read about them in a famous novel by Richard Blackmore. Lorna Doone. Even if that romanticizes the true story behind the Doones."

"Can we go back into the house?" asked Beth. "I'm getting cold."

"Sure, sweetie." Gary grabbed her hand.

Inside, while he got a fire going in the giant fireplace of the living room, Courtney knelt beside him. "I'd like to know more about those robbers. Care to tell me?"

Gary stood up, put his hands on the small of his back, and groaned. He glanced over at his daughter. She was busy combing her doll's hair.

"Beth, I'm gonna show your mom the library. It's on the opposite side of the manor, just beyond the parlor. Do not go around without us, okay? Especially outside. Promise?"

"Promise."

"Good girl."

The library was impressive, containing something like a thousand books on a variety of subjects. There was a large oil portrait depicting a stern-looking gentleman wearing a wig on the west wall, and a stuffed elk or red stag—Gary couldn't say which—was mounted on a pedestal at the center of the room.

"Do not show this to Beth. She doesn't like stuffed animals," said Courtney, caressing the creature's head.

"I know, especially after all the excitement over that deer we saw from the train." He stared at the glassy eyes. "Honestly, I don't like this kind of thing either. Killing a deer, stuffing it, and keeping it inside your house. Bah..."

He sat down in a large armchair and patted his lap. "C'mere. Time to tell you a story."

"You wish," she replied, laughing. "I'm too old for that!" She walked over to a small cabinet and pulled out two glasses and a bottle of mulled apple juice.

"Good," said Gary with a smile. "Really what I need after all that humidity."

She poured a glass for each of them, then offered him one before sitting next to him on the plump arm of the chair. "So, Sir Ashford, tell me about the Doones. I'm curious. They sound a bit like the Goonies."

"Totally different." He sipped the nonalcoholic beverage. It tasted good.

"How different? Gruesomely different?"

He nodded. "It all started in Scotland in 1618. Ensor Stuart of Doune, cousin to the Earl of Moray, assumed the surname of Doune and made a claim for the family castle, enraging the reigning earl. Seems the act repulsed the powerful cousin so much that he became determined to drive Ensor from Scotland; he actually succeeded in entering his cousin's house at Stirling, where he gave him the choice of leaving the country or being kept a prisoner with his wife in Doune Castle. He chose to leave. Disfranchised, he went to London, hoping to obtain redress at the hands of the king. It never came. So Ensor Doune grew disgusted with mankind and resolved to shut himself away from the world in the most remote place he could find. And at the end of a long and tiring march, he, his family, and his retainers found refuge on these moors."

Telling stories had always been one of Gary's special pleasures. When he was young, he had dreamed about becoming a writer, but then life led him into architecture.

"They took possession of a half-ruined farmhouse, which they converted into their home. As time went on, other sons were born to the outlawed nobleman, and they all inherited the bad temper of their father, and they grew up regarding all those not of the family as their enemies. They used threats to obtain whatever they required. They waylaid peaceful travelers on lonely roads, kidnapped the beauties of the village, and became a source of constant terror to everyone in the area. From that time onward, the four sons of Sir Ensor grew to be detested and feared by the country people of Devon and Somerset."

"But how did they become known as the Doones?" inquired Courtney.

"Oh, that's just because the people here warped their name, and it stuck. In fact, with time, it became a way for the Dounes to distance themselves from their past."

His wife finished her glass and poured another. "I see. But how does this connect to the Ashfords?"

"Here is the creepy part." Gary clicked his tongue. "According to a book I bought when we were in London, the Doones slid rapidly into abject depravity and decadence. They turned to barbaric crimes, including cannibalism. Sadistic and merciless, the Doones plagued the counties of Somerset and Devon, avoiding the local militia by hopping across the county borders as the need arose to avoid prosecution. Such was their reputation that the mere mention of the family name induced terror across a wide part of the West Country. Eventually, the Somerset and Devon militias pooled resources and hunted down the renegade clan. Most of the family was killed during a pitched battle, riddled with musket fire or hacked apart by sword and ax. Those who survived the massacre were executed by hanging in Taunton."

"That explains their end, but nothing about your ancestors," pressed Courtney.

"Let me finish," he said. "Now, it seems that during the Doones' reign of terror, other locals were benefitting from the clan's raids. It was rumored that Sir Ashford was one of them. He used to buy all the loot stolen by the Doones highwaymen and resell it for profit."

"Makes me think about that movie we watched together at the drive-in when we were dating. What was that? The one with the guys in the hills..." Courtney finished her second glass.

"The Hills Have Eyes," he said, getting up from the armchair and removing the empty glass from his wife's hand. "Let's go check on Beth."

They went back to the living room. Beth was still there but was now drawing with her crayons. She was bent over the sheet of paper, totally oblivious to her surroundings. He crept behind her to get a better look at what she was drawing, careful to not prompt his daughter's usual reaction of covering her work with both arms and complaining about privacy. Beth wouldn't show you a drawing until it was finished.

On the white sheet, there was a tower similar to that of

the manor, but it looked cruder and rounder than it actually was. It was like a cutout—a sectional view in architecture—because Gary could see that there were two figures inside holding hands. The largest was a boy, while the second looked like a tiny furry creature with big ears. All around them, there was a forest of decorated Christmas trees and gift boxes. The girl surely had a fervid imagination.

He couldn't resist. "What's that, sweetie?"

Surprisingly, there was no defensive reaction this time. Beth kept coloring in the boy…in red? All red from head to toe.

"It's about a dream," she said.

"A dream?" Gary wondered if she was drawing about last night's nightmare but then dismissed the thought. "What's with the chubby one?" He pointed at the smaller figure.

"It's a mogwai. Isn't that obvious?" his daughter replied with a disappointed face.

"Uh, sure," he said. He didn't want to sound unconvinced, but he had no idea what a mogwai was and felt that Beth expected him to know it.

Courtney came to the rescue. "A mogwai? Ooh, that's so cute. Can I see?"

They started talking about "Gizmo," and Gary got even more confused.

Although it was almost lunchtime, he felt the need for more coffee, so he went into the kitchen. He was about to fill his mug when, through the window, he spotted someone in the garden.

9

It turned out that someone was Robert Lockwood, a local farmer and neighbor of the Ashfords.

Bob—as he kindly asked Gary to call him—was a typical West Country rural farmer, slightly overweight and with a ruddy face due to drinking too much cider. He wore some weather-stained, dark brown overalls over an old denim shirt and under a green waxed jacket. His bald head was protected by a narrow-brimmed hat (Bob told him that it was a Trilby, and he was quite fond of it) and his feet by wellies—what Americans called rain boots.

When Gary had questioned him about his presence in the Ashford's property, Bob had apologized and told him he was looking for his cat, Beefcake. He said his tom was a fat boy and usually wasn't too inclined to be chasing the fairy cup (whatever that meant), yet he had the habit of sneaking into Ashcombe to look for coneys (that's rabbits to you yanks, Bob had said), and when he did that, he sometimes forgot the way back home. It had happened many times that Bob had to come over and literally carry Old Beef back.

He had also told Gary that Martha Mullens, the agent responsible for the renting and management of the manor, had agreed to let him trespass to hunt for coneys or pigeons in exchange for him keeping an eye on the property when it was unoccupied.

"Anywhen, I don't mean to disturb your holidays. Should you find me Beefcake," he was saying, handing Gary a business card, "please give me a blow on the horn."

The card said Lockwood Valley Farm.

"Sure," said Gary. And then he added impulsively, "Don't you want to come in for a hot drink?"

Bob hesitated. It seemed to Gary that the guy was not too keen on the idea of stepping inside the manor—for whatever reason—yet, at the same time, he didn't want to act impolite.

"I don't like being a grockel—that's what we call a tourist here—so, I figure, yes, I'll accept your offer."

Gary noticed Bob giving a long, pensive look at the tower before stepping inside. "Ah reckon there is a first time for everything," he said almost under his breath. Then louder, "You know, I'd never a-went inside this house all me life."

"Really? Why?"

Bob shrugged. "Guess I was never invited over."

But Gary felt he was lying. There was something else in the old farmer's eyes. Fear? And if so, what was he afraid of?

"Tea or coffee?"

"Whatever is good," said Bob. His eyes scoured the kitchen. "Say, where's the rest of your family?"

"Oh, they're probably in the living room. Drawing. Or talking about drawing."

Gary filled two mugs with coffee and offered one to his guest. The farmer took it, thanked him with a nod, and was about to lift it to his lips when he changed his mind and looked pensive again.

"Something's wrong?" asked Gary.

"Oh, nothing's wrong, mate" Bob quickly took a swig from the mug as if to apologize. "Coffee's good. I was just wondering if you and your family would like to visit me farm. I've got some cute baby goats and a pair of bigger uns that ain't too joppety. I mean, too nervous. Guessin' your daughter might love them."

Gary didn't know what to say. Part of him was tempted to say yes. Beth loved animals and that would surely make for a distracting day after last night. At the same time, it was Christmas Eve, and he didn't want to intrude. "Thank you, Bob. However, I don't know..."

"You don't know what?"

"We don't have a car..."

Bob laughed. "Got my Rangie just over there. I can bring you all to me farm in time for a morsel. Make some good cheddar over there. And you can try me cider. It's made with the best apples this side of the moor. Don't say no."

"I don't know what to say..."

"Say yes. I promise you'll be back home before it gets dimpsey up the Tor... I mean, before it gets too dark."

"I don't want to disturb your fam—"

"No disturb. As for me family... It's just me and me Daisy. Workers are all off for the holidays. Me kids are no longer kids. The biggun lives in Bangkok. Yeah, he visits from time to time, but this year he decided to go to Japan with his lovely wife. The younger is down under. Australia. He's an herpeto-sumthin... A herpetologist. A bit cakey in the head, if you ask me. Good boy, but risks too much with them crocs down there. Anywhen, we'd be fess right up with some company. I've been up since five in the morning. Can't do a proper job at sleeping anymore. Must be the fact I'm getting old. Got so narked that I wore me wellies and went out looking for that stupid cat." He paused. "Am I rambling, right?"

Gary smiled. "Alright, I'm gonna ask the family."

10

The 'morsel' turned out to be more than Gary had expected, as Daisy Lockwood had unleashed on him and his family all the best of the West Country traditional cuisine. They were served bangers and mash (some flavored sausages served with mashed potatoes, a thick gravy, and peas), Somerset pie (a pastry filled with pork meat, apple, and flavored with cider), a rich potato cake, and some Quantock butter biscuits. And, of course, the famous—at least according to Bob—Lockwood Farms scrumpy, his beloved cider. It was delicious, and Gary forced himself to not drink too much of it, even if Bob insisted on giving him some more.

Gary felt as stuffed as a Thanksgiving turkey and could barely lift his ass from the chair.

The farm was beautiful and very neat, given that it was such a muddy place. There were sheep, goats (and Bob was right; Beth went totally crazy about the baby ones), and a couple of cute-as-button piglets. Most of the land, however, was devoted to farming. It was mainly a cider farm. Bob said he used to have a press room for the scrumpy, but it was in dire need of restoration, so he now sent his produce down to Minehead. Bob owned something like six acres of land—of which four were orchards with seven varieties of apple. The rest was made up of the animal pens, the Lockwoods' home, and a farm shop, where he sold home-made cheddar, biscuits, and cider.

Beth wouldn't stop petting Pumpkin and Spice, the two piglets. And they loved it, for they kept rolling on their back for a rub on the belly. Courtney had been forced to lift her off and carry her inside to have lunch with the Lockwoods.

Now Gary was sitting on the porch with Bob. The old man had produced a long-stemmed pipe and was puffing on it, appearing thoughtful. The porch was long and narrow, with a wooden roof and a balustrade that reminded Gary of an old west saloon. He almost expected to see Clint Eastwood crouching at the edge, his back to the wall, the wide-brimmed hat covering the top of his face, a cigar sending clouds of smoke into the air...

"I hope your time here is gonna be a good one, Gary," said Bob. He said it without a smile, as if something were bugging him. "Why don't we make sure it is? Why don't you spend the night here? We've got plenty of space. In fact, we were thinking of renting the spare rooms to grockels—I'm mean tourists—during summertime. There's plenty of city people that like to visit the country now. You have to see the traffic on the motorway, it's unbelievable..."

"Thanks for the offer, Bob," said Gary, quite surprised by the man's hospitality. "But I paid top dollar to rent that big baby over there." He pointed at Ashcombe.

From Lockwood's porch, the manor looked like an ancient church situated at the top of the hill. The tall tower contributed to that illusion, of course.

"We'll be staying here a couple of days, then we'll be on our way home."

"You came to England just for a week?" Bob's stare made him feel as if he had just insulted the queen.

"No," said Gary, chuckling. "We have been to London, we visited Stonehenge. All in all we'll have spent almost four weeks here."

"Ah..." Bob seemed relieved. He puffed on his pipe and rocked his chair. "Anywhen, my offer still stands. It would be nice spending Christmas together. I'm not pressing you, Gary. Heck, we barely just met. But I like Beth. And your wife. You seem like nice folks." He offered him more cider.

Gary politely refused. "I thank you again and—"

"That's not a good place."

There was silence, then the man added, "I know it may sound crazy, and I really don't know from where to bloody start. I know I'm gonna sound cakey, but I don't want anything bad to happen to you or your family."

Gary was shocked. "Why are you saying that?" He glanced at him, but the man was looking away, toward the hill. His face was stern.

"Ever heard of Rawhead and Bloody Bones?" Bob asked, as if the question justified his disquiet.

"No, I don't know what you are talking about."

Bob took a puff. "It depends on where you hear the legend. Some people call it Tommy Rawhead, or Old Bloody

Bones, or other variations. Most of it's bloody chinny, a load of old codswallop. Stuff made up to make children behave. Like the bogies or the hags. But this one, Gary... This one is something different..."

"Okay..." said Gary. But he was thinking, The guy just wants to impress me. I'm a grockel, after all. He wanted to tell him to stop because it wasn't funny, especially after last night. Instead, he simply said, "Go on."

Bob looked at him. "We've all heard stories of the boogeyman. They are told from Aberdeen to Southampton. From San Francisco to Tokyo. The legend is a universal one. It's the monster under the bed, the one in the closet, inside old cupboards, or under the stairs. In all the dark places. It's the bloody beast that terrorizes, kidnaps, and eats mischievous children, right?"

Gary nodded.

"For centuries, parents have used benevolent and malevolent figures to control their children's behavior. On one hand, you have the jolly myth of Santa Claus, or Father Christmas, as we call him here. It is used to convince children to be nice. You're nice, and Santa will bring you all the presents you can ask for. You're naughty? You'll get a lump of coal in your stocking. On the other hand, the myth of the boogeyman is meant to scare children into submission. Git on to sleep so the boogeyman doesn't get you. Stay in bed, or else the boogeyman will catch you."

Gary raised his eyebrows. "And this leads to?"

Bob lifted a hand. "Let me finish." He moved uneasily in his seat. "Most of these bogies—or hynkypunks, like we call them here—are based on older legends. In Yorkshire, for example, Rawhead and Bloody Bones are kinds of evil spirits haunting old marl pits. In Cornwall, Old Bloody Bones lives in abandoned mines, especially those near the sites of ancient battles. Then there is Black Annis in Leicestershire. Jenny Greenteeth in Lancashire. And many others."

He paused to relight his pipe that had died out.

"'Tommy Bloody Bones. Steals naughty children from their homes. Takes them to his dirty den. And they are never seen again...' That's what we used to sing when we were still in short pants backalong," he said.

"Creepy." Gary shook his head. "I wouldn't want my kids to sing stuff like that. I don't believe in scaring children to behave. It's not healthy."

Bob put the lighter away. "Still, you let kids believe in Santa. Then was a different time. I know nowadays those that study children's psyche have a different approach to the ways we raise kids now. But Gary... there's always a bit of truth behind every legend..."

"Of course. They were cautionary tales to keep nestlings away from trouble. You didn't want them to get lost in an abandoned mine, a tar pit, or something. But I think that explaining why is better than creeping them out," Gary insisted.

"But they wouldn' listen, would they?"

He shrugged. "I understand it was a simpler world, but—"

"What we got here, Gary, is a different kettle of fish. Tommy Bloody Bones is the name that was given by locals to a creature that has haunted this area long before the Romans came to Britain. The Celts that lived here called him Fear Gortha, the ever-hungry one. These tribes worshipped nature spirits, like the Mother-Wife and the Horned Man. The world was full of feral spirits backalong. Folks believed that at certain times of the year, such as the Summer solstice or Yuletide, the Mother-Wife and the Horned Man would mate to regenerate the land. But out of their union, sometimes monsters were born, monsters that preyed on both animals and mankind. They stole away young children and farm animals in a 'natural' culling that was viewed by our ancestors as a necessity. It was a balance of the ferocity and virility of the masculine Horned Man with the fertility and maternity of the feminine Mother-Wife. The balance could be maintained because of this duality. Fear Gortha would not take more than 'necessary.' All was under control in the balance of nature. But then came Christianity, and these pagan gods were banished, and then forgotten. All that was left were the monsters..."

What am I supposed to do? Gary asked himself. Am I going to sit here and listen to all this nonsense?

"There are two legends about the entrapment of Tommy Bloody Bones, both with the same ending. In one, Merlin—you know, the Merlin of Arthurian tales, right him—imprisoned the malevolence of the Fear Gortha into a tower so the land could become civilized. The second version gives the merit to Saint Carantoc, a Welsh evangelist. The legend says he defeated a dragon in Dunster. But it weren't. It was the Bloody Bones. He used the power of the Mother-Wife to trap him inside a tower. Some say that tower became the first abode of a clan of bandits in the fifteenth century."

"Wait," said Gary, now more interested. "Are you saying that the tower of Ashcombe Manor once belonged to the Doones?"

Bob looked at him, surprised. "You know about them?"

"Yes, but I was told a different story."

Bob scoffed. "Well, of course, no one knows the absolute truth. What I know is that the Ashfords got the Doones land after the Bloody Assizes of 1685, after the Duke of Monmouth's rebellion was over."

"Uh," was the only sound that escaped Gary's mouth.

"Ooh, arr." Bob nodded vigorously. "Can't say for sure the tower belonged to the Doones—even if I strongly believe so—but of one thing I'm sure: Ashcombe Manor was built around that tower. And that's the prison of Tommy Bloody Bones."

Gary sniggered softly and shook his head. "Now, suppose I believe this stuff, okay? There's nothing to be afraid of because the thing is imprisoned. So why should I be afraid?"

"You forgot that there are certain times of the year when all the trappings of Christianity, call them wards or just faith, fail. Take Yuletide, for example. Technically, our faith should be stronger, but we are more concerned with 'pagan' rituals that weaken the spirit. We put up 'heathen' trees. We decorate our halls with holly. We exchange gifts. And most of all, we allow our children to focus on a mythical figure rather than on our Lord." Bob stood up and poured another glass of cider.

"Mind you, I'm not saying this because I'm a fervent believer. Quite the contrary. I just think that sometimes things are as they are and that we can't explain everything with science."

"It's getting late, Bob. We should be going." Gary was tired and didn't like those stories at all. "I thank you for the excellent hospitality, and I hope I can do the same for you one day. But I really want to go back, if you don't mind."

Bob opened his mouth, but then closed it again, as if he was unsure about speaking his mind.

"You made it up, right? This story. The boogeyman... Wanna scare a grockel, uh?"

Bob looked grimly at him, then forced a smile. "Sure. But you ain't one to be scared easily, are ya?" He put away the pipe and walked toward the door. "Get your family, mate, I'm gonna get the keys."

Later, at home, while Courtney was giving Elizabeth a bath, Gary recalled the expression on Bob Lockwood's face when he had finally given up and had admitted his prank. He hadn't looked sincere. He had looked like he'd been lying.

11

Once Beth was finally in bed, Gary and Courtney sneaked downstairs to put colorful boxes of gifts under the tree by the fireplace. Then the two of them relaxed in the glow of the Christmas tree, Courtney in her silk nightgown and Gary in his pajamas.

"Do you think it's time we told her the truth?" Gary suddenly asked.

His wife looked at him. "You mean about Santa?"

"Yes. I mean, I don't know if this is healthy." He couldn't stop thinking about Bob Lockwood and his weird stories of how they propagate the myth. "I know Santa is a positive figure... still..."

"You were scared of him, right?"

For a moment, Gary thought she was referring to Bob, but then he realized she meant Santa Claus. "No, I wasn't. But I stopped believing in him quite early. I think I was five." He took her hands. "I was just thinking that maybe...maybe by creating these imaginary things, giving them a myth, a background, a logic behind them... I dunno. It's like giving shape to them. It's like molding them into something real..."

"Gary," she interrupted him.

"What?"

"Did you have too much cider at the Lockwoods?"

He laughed. "No. It may sound like it, but I'm not drunk."

"So why this kind of philosophical approach to something innocent like Santa?"

He couldn't answer. He knew the answer to it was deep inside his primitive brain, provoked by Bob's suggestive tales of pagan gods, spirits, and ruthless bandits, but he couldn't bring himself to tell her that.

She stood up, drawing him with her. "Let's go to bed."

They went upstairs, holding hands like teenagers. Gary felt happy and quickly forgot about bogeys once they got into the bedroom.

It was afterward, while lying naked on his back and staring at the ceiling, his wife fast asleep beside him, that his mind raced back to that creepy rhyme.

Tommy Bloody Bones
Steals naughty children from their homes,
Takes them to his dirty den,
And they are never seen again.

❄ ❄ ❄

Beth sneaked out of her room as soon as she was sure her parents were asleep. She had waited patiently under the bed sheets until she had heard Mom and Dad snoring. That was the signal she had been waiting for. She had quickly put on a pair of jeans and a sweater, and then, barefooted, scampered down the hall. Then she had tiptoed into her parents' room and had taken the flashlight her father kept on the nightstand for emergencies.

Now at the old wooden stairs that led to the attic, she moved stealthily and finally reached the top. She had to do that in the dark because the flashlight's beam might have awakened her parents.

It wasn't a dream, she thought. Tommy is real and is going to give me exactly what I want.

In fact, that morning, when Dad and Mom had gone to the library, Tommy had spoken to her again. This time his voice had come from the fireplace. And he had made a deal with her.

Come up here, he had said. Come up here, and it will be nothing but fun and games forever. Daddy and Mommy will be with you, too. I promise.

Then she had smelled the popcorn again and had heard the sound of cheering kids.

It's gonna be a big surprise, Beth...

Once in the attic, she switched on the flashlight. The beam revealed a small, dark, and dusty corridor leading to four different rooms. The one she was looking for was right in front of her, just like Tommy had said. She moved closer to the big wooden door and examined it. It didn't have a keyhole, but a large latch on this side kept it shut. She had to put the flashlight on the floor to use both hands to lift the latch. Then she pushed the door open...

❄ ❄ ❄

Gary woke up suddenly. Something felt wrong. He immediately checked his surroundings. Nothing unusual. Courtney was sleeping soundly at his side. The window was closed. Same for the door.

So what was wrong?

A noise, maybe?

He listened carefully. Nothing.

Beth...

Beth is sleeping, he told his alert mind. Why would she...

Then he remembered the sleepwalking episode. Could it be that he had heard noises coming from her bedroom? Better check.

He climbed out of bed, careful to not wake his wife.

It's probably nothing, he told himself. Maybe I'm just nervous. But it's not a big deal to check on her, right? Just to make sure...

He reached the door, hesitated, and finally opened it. In the house's stillness, the lock resounded sharply as the spring coiled. He turned to look at his wife. She hadn't moved.

He felt stupid. He really didn't want to bother her again, but after the previous night...

Let her have a nice Christmas.

Carefully, he opened the door. The corridor was dark, but he didn't dare to switch on the lights. He slid out of the room and waited for his eyes to adjust to the dim light coming from the large front windows.

Then he saw that Beth's door was wide open.

❄ ❄ ❄

Beth found herself inside a large storage room. The flashlight illuminated various white shapes, probably old furniture covered by sheets. There was a mannequin close to the left wall, one of those used by tailors in the olden times. It didn't scare Beth, but she found it creepy.

On the right wall, as Tommy had said, there was another door. It was also made of wood, but it was smaller. It looked like one of those dungeon doors she had seen at the Tower of London. That had been a bit scary. She hadn't liked that door.

The same voice that had warned her against Tommy before desperately tried to pull her out of the spell she had fallen into. And it worked for a moment, because Beth turned to leave...

But then she heard the music.

It was the music from Gremlins.

It was Gizmo singing.

Beth stepped closer to the creepy door and cocked her head, listening. The worry on her face melted into a smile. The singing grew louder.

It was amazing. Impossible. Yet irresistible.

She examined the door and saw that this one didn't have a lock, either. Just another latch, but there was something weird on this one. Something that looked like an iron pin.

She lifted the latch and pushed the door. It didn't grind as expected. Instead, it yawned placidly.

Inside, there was the impossible.

A brightly lit hallway, with a red-and-white checkered floor, opened onto a room with an enormous Christmas tree at its center. It was more than ten feet tall and deliciously decorated with twinkling lights, colored glass baubles, and strings of shimmering tinsel. Underneath it, the remains of Christmas morning littered the floor. Shredded paper and unraveled bows. And toys! So many toys! More than she could ever have dreamed for. Empty boxes had been shredded and were scattered all around the room.

And tags, hundreds of tags.

She grabbed one. It read: 'To Beth, from Tommy.'

"F-f-f-finally! You're he-he-here!"

The voice startled her.

She lifted her eyes and saw the boy.

He looked thin and malnourished, as if he had been starving for a long time. A mop of dark hair crowned his head, and big, crazy green eyes topped a smile that made Beth think of the Cheshire Cat.

He rushed to her and grabbed her hand.

"H-h-h-here, look here," he said, pointing at the gifts under the tree. "T-t-these are all yours, Beth!"

She couldn't believe it. Yet it was real. She touched the tree's branches. Then caressed the hair of a doll. She smelled chocolate. It was all real.

"You're Tommy, right?" she asked.

The boy didn't answer and kept shuffling around, picking up toys from the floor and putting them in Beth's hands. He bounced from corner to corner in a frenzied state. It was obvious he hadn't had visitors for a long time.

"Are you Tommy or not? And where are the mogwai?"

"Forget about the mogwai. Here, take this doll." He flashed his big grin again. "It's yours. They are all yours."

The bad smell returned. This time it was stronger, like… that of a butcher shop…

Suddenly, Beth didn't feel safe anymore. "I don't think I'm gonna stay. This is not normal."

But the boy seized her left arm, his hand like steel.

"Hey, you're hurting me! Let go!"

And then Beth saw the boy's face change. It melted like it was made of wax, and the crazy green eyes turned to terribly bright lights. Blinded by the light, Beth's vision started to blur, but she could see that the boy was no longer a boy but a thing made of putrescent and fleshy red worms. The Christmas room was no more; it had been replaced by a moldy and dirty dungeon. And the toys and boxes…

…were the uncountable remains of dead children, their skulls and bones littering the whole damp floor.

"They are yours," the thing said in a guttural voice now. "And they are going to be yours forever."

Beth fought back, struggled against the monster's grasp, but its gross and slimy arms were too strong. She punched and kicked it as hard as she could. Nothing worked. But then, in the end, when the thing pulled her toward its horrible skull-like face, unhinging its fanged jaws like a snake, it was only then that Beth screamed.

❄ ❄ ❄

Gary ran frantically down the stairs with the hope his daughter had sneaked in the living room to spy on Santa. She wasn't there. He checked the front door. It was still locked, and the security chain hadn't been touched.

Besides, she was too smart to go out at night, so he decided to check the library and the dining room. Then he got this idea that she might be in the kitchen, making sure that her forgetful dad had left out a glass of milk for Santa. He had almost forgotten last year, and Beth had thrown a tantrum because she was afraid the jolly old man would take offense and not leave any presents.

She wasn't there.

He went back upstairs, this time by the servant's stairwell that connected the kitchen with the second floor.

It was when he got to the landing that he heard someone moving at the end of the hall.

"Gary?"

It was Courtney.

"I'm down here," he said. He reached for the light switch. It didn't work; the hall remained dark.

"The power went out," she said. "I got up and couldn't find you. What's happening?"

"I can't find Beth. She's not in her room." He tried to not sound too worried, but he heard his own voice trembling.

"What? You're joking, right?"

"No, I'm not. I've checked downstairs. And before you ask, no, she didn't go outside. The front and back doors are still locked, and I've got the keys." He walked toward her.

"So, where is she?"

"I have no idea, but I still haven't checked the attic."

"But...why?"

He felt the tension rising from his abdomen, spreading like fire on a pyre of dry wood. He felt rage, anguish, and... terror? Was that terror?

"Let's not waste time with the whys, Courtney. I don't

know why. It might be another episode of sleepwalking. Or something else."

Tommy Bloody Bones. Steals naughty children from their homes. Takes them to his dirty den. And they are never seen again...

The creepy children's rhyme popped into his mind, and he felt something growing inside him. Something terrible was happening to his baby girl, and he had to stop it. But what? How?

He couldn't reassure himself, so he tried to calm his wife. "I'm sure everything is fine. She just went looking for Santa."

"In the attic?"

"Why not?" he blurted out, exasperated. "Maybe she saw us bringing down the boxes."

Courtney didn't seem convinced.

"I'll need my flashlight." He moved toward the bedroom, but Courtney stopped him.

"It's not there. I checked the nightstand. It was there when we went to sleep. It's gone."

"Damn," he cursed under his breath. "Beth must have it."

"In that case, she can't be sleepwalking, Gary. She consciously took the torch. She planned it, Gary. She—"

A scream resounded through the house, freezing Courtney.

"Shit!" Gary looked up at the ceiling. "It's coming from the attic."

Hell broke loose as Gary and Courtney rushed to the stairwell, ignoring the darkness and bumping into each other. He was first to reach the landing. He couldn't see much, except...

Except there was a feeble light cutting through the darkness of the storage room in front of him. He heard his wife say something, but he didn't understand because his brain was on fire, his temples were pounding furiously with the beat of his heart, and he could only focus on one thing: that that light was the beam of his flashlight. And it was lying on the floor somewhere to the right.

He ran into the room and tripped over something bulky, and he fell and crashed into an old rocking chair that was covered with a thick, white sheet. With a grimace of pain, he pulled himself up and turned to look at the source of the beam.

And he couldn't make sense of what he was seeing.

There was a little door on the west wall. It was open, and the light from the torch was coming from the room beyond it. His daughter was there, too, partially illuminated by the fallen flashlight. Her eyes were frozen in terror, and her mouth was open, but no sound was coming out of it. But what sent his mind over the edge was the impossible crimson-colored thing standing over her, its right claw pinning Beth to the dirty floor like a predator protecting its prey. The thing was tall and almost skeletal, with bones that were clearly visible through its translucent, verminous skin. Sharp talons, like those of a vulture, sprouted out of the mangled flesh of its extremely long fingers. The head was oblong and irregular, and no nose was visible. But the most horrid feature was the eyes; they were large and brighter than the flashlight, burning like fire.

"Ark at 'ee, aren't you a-feard?" snarled the monster, its long tongue lolling out of the fanged mouth. "Come on then, Gary." Its voice sounded like the grinding of a tomb being opened. Stone on stone.

Gary was paralyzed with fear, but a part of him, the part that would die for his daughter, kicked in and sent adrenaline through his petrified body. He stepped forward, ready to fight something that shouldn't exist.

The thing sunk its long claws into Beth's chest. She screamed in pain, and Gary saw dark spots blossoming on her shirt.

"I'll kill her, I swear," growled the monster. Its smell was putrid. "The culling can't be stopped!"

The culling...

Gary remembered Bob's words.

A "natural" culling that was viewed by our ancestors as a necessity...

Fear Gortha — or something like that — the ever-hungry one...

Fear Gortha would not take more than necessary...

"The culling," said Gary, avoiding looking into the creature's eyes. "A sacrifice, right? Then take me and let my girl go. Please."

For a moment, the monster seemed to consider. But then it growled, "Tommy Bloody Bones don't make deals. All I see here is girlmeat, and now manmeat." A long thread of saliva dripped from its mouth.

Gary understood that there was no other way to save his daughter. He gathered all his courage and grabbed the first thing he could find, raised it high, and swung at the creature's hideous head.

But the monster's left claw darted up and blocked the blow by closing its wickedly long fingers around the improvised weapon. It pulled the femur (God! It was a bone!) from Gary's hand and cast it aside. It bounced against the tower's round walls and went clattering to the floor. The thing's jaws snapped like an alligator's, and then the creature lifted its head to the ceiling and laughed in triumph.

Behind him, Gary heard his wife scream. She had seen the Bloody Bones, too.

"Ahhhh... Womanmeat, too!" squealed the monster. "Blood-rich womanmeat!"

The Mother-Wife and the Horned Man, Gary thought. Masculine and feminine...

"Stay away from my daughter!" Courtney shrieked, and then she was inside the tower, too, standing beside Gary holding a rusted poker.

"Not seasoned yet," said the Bloody Bones. "But you will be, you soon will be..."

Courtney thrust the poker forward as if it were a sword. The rusted iron pierced the creature's flesh, and a mix of blood and pus spurted from the wound. Its foul blood drenched Beth's face, and the paralysis gripping the girl broke. She screamed, her cry mixing with the roar of pain from the monster.

Gary gathered all his courage, closed his eyes, and jumped at the Bloody Bones. He no longer felt terror, but anger, anger like when his family had abandoned him. He sank his hands into the creature's gelatinous belly, and he could feel the bones beneath the flimsy skin.

The creature yelled in rage, and its claws descended on him. A piercing pain spread through Gary's body like shrapnel as the talons dug deeply into his shoulders, and he found himself in the creature's grip. It pulled him up as if he were a ragdoll. Then the monster's jaws unhinged impossibly wide and the hideous reddish-purple tongue slithered out. It wormed its way into Gary's open mouth and...

❄ ❄ ❄

...he was inside a strange house. It was round, with a thatched roof made of straw, and there were no windows. There was a dying open-hearth fire in the middle of the floor, its dense smoke climbing up to a hole in the roof. Gary had seen something like that before. Where was it?

In Wiltshire. Yes, in Wiltshire, just before visiting Stonehenge. He and his family had explored that Iron Age replica of a Celtic hut. This was similar, but it felt real.

Someone was kneeling by the smoking embers. It was a woman, and she held something in her arms as she was desperately blowing on the cinders, trying to rekindle the fire. She was wearing a tattered, floor-length dress made of linen topped by a woolen cloak.

"Hush now," she whispered to a bundle snuggled in her arms. "Shhhh..."

Something slithered in the darkness, and as the fire flared back to life, Gary caught a glimpse of a black silhouette on the wall, behind the woman. The form kept shifting, as if trying and failing to give itself a human form. Its appendages were too long. Then too short. The head too big.

"Please, Fear Gortha..." the woman pleaded without looking at the shapeshifting shadow but somehow knowing it was there. "Leave us alone."

"I'm the Eater of Children, I can't let you be," said the guttural voice of the still-invisible creature. "I will eat your baby boy."

"Not my child, please. He's innocent!" The woman retreated to a corner and tried to hide behind rows of dangling smoked meat and fish.

"Says who?" the thing growled. "Who are you, woman, to decide who lives and who dies?"

It took shape now, right on the wall. It came out of the silhouette in all its crimson ungodliness. But it was different from the one in the tower; it looked stretched, even more emaciated, and definitely more inhuman, with what looked like tentacles sprouting from its back, and spikes—no, thorns—growing from its scaly, fish-like skin.

The baby in the woman's arms started to scream, and it sounded like Beth's scream.

"Delicious fear..." said the Bloody Bones, advancing toward the helpless mother. It unhinged its jaws and its horrible tongue darted out. It looked more like a horse penis now, purple, engorged.

"I beg you! Take me!" the woman yelled. And now Gary could see her face brightened by the reborn fire. It was the face of his own mother.

"No!" Gary screamed, but no one in the hut seemed to acknowledge his presence. He was a ghost witnessing events he could not interact with.

"I will take you. And then I'll take the baby. And your husband, and the rest of your worthless family. I will collect your bones in my dark place and lick the sweet marrow from them. I can, and I will."

Gary's mother started to cry.

"Or..." the monster continued. "...if you give up the child willingly..." The bony finger pointed at the bundle in her arms. "I will take him, but you and your dirty family will live. I will no longer hunt your breed..."

The woman seemed to hesitate, but then she stepped forward, sobbing.

"Don't! No, Mama, don't!" Gary yelled.

She kissed the crying baby and put him on the floor.

"I'm sorry... I'm so—"

The greedy hands of Fear Gortha sprung forward, eager to taste the tender meat. They grabbed the baby and greedily lifted him to its face. The jaws unhinged impossibly wide, like those of a python, and then bit down. The baby emitted one last shriek of pain before disappearing into the Bloody Bone's mouth in a bloody mess.

"Nooooo!" Gary screamed.

His mother turned her back. She had stopped crying and was now wearing an expression of acceptance. Grief. But no remorse.

"You monster," shouted Gary at the woman. "You left me! You left me!"

❄ ❄ ❄

And he was back in the tower. Bloody Bones towered above him, its disgusting tongue stuck inside his mouth.

He gagged and tried to lift his arms to pull it out, but they were pinned to his sides, held there by the monster's powerful grasp. He struggled, but he couldn't move.

Then the tongue started going deeper down his throat, and he began to choke while Bloody Bones's steely teeth came closer to his face. It was going to swallow him whole. It was going to chew on Gary's bones like it had done to the baby in his vision. He closed his eyes and waited to die.

But then he heard the creature cry out in pain.

His eyes popped open, and he saw Courtney. She had thrust the poker into one of the monster's eyes. It was now bellowing in pain. It let go of Gary and whirled around to face Courtney, the metal rod sticking out of the now-dark left eye socket. The right one shone brighter, as if trying to compensate. The fiend roared its rage at his wife and then lashed out with one of its claw-tipped hands. It ripped through her nightgown, leaving a trail of blood in its wake.

"You can't kill me!" growled Bloody Bones. "I'm immortal!"

Gary saw that Beth was now standing and watching helplessly as the terrible battle unfolded in front of her.

"Run! Beth, run!" he shouted. "Close the door and fasten it with the iron pin!"

Iron. Iron was the key. He got it now. It wouldn't kill a creature of faerie, but you could keep it at bay.

She looked at him desperately; she didn't want to leave them.

Blood gushed from his shoulder as Tommy Bloody Bones sank its fangs into his flesh. He felt bones cracking and the warm liquid soaking his shirt, then trickling down his pants.

Beth shrieked.

Courtney was holding her belly, and Gary could see glistening intestines between her fingers. She had been badly hurt. Still, there was resoluteness in her eyes. With one hand, she retrieved a small skull from the heap and threw it at the monster.

"Come over here, you bastard! I haven't finished with you yet!"

"Mom!" screamed Beth.

She turned to her daughter. "Get out! Now! You hear me? Get out now or I'll swear I'll make your ass sore!"

Beth wouldn't move.

"Listen to your mother, Beth," Gary said while collapsing onto the heap of bones.

The Fear Gortha turned toward Courtney. "I'm gonna keep you for last. I'm gonna enjoy feeding on your fear."

But there was no fear in Courtney's eyes. Gary could see it. She was fierce. She had only one thing in her mind: protecting her child. She looked at Beth one last time, smiled, and said softly, "I love you."

Then she charged. The Bloody Bones's claws slashed at her, but she ducked, then kicked the fiend right into its belly, pushing it backward. The fiend stumbled but remained on its feet; it reached for her again, and this time it got a good hold of her.

From his position on the floor, Gary could not see what the monster was doing to her, but from her screams of pain and the crunching sounds, he understood that, for Courtney, the nightmare was over.

He felt his own life abandoning him, too. He felt colder and weaker.

He summoned up the last ounce of his strength and

screamed, "Beth Ashford, get out of here! Don't let me tell you again!"

Then Bloody Bones's foot came down on his back, breaking it in two.

The last thing he saw was Beth slamming the tower's door shut.

12

Sylvan Pines Psychiatric Hospital, Hingham, Massachusetts, December 24, 2019

Beth stared out of the padded room. She saw the blinking lights of the Christmas tree in the hall and started singing.

"Tommy Bloody Bones
Steals naughty children from their homes,
Takes them to his dirty den,
And they are never seen again."

Holiday Home Invasion

Robert C. Eccles

The killer stood outside the dark house in the pre-dawn hours of Christmas morning. Every other house on the block was aglow with holiday lights. The fact that this house wasn't decorated filled the killer with rage. His grip on the knife handle tightened as he slipped through the door.

Punishment was meted out in a matter of minutes. His violent lesson was taught to the children first, then the parents. The killer reflected on his work and smiled. The red and green of blood and bile was just the sort of holiday touch the house needed.

WONDERFUL

Marc Sorondo

James Simmons had decided to kill himself. In his opinion, the part of his life worth living had long passed, and for years now, he'd been forcing himself through Hell without even being judged. He'd decided not to do it anymore.

He walked out onto the George Washington Bridge, stopping only when he was right between New York and New Jersey. He liked the idea that maybe, just maybe, there'd be problems with reporting his death because they wouldn't know which state to put on the forms.

As he walked out over the water, the Hudson wind pulling at his hair and clothes, he itemized his life, double-checking to make sure that he hadn't overlooked some good or redeemable quality, making sure that he truly did not have a reason to live anymore.

He blamed it, at least partly, on money. He'd never had much and never seemed to be able to hold on to it when he did. For James, trying to save money was like trying to hold a gust of wind: he never could hold it and couldn't ever be sure he'd really had it in the first place.

His money problems, once a problem separate and apart from the others, had tainted all the other aspects of his life. He tried not to blame it all on money. He'd heard what people said about money not buying happiness, but he'd also learned that the lack thereof could ensure that happiness kept its distance.

James leaned onto the railing, his elbows on the dirty metal, and spit out over the water, where the cold wind caught everything and pulled it away. He looked down at the water, black and glossy as polished onyx, reflecting the moonlight.

Maureen didn't love him anymore; he knew that. Sometimes he wondered if she'd ever cheated on him, but realized that, of course, she hadn't. She spent all of her time working two terrible paying jobs only to come home exhausted and sleep. She had no time for affairs. She wasn't the type anyway, James knew. Though a little part of him wanted her to be, wanted to put some of the blame for his unhappiness on Maureen for infidelity or drugs or some other terrible vice, he knew he couldn't. She was a good person...a hard worker... responsible. She'd have been better off if she'd never met James, he was sure of that.

He didn't lose her love to another man or addiction; instead, she began to see him for the waste that he was...instead, he lost her love to nothing at all.

If he died, maybe she could start over. Maybe then she could make the best of what time she had left, what time she hadn't wasted with him.

He carried a knife along with his empty wallet. He wasn't sure if he should try to make it look like a mugging gone wrong rather than a suicide. He wasn't sure if that would make the news easier or harder to accept.

"How can you be sure things would be better without you?" a voice said behind him.

James turned quickly, startled to see an older man who had somehow managed to get right behind him without his noticing. He had a thin build, a bit under six feet, with thick, gray hair and Italian features.

A car was pulled to the side of the right lane with its hazard lights flashing.

For an instant, he considered pulling the knife, but quickly realized that the old guy was no mugger…and shortly after that, he realized it would be stupid to defend himself to then kill himself.

"What are you talking about?"

"Come on. I know what you're planning to do." The old guy smiled a little.

Something about that smile made James believe that he really did know what he'd planned to do and maybe even the circumstances that had led up to that decision.

"What makes you so sure that this would be a better world without you in it?"

"If you knew me better…" James started.

"I know enough," the old man said, flashing a smile that made James think of Hollywood…classic Hollywood. It was the smile a leading man would have smiled in an old black-and-white movie.

"Yeah, well…it couldn't be any worse without me."

"What if I said I could show you?"

"Oh, man…alright, old-timer. Save the Christmas movie bullshit for someone else."

"Do you really think killing yourself will give Maureen a chance to...'start over.' That it'll wipe the slate clean and she'll just pick up and move on over to Park Avenue?"

James's mouth moved as he searched for something to say.

"You're completely broke, and you've got some of the worst life insurance in existence...which, by the way, won't pay a dime if you kill yourself. What does your death offer her? Hmmm...aside from a chance to go through a fairly miserable life completely alone?"

"How could you possibly know—"

"I just know. And like I've already said, I can show you, if you'd like. You can make sure that you are making an educated decision in knifing yourself and jumping off the bridge."

"Alright...show me." He couldn't believe he'd said it, couldn't believe that even part of him actually expected to see, that he believed the old nut.

The old man extended his hand. "Name's Lou," he said. "Let's get moving."

James shook Lou's hand and followed him to his car, a mundane sedan painted a light blue that looked silver in the light from the bridge.

As the occasional late-night commuter drove past, flashing angry looks at the hazards on the sedan, Lou walked around to the driver's side door, apparently fearless even as angry drivers whizzed past in sports cars and SUVs that would spray him all over the asphalt if they hit him.

"Get in," Lou said, carelessly throwing open his own door as wide as the hinges would allow. He slid into the seat and waited a moment before pulling the door closed.

James got in, feeling like he never should have let the old loon stop him, like he should have just jumped and ended the whole mess already.

There was a faint scent of cheap air-freshener, something floral, along with the musty, ash smell of a smoker's car.

"So where would you like to go?" Lou asked pleasantly. He pulled a box of Marlboro's from the center console and popped one into his mouth.

James sat, staring at the old guy, not answering his question.

Lou held out the pack, offering.

"No, thanks. I quit a long time ago. Too expensive."

"Alright then...let's hear it. Where are we going?" Lou insisted. He started to fiddle with the radio, scanning stations too quickly for James to hear what was on them.

"Home, I guess," James finally answered.

Lou stopped abruptly on a station playing Frank Sinatra. "Chairman of the board," he said with a smile that held his cigarette clamped between his teeth. "Two seventeen Central, coming right up."

"That's not my address," James said. "I'm on Main. Three forty-six. Shouldn't you know that?"

"Three forty-six Main," Lou said with a smoky exhale. "Whatever you say."

"Why don't you know my address if you know so much about me?" James asked. Now that they were in the car, that he was, in a sense, in Lou's control, he was getting nervous. He knew he shouldn't worry. Hell, he was about to kill himself anyway. What could this old guy do that was any worse?

"There are worse things," Lou said, looking at him from the corner of his eye. He blew smoke toward the slightly opened window. "But I'm telling you the truth. I just want to show you how things would be if you'd never been born."

"Yeah, I'm familiar with the premise," James said as the car turned off Route 46 and onto Main Street. "I watch it once a year in December."

Lou slowed and pulled the car over. "Three forty-six," he announced.

James opened the door and extended his right leg. "You're not coming?"

"I'll wait here. Go check it out, and when you're done, I'll take you wherever else you want to go."

James shrugged and got out of the car. He ran up a few familiar steps and slid his key into the front door. He turned the knob with the key, waiting for the door to stick. The door stuck every time, had since they'd first moved in, and he'd always meant to fix it.

The door swung open with a slight creak, but smoothly, without the slightest resistance.

James walked in and was greeted by pale yellow walls rather than the light green he'd expected. Photos lined the walls, every one of a stranger.

"Billy? Is that you?" a woman's voice called from the kitchen.

James panicked, stepped backward out the door, and pulled it closed. He hopped down the few front steps in one leap and got into Lou's car as fast as he could.

"Either you're not crazy, or I am," James said.

Lou sat there smiling at him, the car's engine idling. The front door of 346 Main Street opened, and a tall, older woman with dark hair and graying roots peeked her head out and scanned the street before spotting the blue sedan and the two men in it.

"Shit. Get us out of here," James ordered.

"Sure. Where to?" Lou asked nonchalantly.

"Just hurry before she calls the cops."

"Okay. Where would you like to go?"

James tried to remember the address Lou had mentioned earlier and found that he couldn't. So he said his mother's address, that of his childhood home. "Seventy-four Park Street."

The house was only a few blocks away, and Lou treated speed limits like suggestions. They reached the house in seconds.

Although it was clearly the right address, according to its positioning and the gold "74" that hung against the white backdrop of the front door, the house was not the one in which he'd grown up.

What had once been a small, 1950s style split-level was now a huge home that dwarfed the small plot of suburban property on which it'd been built. Though James could see aspects of the old house shining through (the big window in the front that looked out on his mother's flower garden; the porch that curved from the front door around the left-hand corner and toward the back of the house), this home was three floors and extended out into what had been the side yard when he'd been growing up. At the front, right-hand corner was an octagonal addition that James could see through a window was home to a huge tree covered in gold lights and silver decorations. Two white columns spiraled in gold garland framed the door.

"What the hell?" James said to himself as he walked up the concrete path that led through the landscaped front yard to the door. He ascended the two steps to the front door slowly, unable to shake the idea that he'd finally snapped and he was imagining all of this.

James tried his key and found it didn't work. He rang the bell and waited, glancing briefly over his shoulder at Lou, who sat in the idling car mouthing the words to some Tony Bennett song that could barely be heard where James stood. He waved at James through the smoke that filled the car and seeped out of its cracked-open windows.

"What am I doing?" James whispered to himself. Then he

heard the thump of approaching feet. His mother must have been feeling good today; her steps were quicker than they'd been in years.

The lock clicked, and the door opened.

It was his mother, but it wasn't. She wore a bright blouse and pants with a tropical print. She was a good 40 pounds lighter than his mother and had long hair pulled back in a braid.

"Ma? What the hell is going on?" James blurted out.

"Excuse me?" she said, sliding over a bit to position the door in between them as much as possible.

"Mom?" James ventured.

"I'm sorry. You must be mistaken."

"Mom, it's me."

"You've got the wrong house," she said, louder.

"Honey! Something wrong?!" a sturdy male voice called from upstairs. More footsteps came from above.

"Who the hell is that?" James asked, forcing himself through the hardly opened door.

"Honey?" the voice called again. It was close now.

And then, as if it took her a moment to realize James had forced his way into the house, his mother screamed.

The footsteps from upstairs came faster now, and James headed up to meet them. He only made it up the first few steps before a man reached the landing above him.

"Dad?" James asked, his voice starting to waver

It hit him like a gunshot to the belly. He couldn't breathe for a moment. His father…alive.

"I don't know who the hell you are, but you'd better get out of here before the cops show up," he screamed. He pointed to his wife, telling her to call 9-1-1 with an angry gesture.

"But…dad?" James said again.

"Listen, pal. I can see your confused, and I feel bad, I really do, but I've got one son, and you're not him…so you'd better leave."

"You don't understand," James said.

"Get out now!" his father screamed while pointing at the still-open front door.

James slowly walked to the door. It slammed shut just as he passed through it, and he could hear the deadbolt slide home behind him.

He walked back to the car and got in.

"What's the matter?" Lou asked.

"My dad's alive…my mom's healthy…their house…my old house…" James said.

"That was never your house," Lou corrected. "You've never had a home. You've never been born. You don't exist here."

"What happened? How is my dad…"

"Not dead with a chunk of cancer in his brain?"

James turned to scowl at Lou.

"Hey, don't get offended. You can't get offended. It never happened now," Lou said.

"But why didn't it happen? It's not like I gave him cancer."

"Long story short," Lou started, "you were never born. Thus, your younger brother Henry was an only child. The few resources your parents had, as well as all of their attention, went to him. Thus his grades were better. The scholarships from those grades and your ex-parents' savings got Henry through college. He got himself through law school. Henry is, in this reality, one of the most well-known legal figures on the east coast, so you can imagine the kind of money he makes. He wanted to buy your parents a big new home, but they couldn't bear to leave 'their home,' so he built it up for them and let them retire early. He made sure they saw the best doctors, so your father's cancer was caught early, before it could spread, and treated effectively."

Lou stopped for a moment, and then added, "Oh, and he's sending them to Hawaii for Christmas."

James stared up at the huge house. Then sirens became audible.

"Oops, my least favorite people are coming. Where to now?"

James couldn't think. He just stared up at that huge house. He hated it. It represented everything that his parents would have enjoyed if they'd only never had him.

"You did want to see, didn't you? You did want to be sure that the world would be better without you, right?" Lou asked.

"It wasn't supposed to be..." James said.

"Says who? Come on, what else do you want to see?"

James was torn between Henry and Maureen. Then he decided, "Take me to Hank's house." He was going to apologize to his brother, even though he wasn't his brother anymore. He'd apologize and tell him how proud he was. Even though Hank would think he was crazy, even though he wouldn't recognize him, James felt it was something he had to do.

Then he would kill himself. He'd do it here, to let this better world go on without his influence to ruin it for the few people he'd ever cared about.

"Not your wife?" Lou asked as he pulled slowly away. The lights on the police cars were visible in the rearview mirror as they rounded the corner at the end of the block and sped toward number 74.

"No." He couldn't bare it. Seeing his parents was bad enough. He couldn't stand to see how much better Maureen had turned out without him. He had loved her, and sometimes he still did. Convincing himself that the woman he loved would be better off without him was bad enough, but knowing it as fact…

"You know, if I'm going to be honest with you in this, if I'm going to actually let you see how things would be without you, there's something I should tell you about Maureen."

"No. I'm sure she's better off without me, too."

"That's the thing…" Lou started.

"She's not better off?"

"She is, I just think you might…"

"No," James said. "I don't want to know. She's happier this way. They all are. I just want to see my brother. Then we're done."

"So…you still planning on doing it?" Lou asked.

James looked out the window silently.

"Oh-kay," Lou said. He played with the radio again. James was just about to say that he couldn't bare another Italian crooner when Lou stopped on "Under My Thumb" by the Stones.

"Love the Stones," Lou said. His smile had returned. "They may be my favorite band."

James sighed. "Wouldn't have thought that before, with the Sinatra and stuff," he said, his gaze never leaving the window.

"What can I say, I've got eclectic tastes," Lou said. He slid another cigarette from the bright red pack and placed it between his lips. He lit it and took a long, slow pull. "Sure you don't want one?" he asked with a smile.

James thought about how hard it had been to quite all those years ago. How he'd managed not to take even a single drag in over ten years. He thought about going through the hell of quitting all over again.

Just as James was about to decline, Lou said, "You don't exist, and you're going to kill yourself anyway. What's a smoke going to hurt?"

James snatched one out of the pack and lit it. He coughed for a few seconds, but then the nicotine hit him, caressed his nerves like an old lover, eased his tension and his mind like an opiate.

"Fucking missed these," James said. "Every day, for years, I've missed them."

"So have them," Lou said, grinning at him. He inhaled, and the smoldering cigarette cast a red glow in his eyes. "Think of this as an opportunity. Why should they all get this chance at happiness and you don't?"

"What?"

"Think of the possibilities you have before you right now. You've been faithful to your wife through the whole mess of your marriage; you're going to honestly tell me you've never wanted to have sex with another woman?"

"Are you serious?" James asked. "Are you kidding? The whole reason everyone I care about is happy right now is because I wasn't around to fuck it all up for them. You think..."

Lou's grin changed but never for a moment left. "Don't get so pissy. Just think about it...that's all. I've let you tread where you don't belong, and that makes you a very powerful man here."

"You listen..."

"Two seventeen Central," Lou announced, cutting James off as he slammed on the brakes. He stopped in front of a huge house, a building that James thought should be called an estate or a manor.

Lou had stopped the car at the edge of Henry's property, between the two entrances to a large circular driveway. A marble lion crouched just to the side of the car on the picture-perfect lawn inside the asphalt semicircle.

"Now that's just tacky," Lou said. "Guy makes a few million and he wants a marble menagerie on his property."

That was nothing compared to the roman columns that stood like sentries before the front entrance to the house, holding up a large balcony that James assumed led off some lavish master bedroom.

The whole house was littered with elements of classical architecture. There was even a stained glass window depicting the birth of Athena from the forehead of Zeus over the balcony.

"Talk about money changing you," Lou said.

James grinned. "Hank was into Kiss growing up. He painted his face black and white every year on Halloween. His idea of artwork had been band posters and pin-ups. How could this be the same guy?"

"He's not," Lou said. "You don't totally seem to be getting that."

"I get it. It's just hard to."

James got out of the car and, running the tips of his fingers over the cool marble surface of the crouched lion as he passed it, headed for the front door.

Upon reaching the door, he found himself fighting an urge to turn back. He didn't know what good it would do him to see Hank. It was a sad attempt at getting some closure, he knew, but he would say his piece. He would apologize for ruining a life that no longer existed in a past that was imaginary everywhere but in his own mind.

James pressed the doorbell and listened to an unfamiliar tune played by the struck chimes.

The moment he waited seemed to drag out, accompanied by the fading tone of the doorbell's final note.

Then the door opened.

And it was Maureen who'd opened it. Maureen as she'd been when they'd first fallen in love, before life had gotten a hold of her and beaten her. Before he'd come into her life to ruin it. There were no crows' feet or bags under her eyes. Her face, as well as her body, was slim and firm and youthful.

Then she smiled at him, a bit perplexed, and it broke his heart.

"Maureen?" It came out more as a sad declaration than a question.

She continued to smile, but James could see on her face that she was trying to place him, to come up with his name or a recollection of why she should know him.

"I'm sorry. I'm usually good at this. How do I know you, Mister…?"

A voice in James's head screamed, *You don't know me?! I'm your husband!* It wasn't his own voice, but it was a familiar one.

"Um, James, and you don't, technically. I was looking for Hank, and…" James said.

Maureen laughed, and the sound of it made James want to throw up.

"I don't think I've ever heard anyone other than Henry's parents call him that."

"Oh…that's what I've always called him," James said.

"Well, he worked late tonight. He's got a big trial coming up. But he's on his way home, if you want to wait for him. He called a few minutes ago and said he was close."

"Sure," James said after a pause. "I guess that'll work."

Maureen stepped aside from the doorway, and James entered through a cloud of her perfume. It was a scent that he'd never associated with her: a light, sweet smell in no way similar to the cheap perfume she'd always worn.

"Would you like a cup of coffee?" she asked, already heading for the kitchen down the hall.

James followed her, scanning her from head to toe, amazed by the shape of her body under the jeans and t-shirt she was wearing. She was built like a 20-year-old.

"So how do you know Henry?" she asked as she entered the kitchen.

"I've known him since we were kids," James said, truthfully enough. "But I haven't seen him in...god. He's probably unrecognizable now."

"It's bittersweet, isn't it?" She smiled again. "To go home again, but see it's so different?"

"Painful," James muttered.

"How have we never met before? You weren't at our wedding, Mister James?"

"Oh, James is my first name." That hurt. "I hadn't seen Hank in so long at that point, and I was going through a few...things."

"Hmmm...that's too bad. Cream and sugar?"

"Please. Actually, could I use your bathroom before the coffee?"

"Of course. Second door on the left, back the way we came in."

James thanked her again and hurried to the bathroom. He splashed cold water on his face. "How are they together?" he whispered to himself. He fought the urge to cry and then the urge to vomit.

Think about it, the same voice in his head started. He recognized it this time. It was Lou's. *You met her because her mother and your mother were friends and you two were about the same age. With you out of the picture, she went with Henry...the rest is obvious.*

James shook his head.

You think she could never think of your brother that way? You think she never did? You think she didn't find him attractive, didn't fantasize about him?

James splashed more water on his face.

He couldn't figure out how things had gone so wrong,

how he'd become such a stain on everyone else's lives.

You got screwed, that's how. Some people just get dealt shitty hands in life, and you, my friend, were dealt a hand like a foot.

James turned off the water, wiped his face on a yellow decorative towel, and headed back for the kitchen.

James found Maureen sitting at the kitchen table, a steaming cup of coffee in front of her and another opposite her.

"Okay?" she said, flashing him a smile as he sat across from her.

"Fine," he said. He tried to flash her a smile in return, but it felt more like a snarl to him. "I've just had a very long day."

"The trip itself? Traffic?"

"No. I'm actually here on business." James interrupted himself for a quick sip of coffee. "But the business part of the trip isn't working out so well."

"I'm sorry to hear that."

"I was hoping that seeing Hank would help. He's become so successful in the years since we've fallen out of touch, I thought seeing a real happy ending would do me some good."

Maureen blushed, and it was angelic. "Wow. That's kind of sweet. I never thought of our life as such a happy ending before…not that we're not happy," she stumbled, "just that I never think of it as an ending…still a work in progress."

Maybe she's got doubts, Lou's voice said in his mind like a conscience. *Not so happy after all?*

James leaned in toward Maureen. "Can I ask you something?" he whispered.

"Sure," she whispered back, grinning impishly. She leaned in as well.

"Do you still love him?"

"Of course I do," she laughed.

"Have you always? Never doubted?"

"We've had rough patches. Every marriage does, but I've always known he was the right man for me. Why do you ask?"

James closed his eyes for a moment and heard echoes from Maureen's marriage in his life, his reality, the one he'd ruined. He heard her crying...heard her sobbing...and when he finally had silence, he knew he heard her acceptance, acceptance that it was ruined, acceptance that it was too late.

Maureen reached out and put her hand on his, gave it a gentle squeeze, and asked, "Are you sure you're all right?"

James opened his eyes, and a tear rolled down his cheek. "I love you. No matter how bad things got, I always have."

Maureen's concern fell apart into confusion. She pulled her hand away. "I don't understand."

"Some part of me always thought you were the only thing I'd gotten right. Somewhere, deep down, I thought you'd been the one thing I did right, even if the rightness didn't last. I should have told you once in a while, I guess..."

"James," she interrupted.

"But now I find out that you were the biggest mistake of all." He reached out to grab her hand, but she pulled it away before he'd reached it.

She stood from her stool, took a step back, never taking her frightened eyes from him.

"I ruined you." James wiped at his eyes.

"I think you should go."

"No. I wasn't trying to scare you... I wasn't even looking for you. I wanted to see Hank...to tell him I was sorry, and..."

"You should leave," Maureen said.

He stood and took a step toward her. She matched it with a step back.

"Don't be scared. I'm not crazy, it's just..."

"Get out!" she screamed. The way she screamed, the stern,

angry way she'd screamed those words made him think of his father screaming the very same thing.

Your dead father, Lou whispered musically in his head. *And this is supposed to be your wife. What's left for you when you don't exist, Jimmy?*

"You'd better leave before Henry gets home. He'll be here soon, and if he sees you scaring me..."

James felt his entire universe compressing, all existence as he'd known it being crushed into the infinitesimally small, and then further, into nothing at all.

He stepped toward Maureen again, and she stepped back, backing herself up against the refrigerator.

Her eyes darted to the left.

James knew she was planning to dash to the side and run, probably screaming, from the house.

He reached out and snatched her arm.

Now the real screaming began. The volume of it hit James in the face like a slap.

He grabbed her throat with his free hand and squeezed, just hard enough to quiet her, to make her voice raspy and small. It was still loud enough, he thought, to be heard by neighbors or someone walking past.

He brought his other hand from her arm to her throat and squeezed with both.

Now she was silent. She scratched at his face with her manicured nails, aiming for his eyes but just tearing into his forehead, his cheeks.

She was getting weak, her legs wobbling before finally giving out.

James guided her body gently to the floor, and, looming over her, continued to squeeze, to hold down the scream that still wanted to come.

She clawed at his face again, gouging away skin.

Blood from his wounds dripped onto her face, into her bulging, open eyes.

"You love me," James said. "You love *me*." He repeated it again and again. He wanted to cry, to weep, but he wouldn't let himself. The drops of falling blood would have to serve as his tears.

And then it was over. Her face, which had slowly turned pink and then red, turned a purplish-blue. Her struggling stopped. The pressure of a scream fighting to escape left her throat.

"You love me," he said a final time. An unwelcome tear fell and mixed with his blood on her face.

James heard a key engage the lock on the front door.

He looked quickly around and headed left, the way Maureen had tried to go, into the dining room.

Henry Simmons, in an expensive suit, smiling an expensive smile, walked into his house and was greeted with the sight of his wife's feet on the floor, the rest of her body obscured by the kitchen table. He dropped his briefcase and was already running down the hall when it hit the floor with a soft thud.

He dropped hard to his knees on the tile floor of the kitchen, his hands hovering over Maureen's body as if he worried touching her would do more damage. He finally put his hand to her cheek but quickly pulled it away when he felt how cold it was.

James could see Henry kneeling over her, saw the tears fall from his eyes and patter onto her t-shirt. Then all of a sudden Hank started fumbling in his pocket. James looked around and grabbed the first sturdy object that he could find: a small candlestick off the dining room table.

James stepped into the threshold between the kitchen and dining room just as Henry pulled a cell phone from his pocket.

"I'm sorry, Hank," James said monotonously. But he wasn't...not anymore. He'd been dealt a downright shitty hand. It hadn't been his fault.

As Henry's gaze reached his face, James snarled and brought the candlestick down on Henry's forehead.

Henry fell, but immediately starting moaning and pushing himself back up.

"You bastard," he mumbled as he drooled onto the tile next to Maureen. "Killed her..." He sobbed now. "...bastard."

James hit him again, in the back of the head, and Henry dropped face-first onto the tile.

Henry's right hand lashed out, clutching James's pants, gripping them with more strength than James's brother had ever had.

"Maureen..." Henry sobbed quietly, his face still against the tile.

James could hear it in Henry's lament, some quality to his dying words that revealed that he was already dead, had been since he'd felt her lifeless cheek...something that gave away that they'd been in love, that they had been the right match and one couldn't go on without the other.

James heard this...and it mocked him. It insulted his very existence.

"Ruined..." James said. He brought the candlestick down on Henry's head, smashing it against the tile. Then again. The third time James heard a crack. Either Henry's skull or the tile beneath it had broken.

James shook off the now-loose hand clutching his pant leg and dropped the candlestick to the floor.

His fingerprints and blood were everywhere, but he could care less. He didn't exist here. His files and records were on the other side of the bridge.

He walked outside, closing the door behind him, and saw

the light blue sedan idling right where he'd left it. The windows were down, and light gray tobacco smoke drifted from them. He could hear music faintly but could not recognize the song.

He got in the car and immediately took a cigarette from Lou's pack and lit it.

Smiling as always, Lou said, "Well, you've looked better."

"Fuck you," James said, the cigarette dangling from between his lips.

Lou chuckled. "That's the spirit. I knew there was still some life left in you."

James took a deep drag, deep enough to burn his lungs.

"So what's next, Jimmy? You want to kill your parents?" Lou asked as he changed gear from Park to Drive. "Burn a school full of kids? Blow up a building? There's a pretty good president right now. Up for an assassination?"

"I don't know."

"Well, what do you know?" Lou asked. He turned up the volume on the radio. The song James couldn't make out earlier was Led Zepplin's version of *When the Levee Breaks*.

James smiled, cigarette smoke rising and curling around his bloody face before being sucked out the car window. He looked at Lou, took another huge drag, and said, "I'll ruin everything. It seems that's what I do."

Smiling, drumming his fingers on the steering wheel to the slow beat of the song, Lou drove out into the night, toward whatever was coming next.

Twisted Wishes

Lori Safranek

Ted's head hurt like a bitch. He'd heard his mom say that a hundred times, but now he understood. She'd always been recovering from a hangover, but he couldn't figure out why his brain was thumping and jostling around in his head.

He'd been sleeping so deeply, then he woke up with a jolt, like waking up from one of those dreams where you're falling, and suddenly, with a violent jerk, you're in your own bed, not sure if maybe you've died. In that few seconds of shock, you expect broken bones, a shattered skull, or maybe even a couple burst organs. Then you blink and no, you're fine. It had just been a bad dream.

Ted blinked, but all he saw was blackness. For a heartbeat,

he thought he'd gone blind until he saw a tiny ray of light above him. In a panic, he thrust an arm out, hoping to reach a light switch. He flailed for a bit, then his hand hit something hard. Ted ran his hand over the cardboard, not finding a light source or anything else. A search by his left hand found more cardboard and his heart sank. He tried to sit up and struck his forehead on more cardboard.

He tried thinking, figuring out why he was in a cardboard box. His pounding headache and frantic terror choked out reasonable thought. His hands scrambled over the three walls surrounding him, then behind him, finding nothing. Abruptly he sensed the box sliding sideways.

He screamed as he slammed into one side, then the other before the box steadied. As Ted gulped air like a fish out of water, something squeaked horribly, followed by a metallic clank.

"What's happening? Help me!" Ted shouted.

"Whoever's bellyaching back here, knock it off. I got a schedule to keep," a male voice boomed. "You'll be where you're going soon enough."

Ted heard something being moved, the same sound his box had made. Was it more cardboard boxes? What kind of mess had he woken up to?

The squeak split the air again, followed by the same clank.

"You might as well be quiet, you know," a feminine voice called out. "You're the answer to someone's wish, and you have no choice in the matter. It's a done deal."

"A wish?" Ted shouted. "I'm not a wish! I'm a person, for Christ's sake. Why am I in a box? And who the hell are you?"

A swarm of laughter slipped inside the box with Ted. He punched the wall angrily. "Stop laughing, damn it! What's going on?"

"Ah, stop your squawking." The voice reminded him of

someone, an older man, someone he'd loved, and it calmed him somewhat. "You're not in danger. We're all in the same boat. Or truck, I should say."

"Why am I in a damned truck, then?"

"Because you're on your way to whoever wished for you," the man said. "Probably someone you know, and they missed you so much they wished you'd come back. Hard to say until you get there."

"Are you talking about Santa? Santa Claus is sending me to someone? That's…ridiculous."

Laughter filled his box again. "Of course not. Santa's not real. Wishes, they're real," the feminine voice said. "Wishes come true. Ask Santa for a pony, and see how far that gets you."

"You're panicking, and it won't do you any good," the older man said. "We're all in the same boat, you know."

"No, I don't know!" Ted shouted. "I woke up in this box, in the dark, with no idea of what's going on. Don't tell me to calm down."

The older man cleared his throat. "Young man, you were sleeping for a long time. Now someone has wished for you to come back to them. Their wish has been granted. You're in a box, in a mail truck, being delivered to that person. It's not that difficult to understand."

Ted sighed deeply and closed his eyes again. With any luck, he'd fall back into the perfect, silent dream he'd been living in for months. The last thing he remembered before today was a lot of chaos, a child's sobs, and then the peaceful sleep.

Cold raised goose bumps on his arms. He rubbed them briskly, and they warmed up a bit. His legs didn't seem to be cold. He tried to pull one leg high enough so he could feel it. He groped around the box and couldn't find his legs.

"Oh, my God! My legs are gone!"

Someone sighed. "Sorry, buddy, but it happens sometimes. Wishes are not easily controlled, so sometimes we don't come back the way we used to be," he said. "And don't worry so much. It's just for a couple days."

"A couple days, without my legs?" Ted's voice quivered on the edge of hysteria. "Who the hell cut off my legs?"

"Probably the person who wished for you. They might want to get you back so they can help you."

"Oh, that's fantastic," Ted said. "Someone cut my freaking legs off and now I'm going back to them. Why, so they can cut my head off next?"

"Oh, no. That seldom happens."

Ted clutched the sides of his head and wept. He'd never felt so hopeless, and he still had to face the fiend who cut off his legs. He didn't think he was strong enough to endure that.

The vehicle slowed and then stopped. The screech sounded again, and then the doors thudded open. Ted felt his box rising in the air.

"Now, listen to me," the mailman said. He sounded close. "You gotta stop talking. It's only two days until Christmas. Then you'll see what happens. Most likely it will be over soon. These people wish for things they really shouldn't wish for. They'll get tired of you, send you back, and you can rest in peace again. But if you keep making noise, you'll screw up the timeline. This is not your choice, you know. It's a wish, and wishes are beyond our control."

Ted's mind was still reeling. He'd been dead, he was sure of that. He'd thought it was over, and he'd been okay with that. His life had been tough, and he'd been weary at the end. The sleep had felt so good.

He slid to the bottom of the box as the mailman placed

his box on a dolly, or so he assumed. He shifted around the box several times as the mailman transported him. When the movement stopped, he heard someone say, "Yes?"

"A delivery, ma'am."

"Oh, thank you. Must be from the in-laws for my little boy. Could you possibly bring it inside?"

"Of course," the mailman said. Ted felt the thump as his box was dropped. "Right under the Christmas tree okay, ma'am?"

"That's great. Happy Holidays."

A door slammed, and he thought about yelling to get the woman's attention. Then he remembered what the mailman had told him. It was better to stay quiet.

He was lying on his side now, just like he'd always slept. In spite of his bruises and pain, this thought comforted him. He took a deep breath and smelled something so familiar. A dog was sniffing his box. Things just kept getting better.

Gratefully, he slid back into sleep. When he woke up, he had no idea how much time had passed. He hated not knowing if it was daytime or night. Mostly, he resented not knowing where he was. His memory wasn't working. Some scents seemed familiar. Food was cooking. The dog was snoring.

Something slammed against the top of his box, and it slid sideways. Ted smelled sweat, bad breath, and dirty feet. The pungent odors brought on flashes of the past. It was a little boy named Brandon. Ted gasped. Brandon was the one who had hurt him!

They'd been friends at first. They'd had sleepovers, sharing peanut butter sandwiches and watching movies. They'd gone on adventures. Then Brandon had run out of things to break in his bedroom. That's when Ted's life became hell on earth.

"Ha! I know this is what I wished for!" Brandon whispered.

"I know Santa's not real, but wishes are real. Grandpa told me so. He said if I found a ladybug, to say, "Ladybug, ladybug, fly away home. Your house is on fire and your children are alone." And I did it this summer, and I also was real good all year, and my wish came true."

Ted clenched his jaw. He'd been good? He must have changed dramatically in the time Ted had been asleep. He remembered a naughty boy who had spent a lot of time breaking things with unending enthusiasm. Break the new toy car, break Ted's toys, rip apart the new pillows Mom had put on his bed, and then give the poor dog a smack on the head. Ted began to fear for his life.

He suddenly slammed into the cardboard wall, then rebounded and hit the opposite side. The boy must be trying to shake his box.

"Weird, I can't tell what's inside. It's heavy," he said. "But that's okay. I know what it is. I better get out of here before Mom catches me."

Ted's box got one last kick. Every joint in his body hurt. Not his legs of course. Someone—Ted was pretty sure he knew who now—had taken his legs. The boy had thrown a tantrum and had taken out his anger on Ted. He took some deep breaths and was soon asleep again.

Throughout the next few hours, he heard snippets of the family's life. He heard the boy, and Mom and Dad, then the voice of a young girl. He remembered Megan, a little blonde who smelled nice. He also heard the rustle of gift-wrapping, Mom pouring the kids a glass of milk to have with cookies, and they all talked about what they hoped Santa would bring them. Even Dad was hoping for a video game from Santa. Ridiculous. Why don't they admit they just want their greedy little wishes granted? That Mom and Dad had spent hours and half the family budget making sure everyone got what they wanted for Christmas. Were they really that deluded that they enjoyed the excesses of gift giving and opening gifts? Why not go to the store and buy what they wanted?

Ted had never liked holidays. Either they involved spending a lot of money, or it was loud with fireworks, or noisy like New Year's Eve. Waste of time, all of them. Days were pretty much the same, in his experience. Today could be tomorrow and Wednesday could be Sunday, for all he cared.

That reminded him of how tired of living he had been. He'd been young, barely out of elementary school, but he had been worn out. He'd greeted the sweet sleep of death with open arms.

Damn that kid, wishing for him and waking him from his well-deserved rest. Ted stretched as much as he could in the close confines of the cardboard box. How big was this box, anyway? The kid had seemed to have trouble picking it up, so it must be quite large.

Later, Mom and Dad told the children to get to bed so Santa could come. It seemed to Ted that it took hours before the kids finally quieted down. Ted trembled thinking of the morning ahead. What new torture had Brandon imagined for him? Before he'd torn off Ted's legs, the boy had kicked him, he'd punched him, and at the end, he'd even cut him with a sharp knife he'd stolen from the kitchen. Ted had quit trying to hide the bruises from his own mom, but he shouldn't have bothered. His mom hadn't cared. The family let him stay at their house whenever she needed a "break," and that meant he was there half his life.

Brandon's parents had scolded their son and patched Ted up as well as they could. He became fearful and spent much of his time with the boy hiding under Brandon's bed. Brandon must have found other victims, and Ted had grown hopeful. Inevitably, the day had come when Brandon remembered his old pal, Ted. Ted shuddered. That had been the worst day of his life. He didn't remember everything, but he knew he'd ended up sleeping.

In the morning, the thundering feet of the children woke Ted from a troubled sleep. Brandon insisted on opening Ted's box first. As he ripped open the lid, he shouted with happiness. Ted blinked in the harsh light and wrinkled his nose at the nasty little boy smells.

Mom screamed.

Dad said, "What the hell? Where did that thing come from? Megan, go to your room."

Megan stayed where she was, her eyes fixed on Ted.

Mom was crying. Sniffling, she said, "Well, it came in the mail. I thought it was from your family"

Brandon poked Ted in the stomach. He leaned over the edge of the box and shook him.

"Hmm, I thought he'd come back with his legs," the boy mused. "But that's okay. My wish came true. I told you it would."

Dad said, "This is impossible. Impossible. Ted died."

Brandon pulled Ted's hair sharply. "Not anymore. I wished for Ted to be alive again. I missed playing with him."

"Playing," Mom whispered. "He said he played with Ted. God help us." Dropping her head into her hands, she sobbed.

Dad stood. "Well, it's going back where it came from, mister. This is atrocious."

"Dad! No! I wished for him, just like Grandpa told me to," Brandon said. "I should get to keep him. It's not fair!"

He started bawling like a baby.

"I hate Christmas! I hate you, Dad! You ruin everything!" And he ran from the room.

Dad sighed. "Well, great. Now he's going to need ten years of therapy to get over Dad ruining Christmas."

Mom said, "And we're all going to need years of therapy after seeing half a dead body under the fucking Christmas tree. Our son is insane. We knew it when Ted died. Now..."

Dad hugged her, and they looked sadly at the damaged young boy. She shivered. "Poor, sweet boy."

They sat for a moment, pondering the young bolt of lightning they'd brought into this world. He struck any time, any where, and even sometimes struck the same place twice. They couldn't keep up with his messes, or his tantrums. When he'd cut off the legs of his best friend, they'd been appalled at the viciousness. They never found the missing legs.

It had taken all Dad's intellect to come up with a story for the police and Ted's mother. He had dragged the corpse to the railroad tracks and claimed the boy had wandered outside in the night and been hit by a train. A boy like Ted, no one cared enough to doubt Dad's story. Ted was buried, and his mom moved out of town.

The last year had been hard for Brandon, since his grandfather died. Grandpa could control him, but he gave him some strange ideas. Wishes was the worst lesson he'd taught their son. "Just wish, be a good boy, and you'll get what you want."

They couldn't count the number of wishes the boy made that went unfulfilled. He wished it would snow, but it didn't. He wished they'd go to Disneyworld, but they didn't. Every day, it seemed, he came up with a new wish. The most indulgent parents couldn't have made his wishes come true.

And every unfulfilled wish came with days of tantrums and destruction. Mom kept a close watch on Megan, fearing Brandon would take out his rage on the child. So far, they'd been lucky. Ted had been the only fatality.

"So who do you think sent this?" the wife asked, absent-mindedly stroking Ted's hair.

"Had to be your sister."

She narrowed her eyes at him. "My sister dug up this a boy from his grave and mailed it to Brandon? Seriously?"

He shrugged. "Okay, then who?"

"I knew we should have put it in the garbage," Mom said glumly. Ted's heart sank. That would have been better?

They sat in silence as Megan played quietly with her new toys. She was such a sweet child.

Brandon came thumping back into the room. "I want my presents." He stuck out his lower lip defiantly.

"Well, go ahead and open them," Dad said. He'd give him anything to keep him away from poor Ted's body. "It's Christmas after all."

Brandon ripped and tore and tossed gifts over his shoulder. When all the presents were open, he went back to Ted, his childhood friend. He reached out and gently touched the boy's cheek. Tears filled Mom's eyes, but Dad was unsurprised when the touch turned into a hard slap. "Brandon!"

Mom sobbed again and little Megan laughed.

"I'm glad you're back, Ted. I made up a new game for us to play." His laugh sent a chill down his mother's back. Tears flowed down Ted's face. It was all too much to bear.

She clutched her husband's arm, and they fled to the kitchen. Dad came back and told them to go to their rooms.

"Okay, Dad," they said in unison. Dad return to the kitchen to calm Mom down.

Megan, from the corner of her eye, saw the boy's face.

She lunged toward her brother and pushed him away from the box.

"He's mine now!" she shouted. "You'll just hurt him. He's staying in my room from now on."

Brandon wasn't used to his sister standing up to him. He sat gaping at her. Dad began to take Megan away from the box, but the angelic-appearing little girl bared her teeth at him.

"He's mine! I wished for him, too," she said.

Brandon looked torn. Should he give in or should he reclaim his prize? He'd wished for Teddy to come back. It wasn't fair.

He stepped closer to her, the sweet-faced blonde in her snowflake-dotted nightgown. She didn't flinch. Mom and Dad were still in the kitchen. Brandon would deal with his sister.

He grabbed the box and tugged on it, but she held fast. He leaned in, and she grabbed his arm, pulling him closer. She frowned and shook her head.

"He's mine now. I wished on a ladybug, too, and I wished harder than you, Brandon," she hissed. An unsettling smile darkened her face. "You killed him once, but if you touch him again, I'll hurt you. I'll hurt you bad."

Brandon wanted to laugh in her face, but the wild look in her eyes made him step back. "I don't want the stupid guy anyway. I remember how whiny he was. And he doesn't have any legs." He fled into the kitchen to his parents.

Megan smiled to herself and leaned over the edge of the box. She crooned to Ted. "Aww, poor Teddy. I'll fix you up, I promise," she cooed.

Ted tried to yell for help but his voice was faint and no one could hear him.

"I'll take care of you, sweetie, and if you're a good boy, I won't hurt you."

Memories hit Ted like a freight train. Brandon had stabbed him and thrown him on the floor. Ted had lain there, shocked and angry, but what could he do? Ted had been so relieved when the little girl had wandered into Brandon's room. Maybe she would fix his legs, or tell Mom what had happened.

Hope had died when she sat on his chest. He hadn't been able to breathe. "Hi, Ted. I want to have fun, too."

She pulled out a huge knife Ted had seen in the kitchen.

"Does it hurt very much, not having legs?" She'd cocked her head to one side. "I bet it does."

She'd crawled off his chest and knelt by his legs. The knife had slid into his flesh so smoothly he didn't react. Eventually the sensation had made its way to his brain, and Ted howled with pain. The tiny blonde had giggled. "Okay, I guess it does hurt. Does it hurt as much as this?"

She had pulled a small handsaw from underneath Brandon's desk and dangled it in front of his eyes. He'd screamed as she laid the saw in the groove her cuts had created. Pain had pulled Ted into the blackness at some point.

Then she left Brandon's room, where Mom found Ted later, dead. Megan had tired of sawing through his leg, never realizing how hard it was to cut through human bones. Plus, Ted wasn't screaming anymore, and he stopped begging her to stop, and she was bored. She decided to leave the legs hanging by a bit of flesh.

They had taken Teddy away from her brother then, and Dad had dragged the dead boy to the railroad tracks. There'd been a funeral, and Mom had said Teddy was sleeping.

"It was you!" Ted said, finally remembering everything. "You killed me."

She giggled. "That day was so much fun. Now, let's go play a new game. Brandon got a new pocketknife and I found some matches in the kitchen. We're going to have so much fun."

That's the Spirit

Kurt Newton

"You know Dasher and Dancer..."
"Stop."
"And Prancer and Vixen..."
"Okay, that's enough."
"You know Comet and Cupid..."
"I said, stop!"
"And Donner and Blitzen..."
"Not another word!"
"But do you recall..."
"Don't go there, I'm warning you!"
"The most famous reindeer of all..."
"Mommmm!"
Jenny ran upstairs in tears. Her brother, Zach, still had

the smirk on his face when their mother entered the living room.

"What was that all about?"

"Jenny's just being a Santa-lover. Again."

Zach's mom rolled her eyes. "Zach, just leave her alone, will you do that for me, please? Your sister has a big heart. There's nothing wrong with that."

"Ho-ho-homeless!"

"Okay, that's enough," said Zach's mom, but even she had to smile a little with that comment.

It was true: Christmas and everything Christmas used to entail—the big family gathering, the gift-giving, the good will toward men—had been deemed religiously antiquated, commercially manipulative, and just plain silly. Big families were a dying phenomenon; who could afford them? Gift-giving had become rife with social politics and price-shaming. And good will toward men? Well, that was about as commonplace as phone booths or drive-in theaters. Society had moved on, but Jenny hadn't. Even in the face of ridicule and the occasional tear, she clung to the belief that the true meaning of Christmas was out there somewhere. As rare as a summer snowflake, perhaps, but not dead, as everyone proclaimed.

As she lay on her bed, her face buried in her pillow, she got a gullywhumper of an idea. Zach was right. If she wanted to find out if the spirit of Christmas still existed, she had to go to the source. No, not the North Pole. All she had to do was go to the nearest homeless shelter.

❄ ❄ ❄

The following day, Jenny asked her mom if it was okay if she hung out at the mall with a couple friends from school, and could she drop her off? Jenny's mom was more than happy to oblige. She even commented on the way to the mall how proud she was that Jenny had decided to stop pining over Christmas and decided to do what every other teenager was doing: spending money and trying to meet boys. "Just be careful," Jenny's mother said.

"I will," said Jenny, waving as her mother pulled away from the mall entrance.

Once Jenny's mother was out of sight, Jenny exited the mall, cinched up the hood on her jacket, and began walking toward the seedier side of town.

Society may have rid itself of Christmas, but some things never changed. The poor were still poor, and the homeless population was still a statistical segment of society. In fact, in this particular city, the homeless had grown to the size of a small army. Lucky for them, there was a multitude of abandoned buildings, empty warehouses, and an underground subway system that, in the wintertime, most of the homeless gravitated toward.

As Jenny walked the sidewalks toward one of the places she'd heard about—an entrance to the underground that wasn't on any subway map—she reminded herself of how the homeless came to be thought of synonymously, if not derisively, even mockingly, with the holiday once known as Christmas.

According to Wiki, when Christmas was in its final death throes, the only people volunteering to play Santa were the homeless. They got a warm place to stay, three square meals, and enough pocket change to buy a bottle of Wild Turkey (a creature saved from the brink of extinction, by the way, when Christmas—and Christmas dinners—fell out of fashion). It's rumored that the homeless still celebrated Christmas, much in the same way that non-traditional believers might congregate in private homes or in a clearing in the woods to avoid the eye of persecution. Jenny was counting on this to be so.

Jenny's breath puffed as she walked. The afternoon sun did nothing to warm the cold December air. Wishing she had worn mittens, she kept her hands stuffed deep in her coat pockets. As expected, there came the occasional catcall, but no one approached her. It was just too damn cold. Besides, where she was going, only the brave would follow. Or the foolish. Or the devout.

Jenny chose the latter for herself. Believing in Christmas was a lot like believing in God, she thought. She smiled at that.

Up ahead, the city buildings thinned, and the street dead-ended at an empty rail yard. Tall fencing kept intruders out, but she found a section that had been cut open and put back, held in place by a couple of loosely tied rags She peeled the bottom corner up and squeezed through.

According to her information, there was an entrance, like a bulkhead to a house's basement, that led to an old subway station. Kids from her high school talked of impromptu parties being held there. But the rail yard was huge. Embedded train tracks crisscrossed the uneven pavement. Tufts of dead grass sprouted up through the cracks like island archipelagos in a sea of gray. The only thing that looked like it could be an entrance to the underground was a graffiti-covered guard shack. On closer examination, the guard shack had no windows.

Jenny approached the shack's weather-beaten door, and with a tug, the door scraped open. A long stairway led down into the dark. "Crap," Jenny said to herself. She knew she should have brought a flashlight. She was about to head down anyway when a voice startled her.

"I wouldn't do that if I were you."

Jenny jumped back as a teenaged boy appeared from around the shack. "What are you doing there?"

He was dressed in a heavy army jacket. "I could ask you the same thing." He raised his eyebrows. "The party's not 'til tonight."

"I'm not here for the party," said Jenny. The boy was not half-bad looking. His eyes were kind of dreamy in a sad, rocking-the-homeless-look kind of way. "Is that why you're here?"

The boy smiled. "Maybe."

Yup, definitely hot, thought Jenny. But she had more important things on her mind. "You wouldn't happen to have a flashlight, would you?" she said.

The boy looked her over. "No. But I have the next best thing."

He produced a glow stick from one of his many pockets. "Here. You just shake it."

"I know how it works." Jenny shook the glow stick, and it lit up. "Thanks." She proceeded to descend the stairway, then stopped. "Do you have another one of those?"

"Yup," the boy said.

"Well, c'mon."

The boy followed her.

When they reached the bottom of the stairs, they continued down a long, narrow hallway. The glow from the glow sticks bathed everything in a surreal kind of lime Jell-O fog.

"So, what's your name?" said the boy.

"Jenny. You?"

"I'm Derek."

"Hi, Derek."

"Hi, Jenny."

Their voices echoed off the hard surfaces of the tunnel. When they reached a junction where stairways descended both left and right, Jenny asked, "Which way?"

"Left," said Derek, and Jenny headed down. "So, what school do you go to?" Derek asked, close behind.

"Sixth District High."

"And what is it you're looking for?"

"You'll laugh."

"Try me."

"Christmas! Well, more like the spirit of Christmas."

"Okay."

"That's it? No Santa-lover comments?"

"Nope."

"So, you're a believer, too? Is it true that there's a secret society of homeless Christmas worshipers? And that the Christmas spirit didn't die, it just went underground?"

"Whoa, slow down."

Jenny stopped on the bottom step. "Am I walking too fast for you?"

Derek stared at her. "You're serious."

"What?"

"Nothing. We're almost there."

Derek led her to an old control room that had been refitted with paper lanterns and mirror balls hanging from the ceiling. Refreshment tables lined one wall, leaving an open dance floor.

"Party central?" said Jenny.

"Yup."

"And let me guess, you're the organizer."

"You could say that."

"But Derek, that's not why I'm here. I thought you were going to help me?"

"I am." He placed a finger to his lips. "Shhhh... Hear that?"

At first, Jenny could only hear the annoying tick of time wasted while this homeless boy humored her and no doubt wanted to get into her pants. But there came a quiet sound that started low then rose like the keening of the wind. Only it was music, a gathering of voices to be exact. A choir. It spilled from the vents in the walls and filled the room.

"That's 'Ave Maria'," said Jenny, enchanted. "It's beautiful."

In the green light of glow sticks, Derek looked almost ethereal. He was staring at her. The look in his eyes that Jenny saw previously as sadness wasn't sadness at all. It was remorse.

"I'm sorry," he said, and his hands moved quickly. He had her in a chokehold before she could react. Jenny kicked and flailed, but Derek was much taller and stronger than expected. Soon her limbs became heavy, and the green fog turned to black.

❄ ❄ ❄

Jenny awoke to the muted sound of Christmas carols. She was being held in a damp, dungeon-like room, in a cage made of iron catwalk grates welded together. There were sconces on the walls holding torches flickering with sooty flames. The odor of heating oil hung in the air. But beneath it all, Jenny smelled something bright and familiar: the holiday scent of pine.

"Hello? Helloooo? Can somebody let me out of here?"

No sooner had she called out when the door to the underground chamber opened and in walked two bearded, hooded men dressed in festive-looking robes. Members of the whispered-about secret society, no doubt. And church elders from the looks of it. "Hi!" she said.

"Silence, interloper!" said the first elder.

"Infiltrator!" said the other.

"No, you don't understand. I believe in the spirit of Christmas. I wish it never left!"

The two men looked at each other. "Hmph," they said. They scratched their beards. "So, what do you think?" said the first elder to the other in a soft, conspiratorial whisper.

"My name is Jenny, by the way." Jenny stuck her hand through the iron grate for a shake.

"Shush!" they said in unison.

They scratched their beards some more.

"She could be a real asset," said the first.

"Yeah, but what about the boss? He's expecting a sacrifice," said the other.

There came a knock at the door before Derek entered. "So, who's supposed to pay me?" he said.

"You!" Jenny growled, pointing at Derek. "I trusted you!" She took off one of her shoes and threw it at him, barely missing his head.

"You're here, aren't you?" he said. "That's what you wanted, right?"

One of the elders asked Derek, "So, she is a believer?"

"I guess so," Derek said. "All she talked about was Christmas this and spirit that. She couldn't wait to meet you guys." He stood with his hand out. "My money?"

The two church elders smiled, thinking the same thought.

❄ ❄ ❄

The subterranean church was magnificent; Jenny had never seen anything like it. The underground space was decked out with actual boughs of holly and red carpeting. Pews were old subway car seats with fluffy white trim, and they were arranged in a semi-circular fashion with an aisle down the middle. The pulpit was a sleigh, like the kind seen on old Christmas cards in museums. Behind the pulpit rose the arch of the original subway tunnel, only it had been sealed off, creating a kind of alcove. Red curtains framed the dark recess, lending to it a dramatic, theatrical appearance.

At the moment, a tall man with white hair and beard

stood in the sleigh and spoke of trials and tribulations and the Spirits of Christmas Past, Present, and Future. Each proclamation was greeted by the congregation with the rattle of sleigh bells and a "Ho, ho, ho" in place of an "Amen." Jenny stood at the back of the church with the two elders, watching it all in awe as events unfolded around her.

When the tall man finished his sermon, a hush descended upon those gathered. The doors to the chamber where Jenny had been held opened, and the iron cage was wheeled up the center aisle. In the cage was Derek. He sat in a disoriented stupor, as if drugged.

"Is this really necessary?" said Jenny in as low of a whisper as she could manage.

The two elders nodded solemnly, then spoke as if of one mind speaking through two separate mouths.

"The Spirit of Christmas enjoyed centuries of adulation and worship..."

"It was a sight to behold..."

"Then its meaning became distorted..."

"Misused..."

"Blasphemed..."

"And, through no fault of its own..."

"It was eventually hunted down..."

"Exterminated..."

"Forced into hiding..."

"Forced underground..."

"Where it has slowly regained a following..."

"But it suffers still..."

"A lack of believers..."

"And a reinforcement of that belief..."

"So, on one day of the year..."

"It shows itself..."

"To demonstrate its power..."

"And, we, the faithful..."

"Provide it with an example..."

"Someone to be held accountable..."

"For the sins of the past..."

"And a testament to the future."

"YOU'RE GOING TO KILL DEREK?" Jenny's voice echoed in the subterranean chamber.

"No, no, my child..."

"The Spirit will overtake him..."

"A very special honor, indeed."

By now, the cage Derek was in had been wheeled past the pulpit and placed in front of the dark alcove. The congregation began a low chorus of "God Rest Ye Merry Gentleman." The song had an altered chord structure, and there was no mention of Christ. It sounded more like a funeral dirge than a Christian hymn.

Then the floor began to rumble.

"What was that?" said Jenny, holding on to the two elders to steady herself.

"The Spirit," said the elders.

As the rumbling grew, stone dust fell from the ceiling; candle stands rocked and fell over, creating small fires that had to be extinguished. The church fell into a virtual darkness. The choir kept singing, their voices rising to fill the vacuum. Suddenly, a green light began to emanate from where the cage was parked. Derek had pulled the glow stick out from his coat pocket and was waving it around.

The rumbling stopped.

"It's here," said the elders.

From beyond the curtains that decorated the alcove came a different light. A white light that seemed to coalesce, growing in intensity as the choir reached its crescendo.

Jenny watched in horror and fascination as the light filled

the space the tunnel once occupied. For a moment, Jenny thought she saw what appeared to be a giant face in the shifting intensities of light. Perhaps it was just her perception, but the face appeared anything but kind. She thought she may have even seen horns.

The tunnel of light then pulsed outward, encompassing the cage Derek was in. His screams were like the pealing of church bells. In an instant, the light was gone, leaving the congregation in silence and a sulfurous smell in the air.

One by one, the candles were relit, and the homeless departed. Jenny was once again alone with the two elders.

"It's a lot to take in," said the first elder.

"A lot, indeed," said the second.

Jenny couldn't take her eyes off the now-empty cage.

"So, you'll help us?" Once again, the two elders spoke as one.

At last, Jenny pulled her gaze from the cage. "Yes, I will," she told them. She thought about her Mom and how she went through life as if sleepwalking. Then she thought about her brother, Zach, and all the times she wished he'd never been born. "But does it have to wait 'til next year?" Jenny said. "I mean, why can't the Christmas Spirit be with us every day?"

"That is a lot of sacrifices," said the elders.

"I know," said Jenny. "And I know just where to start."

Christmas Eve on the Rudolph Express

Sheri White

"Bring him home right now, James. You know I have Little Jimmy for Christmas this year. You should have been here hours ago."

Gina closed her eyes. They did this dance every damn time he had Little Jimmy for the weekend. It's not like James cared that L.J. was even there. He just got off on messing with her. If she had her way, James would never get to see his son.

"Come on, Gina. Let's meet up for dinner somewhere. It's Christmas Eve. Let's give L.J. a present and be a family again."

"We weren't a family when you were here, James. Bring him home."

"Fine. We'll be there in a couple hours."

"A couple hours? Uh-uh, James, right now. James?" Silence.

Gina realized he had hung up on her. "You son of a bitch!" she yelled into the emptiness of her house, causing the dog to whimper and run to another room.

"Sorry, Buddy!" she called after him.

Sighing, she pulled out bowls, utensils, and ingredients for Christmas cookies. She and L.J. would decorate them tonight and leave some out for Santa, as well as some eggnog, with a couple shots of bourbon after L.J. went to bed.

❄ ❄ ❄

Gina looked at the trays of gingerbread cookies spread around the kitchen. *We will be up all night decorating,* Gina mused. She checked the time on her watch and gasped. "God damn it." She grabbed her phone and called James.

"Hey, Gina. What's up?"

"Where are you? You said you would bring L.J. home two hours ago. Quit fucking around, James. I *will* take you to court again."

"Well, here's the thing, babe. I'm not going to bring him home."

"What? Don't do this, James. I mean it."

"See, I was thinking. L.J. is going to stop believing in Santa Claus pretty soon. So the three of us are going to take the Rudolph Express tonight. We're going to be a family for L.J. for what could be his last magical Christmas. Surely you won't deny him this joy, Gina."

"I can't believe this. What the hell is wrong with you? Why won't you get it in your head that we are not together anymore? Bring him home right now, James, or I will call the police."

"And tell them what? That your husband wants you to meet him and your son for a Christmas dinner? The divorce isn't final yet, Sweetheart. And we still share custody during our separation.

"Enough arguing, Gina. If you don't meet me at the Tiny Elf Railroad Station, I will tell L.J. that you don't love him enough to come to Christmas dinner."

"Oh my god. You would actually tell our son I don't love him? You are evil, James. Don't do this."

"Don't make me do it, Gina. Meet us at the station for the buffet, and then we're going to take him on the train ride. Be there by seven o'clock."

"James—"

He had hung up again.

She stomped upstairs to her bedroom to get dressed, screaming obscenities the whole way.

❄ ❄ ❄

Gina entered the Tiny Elf Railroad Station, which served commuters every other day of the year except Christmas Eve. Tonight, a Christmas tree blinked merrily in a corner and a buffet featuring a delicious Christmas dinner and treats lined the longest wall. Santa sat upon a throne, handing out candy canes and occasionally busting out a "HO HO HO," to the delight of the children at his feet.

James waved to her from a small table in the back. She panicked for a moment when she couldn't see L.J. *Did he trick me? Where is L.J.?* Then she heard L.J. laugh and saw him in the group with Santa. She sighed with relief.

James pulled out a chair for her to sit down.

"Wow, such a gentleman tonight. You only did that when we first started dating."

"Hey, I'm still charming."

"Yeah, to other women. While I was at home raising our

son and taking care of the house."

"Let's not do this tonight, Gina. I want to have a nice family Christmas Eve."

"We're not a family anymore. We won't be ever again. I'm only here because you were going to traumatize our son." She sat back in her chair and folded her arms.

"Look, I'm sorry I said that. I would never do anything to hurt L.J., you know that. I just couldn't figure out a way to get you to meet us. Come on, let's hit the buffet."

Gina shook her head. "No, I'm not hungry. I just want to take L.J. home now." She pushed her chair back to stand up.

"L.J. wants to ride the Rudolph Express. We can't disappoint him. Besides, this was a sold-out event. I was lucky someone gave up their tickets earlier today."

"James—"

"Hey, L.J.! Your mom is here!"

L.J. looked up in delight and ran over to his parents. "Mommy! I missed you!" He hugged Gina. She hugged him back, glaring at James over their son's head.

"Daddy said we're going on the Christmas train! This is going to be so much fun!"

"I'm sure it will be, L.J."

❄ ❄ ❄

The train, decorated with giant antlers and a red light for a nose, traveled fast through the moonlit night. Here and there, little houses could be seen on the distant mountains, glowing with cheery lights as those inside waited for Santa to arrive.

The kids in their car had their faces pressed to the windows, cupping their eyes with their hands to see better. The Santa Express chugged upwards into the mountains. Below them, deer bounded through snow, and a decorative village with lights and animated figures delighted the children.

Gina and James sat across from each other on bench seats. Gina looked out the window.

"It's really pretty out here. I admit I'm glad you were able to get the tickets. This is something L.J. will always remember."

"See? I knew I was right doing this."

"James, that doesn't mean we're getting back together. Nothing has changed. This is just a train ride, not real life."

"Come on, Gina. It couldn't have been that bad, being married to me. I mean, we had some good times, right?"

Gina thought back to the yelling, the threats, a hard push here and there. She knew it would escalate and wouldn't let L.J. live in that situation.

"Sure, we had some good times. But the bad outweighed the good after a while, James. I became afraid of you. Nobody can live like that."

James stared at her with hardened eyes. "Fine, Gina. I get it."

❄ ❄ ❄

The Rudolph Express pulled into Little Elf Railroad Station #2. They were now up in the mountains, and lights lit up the valley below. Christmas music played through speakers, inspiring a few people to dance and sing along while children stuffed their faces with sugar cookies and burned their tongues with hot chocolate. They yelled and laughed, running back and forth through the station.

Gina smiled at her son, enjoying his excitement.

"Hey, let's get L.J.," James said. "I have something to show you both. It's really special."

"What is it? I don't want to drag him away from the other

kids. He's having a great time."

"It's a surprise. Please. Just give me this one last thing, and then I'll stop bugging you about getting back together. I know there's no chance. Please."

❄ ❄ ❄

James led them out to the parking lot and unlocked a dented, rusted car.

"Wait, why do you have a car here? How did you get it here?"

"It's just a crappy old car from a place called Rent-a-Wreck. I reserved it, and they dropped it off earlier today."

"But *why*?"

"I'm going to drive to this place that is so pretty. I discovered it a while back, and I want to show it to you both. You'll love it. It's magical."

"What about the train? How will we get home?"

James shrugged. "We'll just drive back. The rental place can pick it up from the other station."

"I guess it's okay."

❄ ❄ ❄

L.J. sulked in the back seat. "Are we going back to the train station? I want to play with my friends."

Gina turned to look at him. "Sorry, sweetie. Daddy wants to show us a magical place, and then we'll drive home from there."

"That's not fair! I wanted to ride the train again!" He kicked the driver's seat. James whipped his head around.

"Don't you *EVER* kick my seat again! Do you hear me?"

L.J. cringed. "I'm sorry, Daddy," he whispered.

Gina clenched her hands into fists. "This is why we broke

up. *This.* You are mean and scary. How dare you talk to L.J. like that? How dare you frighten a child?" She turned around and rubbed L.J.'s leg. "Are you okay, honey?"

The little boy sniffled and nodded his head. She smiled and blew him a kiss.

"You're right about one thing, James... He'll remember this night always."

James tightened his hands on the steering wheel. "I'm sorry." He reached around and patted L.J. on the knee. "I'm sorry, little guy."

"Just take us home, James. I think L.J. and I are done for the night."

Yeah, Daddy, I want to go home. I still need to put out cookies and milk for Santa."

"Oh, for god's sake. We're almost there. I'll show you the surprise and then take you home. Okay?"

They drove on in awkward silence, the cheerful mood ruined.

❄ ❄ ❄

Finally, James turned into a wooded area, driving a little ways before he parked the car.

"Where are we? What's so special about this place?" Gina asked.

"Just a second, Gina." James turned off the engine and the headlights. Now Gina and L.J. could see the village with animatronic figures and creatures. Christmas lights colored the snow-covered ground in red and green. A few deer jumped right in front of the car, startling them into laughter. Snow flurries swirled and danced in the air.

"It *is* magic, Daddy!"

"I admit, it's very pretty. Very Christmasy."

James started the car but left the headlights off and turned on the radio. A chorus of children sang "Silent Night" in soft voices.

Gina sat back and closed her eyes. "This is nice. Relaxing. That village looks like the one we passed—" She sat up quickly and stared at it. "Wait, *is* that the same one? James?"

Her husband stared straight ahead, his hands clenching the steering wheel. "Yes."

"James, what is happening?" She looked out her passenger window and realized they were parked sideways on a train track. "Oh my god! JAMES! What are you doing?" She pulled on the door handle, but the door wouldn't open.

"All the doors are locked, Gina."

"No! Let us out, James! Let us out right now!"

"Mommy? What's wrong?"

Then she felt it. A vibration. Subtle, but noticeable. "Move the car, James."

"No. We're a family. I was hoping you would realize that and let me come home tonight. I won't let us be apart any longer, Gina."

"I'm sorry! You're right, we *are* a family. You can come home tonight, okay?"

"Do you think I'm stupid, Gina?"

Now Gina could feel the car shaking. "Mommy, why is the car moving? Daddy didn't turn it on."

"James, please!" Gina screamed. She leaned over and used her fists to pummel his shoulder and arm. She slapped his cheek, his head, but he wouldn't budge.

L.J., not knowing why, yelled and cried along with his mother. "Daddy, please!"

The train whistle screamed its arrival. Rudolph's nose bathed the car in red.

"I love you both so much," James whispered.

Song of the Hunt

Pierce Skinner

Three days before Christmas, Everett Ledbetter broke a bottle of vodka over his skull and fell forward into a bonfire and died.

It was all because his friend, Jason, who used to be the kitchen manager over at The Half Shell Bar and Grill on Cary Street where Everett washed dishes, left the Half Shell for the chance to work up at La Mer, the seafood joint in the fancy-ass Jefferson Hotel. "Can't say no to fifty more cents an hour and a paid vacation," was what he said to Everett. This hurt Everett in a way he didn't know how to describe. Jason's last day, he didn't even show up for work. Didn't even say good-bye. And that hurt Everett even more.

The man who replaced Jason was named Eric Hasslich. There were a lot of things about Hasslich that Everett didn't like right off the bat, and none of them had anything to do with the fact he was white, and none of them had nothing to do with him being a midget. Can't help being born white, and you can't help being born a midget, if that's God's plan for you, but Everett had serious doubts that God's plan was for anyone to be as much of a pompous, dick-swinging son-of-a-bitch as little Hasslich turned out to be. Made things worse how bad he smelled, like onions and wet dog and crotch-rot, and his skin looked like the only baths he'd ever taken were in boiled chicken fat. Constellations of bright pink pimples stood out under his patchy blond beard, and everyone called him Leprechaun behind his back because, for fuck's sake, he looked and smelled and waddled to and fro like an imp from hell.

Eric Hasslich didn't like to be called Eric or Hasslich. He liked to be called "Chef," exclusively, or Mr. Hasslich, if Chef didn't come naturally, which it didn't for Everett, who didn't think grilling burgers and microwaving frozen lobster tails constituted real chef work. Jason had never made anybody call him anything, and he certainly never called himself a *chef*. But, oh baby, Hasslich got himself off on it. He brought in his own little wooden step-ladder so he could reach the grill, and the step-ladder was monogrammed with the word *CHEF* in a big fancy font, for fuck's sake, with the letters inlaid with gold.

It was that patchy blond beard that really kicked the ball down the mad spiral into hell. One Tuesday night, Hasslich came in swinging his big-chef-dick and demanded everyone in his kitchen shave their beards after a plate of beer-cheese fries came back with a hair in it. Made a big show of waddling all through the kitchen, showing everyone the hair, showing all the black men how black the hair was. Even showed Everett.

"Everyone comes into this kitchen tomorrow clean-shaven, is that understood?"

"I ain't," Everett told him. "I don't go near the food."

The Leprechaun glared up at Everett. "Are you in my kitchen?"

"Nah, I'm in the dish pit."

"Dish pit's part of the kitchen, Everett."

"No, it ain't."

"Yes, it is. The microwave is right there."

"I ain't put it there. Don't belong in the dish pit. Belongs in the kitchen."

Everyone else in the kitchen—Dwayne, Price, Kengie—they all laughed loud as hell at that, and Hasslich's face went so pink that for a split second you couldn't even see the pimples. They blended right in.

"Anyone comes in here with a beard tomorrow is gonna be looking for a new job, how about that? That includes you, Everett."

Everyone understood, and they stopped laughing. Dwayne sucked his teeth and said, "Fuck, man."

"Hey!" barked the Leprechaun, "That's another thing. No cussing in my kitchen!"

Dwayne sucked his teeth again, and everyone went back to work. Mr. Hasslich waddled out of the dish pit and back into the kitchen, and Everett covered the sound of himself saying, "Little bitch," by dumping a tray of silverware into the washer and clanking it shut.

The next day, everyone showed up for work without their beards, except for Mr. Hasslich.

"Alright," he barked over the protests, climbing on his step-ladder to address the kitchen. "First thing, my beard is *blond,* so even *if* it fell onto a plate, nobody's gonna *see* it. And, second, I'm the *chef* in this fucking kitchen, so you don't tell *me* what the fuck to do. Ever. And you sure as shit ain't gonna intimidate me."

Dwayne crossed his arms and said, "Thought you said no cussing in your kitchen."

And, just like that, four days before Christmas, Dwayne lost his job. He didn't fight, didn't say a word, just took off his apron and walked out the back into the alley and was gone.

He ever tries to pull some shit like that with me, Everett thought, *I'll knock his ass out.*

His next thought, however, was that it couldn't come to that. It wouldn't. Christmas was four days away, and he still had to make enough on tomorrow's check to finish paying off the Barbie Dream House his daughter wanted, the one with the pool on the roof, the one that came with the neon pink convertible. Thing cost one hundred thirty-nine dollars, which was about what he made in a week, after taxes. He'd had the house on layaway at Walmart since Thanksgiving.

I'll just keep my head down. What was it Jason used to say? Find my Zen, that's what he used to say.

Find my Zen.

❄ ❄ ❄

The following night, The River Front real estate agency rented out the whole damn restaurant for a hundred and some-odd people. Four-course meals, bottomless hors-d'oeuvres, open bar. Everett never saw so many dishes in his whole god-damn life. Stacked from the floor to the ceiling, on top of the microwave, scraps of burger meat and soggy buns and globs of ketchup floating like pieces of people in the chime of cola and beer that rose up over the toes of his shoes. And, in the middle of a wash cycle, the machine sputtered and rattled and clanked and went dead still and wouldn't come back on, no matter what he did to it. Meanwhile, the dishes kept piling up all around him, closing in. The chime rose, soaked into his socks.

The back door swung open. Dwayne stood there, holding a beer, eyes red and glassy staring at the skyscrapers of plates and bowls. The slop on the floor dropped a bit with the amount of it that slipped out the door onto Dwayne's shoes.

Dwayne shook his head, laughed, said, "Want a beer?"

Everett said, "Fuck it." The dishes weren't going anywhere, and it wasn't like he was making a dent anyway, so he went out into the alley with Dwayne and had a cigarette or two and another three or four beers while Dwayne told him how he hadn't found a job yet and didn't know if he was gonna. He might just end up moving back down to Atlanta with his cousin, who cooked dope. Everett always wondered how someone broke into the dope-cooking industry but always ended up figuring it cost more capital than he'd be able to come up with. All the dope-cookers these days were trust-fund kids.

When he finally went back inside, the party was over. The front of the house was emptying out, the bartender and the servers were sweeping up the debris, and the kitchen staff was scrubbing down the grill. Everett found Mr. Hasslich coming out of the restroom.

"Dishwasher broke," he said. "We gotta call Mitch to come fix it."

Mr. Hasslich zipped up his pants—Christ, the stink coming off him, like roadkill—and said, "Wasn't he just here? There was a check for him written in November."

"I guess so. Don't change nothing. Machine's broke now."

"Well, then it sounds like you broke it."

"I ain't break shit."

"It's after midnight, Everett. I ain't calling Mitch 'til tomorrow."

"Oh," Everett said. "All right, then. I'll get here early, then."

Mr. Hasslich laughed. "I don't think so. These dishes are gonna get done tonight."

This plucked a string inside Everett. The note was deafening.

"The fuck you say?" he asked Mr. Hasslich. "Who gone help me?"

Mr. Hasslich shook his head. "You're the *dishwasher,* Everett. You wash dishes. I ain't gonna help you do your job. I'm the *Chef.* And you ain't gonna drag any of my cooks into it, neither. They cook, you wash dishes. Everybody's lives are their own to live. That's something you don't quite get. None of you people do. It ain't nobody's job to do your work for you. That's why this whole fuckin' country's gone to hell, is attitudes like yours. Now, if I were you, I'd be back there five minutes ago. So go on. Get."

Hasslich waddled past Everett. Deaf from the plucked note, struck numb by it, not sure what else to do, Everett followed him.

He watched Hasslich grab his coat off the hook beside the rack that held the mops, and he moved his mouth to say, "Good night," and shoved past Everett again, leaving a smear of stink behind that was almost visible, the way it shivered in the air like a mirage.

And maybe it was the four or five or six beers he'd had with Dwayne, and maybe it was the dollhouse he still had to buy his daughter, or maybe it was Jason leaving without saying goodbye, or the way Hasslich implied that Everett's friends, Price and Kengie, were better than he was because they were cooks, or maybe it was the way he said "you people" there, like he wasn't even pretending, but that string in him got plucked, again and again, strummed by the heavy hand of God until his mind was a blizzard of noise. He didn't feel like washing all these dishes by hand, not when his feet hurt the way they did, socks soaked through with grease and mop water and mayonnaise.

Hasslich had to squeeze through the maze of dishes to get to the back door. To get to his car. To get home.

Everett wasn't thinking about much when he pulled the stack of plates down on the Leprechaun. He didn't hear him scream. Didn't hear the plates crash like an atom bomb. He pulled down another stack. And another. And another, until all that was left was a mountain of broken ceramic and broken glass, and somewhere underneath it all was a Leprechaun.

Eventually, Hasslich managed to drag his bruised and bloodied head out from under the mountain, gasping for air, gagging on the trash water; Everett lifted his boot and brought it down, hard, felt the crack. He stomped again, felt the bone soften. Hasslich went still. Everett just stood there, staring, waiting for something else to happen. Nothing did. He just stood and watched the blood reach out into the chime with thick red tendrils. He watched it swirl and mix with the mustard and the mayonnaise and the soggy burger buns and the soggy napkins, floating like jellyfish in the far-away sea.

And when he got tired of standing there, remembering that his feet hurt, he turned the lights off and left and locked the back door, but not before taking a couple bottles of Skol from behind the bar.

It was too late to catch the bus. He had to walk home.

❄ ❄ ❄

It wasn't 'til morning that Everett realized what he'd done.

For a long time, he lay in bed, staring up at the ceiling, tracing the cracks that ran like rivers through forests of gray mold. He tried to convince himself that it hadn't happened. Not here. Somewhere else, maybe, another world he'd popped into for just a quick visit, long enough to crush Hasslich to death and then zip back over into this world, the world where things were real, and go to bed.

Police'll be here soon, he reckoned. He checked the clock. It was almost eleven, which meant the morning crew had already found the body, which meant they'd already called the police, which meant they were already watching the tape. *Hell. They prolly on they way right now.*

He got up and walked out into the living room, still wearing his work uniform. In the corner by the TV, there was the artificial tree he'd picked up from the curb in front of the apartments across the street from the restaurant. It was crooked, no matter how he had tried to fix it with duct tape. And now the tape was so thick around the central stalk that it showed through the plastic branches. He hated it. His daughter was with her mama up in Henrico. Supposed to come back home today. The tree was supposed to be a surprise. He hadn't had one the past couple years. Hell, even Walmart wanted eighty fuckin' dollars for one, and it was either a tree or the dollhouse with the pool on the roof and a neon pink convertible.

Damn, he thought. *She ain't getting no dollhouse anyway.*

So he wrote a note and made sure his daughter had a snack ready for when Jeanette brought her home, then he built a bonfire in the backyard and drank the first bottle of stolen vodka until he thought he wouldn't feel the fire. The second one he broke over his skull, drenching himself with. He fell forward into the fire with his eyes and his arms open.

He was wrong, of course; he wasn't quite drunk enough.

He felt everything.

❄ ❄ ❄

The first thing Everett thought about when he woke up from being dead was that he wanted to kill someone. This craving was a note played from deep within, a blizzard of sound, a symphony of static, some of which was ancient, older than him or any animal thing, a piece of the Big Bang, and it rang in him and through him like a disease, animating every limb, drowning all other thoughts.

The second thing he thought was, *Fuck, it's dark.*

All around him, a cold, pressing darkness. He tried to move, to sit up. His head clanged against metal. He tried to move his arms, and after another second spent waiting for the nerves to respond to stimulus, he realized he was wrapped in plastic.

Noises then, near his feet, somewhere in the dark. Voices. The beating of hearts and friction of blood and other juices.

Something clicked; the dark parted near his feet, and he was pulled into the light.

Shadows of fingers fumbled with the zipper between his eyes. The voices attached to the fingers were frantic. The hearts behind the voices were trilling, almost in time with the rhythm building inside him, the song rising from the static, flowing where blood used to flow, where now it was just a burnt black paste in his veins.

Killkillkillkillkil. The song went, *killkillkillkill*

The zipper parted. He sat up, saw the cold, gray, fluorescent first circle of hell, the hospital basement. He lifted his fingers to his face, felt the char flake off beneath his touch. His fingers disappeared into his sockets. His eyes were gone. Melted like egg yolk to his cheeks. Yet still, he could see. He could see the attendants backing away from him. Shivering bags of flesh. Alive. Like him. The only difference was what moved inside of them. They were talking to him. One of them was screaming. He couldn't understand what was being said, however. Not over the rush of blood in their veins and the falsetto in his.

Killkillkillkillkillkill

One of the bags of flesh rushed forward, put its hand on Everett's shoulder.

Everett didn't mean to kill him. His limbs acted on their own. The song inside them, those Big-Bang-Blues, they were brains blossoming in each limb, in each finger, like an octopus. His hands bent the man in half until his bones split through his belly like a fish. When he fell, he sat on his own skull before toppling over.

The others ran, screaming from the morgue, piled into the elevator. He didn't follow. They weren't who he was supposed to kill.

Supposed to, he thought. *Weird that I would think that.*

No, but I ain't thinking it. I know it. Same way I know I'm alive at all, same way I know that this is the world I was born into and the world I died in. I'm supposed to be off killing somebody. To get my revenge. And once I get it, I can go back to sleep.

The only problem was, he didn't know *who* he was supposed to kill. Far as he knew, the only person he'd want revenge on was Hasslich, and Hasslich was already dead. That's what got Everett here in the first place.

Well then, who? he thought. *I'm tired.*

It was too cold in the morgue to think clearly. He swung his legs over the edge of the slab and wriggled the rest of the way out of his plastic sheet and walked toward the elevator. It wouldn't open. Someone had pulled the fire alarm.

He took the stairs, which annoyed him because his feet

still hurt.

❄ ❄ ❄

It was warm in the laundry room.

Everett took a white sheet, hot and fresh out of the dryer, and wrapped it around his shoulders and lowered his burnt husk behind the row of machines and thought.

It could be Jerry Gilt, the owner and founder of the Half Shell Bar and Grill. It was Jerry who'd refused to give Jason that fifty-cent raise, the greedy fuck, which was why Jason left. It was Jerry that hired Hasslich. It was Jerry that hadn't replaced the dishwasher since before 9/11.

But the song in him went dull at the thought. And anyway, it wouldn't be fair. Jerry was a good guy. He'd hired Everett, hadn't he? And it wasn't his fault the machine broke, and it wasn't his fault Hasslich was a racist. He probably didn't know. That's not exactly something he figured chefs put on their resume or mentioned in interviews.

Killkillkillkill

Alright, then, who?

Dwayne came to mind. It had been Dwayne who gave him the beers, the ones that ended up tipping him over the edge after he'd walked up to it. But no. The song mellowed. Dwayne was just being a friend. Dwayne would never have meant to enable a break with reality with a few Bud Lights.

What about Mitch? The repair guy. Mitch, the Kitchen Guy, that's what he called himself. On retainer to every restaurant in downtown Richmond.

The song rose in pitch, swarmed the thought like sharks to a whale carcass.

Mitch Leslie. That was it.

The song swelled, an angel choir. Hidden truths revealed

themselves.

KillMitchLeslieKillMitchLeslie.

Mitch Leslie. The man who put the fail-switch in the machine so it'd break down after a certain number of runs. Always right around New Year's, so he could snag his holiday tip at the same time.

Mitch Leslie. That's who it was that ruined his life, who set him up for failure and murder and death. A corrupt, slime-covered toad that made his living off of lies and cunning. The gods of the earth wanted him. The gods of the earth wanted his meat to be ground and his blood to be drained.

Everett's head hurt. This whole thing was shaping up like a *Wheel of Fortune* episode.

The category is Purpose.

Alright, he thought. *I'd like to solve the puzzle.*

The universe said, *Go ahead.*

Kill Mitch Leslie, And Leave This World For Good.

Applause, applause, applause.

Stop. Wait.

It seemed awful stupid. All right, sure, kill Mitch Leslie, but Mitch Leslie wasn't the source of all sorrow. It wasn't Mitch Leslie who got Everett kicked out of the CDL training program at John Tyler Community last year. That was Mike… what was his last name? Mike Something. Mike had told the instructor about the Adderall loose in Everett's bag.

Alright. Kill Mike Something, then.

But he only started taking the pills to stay awake enough to work and go to school at the same time because Jeanette left him alone with the baby so she could run off to Henrico with that architect, Pete Davies.

Fine. Kill Jeanette and kill Pete.

But, fuck it all, if he kept going like this, he'd have hundreds of people to kill, and eventually, the only people to hold responsible for every dumb or rotten thing that had ever happened to him would be his parents for ever dragging him out of oblivion and into this chime-slop world and his mama was dead six years and his daddy was retired and living in Jacksonville. It would take forever, getting all that revenge, with the bodies piling up like dishes at a Christmas party.

Nope. I ain't killing nobody, he decided. *Not anymore.*

But that didn't change the fact that he was alive. Didn't change anything at all.

❄ ❄ ❄

The night was cold, but with the dozen stolen hospital blankets wrapped around him, it was bearable.

I must look like a ghost, he thought, following the guard-rail along the freeway.

It was after two in the morning by the time he got to the Walmart on Sheila Lane. The parking lot was still just about full.

"Fuck," he said to himself. His voice sounded strange. Like many voices speaking at once, but from somewhere far away. The same voices sang in the choir that had replaced his blood.

Of course, he had forgotten that *this* Walmart was open twenty-four hours. He had also, somehow, forgotten that it was, currently, two days before Christmas, and everybody, living or dead, was scrambling in these last precious minutes for anything to put under the tree.

Got to go in through the back, he decided. They'd never let him through the front door. Not looking like a corpse wrapped in white ghost-skins. And, he knew, anyone that got too close to him would be torn and bent all to shit to satisfy the song of the hunt, and there wasn't a damn thing he could do about that except stay clear of the living altogether.

He sighed, stared at the parking lot, sardine-tight, and wondered why nothing was ever easy for him.

The stockroom was poorly lit, the few working fluorescent lights hanging high overhead, and he was able to stick to the shadows mostly, keeping clear of the handful of frenzied employees buzzing and sliding and tearing open boxes and cursing.

As he turned down a darkened aisle, he found a young woman on her knees, weeping with her forehead pressed against a cling-wrapped pallet stacked six feet high with Keurig machines. She looked up at Everett's scoured, lipless, eyeless corpse draped in white. Tears pooled in the dark circles under her eyes; her cheeks were hollow, her skin slick with sweat. He wondered how long she had been here, unwrapping pallets, stocking shelves, wishing people a "Merry Christmas." From the stink of her, she hadn't been home in some time. Several seconds passed with the two staring at each other before the girl, finally, started to scamper away. The tears started fresh, and she said, "Oh, my God. Oh, my God."

Everett lifted his hand and, with his thousand voices, said, "Wait."

The girl did not wait. She ran, screaming down the aisle, bursting through the double doors into the world.

"Fuck," Everett said.

❄ ❄ ❄

Everett walked through the double doors. The world was waiting for him.

A trio of yellow-vested security guards, two police officers, and twenty or thirty others, customers drawn by the racket, stood arranged around him as he emerged, his hands raised, withered, burnt fingers trembling. Overhead, "Here

Comes Santa Claus" played, sung by Michael Bublé.

"Please," Everett said.

Someone screamed. The crowd leaped backward several feet, the circle widening, leaving spaces open between them.

Could make it, Everett thought. *Got to be quick.*

One of the cops drew his gun.

"Please," Everett said. "I just want—"

The bullet tore through Everett's chest in a spray of burnt flesh and black dust.

Inside him, the choir raged.

In the space of a heartbeat, his fingers were inside the man. Ribs snapped like dry twigs, crumbled in Everett's fists. The splinters came out with fistfuls of meat and red strings, and the blood washed over Everett and spread out across the floor, seeping into a stack of boxed futons on sale for $119.

Yesyesyes.

Killkillkillkillkill.

Everett stopped digging when his fingers started scraping linoleum.

He felt another bullet pass through him, this time through his skull, then another through his neck, and another through his left shoulder.

The cop never screamed. Didn't have time to before he was past saving. Not dead. No. Everett let the song do what it wanted, and it wanted this one to shiver and stare at the ceiling until it bled out, throat pulled out like a brake-switch.

Everyone else ran, a screaming stampede surging toward the exit.

Everett stood, every inch of him drenched in blood, and he relished the warmth and the moisture against his ruined flesh, and the song wailed on and on and on as he made his way to the Customer Service counter, where the dollhouse waited.

❄ ❄ ❄

The sound of sirens seemed to come from everywhere, the way he always imagined the angels sounded when Christ was born. He stuck to the backroads at first, and when the sirens started spilling down those, he struck off into the woods. The box was huge, half as tall as he was, cumbersome and heavy and slippery, and he wished he'd had the time to clean himself before leaving the Walmart. He didn't want his daughter's present soaked through with blood. He told himself he'd wipe it down before he went inside.

This walk was harder than the first. He felt the twigs under his feet, felt the bones in his toes start to snap off, one after the other, until he was forced to scuff along through the underbrush, steadying himself with the trunks of the bare trees. Something was leaving him, leaking out of the bullet holes. The song had lowered itself to a dull, monotonous hum.

He could be destroyed now, he knew. The Song was ending, its singers sated, and it almost made him laugh to know that it didn't matter who it was that died, Hasslich or Dwayne or Mitch or Mike or Jeanette or Pete The hunt had no target. The hunt was wild. Revenge was a bloody cloth waved before the nose of the undead. A means to an end. And, hell, he didn't even feel bad about killing those cops. Not really. Only thing that mattered now was getting the dollhouse under the tree.

It was almost dawn by the time he got to Pete and Jeanette's house. A nice house. Two stories. The kind of McMansion an architect's salary can keep afloat. All the lights were still off except for the ones on the tree in the living room.

He set the box down on the patio beside the sliding glass door, went around and got the hose, and sprayed the box down until it was clean of blood, and then he sprayed the blood off the patio into the grass. He shook his head at how silly the dollhouse seemed when he really stood still and looked at it. Three stories, with a pool on the roof. It even came with a car. Neon pink. Nobody in the world had a car that color. Absolutely nobody.

After coiling the hose back up the way he found it, he slid open the door. If it was locked, the mechanism gave out under his strength, and he was glad he still had that much left. He knelt and picked up the box and entered the living room, then slid the box under the tree next to the others, all wrapped and shining. He felt sorry, then, that the dollhouse wasn't. It stood out, a soggy, warped cardboard mess at the base of a mountain of rose gold and ruby, fancy, eleven-dollar wrapping paper Jeanette probably got at Target.

"Um," a small voice said.

Everett turned his eyeless gaze toward the couch. Beside it, his daughter stood. She wore soft-looking white pajamas that made her look like a snowman, with little coal buttons and a scarf sewed into the collar. Probably also from Target. The sleeves hung well past her hands. She was almost six but had been born premature, and she would carry that smallness with her for the rest of her life.

The song hummed at this new living thing before it. It could make room for such a tiny morsel. Barely even a bite, after all.

No, Everett begged. *Please.*

He backed away toward the open door, hid himself behind the tree. He should run. He should disappear into the woods and wait for it all to end quietly. But he couldn't. Not now. Not when he could see his little girl for just a little longer. Just a few more seconds. She took a step toward him. There was fear in her, he could see it. But something stronger, older, even.

"You're not Santa, are you?" she said. Her voice was like the mew of a baby possum.

Everett shook his head. "No," he whispered, so she wouldn't be able to hear what his voice really sounded like. He watched her face stiffen at the answer, watched the fear reach up and close its jaws around the light. He panicked. "I…I work for Santa, though."

She blinked and squinted at the burned, red-colored thing draped in red sheets cowering behind the Christmas tree. "You're an elf?" she asked.

"Well," he hissed, "I sure ain't no Leprechaun."

His daughter laughed, a high, sweet sound, a bird's morning chitter. Everett chuckled. It sounded like bone raked across asphalt. He lifted his finger to what was left of his lips. "Don't wake mommy and Pete," he said.

Something else moved inside her little body now. Her eyes wandered.

"Something bad happened to my daddy," she said.

Everett shivered.

I got to go. I got to go right now.

"I know," he said.

"Can Santa make him be better?"

He already did, he wanted to say. He wanted to tell her everything. About Hasslich and the dish pit and the darkness at the edge of everything, about the hunt and the hunters and the songs they sing, about how dangerous it was to be anything at all and how sorry he was that he had dragged her into existence. But he didn't.

All he could say was, "No, baby. Santa can't do that."

"Oh," she said.

"I brought you that dollhouse you wanted, though." He nudged the box with his foot.

Her eyes fell on the dollhouse, and she squeaked. She scampered across the living room, and with every tiny footstep, the song in him grew louder.

YesYesYes...

No. Please. Not her.

He staggered backward, colliding with the wall.

He opened his mouth to scream, to scare her off, knowing what would happen if she got any closer.

The tiny morsel threw itself at him, wrapped its arms around his middle.

Nothing happened.

He looked down at his limp, trembling hands. Between them, the top of his daughter's head, frizzy and wild from a restless sleep.

On his own, he moved his arms, and he wrapped them around her for the last time.

He began to shake. A moan escaped his blackened teeth. He would have cried, though he had no eyes, and there was no moisture left in his body that hadn't originally run in someone else's veins.

"You smell like a hamburger," his daughter said. "How come?"

He pressed her against him, then released her, peeled her arms from around him. He saw, embarrassed, that her pajamas were stained with black flecks of skin and smears of half-dried blood.

"Go to your room, now," he said, barely forming the words behind the emptiness that was left where the song had once been sung. Where now there was only silence. "It's almost Christmas."

She scuffed her way back toward her room, down the hall, stopping at her door.

"If you see Santa, would you make sure he gives my

daddy good presents in heaven so he can feel better?"

He told her he would.

She said, "Good night Mister Elf!" And shut the door smooth and quiet so as not to wake anyone.

And Everett turned around and walked out the sliding glass door and shut it just as soft.

He walked away without once looking back.

❄ ❄ ❄

The sun came up over the freeway.

Everett walked. The song was over now, and he wondered what was next.

Police cars swarmed. Radios crackled. The sky was the color of butterscotch.

The police cars formed a wall across the highway. Helicopters blinked into the sky. There were other vehicles, shiny as Christmas wrapping and black as the grease between the stars, and out of them spilled men in crisp black suits with angry black guns.

Voices come down the highway out of bullhorns, telling him to stop.

He kept walking.

He thought of his little girl and, how when he was that small, the world had seemed so wide and bright and confusing; how easy it would be to believe that Santa lived in Heaven next to God himself.

The thunder came. Bullets sparked off the highway, and one landed in his knee.

He remembered how, at Sunday School, they had told him to draw a picture of Heaven. He hadn't known what to draw, so he had left the paper blank.

A bullet crashed through his wrist, and his hand fell to

the pavement, curled up like a dead spider.

And that's what Heaven still was. Even now. A blank. A void. Maybe nothing at all.

His body came apart now under a steady metal rain. The dark came back over his sight. He thought of his daughter opening the dollhouse tomorrow morning, and he hoped that, wherever he was going now, there were no restaurants or dishes or pills or racist leprechauns. He hoped there were no jobs where you had to stand up all day and no moldy ceilings. Matter of fact, no slums at all. Just a big, clean house. Maybe one with three stories. Maybe one with a pool on the roof, one that came with a car. He wouldn't even mind if the car was neon pink.

He wouldn't mind one little bit.

Christmas Revenge

Karen Thrower

I hate Christmas. I know, I know. What eight-year-old hates Christmas?

Well, I do!

Every year since I was two, those damn elves torture me. "Were you a good girl? Do you deserve these!" Bouncing around my room like jumping beans. Slapping me in the face as they whiz by, putting sticky candy canes in my hair. Well, no more! It's been six years of torture, and this year I'll have my revenge.

I hid between the couch and the Christmas tree, hoping the drooping ornaments and presents would give me enough cover. I held one of the knives from the kitchen in both hands. The handle was rather thick for my small hands, and I didn't want to drop it if I could help it. I sat hidden for hours after mom and dad went to bed. I knew they didn't believe me about the elves, so I didn't want them to catch me. They'd just march me to my room and lock the door so I couldn't sneak out again. Then it would be another year of torture by those tiny monsters. My parents never took my side. Year after year of telling my parents about my tormenters did nothing. It was always, "It's just a dream, honey," or "Santa and his elves aren't real." But I know they are. And they're horrible.

My ear twitched when something on the roof made a soft thump. *Here we go,* I thought and tightened my grip on the knife. Little thumps on the hardwood told me the elves had already made it down the chimney. I could hear the tiny bells on their shoes jingling as they ran past me to my room. The tinkling came running back into the living room. "She's not in there," I heard one whisper.

"What do we do now, Santa?" My eyes widened; I hadn't heard the big man come down the chimney.

"Keep looking. She's bound to be somewhere," he growled. I never heard that jolly voice everyone speaks of. Never any "Ho-ho-ho'" or "On Dasher!" Just a low grumbling that said to me, "I wish I were dead instead of handing out presents." I flattened myself to the floor and watched four pairs of the little feet in their red-and-white-striped stockings start walking around, looking for me. One set of pointed green shoes got closer to the tree, and I felt my knuckles flex. The feet got within arm's length, and the elf looked under the tree. Its sparkly blue eyes widened when it saw me, but before it could say anything, I grabbed at its legs and pulled it toward me, missing all the hanging decorations between us. It was a perfect catch.

I held the elf against the floor, my hand over its mouth. I could feel its panicked breathing on my skin, and its heart fluttered wildly against the palm of my hand.

I leaned close to its big, pointed ears. "Not gonna get me this year, butt wipe," I whispered and slid the knife into its belly. The breath on my skin stopped, and the tiny body started shaking as I twisted the knife. I could feel the metal scraping on its tiny bones. The smell of its blood hit my nose. Candy canes, cinnamon. I took my hand off the dead elf, and I smiled. "One down," I whispered and tossed the body to the middle of the living room like a grenade. The body made a little thud, and I heard the other elves gasping.

"Jingles!" I heard one yell. I peeked from behind some presents and watched them. The elves were crawling around the body, sniffing and poking at it like wild animals.

"Not Jingles!" one cried out, and the rest of them began sobbing as they licked up their dead friend's blood.

"Fuck, guys, that's so gross. Will you cut it out?" Santa grumbled as he sat in my dad's chair, eating the cookies they'd put out for him. They stopped licking the floor and stood straight, sniffing and started licking the blood from each other's faces instead.

"Sorry, Santa. We'll find that little bitch," one of them said before they scattered and resumed the search. I watched as another pair of feet in blue shoes came close to the tree.

"I think Jingles was over here?" it said as it leaned down to look under the tree.

It saw me, and I smiled. "Yeah, he was," I said, and snatched the little creature up and got to my feet. Santa jumped out of the chair, and the other elves stopped in their tracks and growled at me. "You have tortured me enough!" I yelled at them. "Get out of my house and never come back or I will kill every single one of you. I swear it!" I put the elf's head in my mouth and bit down as I pulled. Sweet, candy cane-tasting blood filled my mouth as I spat the head out and threw the body at Santa. Little blood spatters spread on the dingy white of his coat. "Get. Out!" I brandished the knife at them as I stepped out of my hiding spot.

"You little bitch!" a tiny voice yelled, and I turned as it leaped at me. I slashed the knife down, and it went through its doughy body. The top half landed upside down in the Christmas tree, and the legs landed on the couch. The smell of candy canes was starting to become overwhelming, but I had to ignore it.

"Mittens!" the last two elves screamed and rushed me, but I was ready. I kicked and slashed at the little beasts and watched them land across the room, bruised and bloody.

"Leave, or I'll eat you!" I yelled like a crazy giant and stomped after them.

"That's no way to act, little girl!" Santa roared, and lunged at me, but I was ready. I held the knife out with both hands and let the fat man stumble into me. He smelled like alcohol and dirt, and I fought not to gag. I could feel the knife slide into something, and Santa yelled out as we both went crashing against the tree. The pine needles pricked at my skin, and one of the angel ornaments scratched me on the cheek with its heavenly spear. I pulled myself out of the tree and saw Santa rolling on the ground, holding his stomach. "You little bitch," he said through gritted teeth. His hands were covered in blood, but unlike the elves, it didn't smell like candy. It was human blood, and the metallic tang made me cringe.

"She killed Santa!" a tiny voice to my left yelled. "Get her!"

I turned as the last two elves ran at me once again. One was holding a hand over its right eye, the other looked to be running on a broken ankle, like a tiny zombie.

"I warned you!" I lifted my foot and kicked as hard as I could at the half-blind one. It went sailing across the room and hit the wall with a splat. I rushed over before it slid down and stabbed it in the stomach with my knife. It gurgled and choked, its one eye bulging out of its head. Its blood poured down the wall and drenched the rest of Santa's cookies that were on the bookshelf under it.

A sharp pain in my ankle shocked me, and I looked down to see the last elf biting me like I was a piece of candy. I reached down and picked it up by the neck, but it didn't let go, and I felt my skin rip between its sharp little teeth.

"Ouch! You little butthole, you want something to eat?" I stomped over to the tree and pulled one of the candy canes off a branch. "I'll give you something to eat!" I bit off the end, plastic and all, and gripped the elf's head between my fingers. "Don't say I never gave you anything." I shoved the candy cane in its mouth and down its throat. It started choking on the striped treat and twitched in my hand. It tried biting through the candy cane, but it couldn't close its mouth enough. I shoved the candy cane down as hard as I could until I heard a crack. After that, the sweet treat slid out its backside. It gave a little shudder then stopped moving.

I dropped the body and licked the sticky candy off my hand and turned to see Santa crawling back to the chimney. "Don't ever come back, fat man." He flinched, then scurried up the small hole and out of the house. I stood in the living room, dead elves and blood everywhere. The smell of candy canes was overwhelming. I wondered if I should clean up or let my parents find them in the morning? I mean, their blood is red after all, and red is a Christmas color. I washed my hands and decided to leave them. When my parents saw all the dead bodies, I'd finally get what I wanted for Christmas. For them to believe me.

❄ ❄ ❄

I woke when I heard someone knock on my door. "Mandy?" It was my mom. "Are you awake?"

"Yeah." I sat up and wondered how different this Christmas would be? Peaceful? I slid out of my bed and opened the door. My parents were standing in the hallway, and they looked odd. "Merry Christmas?" I said, not sure what to say. Mom was wringing her hands, and dad's eyes were red, like he'd been crying.

"Merry Christmas, baby," my mom said. "There's someone we want you to meet."

They moved out of the way, and we walked into the living room. It looked like it did when I went to bed, elf blood splattered everywhere, the smell of candy canes overwhelming. There was a man I didn't know sitting on the couch. He was wearing a dark suit and smiled as I walked over.

"Merry Christmas, Mandy. I'm Doctor Martinez."

I shook his hand, still confused as to why he was there. "Hi."

"Your parents want what's best for you, Mandy. Will you come with me?" He held out his hand, and I took a step back.

"No. Mom? Dad? What's going on?"

My mom kneeled next to me. "Mandy, honey, we think this obsession you have about Christmas is getting out of hand. It's more than your dad and I can take. You need help."

"Help what? Killing more elves?"

Mom burst into tears and turned into my dad's chest.

"No, honey, not killing elves," Dad said.

I felt the doctor grab my wrist and start pulling me towards the front door. "Don't worry, young lady, we'll get you all the help you need, and by next Christmas, you'll be with your parents again."

"What?" I struggled against him, but he was too strong.

He picked me up and tucked me under his arm like I

was a sack of potatoes.

"Mom! Dad! What's going on?"

As the doctor hauled me out of the house, I managed to see behind my dad. My cat Dinky's tail was on the floor, but I didn't see Dinky. "No! I didn't hurt Dinky, I swear!" But it was clear they didn't believe me. The doctor put me in the back of his car and strapped me in good and tight. I saw my parents at the door, crying. They thought I hurt Dinky. Those little shits made them think I hurt my lovely cat. Fine, if that's how they wanted to play this… I'll get better, and next Christmas, I'll be ready for them.

Marshmallow World

Vivian Kasley

Sadie sat on the floor against the love seat, sucking on a candy cane. She stared at the fire that her father moved about with the poker, causing it to jump and spit. She had earbuds in, but her mother yanked them out, letting her know it was rude when company was over. *What company?* It was the same as it always was. Her Aunt Eloise and Uncle Jeffrey, her cousins Lois and Graham, Grandma Melody and Grandpa Bill, and, of course, her mom's best friend "Aunt" Opal with her daughter, Julie. She hated Opal and Julie. *Rich little bitches.* Her mother had been friends with Opal since they were kids and forced her to call Opal Aunt.

It got harder every year to listen to the incessant meanderings of all of them. The chatter from her Aunt Eloise about how smart Lois and Graham were, they scored so high on this test or that test. Her Uncle Jeffrey's disgusting way of hugging her too long and whispering into her ear with his rancid breath that he had a little gifty for her under the tree. Her grandma and grandpa compared her to her cousins. "Why don't you dress more feminine, like Lois?" "Graham's involved with so much at school, are you?" Lois and Graham sat in matching holiday finery, tight-lipped, sardonic smiles spread across their faces. *Little dorky fuckheads.*

Opal wore a ridiculous tight red dress and twirled sections of her big hair, laughing at everything her father said. Her daughter, Julie, wandered around in a purple dress, obnoxious scarf, and black boots, staring down at her phone. *Everywhere she walks, you can hear that stupid charm bracelet jingling like a cat collar!* Her father stared at Opal's ass. *Is my mother that stupid?* Sadie looked at her mother then, pathetic in her satin green frock, setting down a plate of appetizers. She was rudely interrupted from her thoughts by a high-pitched voice.

"So, Miss Sadie? Anything you want special this year? Julie wants a car, but Santa might not be able to bring that on his sleigh! More like her father's sleigh." Opal cackled.

"Opal, is Cal not joining us this year again?" Her mother frowned.

"Ha! Don't make me laugh! Cal is in Dubai on business. He hasn't spent the holidays with us in a forever, you know that." She took a long sip of her drink, then looked at her daughter. "Julie, you do know there's no good service up here, right, honey?"

"Duh," Julie said.

"She's always on that damn thing! Kids, right?" Opal shrugged and finished her drink.

Sadie rolled her eyes. Opal drove a Porsche Cayenne, and they lived in a ginormous house. She was sure Julie would get her car. Sadie had just turned sixteen in October and wasn't very good at driving yet. She'd be given her father's old jeep as soon as she got her license. She watched as her dad turned from the fire again and stared at Opal's large, fake breasts. *He looks so stupid with his hair slicked back.* He swirled his scotch on ice and adjusted his prancing reindeer sweater. *Fucking moron.*

"So, have you thought about what schools you might apply to next year, Sade?" her Aunt Eloise asked.

"Nope."

"Well, you don't want to get a late start, you know. Lois is looking, but Graham has already started applying. I think he applied to Brown, Princeton, Columbia, Georgetown, Penn State. Did you do Harvard, Graham?"

"Yes, mom, here, there, and everywhere." He chuckled.

Sadie mocked him in her head. *Here, there, and everywhere, what a douche waffle.* Her Aunt held her glass of white wine up high and toasted, "May you get accepted into whichever one you want the most! I know you will! You've an outstanding resume!" She beamed.

"Yes, well, whichever one we can afford," her uncle chortled.

"Well, Jeffrey, dear, I'm sure he'll have a scholarship. He's applied for those, too, and he may well get a full ride for all we know. He's Captain of the Lacrosse team! And he's a damn fine hockey player, too! And with Lois top in Math and Debate Club, we might not have to fork out much of anything! We're lucky! We really are!" She grinned at her children.

Her grandparents smiled warmly and then turned their attention to Sadie.

"Sadie, are you still playing field hockey?" her grandmother asked.

"Nope."

"Well, why not?"

"Because I hated it."

"You're raising a little quitter, Fran? Dom?" She looked to her parents.

"Mom, of course not! Sadie just didn't like it. She's involved in other things, like writing."

"Yeah, our girl likes to write all kinds of dark poems and stuff. She writes for the school newspaper sometimes. Don't ya, Pumpkin?" Her father winked.

"Well, writing is hard to get into, you know. Isn't it, Bill? Your grandfather has tried to submit his stories to *Reader's Digest* for years. Haven't you, Bill?"

"Yep. No luck yet." Her grandfather shook his head.

"Maybe your stories suck," Sadie mumbled.

"Excuse me? What'd you say?" Her grandmother leaned in.

"Nothing."

"Fran, you need to talk to this girl! Her horrible eye make-up and dyed black hair. What's she even wearing? We're all together on the eve of celebrating the birth of baby Jesus, and she's dressed in... What is it anyway?" Her grandmother scrunched up her face.

"Mom, leave it be. She's just different."

"Yeah, you can say that again! A little freak!" her uncle chimed in.

"She looks like that girl from that creepy movie! The one where the girl comes out of the TV! What's it called?" her aunt asked.

"The Ring," Lois said.

"Sadie, you could've borrowed one of Julie's dresses. Or would it fit? What size are you again? Julie's a size two. I wish I could wear a size two!" Opal smoothed the front of her tight dress, and her father licked his lips.

Sadie held the candy cane tightly, the plastic wrapper wet and sticky in her hand. *What is wrong with everyone? Don't they have any decency? Everyone is a giant fucking asshole! Every year! I hate them!* She closed her eyes and held back the hot tears that sprang to her eyes. She put the candy cane back in her mouth and seethed.

"I'm going to go check the turkey. Anyone want anything?" her mother chirped.

"I'll take another gin and tonic," Uncle Jeffrey said.

'I'll get that, Jeff," her father said.

"I'll join you. I could use another myself." Opal floated over to her father in her candy red heels. They left the room, walking a little too close to one another.

"Sade, what're you listening to?" her cousin, Lois, asked.

"Black Sabbath."

"Black what?"

"Sabbath." Sadie rolled her eyes.

Lois made a face at Graham, then they laughed.

"Something funny?" Sadie asked.

"No, nothing." Lois covered her mouth and looked back at Graham.

Sadie ignored them, put her earbuds in, and sucked her candy cane. Her grandparents looked at her disapprovingly. Then her cousins took their phones out and took selfies by the tree. She took a deep breath and let the sweet peppermint cool her throat and chest. She was startled when her earbuds were ripped from her ears again.

"I told you that was rude, Sade! Can't you just act normal like everyone else, just once? And go put on something else, will you? You look like Morticia Addams, for Christ's Sake!" her mother scolded.

"More like the Grim Reaper's daughter," her aunt added.

They all laughed, and Sadie curled her lip disgust. She

was about to get up, but when her mother asked where her father was, she stayed put. She saw Julie glance up from her phone and smirk. Everyone stopped what they were doing, and her mother looked around the room.

"He went to go make me a tonic, didn't he, Eloise? Taking him a mighty long time, too! Did he go to London to get it?" Her uncle guffawed.

"Yes, he went with your friend, Opal." Her aunt raised her eyebrow.

Her mother's cheeks burned red, and she smiled before she turned to leave. As if on cue, her father and Opal walked back into the room. They were cheerfully singing carols arm in arm. Her father was tipsy and staggered a little. He sang it's cold outside and Opal snickered. Her mother boiled, but they didn't notice. Only when she shouted that she needed help in the kitchen did her father flinch. He removed his arm from Opal's and frowned.

"Fran? You all right?" he asked.

"Kitchen. Now," she said.

"Fran, you need me to help, too?" Opal asked.

"No, you've done enough." Her mother gritted her teeth.

The living room had fallen into an uncomfortable silence. Opal walked over to her daughter and put her arm around her, which Julie shrugged off. Her cousins turned on the TV and went to the Pandora app. They chose a holiday station. Sadie peered at all of them from under her dark bangs. Her uncle drank, his ham-like jowls quivering when he crunched the ice between his yellow niblet teeth. Her grandmother and grandfather beamed at her cousins. Suddenly, a song came on that her aunt liked. She clapped her witch-like hands together, and her earrings bounced excitedly on her large, melted ear-lobes.

"Oh, Jeffrey, 'Marshmallow World'! My favorite!" She

stood, then pulled her uncle up from the couch.

He put his arm around her, and they began to sing. Her aunt sang in a horrible soprano, showing the red lipstick smeared on her two oversized front teeth. Her grandparents wiggled on the couch to the music.

Her cousins swayed side to side, bumping shoulders to the rhythm. Opal's heels scuffed the floor as she danced along, and Julie smiled contemptuously at her mother, but eventually it got the best of even her. Her mother and father came back looking frazzled, but as soon as they witnessed the spectacle in the living room, they soon joined in. The happy tune filled Sadie with blinding rage. *A chorus of idiots, all of them.*

Sadie pulled the candy cane from her mouth. One end had been sucked into a very sharp point. She looked around at all of them, then back down at her candy spear. She got up and walked over to her uncle and aunt. They smiled as if she were going to join them and put their hands out to her, but Sadie shook her head and jabbed the candy cane into her uncle's neck several times. Blood spurted out onto her aunt as he stumbled and grabbed her blouse. He pulled her onto the ground when he fell forward. Sadie then straddled her aunt and stabbed her several times before someone pulled her off.

Everyone screamed as her mother tried holding her back. Sadie swung the candy cane wildly. Her father stood frozen in shock with Opal crying into his sweater. Julie held her phone up toward the ceiling. Sadie broke away from her mother and ran to the Christmas tree. She pulled the cord for the lights out of the wall and tugged until the ornaments fell to the floor and shattered. She dragged the tree on its side and made a growling noise when her mother tried to get close to her.

"Sadie! Stop, please! For god's sake, look what you've done!

What on earth's wrong with you, Sadie!" her mother cried.

Sadie swung the cord and struck her mother in the face, then rushed her and stuck the candy cane into her eye. Her mother fell to the ground, screaming as broken glass went into her hands. Her father finally snapped to and ran towards them, but skidded on the shards of glass. Sadie took the opportunity to grab the pointed star from the treetop and jab her father in the neck. Crimson bubbles formed as he gurgled up at her.

She looked at her cousins, who trembled as they tried to call for help. Opal and Julie ran out of the room. She kneeled over her father and pulled the star from his throat. Blood dripped onto the gray pine floor. Her grandmother was slumped over on the couch, passed out, and her grandfather sat pale as a ghost glued to the couch. Sadie kicked her grandfather's walker out of the way.

"No good cell service up here, especially in winter, remember? There's a landline in the kitchen...if you can get to it." Sadie smirked at her cousins.

Her cousins glanced to the doorway leading to the kitchen. Sadie laughed.

"Well, what'll it be smarty pants?" she asked

They ran toward the kitchen, but Sadie ran faster. She ripped the phone cord out of the wall, placed the bloody star on the counter, then grabbed the knife to carve the turkey and sliced the cord in half. She picked up the star again and held a weapon in each hand. Her cousins ran, and she followed after them. They both fumbled with the front door lock. *That door has always been sticky.* She threw the star at the back of Graham's head, then ran and began to stab them in the back just as the door opened. Snowflakes blew in as Lois fell to the ground. Graham fought back hard, but Sadie stabbed his hands. He tried one last time to flee, but Sadie stabbed him again and again until he fell face-first into the snow.

She went back into the house and saw her grandfather on the floor. He crawled wildly toward his walker, but she kicked it further away. He rolled over, exhausted, and she pranced around him. Finally, she slit his throat and then severed his hand. She grabbed the poker from the fireplace and swung it at the hand, which sent it sailing in the direction of her slumped-over grandmother.

"Goal!" she shouted.

She laughed maniacally and twirled the poker around as she looked for Opal and Julie. "Opal? Julie? Come on out! It's a whipped cream day!"

She crept around until she saw the basement door slightly ajar. She was going to go down, but she shut the door and locked it instead. *Morons!* She went into the kitchen and turned the gas stove on, then went back into the living room and stared down at her parents. Her mother was still alive and moaned softly. Tears and blood streamed down her mother's face. She dropped the poker and pet her mother's head gently, then kissed her cheeks.

"Cara mia," she whispered.

Sadie grabbed the cord and wrapped it around her mother's throat until she stopped breathing, then dragged her body closer to her father's and clasped their hands together.

"Merry Christmas, Mom and Dad."

She yanked the candy cane from her mother's eye and stuck it back in her mouth. She took a magazine, rolled it up, and held it over the fire. Once the magazine looked like a torch, she set fire to the tree. She lit the presents and decorations. Then the curtains and the couch. Once the living room was completely ablaze, she placed her earbuds back into her ears, went outside, and skipped away from the burning house into the gently falling snow.

Aianna

Dan Foley

At midnight, under the glow of a full, pink moon in April, a white pine seedling broke through the forest floor. A tiny silver pinecone was nestled within its branches. A pinecone that grew as the tree grew. On the next full, pink moon, the cone burst open, and Aianna, the seedling's wood sprite, emerged from it. She was a living extension of the tree. In the coming years, she would protect it from insects, disease, and wandering animals. In return, it would provide her with shelter and strength. Aianna and the tree were a single life force, forever linked; neither could live without the other.

* * *

Aianna knew the man was there the moment he stepped into the grove. Visitors were uncommon but not unheard of. They would stroll in, marvel at the peace and solitude, drink in its beauty, and leave more content than when they entered. Aianna welcomed their presence while watching, unseen, from within the shelter of her tree. Small, with skin as rough and brown as bark, hair the color of her trees needles, she was almost invisible. Anyone who managed to catch a glimpse of her quickly put it off to imagination or the flickering wings of a bird. She expected this visit to be no different. Then she saw the ax strapped to the visitor's back, and she knew there was murder in this man's heart.

"Stop! Don't! Leave us in peace," she cried from her hiding place within her tree's branches. Every tree in her grove was special, every loss a wound that tore at her heart. She could only hope he would pass them by.

It was not to be.

"No! Stop," she screamed, panic filling her small heart when the man stood in front of *her* tree and lifted his ax.

❄ ❄ ❄

Brent stopped, stood still for a moment, and then shook his head. Had he heard a voice? *No. Only the wind,* he thought, telling himself that old tales of sprites and spirits in the deep woods were just that...old tales. Nevertheless, a chill ran up his spine.

Quit it, he chided himself. *You're here for a Christmas tree. Pick one and be done with it.*

This one, he thought, eyeing a fat, eight-foot-tall, white pine. It didn't have the classic, trimmed shape of the ones in the church parking lot, but it had charm...and it wasn't going to cost him sixty bucks. Instead, he could use the money for the bike Jamie had been begging for. Shrugging off his sudden unease, he raised the ax and started chopping.

❄ ❄ ❄

"No!" Aianna screamed in pain when the ax cut into her tree's side. How could the man not hear it? How could he not feel their pain? *"No!"* she screamed again, but her cries fell on deaf ears. The man chopped and chopped and chopped until her beautiful tree toppled and lay on the ground, its life sap bleeding from its stump and trunk.

Aianna huddled in her tree's branches, clinging tight to the trunk as the man dragged them from the woods and dumped them into the bed of his pickup. Then the wind was whistling past them like a storm, and every bump threatened to rip her from her perch.

❄ ❄ ❄

Gooseflesh rose on Brent's neck and arms as he dragged the tree from the forest. He ignored the wind that sounded like wailing in his ears. He had the uncomfortable feeling that someone, or something, was watching him, following him as he made his way out of the woods. The feeling didn't stop until he had loaded the tree in the back of his pickup and driven away. When he arrived home, the smile on his wife's face and the excitement in his son's eyes as he unloaded the tree from the back of the truck drove all thoughts about the voices in the wind and the feeling of being watched from his mind.

"When can we put it up?" Jamie demanded, bouncing with excitement once Brent had it off the truck.

Brent laughed and ruffled his son's hair. "Patience. I have

to trim the trunk and get it into the stand. That's going to take a while. Tomorrow's Saturday. I'll do it in the morning. Then we can take our time and enjoy it."

"But I want to decorate it tonight," Jamie whined.

Brent looked to his wife for support. "Your Dad's right," she said. "We can decorate it tomorrow. We'll make hot chocolate, string popcorn, and put the ornaments on. You can put the angel on top."

"Okay," Jamie reluctantly agreed, disappointment evident in his voice.

❄ ❄ ❄

Brent had to hide a smile as he watched Jamie scarf down his pancakes and squirm in his chair.

"Come on, Dad, hurry! We're decorating the tree today."

"Let me finish my breakfast and drink my coffee. Then we can get started. You can help me get it ready."

"Okay," his son agreed, but he didn't stop his squirming.

Brent finished the last of his coffee. He was tempted to pour himself a second cup but took pity on Jamie. "Okay, let's go," he said, standing up.

The boy was off his chair like a shot.

Brent laughed as he followed his son outside to where the tree was standing in a bucket of water next to the house.

❄ ❄ ❄

Aianna slipped from her tree and took cover in a rhododendron next to the house when the man and boy came toward them with a saw. She watched in horror as the man used the saw to cut off part of the trunk before placing it into a metal holder and dragging it into the house. Her spirits plummeted with every step the man took. She had never been more than a few feet from her tree her entire life.

Aianna shared her tree's relief when its stump was placed in water. The freshly trimmed trunk allowed it to drank heavily, replacing some of what was lost, but it would only delay death for a few days. Days in which it would slowly wither and dry. Its branches would droop, its needles would fall. Aianna's life would fade with it.

❄ ❄ ❄

His wife and son watched as Brent strung the lights on the tree. This had to be done before the first ornament could be hung. Jamie could barely contain his enthusiasm. "Come on, Dad," he pleaded repeatedly until the last string was hung. Then, as soon as Brent stood back to evaluate his work, Jamie rushed past him and attached the small rocking horse that was the special ornament he had picked out for this year. He reached for another until Brent stopped him. "Let your mother and me place ours first, and then you can hang all you want. Okay?"

"Okay," Jamie agreed and stood ready to go as soon as his parents had hung their special ornaments. He didn't even notice that his mother's ornament of choice was an ultrasound picture of the sister that would be joining the family in June.

Outside, Aianna watched from her perch in the rhododendron as the man, woman, and boy desecrated her tree by wrapping it with lights and hanging tiny objects from its branches. The heat of the lights assaulted her skin while the weight of the objects dragged at her limbs. Why were they doing this? Were they making a mockery of its death? Their death? As she watched, a feeling she had never experienced started to grow within her—sadness. Over the next few days, as she and her tree grew weaker, her sadness would deepen...and then turn to hate.

As the days passed, Aianna grew weaker as her tree slowly died. The air inside the house was too dry. It sucked the water from her tree's branches like a hot wind in summer. The woman in the house gave it water every day, but her tree was dying and drank less and less of it. Outside, no matter how much water Aianna managed to gather from frost and snow, it couldn't quench her thirst. Nothing could.

❄ ❄ ❄

So weak she was barely able to cling to the branches of the rhododendron that had been sheltering her, Aianna watched as the man and woman placed colorful packages under and around her tree. They were laughing and hugging while she and her tree were straining to cling to the last vestiges of life. Her tree no longer drew in any of the water the woman offered it every day. Its needles were dropping, and what little moisture that was left inside its trunk and branches would soon be gone. Aianna knew her death was close. She wouldn't see another morning.

❄ ❄ ❄

"Let's go to bed," Brent's wife told him after he had placed the new bike with the big red ribbon attached to its handlebars next to the tree. "Jamie's going to get us up at the crack of dawn. And... I've got a special gift for you if you're good," she added with a grin.

"You go ahead, I'll be up in a minute," he told her.

Brent took a minute to admire the scene in the living room. The tree looked better than he had imagined when he first cut it down and brought it home. It was perfect, round and full, covered with lights and filled with ornaments and strings of white popcorn and red cranberries. He considered going straight upstairs, but instead, he stepped outside for a cigarette. The last one he would ever smoke. He was finally going to give up the damn things. That was his special Christmas present for Evie this year, one she had been asking for since Jamie had been born.

❄ ❄ ❄

Aianna was shocked to see a flame blossom in the man's hands. Was he crazy? Fire was dangerous. Fire was the enemy. Fire was to be feared. Before shaking out the tiny flame, he touched it to something in his mouth, something that glowed every time he sucked on it. A second later, smoke would issue from his mouth and nose. Was he on fire inside? Was that even possible? Then, as she watched, he flicked the glowing thing into the night. Sparks flew from it when it hit the ground at the base of the rhododendron. Aianna studied it, shuddered, climbed out of the rhododendron, and crawled toward it. When she reached it, she gathered it into her dry, withered arms. Inside the house, her tree burst into flames. Aianna's last thought was, *Now we will all die together.*

Away in a Manger: A Christmas Tale of Terror

Tim Kane

"It's not even snowing," Marissa said, tapping on the car window. "Isn't that the point of living all the way up on bum-fuck mountain?"

Bill kept his gaze riveted to the road. The sleet poured down in wet globs, adding a sheen to the ribbon of asphalt.

"We deserve some snow for trekking out here," she added. "Instead, we get this sleety slush."

"It's Christmas," Bill said.

"Nope, tomorrow's Christmas."

Bill hunched his shoulders and concentrated on the curve up ahead.

"I could be at the Pearl Oyster enjoying a chocolate martini." She twirled a lock of black hair with one finger. "Maybe find a lonesome guy missing his family." She sighed and leaned her head against the glass but then jerked away. "Crap, that's cold."

As the Audi banked around the curve, the tires slid on the glossy road and kissed the rocky embankment. Bill cranked the wheel, veering away from the steep drop-off.

"Easy Tex. I'm still making payments," she said.

"Then you should have driven." He drew himself up over the steering wheel.

"Why? You're doing such a bang-up job."

"Gives you more time to bitch and moan," he murmured under his breath.

"Come again?"

The road leveled off, and he pried his gaze away. "Come on, Sis. It's Mom and Dad. We do this every year."

"I know. You'd think they'd give us at least one year off."

"It's Christmas."

She shook her head. "Not yet."

The sun sank behind the mountains fifteen minutes before the Audi turned onto the access road. The tires sloshed through the gravel ruts, now a soup of mud and ice. Bill pulled up behind the Lincoln Navigator parked in the drive and killed the headlights. The forest loomed like a black wall. The closest neighbor lived a mile down the road.

He peered through the windshield at the darkened house. "Well, the car's here."

"Maybe they're conserving electricity. Who knows." Marissa shoved open the passenger door. "Let's get this show moving. You grab the gifts."

She zipped up her parka and flipped up the hood.

"You could help me, you know," he said, eyeing the sleet still filtering through the tree branches.

"I love you, too." She winked and dashed out of the car.

She made a beeline for the courtyard. Even with the coat, she instinctively wrapped her arms around her shoulders. Once under the eave by the front door, she rang the bell, stomping her feet to remove the slush from her Kate Spades.

"Come on, Mom. Break away from the cookie baking for five seconds." She jabbed the doorbell three more times.

Bill popped the trunk and stepped out of the car. Even though the trees blocked most of the sleet, fat gobbets of half-frozen rain still dribbled onto his head. He tossed a scarf around his neck and trudged to the rear of the Audi. Marissa's three presents sat neatly arranged in an oversized Christmas bag, all looking far too festive to be her own shopping taste. His six presents fit like jigsaw pieces into a cardboard banker's box. Bill grabbed the lid and tried to cover his gifts, but the bottle of wine for Dad jutted up. He canted the cardboard lid sideways and propped the whole thing under one arm. With one finger, he hooked his sister's bag and then elbowed the trunk closed. He hustled past the courtyard wall and onto the stoop next to Marissa's bundled-up form.

"Quick, open the door," he said.

She raised her hands. "Houdini I am not." She grabbed the knob and shook it. The door rattled in its frame but stayed shut. "Did you remember your key?"

"No." He unloaded the bag and the box onto the stoop. The eave kept most of the sleet off the packages. "Don't they keep a spare somewhere?"

She smiled, opening her hands in a gesture meant to say, "Be my guest."

"Some help you are."

"I didn't want to come, remember?"

He rolled his eyes and scanned the courtyard. Perhaps forty potted plants cluttered every conceivable nook. He ran his hands over his face. The key could be anywhere.

"Let me check the other doors."

"Knock yourself out," she said, leaning against the wall. "I'll wait here."

He flipped up the collar on his coat and disappeared around the side of the house. She began humming "Jingle Bells" and peered through the darkened window. Something crashed inside. It sounded like a plate shattering.

"Bill! Is that you?" she called through the window. "Hurry up, will you? It's freezing out here."

She stomped her feet once more, though the gesture didn't bring her any relief.

"Bill?"

"What?" The voice came from the courtyard. She spun around and saw her brother round the corner of the low wall.

"I went around the whole place," he said.

"Something broke inside. I thought it was you."

"Nope. All the doors are locked. Even the windows. I checked."

"Well, something fell over."

"It must be them." He rushed to the door, pounding. "Mom! Dad! Can you hear me?"

"Why not turn on a light?" she wondered.

"Maybe the power's out." He hammered on the door again. "Mom! Dad! It's Bill. Open the door!"

She flipped her hands up. "I say we call it a loss and head back."

"No, Mom and Dad could be hurt in there."

"Or they could be at a friend's house."

He glanced at the car. "The phone." He dashed toward the parked Audi.

Marissa watched as he sat in the driver's seat and dialed his cheap Samsung. No way was she diving back through the sleet for her iPhone.

She heard something scuttle across the wood floor just on the other side of the window. She wrinkled her forehead and leaned closer. As far as she knew, her parents didn't have any pets.

Then the phone rang inside, blotting out the sound. When the first ring abated, she leaned in again but heard nothing. After eight rings, the phone stopped as the call went to the machine. A glance toward Bill showed that he was leaving a suitably concerned message.

Marissa kissed two fingers, and touched them to the door. "Merry Christmas, Mom and Dad." She jogged back to the car and slid onto the passenger seat just as Bill ended the call.

"What are you doing?" he asked.

"They're not home," she said.

He stared at her, and she shrugged.

"What? I left the gifts. Let's go."

"We can't just leave."

"It's freezing, and I am not staying out here all night."

"But..." He glanced across the courtyard. "The gifts will get soaked."

"No, they'll be fine."

He stepped out of the car and plodded toward the front door.

She cracked open her door. "Just throw something over them."

He shouted back, "The door's open."

"Oh, for Chrissakes." She summoned up her courage and scurried through the sleet.

"Are you sure you checked the door?" he asked.

"Yes, I checked." She stomped her feet again. "Do you think I wanted to stand out in this muck?"

He twisted the doorknob, and the door creaked open. A

gust of wind blew the rain in, spattering the wood floor.

"I swear it was locked."

Bill hefted up his box of presents. She stepped over her bag of gifts and entered the house. He frowned and curled a finger under the handle of her bag.

She flipped the light switch, and a scene of true Christmas splendor greeted her. The tree stood in the corner of the living room, festooned with ornaments and subdued lights.

"Wow," Marissa said. "Every year they get more of these things." She tapped the top of a crocheted Wise Man. "I swear they're breeding on their own."

Scenes of the nativity infested nearly every surface of the room. An embroidered pillow showed Joseph and Mary around the baby Jesus. Collages of Christmas cards depicting the nativity were framed and hung about the room. On every available flat surface sat a carved or cast version of that famous manger scene. There were versions of Joseph and Mary in ceramic, straw, and even crystallized salt.

Bill struggled through the door. "You want to help me?"

She plucked her bag from his outstretched hand.

"Hello?" she called as they walked down the hall to the dining room. "Mom? Dad?"

He elbowed the lights on and slid the box onto the table. She set her presents next to his and draped her parka over the back of a chair.

"Is that all you got them?" he asked.

She shrugged, scanning this room's nativity decorations. Some of the scenes looked like full villages of miniature people.

"Did you re-gift?"

She gave him a look, and the corner of her mouth hitched up. "Maybe."

He rolled his eyes and stepped into the kitchen.

"Listen, I'm not into all that Christiany stuff. Mom and Dad are. So why put them to waste?"

Propping the refrigerator door open, he reached behind the carton of eggnog for a can of V8.

"Unbelievable."

"Yeah, like you go to so much trouble." She flicked the bows on one of his packages. "I bet Sara bought those for you."

He popped the can and downed the contents. When he turned back, a frown crossed his lips.

"Ha!" She pointed an accusing finger. "Told you."

"Scrooge," he said.

"Grinch," she fired back.

He dumped the empty can in the trash and looked around. "Where are Mom and Dad?"

"Maybe they're really not here."

"I'm going to check upstairs."

He took the stairs two at a time. She could hear the floor creaking as he walked around up there.

She wandered toward the game room, but something crunched on the floor.

"Shit." She lifted her foot and glanced down. Too dark to see anything.

Marissa fumbled for the light, finally finding it and flicking it on. What was once a pool table sat drowned in half-finished baskets, strands of raffia, various thrown pots, and several painted nutcrackers shaped like soldiers.

She looked down and spotted the culprit—a tiny ceramic Wise Man, now shattered.

"Dammit."

She leaned down to retrieve the figure. The pieces around the arm flaked away to reveal a wire framework with miniature hinges. The rest of the porcelain looked cracked but managed to hold together.

A scan of the table revealed a new nativity scene next to a wooden box. All the figures looked like ceramic but had movable joints. A thin brass lever jutted out of the bottom of the manger. She pulled it, and the scene sprang to life. Baby Jesus sat up in his crib. Joseph and Mary bent forward under the roof of the manger. A pair of shepherds wiggled their crooks. The angel flapped its wings, and the two remaining Wise Men swiveled to face her.

"Cool."

After a moment, the scene wound down, and the figures sputtered into statues again. She inspected the crushed figurine. It seemed to fit next to the other Wise Men. She clicked it back into place.

"There."

Bill tromped down the steps. "They're not upstairs."

"You should check this out. Mom and Dad really outdid themselves this time."

He stepped into the game room. "Maybe they're not home."

"Yeah. What I said." She pulled the lever back, but nothing happened. A jiggle on the handle produced no movement. "There's got to be some way to... Aha!" She found a winding key on the side. Cranking it caused gears inside to click as the spring tightened.

"Maybe we should look in the bedrooms."

"Check this out."

"Since when have you been interested in nativity scenes?"

"This is cool. Just watch." She pulled the lever. At first, nothing happened; the figures remained still. Then Joseph and Mary quivered, as though some mechanism were stuck. Suddenly the whole scene came to life. All the figures went through their motions. The cows rotated their necks, and the camels fluttered their eyes.

There came a snapping sound, and the third Wise Man

tumbled to the ground. The fall shattered the remnants of its porcelain façade.

"Great, Marissa. You explain that to Mom and Dad."

"But I found him that way. He must have dropped before." She picked up the remains of the figure, now only a skeleton of wire. "He fell off and cracked."

"Great. Let's see if it holds water with Mom."

She stuck out her tongue.

"I'm going to check the bedrooms." He trotted to the hall that led away from the dining room.

"Knock first," she said.

He shook his head and proceeded down the hall.

Marissa knelt and collected all the ceramic bits of robe. Her head now level with the mechanical nativity scene, something caught her eye.

"Huh." She peered at the figure of Joseph. "Looks a little like Dad."

She went back to cleaning the floor. The remaining figures of the Wise Men clicked their heads, their tiny eyes trained on Marissa. When she stood, the heads rotated back to their original position.

She held the shattered Wise Man in one hand. "What am I going to tell Mom and Dad?" She placed the pieces inside the wooden box. The label on the side said: PRODUCT OF ARKHAM.

❄ ❄ ❄

Bill checked the two guest rooms and the storage room. All empty. Finally, he came to the master bedroom. He hesitated, glancing over his shoulder, and knocked on the door.

"Mom? Dad?"

No answer.

He turned the knob and entered the darkened room. He felt along the wall but then remembered that he had to walk over to the nightstand lamps if he wanted light. Instead, he maneuvered around the bed and flicked the switch in the master bath. The light reflected against one wall and seemed to intensify the shadows in the room.

He sighed. "Where are you guys?"

A momentary shudder passed through him as terrible scenarios played out in his mind. He shook his head. "Marissa's right. They're not home." He reached to flip off the light, and his shoe knocked into something.

He bent down and picked up a small, hard object. At first, he couldn't tell what it was. There were little bits of metal and wire. When he turned it over, he noticed the ceramic face. The figure Marissa had broken from the nativity. *But how did it get in here?* he wondered.

Something scurried up his arm. Reflex action took over. He flicked at his sleeve with his free hand and knocked something loose. Whatever it was flew across the room. It bounced off the mattress and *thumped* on the carpet.

He moved over to examine the remains. Another of those Wise Men from the nativity scene in the game room. He furrowed his brow. The little figure jerked its arms and legs and stood. It swiveled its head toward Bill and charged. Several more figures emerged from under the bed and scurried up his pant legs.

Bill dropped the shattered figure of the first Wise Man and began sweeping at his body, trying to dislodge the tiny people.

Two had reached his arms. *Damn, they were fast.* He shook them loose, but the third Wise Man and one of the shepherds had climbed up his back and reached the nape of his neck. The Wise Man removed his crown and, together with the shepherd's crook, they repeatedly jabbed at the skin.

Bill swatted at his neck but failed to dislodge the tiny figures. The Wise Man used the jagged pieces of his broken jar of myrrh to slash at Bill's neck. By now the other discarded figurines, another Wise Man and a shepherd, had recovered and scrabbled up his pant legs.

Bill plucked the first shepherd off his neck and saw the end of the crook stained crimson with his blood. He tossed this one away and grabbed the Wise Man from his shoulder, holding this figurine aloft. Thin cracks zigzagged through the ceramic robes. He closed his fingers around the figure, crushing the Wise Man in his fist.

The other figures had skittered up his shirt and reached his head. The second shepherd hooked the corner of his mouth with one end of the crook. The Wise Man seized the other corner, and together they yanked the mouth open. Bill threw the squashed Wise Man aside and grasped the two figures with his hands. Both kept their grip on his mouth, pulling his lips open.

Now he spied the angel, hovering above him.

It clasped the shattered remains of the first Wise Man in its arms. The angel dive-bombed his open mouth. His scream was cut short as the angel shoved the metal and wire skeleton down his throat.

❄ ❄ ❄

Marissa stooped under the Christmas tree, arranging the gifts. She cocked her head.

"Bill?" She stretched out the word.

It had been a while since he went to check the bedrooms. He would have come back if he'd found Mom and Dad. Even if he hadn't, he should have been back by now.

She set down the wrapped snow globe and stood. Hundreds of tiny ceramic and wooden eyes stared placidly out of their mangers. She walked back into the dining room.

"Bill, is that you?"

She peered down the hallway leading to the bedrooms. There was only one light, muffled under plexiglass in the ceiling, which created a gloomy glow. Marissa hated this hall. As a girl, she would charge down it to the safety of her bedroom, but now she proceeded slowly.

The door to the master bedroom lay open, and light shone out from the bathroom light. She stepped inside and glanced around. Empty.

"Bill! This is not funny."

She padded over to the bed and flicked on one of the lamps. Bill wasn't hiding in the shadows. She tiptoed over to the bathroom, pausing at the door, and then sprang out.

"Boo!"

The bathroom was vacant. She flipped off the light.

"Okay, you can come out now."

She headed back into the hall and peeked into the storage room and the two other bedrooms—all empty. Finally, she jogged upstairs, positive she heard the floor creak under Bill's weight, but no one was there.

She wrapped her arms around herself, feeling alone in her parent's house.

She hustled back to the dining room.

"Quit it, Bill. I'm warning you."

From the game room, she heard a clicking sound. As she approached the edge of the pool table, she saw the mechanical nativity winding down.

She knelt to examine the scene. The third Wise Man—the one she'd stepped on—was there, the clothes whole and looking as though it had been painted today. But the face. It didn't look the same.

Her heart froze.

It was Bill's face.

She let out a little yelp and jumped back. Her heart banged against her ribcage, ready to leap out any second.

She forced herself to breathe easy, calming down.

She stepped closer. *Damn, if that doesn't look like Bill,* she thought. A glance at Joseph told her it didn't just look like Dad—it was Dad. Down to the little mole on his neck. And Mary, too. Totally Mom.

"Okay, is this some kind of joke?" There was no answer. "You guys got me, all right." She scanned the area around her. The various quilted figures from the nativity wall hangings glared at her with empty eyes.

When she returned to the nativity scene, she could swear that some of the figures had shifted. Had the shepherds been looking at her before? She reached out to touch the third Wise Man, the one that looked so much like Bill, but paused and furrowed her brow. She glanced in the wooden box. The shattered remains were missing.

"How did they do that?"

She bent closer to examine the figures. Looking at the Wise Man felt like she was looking at a costumed version of her brother, a perfect copy of Bill. Too much like him, in fact. Her gut clenched. The figures of Joseph and Mary quivered as though resisting the spring inside. Then the eyes of the Wise Man jerked open. They weren't mechanical eyes. They were Bill's eyes.

Marissa screamed and lashed out at the nativity, striking it with her fist. Two of the Wise Men fell to the floor. She instantly pulverized them, stomping on them repeatedly.

Finally, better senses took control, and she stopped crushing the tiny figures underfoot. When she took a step back, two very different remains littered the floor. The first Wise Man showed shattered ceramic shards over a metal skeleton. The other looked different. Some sort of pulpy red liquid oozed out. She bent over to examine it. Under the fractured shell, she saw blood, torn muscle, and bits of bone. The face she recognized. It was Bill's. She'd smashed him, crushed her own brother underfoot.

Marissa glared at the nativity scene. Now she didn't have to imagine. The figures of the shepherds, the angel, and the lone Wise Man all swiveled to look at her. The angel flapped its wings and leaped into the air. The other figures also came to life, scurrying away from their posts.

She seized one of Mom's glazed pots and brought it down on top of the nativity. The pot smashed into wicked-looking shards. She grasped a massive three-foot nutcracker and beat at the nativity. One of the arms sheared off after the second blow. The head snapped away by the tenth.

She abandoned the mangled nutcracker and staggered away. Bits of the broken figurines lay scattered amidst the wrecked pot. She noticed that the figures of Joseph and Mary were also split open, revealing bloody interiors.

Marissa held one hand up to her mouth. Tears, hot and stinging, filled her eyes. She retreated, wanting to escape the ghastly scene. Her back banging into the dining room table jarred her to her senses. She would get in the car and drive away.

But before Marissa could reach the front door, the angel from the mechanical nativity hovered in the air before her. She raised one hand to swat it, but then the other figurines caught her eye, hundreds of nativity scenes set all around the room. Were they moving, too? She felt their gazes—wooden, ceramic, painted, and unpainted—all staring at her.

The angel dove forward, and Marissa threw herself against

the wall, knocking down a quilted scene of baby Jesus. The angel zoomed past. She rushed for the door, pawing at the handle. Every second that passed she imagined the other figurines crawling off the shelves to get her. Yet a glance told her that they were still motionless.

The lock clicked, and she flung open the door. Racing to the car, her feet slid on the icy cement. Her parka was still inside, and globs of semi-melted sleet plopped onto her shoulders and head. As she dashed for the car, a thought seized her. *The keys!* Had Bill had left them in the ignition? She threw open the driver's door and groped around the steering column. The keys jangled. *Yes!*

She grabbed them and twisted. The car started up immediately. Thank God for preventative maintenance. She yanked the door shut.

Her gaze flicked back to the house. Any second, an army of figurines with robes and crooks would pour through the open doorway. Her heart thumped in her ears, drowning out the engine.

When she had the car turned around, she stomped down on the accelerator. The tires spun on the slick driveway but finally found purchase. She hurtled down the access road, taking the turn onto the asphalt strip at top speed. The Audi skidded to the shoulder, the tires popping on the rocks along the drop-off.

She pumped the brake.

The car rocked over the embankment, threatening to slide into the woods.

Her fingers tightened on the steering wheel. The tears came in a flood. She couldn't control them. One hand flew up to cover her face. She cried for Bill and Mom and Dad. She cried for the sheer horror of it.

A cracking sound caught her attention. She peered through

her fingers. A star marred the windshield. A stray rock must have hit the glass. Had that been there when she'd stopped? Probably. She hadn't been thinking clearly. The sight of the damaged glass steadied her. She gripped the wheel again and put the car in gear.

Something shot at the windshield and hit the same spot. She jumped back in her seat, her heart revving. That was no rock. The angel figurine hovered on the other side of the glass. The crack spiderwebbed across the windshield, the hole in the center now large enough for it to poke its diminutive head through. It stared at her for a moment and then leaped up into the night air.

Marissa floored the accelerator. The engine gunned, and she nearly drove off the embankment. She yanked on the steering wheel and swerved onto the road. As she drove, she kept glancing toward the sky, unsure when the angelic kamikaze might strike next.

Then she spied it.

Somehow the angel had gotten in front again and was speeding toward her. She jerked the wheel to the right. The fender scraped along the rock face. The Audi rebounded off the wall and careened across the two lanes and off the other side.

Marissa screamed.

For one brief moment, the night sky filled the windshield, the stars looking like glistening drops of dew.

Then the Audi struck the tree—a detonation of splintered wood and crumpled metal. A globe of white eclipsed her vision. As the airbag deflated, she could see the windshield. Teeny cubes of safety glass dotted the dash like shimmering snowflakes. Her body caved under the weight of her injuries. She fought off fatigue.

Rain cascaded down through the shattered windshield

onto her face, but she craned her head toward the sky.

The angel landed on the crumpled hood with a *plink*—its ceramic form pulverized and the frame underneath distorted. It folded its wings and marched straight for her.

She tried to squirm away, but her body was slow to respond. As her consciousness faded, she felt the tiny figurine grab her by the lips.

Then the blackness took her.

❄ ❄ ❄

Marissa blinked awake. Her muscles ached, and she could hardly move. Had Bill found her and brought her back home? But why had he left her in the game room? She could just make out the dining room table with the cardboard box Bill had brought. She tried to look down, but her neck felt stiff. The extent of her vision showed her that she sat on the pool table. She shifted her gaze left. A giant nutcracker sat beside her—impossibly large. In fact, everything in the room seemed gargantuan.

A sickening chill coursed down her spine.

She was *in* the nativity scene. Mom, Dad, even Bill stood back in their places.

Her heart crescendoed, creating an unbearable tattoo inside her chest.

Marissa wanted to scream, but the sound died behind her frozen ceramic lips.

The Vices and Virtues of Gideon Thomas

James Carlson

Hidden a fair distance behind the respectable residential areas and quaint mom-and-pop shops of a small Pennsylvania town was a charmless industrial district. And in this industrial district, across a dirt lot scattered with rubble and broken glass, was a large brick building that had certainly seen better days. But for all of its boarded-up windows, weathered doors, and crumbling exterior, this building, which stood quite apart from the factories and warehouses in this bleak part of town, wasn't a complete ruin. In fact, it looked as though it could stand for decades more.

What this building's use might be was not evident, as nothing advertised such information. On the ground, however, was a rusted metal sign that had once graced the arched brickwork above the main entrance before the passing of time and the elements had conspired to render it unreadable. Several "No Trespassing" postings, all of them of the thin plastic variety, were attached to the walls and lampposts about the property—the only indication that it might still have a purpose.

Whatever the case, the place had a very uninviting quality, which gave its current visitor an uneasy feeling.

Gideon Thomas stood in the lot and stared for some time at the structure. There was something undeniably dark and disturbing about it—a foulness more commonly assigned to people than places. Strange that his next story waited behind those crumbling brick walls. Even stranger still was that he had been summoned there by a representative of the Church. Part of him wanted to turn around and walk away with haste and never look back. Another part of him, the decidedly more dominant of the two, was compelled to continue forward and see this through.

The December evening was cold and breezy, and the ashtray sky was streaked with a soft orange as the sun set in the west. The naked branches of nearby trees swayed, knocking gently against one another, as a gust of wind blew a cluster of brittle leaves tumbling down the street.

Gideon let out a long sigh, his breath forming a white cloud in the crisp air. It was Christmas Eve, for fuck's sake. He should've been home with his loved ones, not chasing down stories in Pennsylvania. But the person with whom he spoke on the phone assured him it would be worth his while.

Crossing the lot, Gideon noticed dozens of large black birds perched watchfully along the edge of the roof. Because of this winged presence around the property, the upper portion of the building was crusted over with an astonishing accumulation of white bird feces.

When he was ten paces from the building, give or take, Gideon crossed paths with a stray cat, its fur entirely gray save for a patch of white on its chest. The cat shot Gideon a curious glance with its big green eyes before quickly losing interest and moving on to whatever feline business it had in the area.

At the main entrance, Gideon faced a door, whose long years of neglect had turned the wood from a healthy, attractive brown to a faded gray with countless surface cracks. As he knocked on the ugly thing, he realized it still seemed remarkably sturdy and secure for something in such poor condition.

He waited.

The seconds ticked slowly by, and Gideon still waited. He considered knocking again, harder this time but decided against it for now.

Gideon's waning patience was at last rewarded when a dour young man opened the door and allowed him to enter.

❄ ❄ ❄

The man's unwashed hair was long and hung about his face in greasy black strands. A brief glimpse of the pale face hiding behind the hair showed Gideon that he'd had corrective surgery to a cleft lip and palate. He avoided eye contact with Gideon utterly. Once inside, the young man pushed a hinged latch into place between the door and the wall, slid a large, positively antique-looking padlock into the eye mount, and snapped it shut. The fact that Gideon was now locked in did not escape his notice, and he didn't like the thought of it one bit.

"Right this way," Gideon's laconic greeter said without

proper introduction.

Gideon was led through a labyrinth of dim corridors and rickety stairways to an equally ill-lit office cluttered with stacks of tobacco-stained papers and old books. Behind a mahogany desk, seated in a worn-leather chair was an obese, balding man whose small hazel eyes peered out from behind circular, wire-framed glasses. Gideon guessed his age to be between fifty-five and sixty, but it was possible that he was younger and had simply aged poorly. Gideon could see that although this person was a member of the clergy, he was no stranger to excess. A repurposed coffee can on the desk overflowed with cigarette butts. Dirty plates were precariously piled on an aged Windsor chair by the door. And a lone wine bottle on the desk—its red contents nearly drained—would undoubtedly soon join the several empty bottles in a crate in the corner.

Gideon didn't judge the man harshly. He had grown rather fond of drink himself in recent years, certainly more than he cared to admit. Then again, it was less of a fondness for drink that drew Gideon to the bottle than a need to medicate his ailing soul. And the more he observed and experienced in this world—this strange, wonderful, terrible world—the more unwell his soul became, and consequently, the closer his relationship to the bottle.

Grunting, the man behind the desk rose from his seat with some effort when he saw Gideon. "Ah, Mister Thomas, do come in," the man said in a deep, friendly voice. "I've been expecting you." He extended a plump hand. Gideon took the hand and gave it a firm shake. It was quite sweaty. "Have a seat, won't you?"

"Thank you," Gideon said, lowering himself into the chair opposite the other man.

"I'm Father O'Halloran. I run this...er, facility, for lack of a better word."

"And what is this facility, Father?"

"Straight to the point, eh, Mister Thomas? You know, we've never officially given this place a name. But it's used for storage. A spiritual warehouse, you might say."

"Why would I have been asked to visit a storage facility?"

"Perhaps storage is the wrong word," Father O'Halloran contemplated. "Let's call it a containment unit instead."

"What's it meant to contain, exactly?"

"Vile things that you do *not* want out there wandering the streets, Mister Thomas."

Now this is getting interesting, thought Gideon.

"I guess what I want to know," Gideon said, "is why I'm here."

"Well, that's easy. You were requested."

"Requested by whom?"

"Our resident," the priest stated simply.

"That doesn't really answer my question, Father."

"Quite right. But before we get into all that, I think it pertinent to discuss a few other things."

"Such as?"

"First, you are free to write about what you experience here today with only one condition: You refrain from painting the Church in an unflattering light. Some, myself included, think that your history with the Church may have a less than desirable impact on the telling."

"That won't be an issue," Gideon assured him.

"Glad to hear it."

"Anything else?"

"I'm sure you're aware," O'Halloran continued, "the Church would typically insist you sign a strict non-disclosure form and forbid you from recording what you see here today. Although, in the past, it's more likely they would have refused you access, period. But, being that this facility has served its purpose and will probably be retired soon, our resident's request to visit with you has been granted, as has the telling of his story."

"I appreciate that," Gideon said, not quite sure how to respond to O'Halloran's statement. "What else?"

"You have witnessed some extraordinary things in your line of work, dealing with the occult and all, isn't that right?"

"Yes, I've seen many things in my line of work, some of which I'd say were extraordinary. But I don't deal with the occult, as you say. I document spiritual phenomena and work towards substantiating or disproving fantastic claims. But my focus is a broad one that includes many faiths, both the sacred and the profane, and everything in between. My research has taken me to dark places, where I have witnessed strange and fearsome things, granted, but I am in no way tied to the occult."

"Of course not," O'Halloran said in a somewhat apologetic tone. "I misspoke. It wasn't my intention to offend."

"No offense taken."

"I understand you were a man of the cloth once upon a time, Mister Thomas," O'Halloran uttered in a way that could just as easily have been a statement as a question, but also in a way that suggested disapproval.

"Seems like a lifetime ago, but yes, I was. All told, I was only a priest for two years, slightly longer than I spent as a transitional deacon. So, regrettably, my education lasted longer than my vocation."

"And why, if I may ask, did you leave the priesthood?"

"A crisis of faith that ultimately resulted in an altered spiritual point of view. There are so many religions in the world, all with very different stories and sets of beliefs, and each of them is convinced that it's the one true religion. I began obsessing over this, eventually doubting that Catholicism was the one. Maybe another of them is the one, or perhaps none of them are. It's also possible that they all have some truth in them. Therefore, I decided to begin researching spiritual matters all over the globe. To fund this research, I write and sell books about my experiences and findings."

"Your books have become rather popular, to my understanding."

"They do well enough."

"Any experience with demons?" O'Halloran asked in earnest.

"I've encountered a few things that have led me to believe demons may truly exist."

"Oh, make no mistake, Mister Thomas, they *do* exist. You will undoubtedly see proof of that today."

"What do you mean by that?"

"Have you ever heard of Father Peter Martin?"

"No, I don't believe so. Should I have?"

"Not if the Church has been doing its job properly, no."

"So...who's this Father Martin fellow?"

"Every diocese has at least one priest who is trained extensively in the rites of exorcism. Rarely in the life of a priest is he called upon by the bishop of his district to carry one out, though it does happen. For this district, I was that priest. Do you know how many exorcisms I did?"

Gideon shook his head.

"None, Mister Thomas. Not a one. And the sole reason: Father Peter Martin. To say demonic possession was his expertise would be a gross understatement; it was his calling, assigned to him from on high. He did all the exorcisms in this district and many others. Some of his exorcisms took place in other states, some in other countries. God truly made Father Martin His instrument in combating the agents of Hell.

Be that as it may, his last exorcism took quite a toll on him, and he's been here in our care ever since. It's been, oh, six years or so."

"This is all very fascinating, Father, but what's it got to do with me?"

"Father Martin is dying, Mister Thomas. His end is likely to be very soon. Whether he's down to days or hours, we're not certain. And for reasons he has not shared with us, he has requested to speak with you specifically."

"Well, this is highly unexpected."

"I'm sure it is."

"You honestly have no idea why he wants to see me?"

"In truth, I have no idea," O'Halloran said as he lit a cigarette and inhaled deeply. Exhaling a sizable cloud of smoke, he added: "I'll admit to some misgivings about allowing this meeting. But, alas, it's not up to me. It's been approved, and that's that."

"What else can you tell me about Father Martin?"

"Father Martin performed forty-seven rituals during his years as an active exorcist, the last of which took place at the start of 2012 in Philadelphia. This last demon, which he extracted from a thirteen-year-old Dominican girl, was something much different than he'd encountered previously—darker, stronger, more malevolent—and it proved to be more than he could handle. Or maybe all the exorcisms had finally irreparably damaged the man in both body and spirit, forcing him into retirement."

"How's that?"

"You see… Father Martin, while gifted by Heaven with a remarkably unique ability to deal with demonic presence on Earth, was never truly able to banish demons from the possessed. He was only able to draw them into himself and imprison them there."

"You mean to tell me that Father Martin has forty-seven demons imprisoned within him?" Gideon asked, shocked.

"That's precisely what I'm telling you, Mister Thomas."

"And he has requested to see me?"

"He has."

"But why?" Gideon asked again, not really expecting an answer.

"That's the question, isn't it, Mister Thomas? I mean, Father Martin is on his deathbed, as the saying goes, and instead of receiving his last rites, he is asking to speak with you. It's very curious indeed."

"We mustn't keep him waiting, then," Gideon said, rising from his chair.

"I suppose we shouldn't," O'Halloran agreed, extinguishing his cigarette by pushing it into the filthy collection of cigarette butts that had already been snuffed out in the coffee can. "Here, I'll walk you down to Father Martin's room."

Father O'Halloran, pallid and sweating, started to stand. Before he could get to his feet, however, he appeared to be overcome by some sort of unpleasantness. He reached for a nearby wastebasket, lifted it to his face, and vomited. Afterward, breathing heavily, he wiped his mouth with a black handkerchief he had retrieved from his back pocket.

"Are you okay?" Gideon asked with concern.

"Yes, yes, I'm fine." O'Halloran waved his hand in the air, collecting himself. "I'm terribly sorry you had to see that. Happens almost every time I prepare to venture into the wretched bowels of this infernal place."

"Should we get someone else to escort me to him?"

"No, I'll take you," O'Halloran insisted.

❄ ❄ ❄

Gideon, accompanied by the corpulent priest, moved through the complicated corridors and down a long flight of stairs to the basement. Father O'Halloran carried a battery-powered lantern with him, explaining that the wiring in the building was very old and therefore occasionally unreliable. Gideon had noticed this already. Since they began walking the corridors, the lights had flickered intermittently. The bare bulbs hanging from electrical wires in the ceiling of the basement did the same.

Gideon and O'Halloran crossed the length of the basement, a vast open space with steel supports extending from ground to ceiling and wide planks of wood, now half-rotted, over a badly deteriorating and cracked concrete floor. The basement smelled of the long years it had been in existence, in addition to a musty dampness, and the urine and feces of vermin. Gideon could hear these vermin as they scuttled about in the dark.

"You keep Father Martin down here?" Gideon asked with a note of incredulity.

"No, of course not." O'Halloran stopped at a green hatch door and pointed to it. "He's down there."

O'Halloran, rivulets of sweat running down his temples and over his jowls, groaned and wheezed as he lifted the heavy door to its open position.

"This underground portion is why the Church purchased this property," the priest panted. "Even though the tunnel and its chamber predate the construction of this building by more than thirty years, it wasn't in the architectural design or site analysis as a pre-existing feature. Nor was it mentioned in the real estate listing. We happened upon it during our walkthrough of the place and knew instantly it was the one. A fine example of God leading the way."

"What was it used for originally?"

"That's an excellent question, for which I don't have an answer. Sorry to disappoint. But I admit I've been rather curious about that myself."

Gideon leaned over the entrance. It was dark, very dark, like a toothless mouth yawning into an abyss. All he could see was a rusty metal ladder descending into the blackness.

"We're going down there?" Gideon asked warily.

"Indeed, we are, Mister Thomas."

"This doesn't feel right," Gideon confessed.

"Nothing about this place is right," O'Halloran pointed out. "But you're welcome to turn back and leave. I can tell Father Martin you weren't able to make it to see him. It's all the same to me, quite frankly."

Gideon considered this for a moment.

"No," he said finally, "I think I'd like to continue."

"Very well," O'Halloran said as he tied a rope around his lantern and lowered it into the tunnel below. "Shall we?"

O'Halloran struggled somewhat with moving his bulk onto the ladder. Once he succeeded in this graceless endeavor, he climbed down without incident.

"Now you, Mister Thomas," O'Halloran called out from the bottom.

Gideon climbed down, the rungs of the ladder staining his hands orange with rust. O'Halloran was waiting for him at the bottom, a newly lit cigarette hanging from his mouth.

Gideon found himself in a narrow tunnel with thick stone walls and a floor of wooden planks much like the basement floor above. Along the top of the wall, to Gideon's right, ran a bundle of pipes and wires that were presumably for electricity, water, and ventilation. A large, brown rat scurried along the top of the largest pipe, stopping briefly to sniff the air around Gideon and the priest. O'Halloran flipped a switch. Little lights came to life along the tunnel, filling it with a murky yellow glow.

For a moment, Gideon was sure he could hear disembodied voices whispering and murmuring around him, all of them speaking unintelligibly at once. Then he realized that the voices weren't in the tunnel; they were in his head. Suddenly, his head was swimming and his thoughts unfocused. He placed a hand against the damp wall, leaning his weight against it, as he became slightly unsteady on his feet.

Was he imagining this?

But just as Gideon began to question what was happening, the voices stopped, and there was silence. Equilibrium returned. The only sounds were O'Halloran's breathing and the occasional droplet of water falling from the ceiling to land with a faint liquid plop on the planks below.

"Are you okay?" O'Halloran asked, looking at Gideon with an expression of worry.

Gideon nodded, hiding the truth that he wasn't entirely convinced he was okay.

The tunnel went on for as far as Gideon could see, sloping steadily downward. As they walked, O'Halloran noticed Gideon looking curiously at the large images of the cross that had been painted on the walls of the tunnel in black.

"Originally," O'Halloran explained, "we hung crucifixes on the walls. But every morning we found them hanging upside-down. So, rather than right them every day, we took them down and painted crosses right on the walls. Turned out to be a wise solution to the problem—they haven't been altered since."

When Gideon and O'Halloran reached the end of the tunnel, they were met by a tall, muscular, middle-aged man with stony gray eyes and a shaven head peppered with dark stubble. This man, who had been sitting in a folding chair behind a small table by lantern light, stood respectfully when he saw Gideon and O'Halloran approaching. Behind the man was a thick steel security door that seemed more focused on keeping someone from getting out rather than preventing someone from getting in. A large black cross had been painted on the door, and surrounding the cross were esoteric symbols with which Gideon was not in the least bit familiar.

"Good evening, Liam," O'Halloran addressed the man at the door.

"Father," Liam said with a nod.

"We have a visitor for Father Martin," O'Halloran said. "This is Gideon Thomas."

"How d'you do, Mister Thomas?" Liam asked, turning his attention to Gideon.

"Somewhat unsettled and overwhelmed, to be perfectly honest," Gideon confessed. "Even so, I'm pleased to make your acquaintance, Liam."

"Liam mans the door to Father Martin's chamber," O'Halloran explained, "and keeps a vigilant watch over things on his end, don't you, Liam?"

"Aye, that I do, Father."

"I shan't be long, Liam, though Mister Thomas may be a while. It's difficult to say. Depends on the state of poor Father Martin. At any rate, I'll return in just few minutes."

Liam pulled a lever that moved a heavy-duty bolt lock to its open position. He then pulled the door toward them. Hot, fetid air flooded the cool tunnel. With a look of revulsion, Gideon took a step back and raised his hand to cover his nose and mouth.

"I know, it's quite unpleasant," O'Halloran remarked.

"What the hell is that?" Gideon asked through the hand cupping his nose and mouth.

"Exactly that, Mister Thomas; it's Hell."

"What's that supposed to mean?"

"Quite simply, even though it's a damp, gloomy hole in the earth, this place is climate controlled. Or at least it's supposed to be. No matter how cool we try to keep Father Martin's chamber, it remains inexplicably, unreasonably hot. As for the smell, Father Martin breathes and excretes sulfur, an unfortunate side effect of having demons trapped within him. That, and he doesn't bathe very often. We try to encourage daily ablutions, but Martin's not always in full control of himself and tends to remain unwashed for days, sometimes weeks at a time."

"Just to give you an idea of what to expect in there," O'Halloran said, producing a shiny red apple from his pocket and extending the arm holding it into the room. He held his arm there for a few moments. When he withdrew it, the apple in his hand was shriveled, black, and moldy. Had someone on the other side of the door swapped the healthy apple for the rotten one? Or was this truly the effect this room had on earthly things and organic matter?

"And you'll need this." O'Halloran picked up an hourglass from the table where Liam had been sitting when they'd arrived.

"What's this for?" Gideon asked, taking the hourglass from the priest.

"As my display with the apple so adequately proved, what's in this room is good for neither body nor soul. People who stay in the room too long have gone mad. In some cases, people have even died. We don't want such an incident with you, Mister Thomas."

"This is too much," Gideon said in disbelief.

"Shall we?" O'Halloran gestured toward the door.

❄ ❄ ❄

Gideon was not prepared for what awaited on the other side of the door. Upon crossing the threshold, he stopped, wide-eyed and open-mouthed, taking in the terrible spectacle of it all. The room was enormous, almost cavernous, with high walls of rock and earth through which large, gnarled roots penetrated and lay across the floor. The floor was smooth, damp stone. From parts of the ceiling there hung rusty iron chains. Strips of rusty iron were fastened to the walls so that they formed crosses. In each corner of the chamber was a stationary holy water font of hand-carved marble. And around the room there knelt rosary-clutching men and women in prayer, perhaps seven altogether.

At the center of the room, sitting on a dingy, threadbare blanket, was a haggard old man. The whites of his eyes were entirely yellow save for pronounced networks of red, swollen blood vessels. A hawkish nose sat above a straight line of a mouth that was almost lost in the man's thick, white beard. A shirtless torso, shoeless feet, and ill-fitting pants revealed ashen skin stretched over a skeletal frame. Bible verses had been tattooed into the old man's flesh, along with lines inked in several different languages. Gideon recognized only one of the languages: Latin. He'd learned Latin at the seminary. Or rather, he'd achieved a passable grasp of the language during his studies, even though the Church had long since changed the liturgy to the vernacular.

"They're binding prayers to aid Father Martin in keeping the demons from escaping," O'Halloran said when he noticed Gideon's gaze lingering on the strange words. "I know what you're thinking, the Church frowns upon marking one's skin in such a way. Yet, despite what it says in the Bible, the Pope has recently declared tattoos to be an acceptable way of celebrating one's faith. He even said it was okay for priests to get tattoos to better connect with today's Catholic youth.

And, in the case of Father Martin here, I'd say it's doubly acceptable."

O'Halloran strode over to a vintage record player, the kind you might find at a flea market and take home only to discover it doesn't work. This one, however, did work, and quite well. O'Halloran carefully placed the needle into a groove in the vinyl, and what sounded much like an old field recording of blues music began to play.

Before Gideon could ask, O'Halloran explained: "We tried hymns and sacred classical pieces, none of which had any effect on the demons. But this one—a gospel blues song recorded in the 1920s by a sightless street musician and evangelist named Blind Willie Johnson—well, it gets 'em every time. They absolutely hate it. 'Dark Was the Night, Cold Was the Ground' it's called. If I'm not mistaken, Mister Johnson was a Baptist, but we can forgive him for that."

From the record player there emanated the sound of passionate slide guitar and fingerpicking. This was coupled with gravelly vocals that didn't convey any clear lyrical message but were more of an accompanying instrument of hums and moans. There was something utterly inspired and sublime in it.

The very air of the room seemed to shriek in agony and hiss in anger at the sound of the sacred blues song, a host of voices suffering in unison. Father Martin's weak and sickly body twitched with each note masterfully wrung from the guitar, with each impassioned utterance of the singer.

Gideon and Father O'Halloran moved closer to the old man at the center of the room, stopping at a line made from a whitish granular substance that encircled the man.

"What's that?" Gideon pointed to the white circle around Martin.

"Salt. It acts as a barrier of purity that the demons cannot cross. At least in theory. Hasn't been tested yet. And I pray it never will."

The old man looked up at the priest and the writer.

"Father Martin," O'Halloran said, "this is Gideon Thomas, the young man you've been asking for."

Father Martin said nothing to this. He seemed to be inwardly preoccupied.

O'Halloran turned to Gideon. "If you need anything, just ask Liam."

"Thank you, I will."

"We hired Liam after he was released from prison," O'Halloran whispered confidentially, "but he's a good Catholic who not only needed work but a second chance. He's strong and loyal. And besides, forgiveness is given to the repentant, is it not?"

Gideon didn't say anything to this.

"Strange," O'Halloran continued, changing the subject, "that while the rest of the world is peacefully awaiting to commemorate the birth of Christ through song and prayer and spending quality time with loved ones, we are here witnessing the workings of the devil. They rejoice at Heaven as we look in dread at the Infernal."

"Good point," Gideon agreed.

"Well," O'Halloran said, "I'll leave you to it, then."

After O'Halloran had started back toward the door, he paused and turned to Gideon. "Remember, Mister Thomas, use the hourglass. When the last of the sand sifts through to the bottom, take a break from this room. You'll regret it if you don't."

And with that, O'Halloran made his exit.

❄ ❄ ❄

Gideon sat in a chair that had been set out for his meeting with the retired exorcist. It was the kind of exceedingly ordinary and uncomfortable chair one finds in hotel conference rooms across the country—a metal frame with two irremovable red cushions, one for the back and one for the rear end.

As he sat in this ordinary and uncomfortable chair, Gideon felt himself beginning to sweat.

Was it the heat? Or was it being in this bizarre and disquieting place with this broken vessel of evil before him?

Probably both, Gideon decided.

"Father Martin," he said, "good evening. My name is Gideon Thomas. I believe you've been expecting me."

Martin straightened himself from a slumped-over position. His eyes, which had been sort of rolling around in his head, regained a degree of focus as he set them on the one who'd spoken his name.

"Yes, I'm Father Martin," the old man said in a weak, tremulous voice.

"I'm Gideon Thomas, Father," Gideon repeated, "I believe you've been expecting me."

"No, I don't think I have," Martin said, clearly confused.

"But Father O'Halloran said—"

"That man has less wits than I do," Martin stated bluntly, "and I'm a badly damaged parcel about to be delivered to death's doorstep."

"I'm sorry for the misunderstanding. Would you like me to go?"

"What's your name again, young man?" Martin asked.

"Gideon Thomas."

"Well, Gideon Thomas, I get so few visitors here. You're welcome to stay awhile, if you'd like."

Gideon looked at the men and women in prayer around

the room.

"Oh, they make for lousy company, that lot," Martin grumbled. "All they do is pray. Not that there's anything wrong with prayer. I'm a big fan, personally. But between you and me," Martin lowered the volume of his voice considerably, "I'm fairly certain their efforts are wasted here."

"Who are they, anyway?" Gideon inquired.

"Terminally ill people, all of them—devout Catholics, too—recruited by the Church from the hospital rooms of St. Jude's. They just kneel there praying till they quite literally drop dead. You know how people elect to be organ donors when they die? Well, these people have donated both body and soul to the Church to keep this unholy scourge bottled up inside of me. But, as I said, I'm not convinced of its efficacy."

Just as Martin finished explaining this to Gideon, as if to add validity to the priest's words, one of the supplicants fell forward with a thud, face-down on the stone floor. Dead.

"See, I told you."

"That's awful!" Gideon exclaimed.

"Agreed. It's a most disagreeable way to spend one's final days of life."

"The same could be said for what you do, imprisoning demons inside of yourself and suffering for years in this miserable hole in the earth."

"It's a price I gladly pay in service to God."

"You're a better man than I."

"Please," Martin said, changing the subject, "tell me about yourself."

And Gideon did.

❄ ❄ ❄

"That's a fascinating story," Martin commented when Gideon had finished speaking.

"Thank you."

"So," Martin said, "if I've got this right, you left the priesthood. And because you'd lost your own faith, you thought it somehow appropriate to assist others in doubting their own."

"That's not it at all," Gideon defended himself. "I'm merely looking for answers, for the truth."

"One cannot take a purely academic approach to religion, Mister Thomas. Faith is not an altogether intellectual pursuit; it is first and foremost a spiritual one. Either you believe it as strongly as you do your own existence, or you don't."

"I believe in something. I just don't know exactly what it is yet."

"How spiritually inconvenient for you."

"But I've seen things, Father."

"Such as?"

"In the Appalachian Mountains, I witnessed a preacher put his hand into the mouth of a seemingly normal eight-year-old boy and pull out a living, four-foot rattlesnake. In Texas, at a tent revival, I saw a young woman heal an infected compound fracture just by laying hands on the affected area; it was as if the wound had never been there at all. At a Gypsy encampment in eastern Europe, a woman walked naked into a raging bonfire and emerged minutes later without so much as a first-degree burn on her body. In the Louisiana bayou, I was present when a voodoo priestess and some of the townsfolk bound a serial pedophile to a cypress tree and stabbed him repeatedly. Then, for two days and two nights, every time the man died, the priestess pulled his soul back from the afterworld, returning it to his body so the townsfolk could kill him again. During an expedition to the Congo, I came across an obscure tribe of cannibals that not only ate human flesh but also devoured the soul. And those are only a few of the things I've seen."

"And now you've met an old exorcist who has sacrificed his physical and spiritual health to spare the world the evil that now resides within him."

"Tell me more about you, Father?"

"Oh, I'm sure Father O'Halloran told you all about me."

"He told me some," Gideon admitted, "but—"

"But you want to know if it's all true, if I really have forty-seven demons imprisoned inside of me?"

"Yes, I suppose so."

"And you require proof?"

"If I am to fully believe the claim, yes, I require proof."

"Can't you feel it?"

"Feel what?"

"The concentration of evil occupying this room with us."

"I can't deny that I feel something. It makes me feel dirty and a little sick to my stomach. And, quite frankly, it's almost akin to an invisible battering ram aimed at the moral wall behind which all of my worst impulses are held at bay."

"Then, why the skepticism?"

"It's my job to question everything, even if it seems legit."

"Take my word for it, Mister Thomas. I wish I didn't have these terrible things inside of me. But I was chosen to do God's work. And that's what I am going to do until I die... which will no doubt happen very soon."

"I can't even imagine what you've had to endure."

"No, Mister Thomas, you can't."

"Is it very painful?"

"It's rather unbearable, I'm afraid. But worth it."

"Why?"

"Did you know," Father Martin asked, "that the end times were supposed to begin six years ago?"

Gideon shook his head.

"Had I not performed that last exorcism," Martin continued, "we would neither of us be here today to have this conversation. We'd be long dead, and so would the world as we know it. The demon has shown this to me."

"That would mean," Gideon began, "that the last demon you took into yourself wasn't just any demon. It was..." He paused, not believing the word he was about to speak. "It was..."

But Gideon couldn't say it, as if by saying it aloud, he was automatically agreeing to the reality of it.

Father Martin nodded gravely, his sickly eyes never breaking contact. Then his expression changed drastically. His eyes narrowed, and a wicked smile spread across his face to reveal teeth that were black with advanced decay.

"Father Martin?"

"Not Father Martin," the priest answered in a raspy, sinister voice, the words slithering from his mouth like snakes through the dry autumn brush.

"Then, who are you?"

"I am he, and we are me."

"He who?" Gideon insisted, attempting to tame the shakiness in his voice.

"I am he...and we are me," repeated the voice.

Gideon stared at the wretched old man as the sinister smile spread even wider, revealing more of his horribly rotten teeth.

"By the hand of the apostate," slithered more words from the mouth, "shall the door be unlocked. He has waited for the fourth key, and it is here."

And with that, Gideon watched the last grain of sand circle the mouth of the upper bulb, fall through the neck, and join the rest of the sand at the bottom of the hourglass.

❄ ❄ ❄

Liam opened the door for Gideon when he knocked to be let out. Sweating, head spinning with thoughts too terrible to entertain, Gideon walked unsteadily back through the tunnel, climbed the rusty ladder, and returned to the basement.

The wooden planks creaked underfoot as Gideon made his way to the stairs, then to the upper levels of the building. His thoughts flitted from one to the next without gaining proper purchase, all of them eventually falling from his mental branches into oblivion. And he continued to walk on in this haze until he reached the restroom on the first floor.

Once in the restroom, Gideon stood in front of a large mirror fixed to the wall above a row of porcelain sinks; the faucets dripped a slow rhythm into their filthy basins. Through the surface of the mirror ran a network of cracks like a map of sharp, irreparable injury. His fragmented reflection showed wild eyes, sweat glistening on his brow, and a thoughtful mouth presently capable of neither smile nor frown. Leaning over the sink directly in front of him, Gideon let cold water run into his cupped hands and then splashed it on his face. When he stood, his reflection showed a slightly more composed and rational man.

After running his fingers through his thick brown hair, which he deliberately styled in a messy fashion, Gideon wiped his damp hands on his jeans. He then reached into the inside pocket of his charcoal gray blazer and pulled out a stainless steel flask. He downed a good portion of its contents—a middling label of Irish whiskey—capped the flask and returned it to his pocket.

Gideon had an unconventionally handsome face. His nose was perhaps a touch too wide, his lips neither pencil-thin nor sensuously full, and his eyes a turbulent blue that recalled stormy seas. Covered in long stubble, his chiseled jaw only met with a shaving razor once every three or four days. There was something of the tortured artist in his appearance. Though a writer, Gideon had never considered himself an artist. Rather, he thought of himself as more of a documentarian—someone whose mission was to provide an empirical, logical voice to the spiritual, the supernatural, and the weird and mysterious happenings of the world. To this end, he had been somewhat successful, though it had brought him no closer to God. In fact, although he never would have admitted it to be true, his pursuits had moved him even further from the God to which he had once sworn love and devotion.

Gideon's thoughts returned to Father Martin and what he had revealed.

"The crazy old bastard is just fucking with you," Gideon told his reflection in the mirror. "Or he's dying and confused and doesn't know what the hell he's saying. Either way, it's all bullshit."

Still, Gideon retrieved his wallet from his back pocket and withdrew a photo of a young girl—a daughter he'd unintentionally fathered while out of the country investigating incredible claims surrounding an Indonesian mystic. Lust can be a powerful thing, even for the celibate, and although he had divorced himself from the Church and was no longer under any obligation to abstain from sexual intercourse, he didn't give in to his urges often. But with this young woman, it had been something more than lust. She had been so very beautiful and kind, and she'd taken quite an interest in the strange foreigner. After forsaking his spiritual vows and leaving the priesthood, Gideon had only two carnal encounters out of wedlock—the first a guilty visit to a German brothel, and the second in Indonesia with Leti, who not only became the mother of his daughter but his wife.

A year after he'd returned to the States, Gideon received a letter from Leti telling him they had a child. A week later, he flew back to Indonesia to collect his new family and bring them back to America. This turned out to be more of a process than he'd anticipated, but eventually, after roughing it in a Jakarta tenement for nearly a year, father, mother, and daughter safely made it the United States.

Staring lovingly at the little photograph, Gideon went over his daughter's features for several minutes, committing them all to memory again and again as if they would begin to fade as soon as he stopped looking at them. He wished he could see her face this instant, in person. Then it occurred to him that, if he left now, he could be home in two hours, where his family would be waiting for him. He should be there anyway. It was nearly Christmas morning, after all.

Pocketing his wallet, Gideon noticed something he'd missed when he had first entered the restroom. Reflected in the mirror was a pair of feet under one of the stalls behind him.

"I'm sorry," Gideon addressed the owner of the feet, remembering his little outburst a few moments ago, "I didn't know you were in here."

The occupant of the stall didn't respond.

That's when Gideon saw the blood. It was pooling beside the feet and running into the adjacent stall toward a drain in the tiled floor. There was too much of it. This person was clearly not all right.

Rushing across the restroom, Gideon flung open the door of the stall to reveal a scene of unspeakable horror. Sitting on the toilet was the taciturn young man that had greeted him at the entrance of the building when he'd arrived. There was no question that the young man was dead. The bottom half of his jaw had been almost entirely torn away from his face so that his tongue dangled limply from what was left of the devastated orifice. Carved crudely into the man's left forearm were words that made no sense to Gideon whatsoever: *The silent prophet.*

In shock, Gideon fled the restroom. He ran down the corridors, turning this way and that, without much sense of direction in the confusing design of the place. It took him some time, but he eventually made it back to Father O'Halloran's office.

What awaited him in the priest's office proved just as horrific as what he had seen in the restroom downstairs, perhaps even more so.

In the flickering light of the office, Gideon could make out O'Halloran on his knees in front of his desk. Just as dead as the young man in the restroom, O'Halloran's hands were held out, palms-up, and in each of them was cradled an eyeball that had once resided in one of the two empty cavities in his face. He had been opened from sternum to belly button, his guts spilling from the wound onto the floor. Two large, black vultures, one on either side of the desk, tore at bloody, maggot-covered meat with jerky, aggressive movements, their black talons glinting in the inconsistent light. Gideon knew the meat on which the carrion birds feasted had once been housed within O'Halloran's living trunk. Like the body downstairs, words had been carved into O'Halloran's left forearm: *The sightless witness.*

The carpeted floor was saturated with blood. When Gideon took a step back, his feet made a squishing sound. He was suddenly struck by a wave of nausea, but he managed to hold the contents of his stomach where they belonged.

What the hell was going on?

Was any of this even real?

Had he finally gone mad?

Gideon's mind went from questioning what was happening to being possessed by a singular thought: he needed to get out of here. Out of this office, out of this building. But he didn't have the key to the main door and knew no other way out. The key, Gideon knew, was somewhere on the person of the dead young man in the downstairs restroom. Or at least that was the last place he had seen it. The last thing he wanted to do, however, was rifle through the pockets of a corpse.

Wait, Gideon thought, *perhaps Liam has a key and can let me out.*

Not quite remembering the route he'd taken to arrive at O'Halloran's office, Gideon did his best to retrace his steps to the basement. After losing his way in the corridors a few times, reaching abrupt and curious dead-ends and several locked doors, he found the basement, then the hatch door leading to the tunnel.

Gideon stumbled through the dark toward a point of light in the distance.

When Gideon neared the end of the tunnel, he could see in the soft glow of the lantern on the table Liam sitting in his chair, his back to Gideon.

"Liam," said Gideon, breathless from exertion and panic, "you'll never believe what's happening. We need to—"

As he moved around the chair to face Liam, Gideon's heart sank into a pit of hopelessness. Fear surged through his veins like an electric current. Liam's skin was blue, his eyes a milky white. From his open mouth poured forth a steady stream of water that had no discernable source. Water also leaked from his ears and fell from the corners of his eyes like so many tears. And like the young man in the restroom and O'Halloran in his office, Liam had words carved into the flesh of his left forearm: *The baptized sinner.*

After finding three dead bodies of people who'd been alive and well only two hours prior, and noting the impossible state of each of them, Gideon knew this was not his usual sort of case. This was something else altogether. And if he was being completely honest with himself, he was shaken to his core. No; the truth was that he was completely fucked up—emotionally and psychologically. But there would be time for therapy later. That was, if he got of this place alive.

Gideon struggled briefly with the stubborn lever to the bolt lock, eventually succeeding in what should have been the simple task of manipulating the mechanism to disengage. As soon as he opened the door, he was met again by the smell of sulfur, poor hygiene, and hot, damp air that was in dire need of improved ventilation.

If the spectacle that greeted him the first time he'd visited this room had been strange and horrible, it was many times that now. All the supplicants had been strung up by their necks and asphyxiated by their own rope-like entrails. Eyes bulged from horror-stricken faces as their naked, lifeless bodies hung from the wooden support beams overhead. Blood dripping from their bare feet to land in thick crimson puddles on the stone floor. Even in death, some of them managed to continue clutching their rosaries.

Turning, Gideon saw at the center of the room the body of Father Martin lying on its back. The old man wasn't moving. Nor did he appear to be breathing.

Gideon ran to the priest, his foot brushing right through the salt circle, and knelt beside the body. There were no apparent injuries to the old man—nothing so ghastly as what had befallen Martin's fellow clergyman, the two poor souls who had been employed here, and the unfortunate supplicants—so Gideon placed the middle and index finger of his right hand over Martin's carotid artery. He couldn't detect a pulse. Nor was there any life left in Martin's lungs. But when Gideon removed his fingers from the expired exorcist's neck, the area he had touched glowed a fiery red. This red glow spread throughout the corpse until all exposed flesh seemed to be affected by it. After a few moments, the glow began to fade, like embers cooling in a fireplace, until Martin's skin was the same sickly pallor it had had before. Then the body began to twitch and convulse violently. Startled, Gideon fell backward. Using his hands and feet, he began to scurry away.

As Gideon watched in quaking terror, Martin's chest cracked open from the inside, the ribs snapping outward like dead tree branches. Stretched by some unseen force within, the skin split open from throat to pelvis. And from this ragged hole in Martin's body there rose a head, then broad shoulders, and finally the rest of something that resembled a man but was very clearly not human.

Covered in gore, the dark figure stretched and sighed. Long black wings unfurled from its back before being retracted and hidden from sight. The bits and pieces of Father Martin still clinging to the figure began to fall away as it moved, its naked, grayish-green skin glistening wet like a terrible newborn thing. Then it opened its eyes to reveal vertical slits for pupils and irises the color of sunlight filtered through amber. It fixed its menacing eyes on Gideon as it walked toward him.

Trapped in a tarpit of fear, Gideon was no more able to flee than he was able to fully process what was transpiring right before his eyes. The thing advanced, and Gideon remained still as if rooted to the floor. When it reached him, a blue forked tongue darted from its mouth of incredibly sharp teeth. It towered over him by at least two feet, looking down on him with its yellow eyes. Grabbing hold of Gideon's left arm, it pushed up his sleeve. It then placed one of its long, curved claws against the tender flesh, pressing until there was blood. With that, it began to tear this way and that, in small, precise movements.

Tears streamed down Gideon's face as much from fear as from the pain. As the thing carved into his arm, he felt himself slipping from consciousness.

❄ ❄ ❄

A familiar voice sounded from what seemed like quite a distance away. "Mister Thomas."

Gideon tried to call out to the voice, but his voice defied his brain's command to do so.

"Do wake up, Mister Thomas," came the voice again through the blackness, only closer this time. "Are you all right, young man?"

With some effort, Gideon willed himself to rise from the blackness into what he could only refer to as a blur. He continued to rise until his eyes slowly opened and the world came into focus. Kneeling over him was Father O'Halloran, whose round, fleshy face wore a most worried expression. Gideon looked at the priest without responding, puzzled.

"Oh, Mister Thomas, thank heavens you're okay."

Then the events of the night came flooding back through Gideon's mind in an intense barrage of images.

"I am not okay, Father," Gideon said, panicked and afraid, "and neither are you. You were dead earlier tonight. So we're pretty fucking far from okay."

For a moment, O'Halloran looked at Gideon as though he'd gone mad. Then he began laughing a hearty, good-natured laugh.

"You've had quite an evening, Mister Thomas, haven't you?"

"Yes," Gideon answered, "I have."

"Well, I am pleased to say that I'm still very much alive.

Father Martin, I am sorry to report, is no longer with us."

"This doesn't make goddamn any sense."

"Easy on the blasphemy, if you don't mind."

"Sorry, Father."

"Here," O'Halloran said, putting his arm under Gideon's shoulders. "Let's sit you up."

From where he sat, Gideon could see Father Martin's body. It lay there unbloodied and in one piece. Gideon scanned the room. There weren't any supplicants strung up by their own intestines. In fact, he and O'Halloran were the only two in the room apart from the deceased exorcist.

"Perhaps the shock of seeing Father Martin pass away caused you to faint," O'Halloran suggested.

"Yeah, maybe," Gideon said doubtfully.

"Are you able to stand?"

"I think so."

"How about we get out of here, then?"

"But, Father, what about the demons?" Gideon asked with unmasked trepidation. "What's happened with them?"

"Your guess is as good as mine, I'm afraid. Perhaps upon Martin's passing they were returned to Hell. Or perhaps they've been loosed into the world all over again. I truly can't say with any degree of certainty."

"Hopefully, the former."

"Yes, hopefully."

Gideon winced in pain as he stood. He hurt all over.

"Are you ready to go home, Mister Thomas?"

"Oh, yes, I really am."

❄ ❄ ❄

As Gideon and O'Halloran walked through the building to the main entrance, Gideon described the awful things he thought he'd witnessed throughout the evening. He spared no detail, from lolling tongues and blood-soaked tiles to disemboweled corpses that had been relieved of their eyes, and from human fountains and hanging supplicants to creatures too horrible to properly put into words.

"That's quite a story, Mister Thomas."

"It just felt so real."

"Perhaps your imagination took over after you passed out," O'Halloran submitted for Gideon's consideration. "Sometimes dreams can seem so very real."

Gideon ignored O'Halloran's words.

"Before he died," Gideon thought aloud to himself, "Father Martin said something about the end of days. Then he mentioned an apostate and four keys. Only it wasn't Father Martin speaking. I don't think it was, anyway. I can't be sure of anything."

"What do you think it all meant?" O'Halloran asked.

"I think," Gideon continued, "that sometimes hellfire can be fashioned into something resembling a halo. I think what might seem very much like a divine ability may actually be a curse from the pit, and that a task from the Devil can be disguised as God's work."

"What about the apostate and the four keys?" O'Halloran wanted to know.

"I think there were steps, or rituals necessary to free the demons from Father Martin. I think each of the dead people in my dream was a key."

"Interesting."

"Awful is more like it."

"Yes, obviously that, too."

Once at the door, O'Halloran inserted the key into the padlock, and the shackle sprung loose from the locking bar in its metal body. Gideon stepped forward. As he began to open the door, he noticed a raw pain throbbing in his left forearm. Maybe he had scraped it when he'd lost consciousness earlier and was just now beginning to feel it because the evening's wave of adrenaline was subsiding. He looked down at his arm; the fabric of his shirt and blazer were saturated in blood. With a trembling hand, he rolled up his sleeve to reveal words carved into the flesh of his arm: *The wandering apostate*.

Panic gripped him anew, its fingers tightening around his frantic mind.

His heart pounded wildly in his chest.

It had all been real, after all. It had happened.

Gideon turned to tell this to O'Halloran, but standing there was not the priest with whom he had been walking and talking just moments before. Instead, it was the grotesque face he'd seen in O'Halloran's office earlier in the evening, which is to say, the face of the same man, only without any eyes. From the sockets where O'Halloran's eyes once resided now stared two deep cavities of red, wet tissue. O'Halloran took a step toward Gideon, dragging entrails behind him, opening his hands to show that held in each was a hazel eye.

For the first time since he arrived at this godforsaken place, Gideon screamed.

He took a frightened step backward from the revolting thing, his scream freezing in his throat as he tripped through the doorway, landing hard on his backside in the lot outside.

The door slammed shut.

❄ ❄ ❄

From his backside in the dirt lot, among the rubble and litter, Gideon observed a town on fire. Flames burned within houses and business, licking the sky from windows and rooftops like the reddish-orange tongues of so many demons. Black smoke billowed into the heavens, eclipsing the low-hanging autumn clouds. Nearby, the asphalt of a street cracked open, devouring the cars parked at its edge. Streetlights toppled, the exposed electrical wires at their bases sending out showers of sparks. Great claps of thunder sounded from much higher in the heavens, like an unseen war waged by great beings. And the crows perched along the building's edge took flight in all directions, some disappearing into the smoke, some flying directly into the flames to be burned alive, and some circling wildly overhead.

The gray-haired, green-eyed cat that had crossed paths with Gideon when he first arrived had returned. It sat down in front of Gideon and watched him intently, indifferent to the town on fire.

Gideon stood and brushed the dirt from his pants. A resigned sort of calm suddenly replaced the fear and panic that had taken up residence in his tortured mind and heart, like a switch had been flipped somewhere deep within him. He reached into his blazer and retrieved his flask. Draining the remainder of its contents, he looked down at the cat.

"I guess I won't be writing that book, after all," he said to the animal.

With the sky rumbling overhead, and with the world trembling and burning all around him, Gideon began to laugh a maniacal laugh that joined with the apocalyptic din.

Gideon chose a direction and began walking. He didn't have a specific destination in mind. None of that mattered. East, west, north, south—they all led to Hell now. Maybe they always had.

ABOUT THE AUTHORS

Dan Allen is Canadian and enjoys spending time off the grid in Northern Ontario. His story "Above the Ceiling" (originally published in *Home Sweet Home* by Millhaven Press, September 2018) is featured in Bards and Sages collection of the *Best Indie Speculative Fiction Volume 2.* Another popular release this year, "Sympathy for the Zingara," can be found in the March 2019 edition of *ParABnormal Magazine.* He is honored that "The Basement" has been chosen to appear along with an elite group of authors in the upcoming Horror Zine's Book of Ghost Stories.

Also out this year: "Where Only the Mosquitoes Sing" (*Monsters We Forgot*), "Munchers" (*Halloween Party 2019*), "Footprints" (*Through Death's Door*), "Become the Beast" (*Erie Tales*), and "Corn Stalker"(*Bloody Red Nose — Fears of a Clown*). And sometime very soon - a new and yet to be published story will be performed on the "Tales to Terrify" podcast.

Dan is currently working on the final edits of his first novel, an epic tale spanning the decade before and after a devastating disaster that alters the lives of the people in Joshua Ridge. It's a nostalgic tale of young love and heartbreak, loaded with both real and supernatural horrors. You can visit Dan at www.danallenhorror.com and follow him on Facebook and Twitter at @danallenhorror. You can write to Dan at contact@danallenhorror.com.

Rose Blackthorn lives in the desert but longs for the sea. She is a writer, dog-mom, jewelry-maker, avowed coffee drinker, and photographer. Her short fiction and poetry have appeared online and in print with a varied list of anthologies and magazines including the collection *Beautiful, Broken Things.*

More info can be found at: http://roseblackthorn.wordpress.com/; http://www.facebook.com/RoseBlackthorn.Author; http://amazon.com/author/roseblackthorn; https://twitter.com/rose_blackthorn; https://www.instagram.com/roseblackthornauthor/

James Carlson began writing as a young man by scribbling journal entries while hitchhiking and traveling on Greyhound buses across the US. Later, as a music journalist, James reviewed countless albums and interviewed artists for publications such as *Punk Globe* and *No Depression.* More recently, James has discovered a passion for penning fiction, especially in the genres of horror, science fiction, and dark fantasy. His stories have appeared in such books as Gypsum Sound Tales' Colp anthology, *Solitude*, and Breaking Rules Publishing's short story book project, *Horror.* James resides in

Pennsylvania with his family and many pets.

Matt Cowan's love for the horror genre stretches back beyond his earliest childhood memories. At a young age he stopped having nightmares when he began enjoying them too much. His primary literary influences are Ramsey Campbell, M.R. James, and Algernon Blackwood. In addition to writing fiction, Matt also writes about some of the legendary names in the field at his Horror Delve blog (horrordelve.com) as well as the movie review column *Matt Cowan's Threat Watch for Black Infinity* magazine from *Rocket Science Books.* He lives with his wife Lynne in Indianapolis, Indiana where he's currently working on more stories. His publishing credits include "The Collective of Blaque Reach," originally published in 2008 by Dead Letter Press as the bonus story chap book for the *Bound for Evil: Curious Tales of Books Gone Bad* anthology. It was also featured on The Tales to Terrify Podcast in 2013 (read on episode #90). He's had stories in *Indiana Horror Anthology's 2011* and *2012*, *Indiana Science Fiction 2011*, and *Indiana Crime Review 2013* from James Ward Kirk Fiction, Cellar Doors: Words of Beauty, Tales of Terror anthology from James Ward Kirk Fiction, *O Little Town of Deathlehem,* and *Deathlehem Revisited.* "Here He Comes A-wandering" was originally read by Mark Justice on The Pod of Horror Podcast (Episode #58) as the winning entry in their Christmas Horror Story Contest that year. His movie review column, "Matt Cowan's Threat Watch" appears in *Black Infinity.*

Scott Deegan is a stay-at-home dad from the little town of Pequot Lakes, MN. I have always wanted to write horror stories, but before this I've never showed anyone. I left high school during Christmas break in tenth grade and took my GED. Because of this I didn't think anyone would even look at my writing. I'm not a dumb person, but dropping out of school I now believe was a stupid thing to do.

I did try writing a number of years ago but was told by my now ex-wife that I wasn't any good and shouldn't waste my time. I trashed all my stories.

I've always loved horror, both reading and writing. I feel I have a talent for it and wanted to start seeing if others agree. I'm getting a bit of a late start, but I'm good at this and just too out of shape and too old to become a professional wrestler. I have written reviews of horror books that can be found on Goodreads, Amazon, and the Facebook group Books of Horror.

Robert C. Eccles is a member of the Horror Writers Association, the Great Lakes Association of Horror Writers, and The Fictioneers. His stories have appeared in Necrotic Tissue Magazine and numerous anthologies. He's a 30-year radio broadcasting veteran who also narrates the occasional story for the Pseudopod horror podcast.

Dan Foley grew up in Northern New Jersey. He has lived on the east coast, the west coast and points in between, including two nuclear submarines. He has lived in Manchester, CT. since 1985. His genres of choice are horror and paranormal suspense.

He is the author of the novels *Death's Companion, Reunion, Abandoned,* and *Wolf's Tale*, the novellas, *Intruder* and *Gypsy,* and a collection of short stories *The Whispers of Crows.* All are available through Amazon and B&N. He has also published in various anthologies and magazines in the U.S. Canada, England and Australia. Find him at www.deathscompanion.com, or on Facebook at www.facebook.com/dan.foley.31

R.A. Goli is an Australian writer of horror, fantasy, erotic, and speculative short stories. In addition to writing, her interests include reading, gaming, the occasional walk, and annoying her dog, two cats, and husband.

Her short story collection Unfettered is available at Lulu. Her fantasy novella, *The Eighth Dwarf,* is available at Amazon and Fantasia Divinity Magazine. Check out her numerous short story publications at her website, https://ragoliauthor.wordpress.com/, or stalk her on Facebook.

Kev Harrison is a writer of horror and dark fiction from the UK, living in Lisbon, Portugal. His work has featured in *Lost Films* from Perpetual Motion Machine Publishing, *In Darkness, Delight: Creatures of the Night* from Corpus Press, and on *The Other Stories and Tales To Terrify* podcasts. His folk horror novelette, *Cinders of a Blind Man Who Could See,* is available now from Demain Publishing and his debut novella, *The Balance,* is coming at the turn of the year from Lycan Valley Press. Find out more at www.kevharrison fiction.com.

Dave Jeffery is author of 15 novels, two collections, and numerous short stories. His Necropolis Rising series and yeti adventure *Frostbite* have both featured on the Amazon #1 bestseller list. His YA work features critically acclaimed Beatrice Beecham supernatural mystery series and *Finding Jericho*, a contemporary mental health novel that was featured on the BBC Health and the Independent Schools Entrance Examination Board's recommended reading lists.

Jeffery is a member of the Society of Authors, British Fantasy Society (where he is a regular book reviewer), and the Horror Writers Association. He is also a registered mental health professional with a BSc (Hons) in Mental Health Studies and a Master of Science Degree in Health Studies.

Jeffery is married with two children and lives in Worcestershire, UK. Visit https://davejeffery.webs.com/ for further information.

Tim Kane loves things that creep and crawl. His first published book is non-fiction, *The Changing Vampire of Film and Television*, tracing the history of vampires in television and movies. Most recently published stories in *Ripples in Space*, *Drunk Gekko*, and the upcoming *Lovecraftia*. Find out more at www.timkanebooks.com.

Vivian Kasley lives in the land of the strange and unusual, Florida! She's an educator who writes in her spare time. Her stories have appeared in Gypsum Sound Tales, Dark Moon Digest, HellBound Books, Castrum Press, and Sirens Call Publications. She has more on the way, including her first novella. When not spinning twisted tales, she's reading or enjoying life with her other half and fur babies. You can find her online at https://www. facebook. com/bizarrebabewhowrites/ and on Amazon at amazon.com/ author/viviankasley.

Jeffrey Kosh is the author of three novels, some novelettes, and a long series of short stories. His works have been published by Alexandria Publishing Group, Grinning Skull Press, May-December Publications, Optimus Maximus Publishing, and EFW.

He is the owner of Jeffrey Kosh Graphics, where he creates book covers for various authors and publishing companies, movie posters, and DVD jackets. His various careers have led him to travel extensively worldwide, developing a passion for cinema, wildlife, history, and popular folklore. All these things heavily influence his writing style.

W. Brice McVicar's non-fiction work has appeared in *Rue Morgue*, *Fangoria*, and *Delirium* magazines. He lives in Ontario, Canada with his wife, three sons, and their dog.

Damascus Mincemeyer was exposed to the weird worlds of horror, comics and science fiction as a boy and has been ruined ever since. He's now an artist and writer of various strangeness and has had stories published (or set-to-be published) in the anthologies *Fire: Demons, Dragons and Djinn*, *Earth: Giants, Golems and Gargoyles*, *Hear Me Roar* (Tyche Books), *Bikers Vs The Undead*, *Psycho Holiday*, *Monsters Vs Nazis*, *Mr. Deadman Made Me Do It*, *Satan Is Your Friend* and *Monster Party* (all from Deadman's Tome publishing and books for which he also provided cover art), *Crash Code* (Blood Bound Books), *Hell's Empire* (Ulthar Press), *Appalachian Horror* (Aphotic Realm), *On Time* (Transmundane Press), the *Sirens Call* ezine, and the magazines *Gallows Hill*, *Aphotic Realm* and *StoryHack*. He lives near St. Louis, Missouri, USA and can usually be found lurking about on Twitter @DamascusUndead.

Kurt Newton's dark fiction and poetry have appeared in numerous magazines and anthologies including *The Shadow Over Deathlehem*, *O Unholy Night in Deathlehem*, *Revisiting the Dead*, *Weird Tales*, *Dark Discoveries*, *Weirdbook*, and *Hinnom Magazine*. He is the author of two novels, *The Wishnik* and *Powerlines*, and recently sold a short story collection to Lycan Valley Publications. He lives in Connecticut.

Joseph P. Pietris is a Chief Electrician's Mate in the United States Coast Guard and currently resides in Williamsburg, VA. When not training future Electrician's Mates, Joseph is working on his Electronics Engineering Degree and dabbling in horror.

Tristan Ryan is a self-published author from Chicago. In their spare time they paint, write music, create board games and are an avid horror fan. They are the author of the novel Young Ghost Investigators and the co-author of the Ghost Seekers Club series (which they write with their twin, Steve Ryan). While their currently published works are labeled as "Young Adult" novels, they are enjoyed by readers of all ages. Find out more about Tristan Ryan at their website: author-tristan-ryan.weebly.com.

Lori Safranek started her writing career as a small-town newspaper reporter in Nebraska. She released a collection of short stories named *Freakshow: The Complete Freaked Out Series*. She's currently writing a sequel to her collection, titled *Julia, The Pearl of the Prairie*. Her short horror fiction has been published in anthologies such as *Dark Harvest*; *Slaughterhouse: The Serial Killer Edition Volume I*; *Simple Things*; *Final Masquerade*; *Tales from the Zombie Road: The Long Haul Anthology* and several issues of Sirens Call online anthologies.

Paul A. Sheppard is a digital nomad and homeschool teacher to his young son as they travel the world. Currently based in rural Thailand. Paul spends most of his time butchering the Isan dialect, explaining the laws of motion to a nine-year-old, and writing swashbuckling action-adventures.

An avid traveler, accomplished martial artist, and less-than-accurate archer. Paul's bucket list is his blueprint for life. His debut novel, *The Wolf We Feed*, is available on Amazon.

Pierce Skinner lives in Richmond, VA with his wife and four cats. He is aware that this is probably too many cats, he simply does not care. When he's not writing, he can likely be found waiting tables, studying to be a mortician, or enjoying some downtime at his favorite Thai restaurant, arguing with strangers about *Star Wars*. His work has appeared in PseudoPod, *Shock Totem*, *Aurealis Magazine*, *LampLight Magazine*, and others.

He also reviews comic books at http://polaroidsandpolarbears.co.uk.
Marc Sorondo lives with his wife and children in New York. He loves to read, and his interests range from fiction to comic books, physics to history, oceanography to cryptozoology, and just about everything in between. He's a perpetual student and occasional teacher. For more information, go to MarcSorondo.com.

Christopher Stanley lives on a hill with three sons who share a birthday but aren't triplets. His stories have been published by Unnerving Magazine, The Arcanist and in The Third Corona Book of Horror Stories. His novelette, The Forest is Hungry, was published by Demain Publishing in April 2019. Follow him @allthosestrings

Karen Thrower is a native Oklahoman, wife and mother. Her story "The Lost Ones" appears in the bestselling *Secret Stairs: A Tribute to Urban Legend.* You can find more of her work on Amazon. amazon.com/author/karenthrower.

Sheri White lives in Maryland with her husband Chris, as well as two of their daughters, their significant others, three dogs, and three cats. Her oldest daughter and her first granddaughter live nearby. Life is not dull!

Her stories have been published in many anthologies, including *Tales from the Crust* (edited by Max Booth III and David James Keaton), *Be Very Afraid* (edited by Edo Van Belkom), *When the Clock Strikes 13* (edited by Kenneth W. Cain and Steve Thompson), *Once Upon an Apocalypse* (edited by Scott Goudsward and Rachel Kenley), and the upcoming *New Scary Stories to Tell in the Dark* (edited by Jonathan Maberry). Magazine appearances include *Lamplight*, *The Sirens Call*, *Devolution Z*, and *Beware the Dark.*

Find her on Facebook - https://www.facebook.com/sheriw1965

Grinning Skull Press Presents

The Place where it all started

O Little Town of Deathlehem

Twas the fright before Christmas,
And all through the town,
Not a soul stirred,
No one dared make a sound…

Welcome to Deathlehem, where…
…Krampus, not Santa, brings the holiday cheer…
…the lights on the tree, so festive and bright, skitter and crawl and possess a lethal bite…
…malicious little elves, not a jolly one, know if you've been naughty—or nice…
and
…family gatherings often turn deadly.
So enter…if you dare.

A collection of 23 holiday horrors benefiting the Elizabeth Glaser Pediatric AIDS Foundation.

Return to Deathlehem

Slay bells ring,
Kids are screaming,
In the lane, snow is blood stained.
There's nowhere to hide,
Krampus has arrived,
There'll be feasting in a winter slaughter land…

Welcome back to Deathlehem,
…where the office Secret Santa proves more dangerous than a game of Russian roulette…
…where trips to Grandma's house are fraught with danger…
…where a traditional Nutcracker poses a threat to a pair of would-be thieves…
…where ghosts of Christmases past haunt and take vengeance against the living…
…and many more!

Twenty-three more tales of holiday horror benefiting the Elizabeth Glaser Pediatric AIDS Foundation

Deathlehem *Revisited*

You make this a Christmas to dismember,
Killing feelings in the middle of December,
Strangers meet, one unwillingly surrenders,
Oh, what a Christmas to dismember…

Welcome back to Deathlehem…again!…
where a mutated Christmas has a taste for human flesh…
…where a trio of trespassers are terrorized at an abandoned holiday-themed tourist attraction…
…where elves thrive on the torment delivered to others…
…where holiday shopping drives people to commit extreme acts of violence…
…and many more!

Twenty-three more tales of holiday horror to benefit The Elizabeth Glaser Pediatric AIDS FoundationPediatric AIDS Foundation

The Shadow over Deathlehem

O little town of Deathlehem,
Within you death doth lie!
Beneath thy deep and rutted streets
Tormented souls do cry.
Yet in your dark streets shineth
A cold and ghostly light.
The fears and tears of all the years
Are met in thee tonight.

Well, here we are again, folks — Deathlehem …
… where Krampus isn't the only creature to fear
when the holiday draws near…
… where holiday treats aren't safe to eat …
… where not even the apocalypse will keep
people from celebrating the holiday …
… where even Chanukah isn't safe to celebrate …

Twenty-five more tales of holiday horror to benefit
The Elizabeth Glaser Pediatric AIDS Foundation

O Unholy Night in Deathlehem

Said the little child to his mother dear,
do you hear what I hear
Shrieking through the night, father dear,
And do you see what I see
A cry, a scream, blood coloring the snow
And a laugh as evil as sin
And a laugh as evil as sin

Well, folks, looks like we're back in Deathlehem, where…
…Santa's gift turns a mindless horde of bargain-hungry shoppers
into…well… a horde of hungry shoppers…
…defective toys aren't just dangerous; they're deadly…
…holiday ornaments prove to be absolutely captivating—permanently…
…those ugly Christmas sweaters are to die for…

Twenty-five more tales of holiday horror to benefit
The Elizabeth Glaser Pediatric AIDS Foundation

And don't miss these exciting titles...

Midnight.

The Witching Hour.

But the creatures of darkness are not
confined to the shadows of the night.

Lonely stretches of highways...
Bustling college campuses...
Quiet suburban neighborhoods...
Pricey, upscale day spas...
They're everywhere.

Earl and Dale, a pair of burly truckers,
seem to be drawn to those that dwell in the darkness.
Monster hunters by default, they
confront the evil fearlessly—and with just a bit of humor.
Vampires, werewolves, half-human spider demons,
and those that prey on the innocent...
All will realize they've met their match
when they go head to head with...

The Midnight Men

THE FEAR IS GROWING

From the moment he saw the ancient castle rising out of the picturesque Scottish countryside, filmmaker Dan Martin knew he'd found the ideal location for his vampire horror movie. And nothing could make him leave. Not the eerie legends of soul-stealing beasts of the night…nor a bizarre series of freak accidents. Not even his pregnant wife's tragic miscarriage.

THE TERROR IS BORN

Except that now there is another fetus growing in Vicki's womb. But little Darian is not going to be a normal baby. The Martins' adopted ten-year-old son Marty will soon find that out. In fact, Marty will soon know exactly what his new brother really is.

Shrouded in Mystery

The locals call it *Isla de los Perdidos.*
Island of the Lost.
According to the legends, those who venture onto the shores of this cursed island never return.

Abandoned

Valarie DeNola and her sister Julie have chosen to ignore the legends and the warnings. They have been selected to lead a team of explorers to the island to discover the mystery surrounding it. But once ashore, they become cut off from the outside world, and what they discover is something they could never have prepared for.

Inhabited by Death

Now they must fight against an unknown presence that is picking them off one by one. No one can be trusted, and when even nature rises up against them, all seems lost. Their one hope is the extraction team they know is coming.

But will any of them survive to see it arrive?

Printed in Poland
by Amazon Fulfillment
Poland Sp. z o.o., Wrocław

54584097R00208